THE FINAL

<<<<<<<<<<<<<<<<<<

ENCYCLOPEDIA

Volume

> >**ONE**< <

Gordon R. Dickson

THE FINAL
‹ ‹ ‹ ‹ ‹ ‹ ‹ ‹ ‹ ‹ ‹ ‹ ‹ ‹ ‹ ‹
ENCYCLOPEDIA

Volume

› ›ONE‹ ‹

ORB

A Tom Doherty Associates Book
New York

This is a work of fiction. All the characters and events portrayed in this novel are either fictitious or are used fictitiously.

THE FINAL ENCYCLOPEDIA: VOLUME ONE

An Orb Book
Published by Tom Doherty Associates, Inc.
175 Fifth Avenue
New York, NY 10010

Tor Books on the World Wide Web:
http://www.tor.com

Design by Basha Durand

Library of Congress Cataloging-in-Publication Data

Dickson, Gordon R.
    The final encyclopedia / Gordon R. Dickson.
        p.   cm.
    "A Tom Doherty Associates book."
    ISBN 0-312-86186-9 (v. 1).
    1. Dorsai (Imaginary place)—Fiction.   I. Title.
PS3554.I328F56   1997   96-29217
813'.54—dc20   CIP

First Orb Edition: January 1997

Printed in the United States of America

0 9 8 7 6 5 4 3 2 1

The Final Encyclopedia, *and the Childe Cycle of books of which it is a part, are dedicated to my mother, Maude Ford Dickson, who in her own way in ninety-five years has achieved far greater things.*

The Worlds of
The Childe Cycle

- ● Planet
- ○ STAR
- ‑ ‑ ‑ Distance from Sol in
  light years (not to scale)

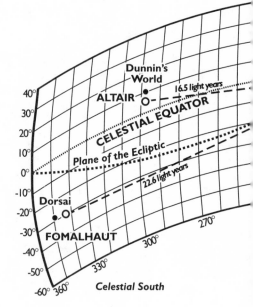

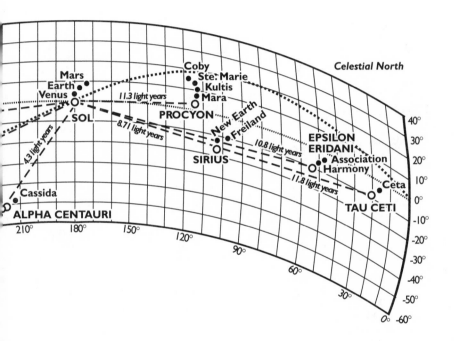

Celestial North

Coby
Ste. Marie
Mars
Earth
Venus
SOL
Kultis
Mara
11.3 light years
PROCYON
Coby
8.71 light years
43 light years
New Earth
Freiland
EPSILON
ERIDANI
SIRIUS
10.8 light years
Association
Harmony
11.8 light years
Ceta
Cassida
TAU CETI
ALPHA CENTAURI

40°
30°
20°
10°
0°
-10°
-20°
-30°
-40°
-50°
-60°

210° 180° 150° 120° 90° 60° 30° 0°

THE FINAL
< < < < < < < < < < < < < < <
ENCYCLOPEDIA

Volume

> >ONE< <

Chapter

> > 1 < <

The low-angled daylight dimmed suddenly on the page of a poem by Alfred Noyes that Walter the InTeacher was reading. It was as if a little cloud had passed over the face of the late afternoon sun that was slanting its rays through the library window beside him. But when Walter glanced up, Earth's star shone bright and round in the sky. There was no cloud.

He frowned, set the antique book aside and reached into his now old-fashioned Maran robes to take out a small, transparent cube filled with liquid, within which normally drifted a thin pink strip of semi-living tissue. It was a cube sent to him here on Earth fourteen years back, from what remained of the old Splinter Culture of the men and women of Mara—that with Kultis had been the two Exotic Worlds. In all those years, as often as he had looked at it, the appearance of the strip had never changed. But now he saw it lying shrivelled and blackened and curled as if burned, at the bottom of the liquid enclosing it. And from the implications of this it came to Walter then, coldly and like something he had been half-expecting for some time, that the hour of his death was upon him.

He put the cube away and got swiftly to his feet. At ninety-two he was still tall, spare and active. But he did not know how long the life gauge had been shrivelled, or how much time remained. He went quickly, therefore, along the library and out through a tall french window, onto the flagstone terrace, flanked at each end by heavy-blossomed lilac bushes and standing a sheer forty feet above the half mile of lake enclosed by the Mayne estate.

On the terrace, legs spread and big hands locked together behind him, Malachi Nasuno, once an officer and man of the Dorsai, but now a tutor like Walter, stood watching an eggshell plastic canoe and the canoeist in it, paddling toward the house. It was almost sunset. The sun, dropping rapidly behind the sharp peaks of the Sawatch Range of the Rocky Mountains around them, was growing a shadow swiftly across the lake from its farther end. This shadow the canoeist was racing, just ahead of its edge on the dark blue water.

Walter wasted no time, but hurried to the flagstaff at one end of the terrace. He loosened the cord on the staff; the sun-warmed, flexible length of it ran through his fingers, burning them lightly, and the flag with its emblem of a hawk flying out of a wood fluttered to the terrace stones.

Out on the lake, the canoeist's paddle beat brightly once more in the sunlight and then ceased. The living figure vanished overside. A moment later, the canoe itself heaved up a little, filled and sank, as if it had been ripped open from beneath and pulled down into the depths. A second later the advancing edge of darkness upon the water covered the spot where the craft had been.

Walter felt the breath of Malachi Nasuno suddenly warm against his left ear. He turned to face the heavy-boned, deep-lined features of the old professional soldier.

"What is it?" asked Malachi, quietly. "Why alarm the boy?"

"I wanted him to get away—if he can," answered Walter. "The rest of us are done for."

Malachi's craggy, hundred-year-old face hardened like cooling metal and the thickets of his brows pulled close together.

"Speak for yourself," he said. "When I'm dead, I'm dead. But I'm not dead yet. What is it?"

"I don't know," said Walter. He lifted the cube from his robes and showed it. "All I know is I've had this warning."

"More of your Exotic hocus-pocus," growled Malachi. But the growl was only half disdainful. "I'll go warn Obadiah."

"There's no time." Walter's hand on a still-massive forearm stopped the ex-soldier. "Obadiah's been ready to meet that personal God of his for years now, and any minute we're liable to have eyes watching what we do. The less we seem to be expecting anything, the better Hal's chance to get away."

Far up along the shadowed margin of the lake, the gaudy shape of a nesting harlequin duck, disturbed from some tall waterweeds below overhanging bushes, burst suddenly into the open, crying out, and fluttered, half-running, half-flying, across the darkened surface of the water to another part of the shore. Walter breathed out in relief.

"Good lad," he said. "Now, if he'll just stay hidden."

"He'll stay," said Malachi, grimly. "He's not a lad now, but a man. You and Obadiah keep forgetting that."

"A man, at sixteen?" said Walter. The ready tears of age were unexpectedly damp against the outer corners of his eyes. "So soon?"

"Man enough," grunted Malachi. "Who's coming? Or what?"

"I don't know," answered Walter. "What I showed you was just a device to warn of a sharp pressure increase of the ontogenetic energies, moving in on us. You remember I told you one of the last things I was able to have them do on Mara was run calculations on the boy; and the calculations indicated high probability of his intersection with a pressure-climax of the current historical forces before his seventeenth year."

"Well, if it's only energies—" Malachi snorted.

"Don't fool yourself!" said Walter, almost sharply for a Maran. "There'll be men or things to manifest its effect when it gets here, just as a tornado manifests a sudden drop in air pressure. Perhaps—" He broke off. Malachi's gaze had moved away from the Maran. "What is it?"

"Others, perhaps," said Malachi, quietly. His generous nostrils spread, almost sniffing the cooling air, tinged now by the sky-pink of the sunset that was beginning to flood between the white-touched mountain peaks.

"Why do you say that?" Walter glanced covertly around, but saw nothing.

"I'm not sure. A hunch," said Malachi.

Walter felt coldness within him.

"We've done wrong to our boy," he almost whispered. Malachi's eyes whipped back to focus on him.

"Why?" demanded the Dorsai ex-soldier.

"We've trained him to meet men—men and women at most," whispered Walter, crouching under his feeling of guilt. "And these devils are loose now on the fourteen worlds."

"The Others aren't 'devils'!" snapped Malachi, not bothering to keep his voice down. "Mix your blood and mine, and Obadiah's in with it—mix together blood of all the Splinter Cultures if you want to, and you still get men. Men make men—nothing else. You don't get anything out of a pot you don't put into it."

"Other Men and Women. Hybrids." Walter shivered. "People with half a dozen talents in one skin."

"What of it?" growled Malachi. "A man lives, a man dies. If he lives well and dies well, what difference does it make what kills him?"

"But this is our Hal—"

"Who has to die someday, like everyone else. Straighten up!" muttered Malachi. "Don't they grow any backbones on the Exotics?"

Walter pulled himself together. He stood tall, breathed deeply and with control for a few seconds, then put on peace like a cloak.

"You're right," he said. "At least Hal's had all we could give him, the three of us, in skill and knowledge. And he's got the creativity to be a great poet, if he lives."

"Poet!" said Malachi, bleakly. "There's a few thousand more useful things he could do with his life. Poets—"

He broke off. His eyes met Walter's with abrupt warning.

Walter's eyes acknowledged the message. He folded his hands in the wide sleeves of his blue robe with a gesture of completion.

"But poets are men, too," he said, as cheerfully and casually as someone making light argument for its own sake. "That's why, for example, I think so highly of Alfred Noyes, among the nineteenth-century poets. You know Noyes, don't you?"

"Should I?"

"I think so," said Walter. "Of course, I grant you no one remembers anything but *The Highwayman*, out of all his poems, nowadays. But *Tales of the Mermaid Tavern*, and that other long poem of his—*Sherwood*—they've both got genius in them. You know, there's that part where Oberon, the king of elves and fairies, is telling his retainers that Robin Hood is going to die, and explaining why the fairies owe Robin a debt—"

"Never read it," grunted Malachi, ungraciously.

"Then I'll quote it for you," said Walter. "Oberon is talking to his own kind and he tells about one of them whom Robin once rescued from what he thought was nothing worse than a spider's web. And what Noyes had Oberon say is—listen to this now—

> " '. . . He saved her from the clutches of that Wizard,
> 'That Cruel Thing, that dark old Mystery,
> 'Whom ye all know and shrink from . . . !' "

Walter broke off, for a thin, pale-faced young man in a dark business suit, holding a void pistol with a long, narrow, wire coil–shielded barrel, had stepped from the lilac bushes behind Malachi. A moment later another gunman joined him. Turning, Walter saw yet two more had appeared from the bushes at his end of the terrace. The four pistols covered the two old men.

" '. . . Plucked her forth, so gently that not one bright rainbow gleam upon her wings was clouded. . . .' " A deep, vibrant voice finished the quotation, and a very tall, erect man with dark hair and lean, narrow-boned face, carrying the book Walter had just been reading with one long finger holding a place in its pages, stepped through the same french window from which Walter had come a few moments before.

". . . But you see?" he went on, speaking now to Walter, "how it goes down-hill, gets to be merely pretty and ornate, after that first burst of strength you quoted? Now, if you'd chosen instead the song of Blondin the Minstrel, from that same poem—"

His voice took on sudden strength and richness—half-chanting the quoted lines in the fashion of the plainsong of the medieval monks.

> "Knight on the narrow way,
> Where wouldst thou ride?
> 'Onward,' I heard him say,
> 'Love, to thy side!'

". . . then I'd have had to agree with you."

Walter bent his head a little with bare politeness. But there was a trai-torous stir in his chest. The magnificent voice, the tall, erect figure before him, plucked at Walter's senses, trained by a lifetime of subtleties, with the demand for appreciation he would have felt toward a Stradivarius in the hands of some great violinist.

Against his will, Walter felt the pull of a desire—to which, of course, yielding was unthinkable—to acknowledge the tall man as if this Other was a master, or a king.

"I don't think we know you," said Walter slowly.

"Ahrens is my name. Bleys Ahrens," said the tall man. "And you needn't be worried. No one's going to be hurt. We'd just like to use this estate of yours for a short meeting during the next day or two."

He smiled at Walter. The power of his different voice was colored by a faint accent that sounded like archaic English. His face held a straight-boned, unremarkable set of features that had been blended and molded by the character lines around the mouth and eyes into something like handsomeness. The direct nose, the thin-lipped mouth, the wide, high forehead and the brilliant brown eyes were all softened by those lines into an expression of humorous kindness.

Beneath that face, his sharply square and unusually wide shoulders, which would have looked out of proportion on a shorter man, seemed no more than normal above the unusual height of his erect, slim body. That body stood relaxed now, but unconsciously balanced, like the body of a yawning panther. And the pale-faced young gunmen gazed up at him with the worshipping gaze of hounds.

"We?" asked Walter.

"Oh, a club of sorts. To tell you the truth, you'd do better not to worry about the matter at all." Ahrens continued to smile at Walter, and looked about at the lake and the wooded margin of it that could be seen from the terrace.

"There ought to be two more of you here, shouldn't there?" he said, turning to Walter again. "Another tutor your own age, and your ward, the boy named Hal Mayne? Where would they be, now?"

Walter shook his head, pleading ignorance. Ahrens' gaze went to Malachi, who met it with the indifference of a stone lion.

"Well, we'll find them," said Ahrens lightly. He looked back at Walter. "You know, I'd like to meet that boy. He'd be . . . what? Sixteen now?"

Walter nodded.

"Fourteen years since he was found . . ." Ahrens' voice was frankly musing. "He must have some unusual qualities. He'd have had to have them—to stay alive, as a child barely able to walk, alone on a wrecked ship, drifting in space for who-knows-how-long. Who were his parents—did they ever find out?"

"No," said Walter. "The log aboard showed only the boy's name."

"A remarkable boy . . . ," said Ahrens again. He glanced out around the lake and grounds. "You say you're sure you don't know where he is now?"

"No," answered Walter.

Ahrens glanced at Malachi, inquiringly.

"Commandant?"

Malachi snorted contemptuously.

Ahrens smiled as warmly on the ex-soldier as he had at Walter, but Malachi was still a stone lion. The tall man's smile faded and became wistful.

"You don't approve of Other Men like me, do you?" he said, a little sadly. "But times have changed, Commandant."

"Too bad," said Malachi, dryly.

"But too true," said Ahrens. "Did it ever occur to you your boy might be one of us? No? Well, suppose we talk about other things if that suggestion bothers you. I don't suppose you share your fellow tutor's taste for poetry? Say, for something like Tennyson's *Morte d'Arthur*—a piece of poetry about men and war?"

"I know it," said Malachi. "It's good enough."

"Then you ought to remember what King Arthur has to say in it about changing times," said Ahrens. "You remember—when Arthur and Sir Bedivere are left alone at the end and Sir Bedivere asks the King what will happen now, with all the companionship of the Round Table dissolved, and Arthur himself leaving for Avalon. Do you remember how Arthur answers, then?"

"No," Malachi said.

"He answers—" and the voice of Ahrens rang out in all its rich power again, *"The old order changeth, yielding to new . . ."* Ahrens paused and looked at the old ex-soldier significantly.

"—And God fulfills himself in many ways—Lest one good custom should corrupt the world," interrupted a harsh, triumphant voice.

They turned, all together. Obadiah Testator, the third of Hal Mayne's tutors, was being herded out through the french window into their midst, at the point of a void pistol, by a fifth young gunman.

"You forgot to finish the quotation," rasped Obadiah at Ahrens. "And it applies to your kind too, Other Man. In God's eye you, also, are no more than a drift of smoke and the lost note of a cymbal. You, too, are doomed at His will—like that!"

He had come on, farther than his young guard had intended, to snap his bony fingers with the last word, under the very nose of Ahrens. Ahrens started to laugh and then his face changed suddenly.

"Posts!" he snapped.

Tension sprang like invisible lightning across the terrace. Of the four gunmen already there, three had left off covering Walter and Malachi to aim at Obadiah, as he snapped his fingers. One only still covered Malachi. Now, at the whip of Ahrens' voice, the errant gunmen pulled their weapons almost in panic back to their original targets.

"Oh, you fools, you young fools!" said Ahrens softly to them. "Look at me!"

Their pale and guilty glances sidled back to his face.

"The Maran"—Ahrens pointed at Walter—"is harmless. His people taught him that violence—any violence—would cripple his thinking processes. And the Fanatic here is worth perhaps one gun. But you see that old man there?"

He pointed at the unmoved Malachi.

"I wouldn't lock one of you, armed as you are, with him, unarmed, in an unlighted room, and give a second's hope to the chance of seeing you alive again."

He paused, while the gunmen cringed before him.

"Three of you cover the Commandant," he went on at last, quietly. "And the other two watch our religious friend here. I'll"— he smiled softly at them—"undertake to try to defend myself against the Maran."

The aim of the pistols shifted obediently, leaving Walter uncovered. He felt a moment's pang of something like shame. But the fine engine of that mind of his, to which Ahrens had referred, had come to life; and the unprofitable emotion he had briefly felt was washed away by a new train of thought. Meanwhile, Ahrens had looked back at Obadiah.

"You're not exactly a lovable sort of man, you know," he told the Friendly.

Obadiah stood, unawed and unchangeable. Fanatic against fanaticism, apostate to the totalitarian hyper-religiosity of the Splinter Culture that had birthed him, the Friendly loomed almost as tall as Ahrens. But from that point on, any comparisons between them went different ways.

Face-to-face with the obvious necessity now of his own death to protect the boy he had tutored—for Obadiah was no fool and Walter, from fourteen years of living with the Fanatic, saw that the other had already grasped the situation—Obadiah was regarding the terminal point of his life neither with the workmanlike indifference of Malachi, nor with the philosophical acceptance of Walter, but with a fierce, dark, and burning joy.

Grim-countenanced, skull-featured and lath-thin from a life of self-discipline, nothing was left of Obadiah in his eighty-fourth year but a leathery and narrow lantern of gray-black skin and bones. It was a lantern illuminated by an all-consuming inner faith in his individually-conceived God—the God who in gentleness and charity was the direct antithesis of the dark and vengeful Lord of Obadiah's Culture, and the direct, acknowledged antithesis of Obadiah himself.

Oblivious now to Ahrens' humor, as to all other unimportant things, he folded his arms and looked directly into the taller man's eyes.

"Woe to you," he said, calmly, "to you, Other Man, and all of your breed. And again I say, woe unto you!"

For a second, meeting the deep-sunk, burning eyes in that dark, bony face, Ahrens frowned slightly. His gaze turned and went past Obadiah to the gunman covering him.

"The boy?" Ahrens asked.

"We looked. . . ." The young man's voice was husky, almost whispering. "He's nowhere . . . nowhere around the house."

Ahrens wheeled sharply to look at Malachi, and Walter.

"If he was off the grounds one of you'd know it?"

"No. He . . . ," Walter hesitated uncertainly, "might have gone for a hike, or a climb in the mountains . . ."

He saw Ahrens' brown eyes focus upon him. As he looked, without warning the dark pupils of them seemed to grow and swell, as if they would finally fill the whole field of Walter's vision. Again, the emotional effect of the strange voice and commanding presence rang in his memory.

"Now, that's foolish of you," said Walter, quietly, making no effort to withdraw his attention from the compelling gaze of Ahrens. "Hypnotic dominance of any form needs at least the unconscious cooperation of the subject. And I am a Maran Exotic."

The pupils were suddenly normal again. This time, however, Ahrens did not smile.

"There's something going on here . . . ," he began, slowly. But Walter had already recognized the fact that time had run out.

"All that's different," he interrupted, "is that you've been underestimating me. The unexpected, I think some general once said, is worth an army—"

And he launched himself across the few feet of distance separating them, at Ahrens' throat.

It was a clumsy charge, made by a body and mind untrained to even the thought of physical violence; and Ahrens brushed it aside with one hand, the way he might have brushed aside the temper tantrum of a clumsy child. But at the same time the gunman behind Obadiah fired; it felt as if something heavy struck Walter in the side. He found himself tumbling to the terrace.

But, useless as his attack had been, it had distracted at least the one armed guard; and in that split second of distraction, Obadiah hurled himself—not at either of the gunmen guarding him, but at one of those covering Malachi.

Malachi himself had been in movement from the first fractional motion of Walter's charge. He was on one of the two still holding pistols trained on him, before the first man could fire. And the charge from the gun of the other passed harmlessly through the space the old soldier had occupied a second before.

Malachi chopped down the gunman he had reached as someone might chop a flower stalk with one swipe of an open hand. Then he turned, picked up the man who had missed him, and threw that gunman into the fire-path of the discharge from the pistols of the two who had been covering Obadiah—just as the remaining armed man, caught in Obadiah's grasp, managed to fire twice.

In that same moment, Malachi reached him; and they went down together, the gunman rolling on top of the old man.

From the level of the terrace stones, lying half on his side, Walter stared at the ruin his charge had made. Obadiah lay fallen with his head twisted around so that his open and unmoving eyes stared blankly in Walter's direction. He did not move. No more did the man Malachi had chopped down, nor the other gunman the ex-soldier had thrown into the fire from his companions' pistols. One other gunman, knocked down by the thrown man, was twitching and moaning strangely on the terrace.

Of the two guards remaining, one lay still on top of Malachi, who had ceased to move, and the other was still on his feet. He turned to face Ahrens and cringed before the devastating blaze of the Other Man's gaze.

"You fools, you fools!" said Bleys softly. "Didn't I just get through telling you to concentrate on the Dorsai?"

The remaining gunman shrank in on himself in silence.

"All right," said Bleys, sighing. "Pick him up." He indicated the moaning man and turned to the gunman on top of the silent figure of Malachi.

"Wake up." Bleys prodded the man on top with his toe. "It's all over."

The man he had prodded rolled off Malachi's body and sprawled on the stones with his head at an odd angle to his body. His neck was broken. Bleys drew in a slow breath.

"Three dead—and one hurt," he said as if to himself. "Just to destroy three unarmed old teachers. What a waste." He shook his head and turned back to the gunman who was lifting the moaning man.

They think I'm already dead, too, then, thought Walter, lying on the flagstones.

The realization came to him without much surprise. Bleys was already holding open the french window so that the wounded man could be half-carried inside the library by his companion. Bleys followed, his finger still marking a place in the volume of Noyes' poetry Walter had originally been reading. The french window closed. Walter was left alone with the dead, and the dying light of day.

He was aware that the charge from the void pistol had taken him in the side; and a certain feeling of leakage inside him confirmed his belief that the wound was mortal. He lay waiting for his personal end and it grew in him after a moment that it was something of a small victory that neither Ahrens nor the surviving gunman had realized he was still alive.

He had stolen several minutes more of life. That was a small victory, to add to the large victory that there was now no one from whom the lightning of Bleys' multi-talented mind could deduce the unique value of Hal. A value that, since it was connected to a possible pressure-climax of the ontogenetic energies, could be as dangerous to the Other Men as they would be to Hal, once they realized he might pose a threat to them.

It was this awareness of Hal as a possible danger that Walter had been so concerned to hide from Ahrens. Now he had done so. Now, they would probably search the grounds for the boy, but not with any particular urgency; and so, perhaps, Hal could escape. Walter felt a modest surge of triumph.

But the sunset was red, and deepening around him as well as around the other silent bodies; and the feeling of triumph faded. His life was leaking fast from him, and he realized now, for the first time, that he had never wanted to die. If only, he thought, I could have lived to think a little longer.

He felt a moment's unutterable and poignant feeling of regret. It seemed to him suddenly that if he had existed only a few more hours, some of the answers he had sought all his life might have come to him. But then that feeling, too, faded; the light seemed to darken swiftly about him, and he died.

The sun was now setting. Shortly, its rays left the stone terrace and even the dark slates of the house rooftop. Darkness brimmed in the area below the mountains, and the french windows above the terrace flagstones glowed yellow from the lights in the library. For a little while the sky, too, was light; but this also went, and left only the brilliant pinpoints of gleaming stars in a velvet-black, moonless sky.

Down by the margin of the lake, the tall weeds rising out of the black water by the shore stirred. Nearly without a sound, the tall, sapling-thin, shadowy figure of a sixteen-year-old boy hoisted itself up on the grassy bank and stood erect there, dripping and shivering, staring off at the terrace and the lighted house.

Chapter

> > **2** < <

For a moment only, he stood staring. He felt numb, set apart from reality. Something had happened up on the terrace. He had witnessed it, but there was a barrier, a wall in his mind that blocked him off from remembering exactly what had taken place. In any case, there was no time now to examine it. An urgency implanted long since against just such a moment as this was pushing him hard, thrusting him along a path toward certain rehearsed actions that had been trained in him against this time when even thought would be impossible. Obeying that urging, he slipped back out of sight among the greenery that surrounded the lake.

Here, in the dimness, he went swiftly around the lake until he came to a small building. He opened its door and stepped into its unlighted interior.

It was a toolshed full of equipment for keeping the grounds in order; anyone unfamiliar with it would have tripped over any of several dozen pieces of such equipment within two steps beyond the door. But Hal Mayne, although he turned on no illumination, moved lightly among them without touching anything, as if his eyes could see in this kind of darkness.

It had been, in fact, one small part of his training—finding his way blindfolded about the interior of this shed. Certainly now, by practice and touch alone, he found a shelf against the wall, turned it on a hidden pivot at its midpoint and opened a shallow secret compartment between two studs of the building's back wall. Five minutes later, he slipped back outdoors with the compartment reclosed behind him. But now he wore dry clothes, gray slacks and blue half-jacket. He carried a small travel bag, and had tucked into an interior pocket of the half-jacket papers that would authorize him to travel to any of the fourteen inhabited worlds, plus the cards and vouchers that would make available to him enough Earth and interplanetary funds to get him to a number of off-world destinations.

He went now, among the night-dark trees and bushes once more, in the direction of the house. He was deliberately not thinking—he had not thought from the moment he had seen the flag dipped and had responded by hiding in the lake. Thought was trying to come back, but training still held it at bay; and for the moment there was no will or urge in him to break through the wall in his mind.

He was not thinking, only moving—but he moved like a wisp of mist over the night ground. His lessons had begun as soon as he could walk, at the hands of three experts who had literally lived for him and had poured into him everything that they had to teach. From his standpoint, it had all seemed merely natural and normal, that he should come to know what he knew and be able to do what he did. It was without effort, almost uncon-sciously, that he went through the dark woods so easily and silently, where almost anyone else would have blundered and made noise.

He came at last to the terrace, now deep in shadow—too buried in dark-ness to show what still lay there, even though light shone from the library windows at its inner edge. His training kept him apart from the shadow, he did not look into it, did not investigate. Instead, he went toward the edge of one of the windows of the house, from which he could look down into the library itself.

The floor of the library was nearly two meters below the level of the ter-race; so that, from within, the window he looked through was high in an outer wall. The room itself was both long and high, its floor-to-ceiling book-shelves warmly stuffed with some thousands of antique, printed and bound volumes holding works like those poems of Alfred Noyes which Walter the InTeacher had been fond of reading. In the fireplace at one end, a fire had just been lit, to throw the ruddy, comforting light of its flames upon the heavy furniture, the books, and the ceiling. The two men in the room stood talk-ing. They were both so tall that their shoulders were almost on a level with Hal's feet. They stood face-to-face; and there was a certain tenseness about the two of them, like partners who might at any moment become adversaries.

One was the tall man he had seen earlier on the terrace. The other was a man the same height, but outweighing the slim man by half again as much. Not that the other man was fat. He was merely powerfully built, with the sort of round, thick arms and body that, even in lesser proportion on some-one of normal height, would have made him seem formidable. His face was round and cheerful under a cap of curly, jet-black hair, and he smiled mer-rily. Facing the slimmer man, he appeared coarse-bodied, almost untidy, in the soft material of the slacks and cloth jacket that made up the maroon busi-ness suit he wore. In contrast, his companion—in gray slacks and black half-cape—seemed tailored and remote.

Hal moved close to the edge of the pane to see if he could hear their talk; and the words inside came faintly through the insulated glass to his ear.

". . . tomorrow, at the latest," the first man was saying. "They should all be here, then."

"They better be. I hold you responsible, Bleys." It was the big, black-haired man speaking.

"When didn't you, Dahno?"

Distantly, a point of information clicked in the back of Hal's mind. Dahno, or Danno—it was spelled various ways—was the one usually spoken of as the leader of the loose Mafia-sort of organization by which the Other Peo-ple were said to be increasing their hold upon the inhabited worlds. The Oth-ers tended to be known to their people by first names only—like kings. Bleys . . . that would be Bleys Ahrens, one of the lesser leaders of the Others.

"Always, Bleys. As now. Your dogs made something of a mess taking over here."

"Your dogs, Dahno."

The thick-bodied giant brushed the answer away.

"The dogs I lent you. It was your job to set up for the Conference here, Mr. Vice-Chairman."

"Your dogs aren't trained, Mr. Chairman. They like killing because they think it proves their value in our eyes. That makes them unreliable with void pistols."

Dahno chuckled again. His eyes were hard and bright.

"Are you pushing me, Bleys?"

"Pushing back."

"All right—within limits. But there'll be fifty-three of us here by tomorrow. The bodies don't matter as long as they're cleaned up, out of the way. Then we can forget them."

"The boy won't," said Bleys.

"Boy?"

"The ward these three were raising and tutoring."

Dahno snorted faintly.

"You're worried about a boy?" he asked.

"I thought you were the one who talked about neatness, Dahno. The old men died before they could tell us about him."

Dahno brushed the air again—a little impatiently. Hal watched him, standing in darkness outside the swath of light from the window.

"Why would the dogs think to keep them alive?"

"Because I didn't tell them to kill." Bleys' voice did not seem to have been raised, but it came with peculiar clearness to Hal's ears through the glass. Dahno cocked his head to look at the slim man, his face for a moment not cheerful, but merely watching.

"Aside from that," he said, his own voice unchanged, "what could they tell us?"

"More." Bleys' voice was again as it had been earlier. "Didn't you look at the prospectus on holding our Conference here? This place was set up under a trust established from the sale of an unregistered interstellar courier-class ship, which was found drifting near Earth, with the boy in it as a two-year-old child, or younger. No one else was aboard. I don't like mysteries."

"It's all that Exotic blood in you that doesn't like mysteries," Dahno said. "Where would we be if we took the time to try to understand every mystery we came across? Our game is controlling the machinery, not understanding it. Tell me about another way a few thousand of us can hope to run fourteen worlds."

"You could be right," said Bleys. "But still it's a careless attitude."

"Bleys, my buck," said Dahno. His voice changed only as slightly as Ahrens' had a moment before, but his eyes reflected the red light of the fire. "I'm never careless. You know that."

The night breeze freshened off the lake and a sudden small gust sent the branches of a lilac bush lashing against the pane of another of the library windows. Both of the men inside looked toward the sound at once. Hal stepped back noiselessly from the window, deeper into the shadow.

His training was urging him away, now. It was time to go. He half-swung toward the terrace, still not forming clearly in his mind the true picture of what was there, but with the empty feeling that what he was leaving was something to which he would never have a chance to return. But his training had anticipated that feeling also, and overrode it. He turned away from terrace and house alike, and moved off through the surrounding trees at a silent trot.

There were gravel-bed roads in the area for the traffic of air-cushion vehicles, but the way he took avoided them. He ran steadily, easily, through the pine-scented night air of the forest, his footsteps silent on the dead conifer needles underfoot and making only little more sound on the patches of bare rock and hard earth. His pace was a steady twelve kilometers an hour, and in a little less than an hour and a half, he reached the small commercial center known as Thirkel. There were a dozen other such centers and two small towns that he could have reached in less distance and time; but an unconscious calculation from his training had led him to choose Thirkel.

Thanks to that calculation, at Thirkel he had only a fourteen-minute wait before a regularly scheduled autobus stopped on its way into Bozeman, Montana. He was the only passenger boarding in the soft mountain night. He stepped aboard and displayed one of the credit tabs he now carried to the automatic control unit of the bus. The unit noted the charge for his travel, closed the doors behind him with a soft breath of air, and lifted the vehicle into the air again.

He came into Bozeman shortly after midnight and caught a shuttle to Salt Lake Pad. Then, as the early dawn was pinkening the sky beyond the surrounding mountains, he lifted in an orbital jitney on its run from that Pad to the gray-clad globe that was the Final Encyclopedia, swimming in orbit around Earth at sixteen hundred kilometers from its surface.

The jitney carried no more than fifty or sixty passengers—all of them having passed pre-clearance at the Earth end of the trip. Among Hal's papers had been a continually renewed scholar's passport for a single visit, under his own name. Earth, the Dorsai, Mara and Kultis were the only four worlds where the Others had not yet gotten some control of the internal government. But on Earth, only the records of the Final Encyclopedia could be regarded as secure from prying by the Others; and so all credit and record transactions Hal had made since leaving his home had been achieved with papers or tabs bearing the name of Alan Semple. These he now destroyed, as the jitney lifted, and he was left carrying nothing to connect him with the false name he had temporarily used. The automated records at the Final Encyclopedia would be too well informed for him to hope to use a false name; but, in them, his real name would be safe.

Twelve hundred kilometers out from Earth's surface the jitney began its approach to the Final Encyclopedia. On the screen of his seat compartment

Hal saw it first as a silver crescent, expanding as they moved out of Earth's shadow to a small silver globe of reflected sunlight. But as they came closer, the small globe grew inexorably and the great size of the Encyclopedia began to show itself.

It was not just its size, however, that held Hal fixed in his seat, his attention captured by the screen as the massive sphere on it swelled and swelled. Unlike the other passengers aboard this jitney, he had been trained by Walter to a special respect for what the Encyclopedia promised. He had gazed at it countless times on screens like this one, but never when he himself was about to set foot in it.

The jitney was slowing now, matching velocities as it approached the sphere. Now that they were closer, Hal could see its surface, looking as if it were shrouded in thick gray fog. This would be a result of the protective force-panels that interlocked around the Encyclopedia—a derivation of the phase-shift that had opened up faster-than-light communication and transportation between the worlds, four hundred years before. The force-panels were a discovery, and a closely-guarded secret, of those on the Encyclopedia. It had been these which had given the structure the silvery appearance from a distance—as the gray mist of dawn close above the water of a lake seems silvered by the early light of day.

Within those panels, the Encyclopedia was invulnerable to any physical attack. Only at points where the panels joined were there soft spots that had to be conventionally armored; and it was to one of these soft spots the jitney was now headed to find a port in which to discharge its passengers.

Hidden within the shield provided by those panels was the physical shape of the Encyclopedia: a structure of metal and magic—the metal from the veins of Earth and the magic of that same force that made possible the phase-drive and the panels—so that there was no way for anyone to tell from observation alone what was material and what was force-panel about the corridors and rooms that made up the Encyclopedia's interior. People within that structure did not move about as much as they were moved. The room they were occupying, on proper command, would become next door to the room to which they wished to go. Yet, also if they wished, there were distances of seemingly solid corridors to traverse and solid doors to open on places within the structure. . . .

Metal and magic . . . as a boy Hal Mayne had been led to an awe of the Encyclopedia, from as far back as he could remember. For the moment now, that awe reinforced the wall protecting him from what he might otherwise remember from only a few hours before. He remembered that it had been an Earthman, Mark Torre, who had conceived the Encyclopedia. But Mark Torre, or even Earth, would never have managed to get it built on its own. A hundred and thirty years had been required to bring it to completion, and all the great wealth that the two rich Exotic Worlds of Mara and Kultis could spare for its construction. Its beginnings had been put together on the ground, just within the Exotic Enclave in the city of St. Louis, in North

America. A hundred and two years later, the half-finished structure had been lifted into its first orbital position only two hundred and fifty kilometers above the Earth. Twelve years after that, the last of the work on it had been finished, and it had been placed here, in its final orbit.

Mark Torre's theory had postulated a dark area always existing in Man's knowledge of himself, an area where self-perception had to fail, as the perception of any viewing mechanism fails in the blind area where it, itself, exists. In that area, ran Torre's theory, the human race would at last find something which had been lost in the people of the Splinter Cultures on the younger worlds; and this, once found, would be the key to the race's last and greatest growth.

There was a largeness of dream and purpose about that theory, and the Encyclopedia itself, that had always resonated powerfully within Hal. That resonance touched him now as the jitney reached the point where the corners of four of the huge, insubstantial force-panels came together, and the jointure where their forces met dilated to reveal an aperture into the docking area that awaited them.

The jitney drifted in, very slowly it seemed, and settled into the cradle that waited for it. Abruptly, they were enclosed by a blaze of light. The aperture that had seemed so tiny as they had approached, now revealed itself to have the diameter of a chamber that dwarfed the jitney and was aswarm with human workers and machines.

Hal got to his feet and joined the procession of passengers moving to the exit port of the jitney. He stepped through the port, onto a sloping ramp and into a roar and clangor of sound, as the busy machines moved about the jitney on the metal floor and walls. Metal and magic . . . he went down the slope of the ramp and through a faintly-hazy circle that was an entrance to the interior parts of the Encyclopedia. As he stepped through that circle, all the noise behind him was cut off. He found himself being carried forward by a movable floor, down a corridor walled in soft light, in a muted hush that welcomed him after the noise he had just left, and seemed to soften even the low-voiced conversations of his fellow passengers.

The line slowed, stopped, moved forward a couple of paces, stopped again, moved, stopped. The passengers ahead were displaying their clearance papers to a wall screen from which a thin-faced, black-haired young man looked out at them.

"Fine. Thank you." The young man nodded at the passenger ahead of Hal, and the passenger moved on. As Hal stepped level with the screen, the man moved aside out of camera range and a lively female face under a cloud of bright blonde hair, young enough to be that of a girl rather than of a woman, took the vacated space. Under the bright gold hair, she had a round, laughing expression and green eyes with flecks of gold swimming in their irises.

"I see . . ." She looked at Hal's papers as he held them up to the screen, then back to him. "You're Hal Mayne? Fine."

It seemed to Hal that her eyes met his with a particular friendliness; and a comfort came to him from seeing her that for a second dangerously weak-ened the wall that hid things in the back of his mind. Then he moved on.

The corridor continued. The people in front of him were moving more quickly now, single file down it. Ahead, a voice was speaking to them out of nowhere in particular.

". . . If you'll please pause at the point where the corridor widens, and lis-ten. Tell us if you hear anything. This is the Transit Point, at the center of the Index Room. You are now at the exact center of the communication sys-tem of the Encyclopedia. We do not expect you to hear anything; but if any of you do, will you speak up. . . ."

More magic . . . they had moved what seemed like only a hundred me-ters; but now they were at the very center of the sphere that was the Ency-clopedia. But neither Walter the InTeacher nor anyone else had ever mentioned to him anything about a Transit Point. He was not yet at the wide stationary spot that had been spoken of, but he found himself listening, as if there might be something he could hear even before he reached it. Vaguely, he felt the request to listen as if it had been a challenge. If there was some-thing to hear there, he should be able to pick it up. He found himself strain-ing to hear.

Almost—he could see the wide, unmoving spot now and he was only two people back from it—he could imagine that he was hearing something. But it was probably only the people who had already passed the Transit Point, discussing it among themselves. There was something familiar about their voices. He could not identify them but there was still a feeling of familiar-ity, although they seemed to be speaking a language he did not know. He had been trained to break down unfamiliar languages into familiar forms. If it was Indo-European . . . yes, it seemed to be a Romance tongue of some sort, one of the modern derivatives of Latin.

But their conversations were very loud now, and there seemed to be a number of them all talking at once. There was a single person left in front of him before he would reach the Transit Point. How could they expect any-one to hear anything at the Point if they were talking like this ahead of it— and behind, too, for that matter? The voices were all around him. Every-body in the line must be talking. The man just ahead of him stepped on, clearing the Transit Point. Hal stepped into it, stopped there, and the voices exploded.

Not tens of them, not hundreds or thousands, or even millions—but bil-lions and trillions of voices in countless languages, arguing, shouting, call-ing to him. Only, they did not merge into one great, voiceless roar, like the radio roar of a universe. They each remained distinct and separate—unbe-lievably, he heard each one; and among them there were three he knew, call-ing out to him, warning him. The voice of Walter the InTeacher, of Malachi Nasuno, of Obadiah Testator—and with his identification of those three voices, the mental wall that had been protecting him finally crumbled and went down.

The Transit Point whirled around him. He was conscious, as of something heard from a little distance, of a sound coming from his own throat. He spun, staggered, and would have fallen—but he was caught and held upright. It was the young woman from the screen, the one with the green eyes, who was holding him. Somehow she was here, physically, beside him; and she was not as small as he had thought her to be when he had seen her face on the screen. Still, his awkward, long-boned length was not easy to support; and, almost immediately, there were two men with her.

"Easy . . . hold him . . . ," said one man; and something touched deep inside him, triggering a darkness like the spreading stain of biologic ink pushed out by a fleeing octopus. It flooded all through him, hiding all things in utter darkness, even his memory of what had happened on the terrace.

Gradually he roused once more, to silence and to peace. He was alone, naked, in a bed in a room walled by slowly-changing, pastel colors. Besides the bed, and the table-surface beside it, there were a couple of chair-floats hanging in the air, a desk, and a small pool with blue sides and floor that made the water in it seem much deeper than he guessed it actually to be. He propped himself up on one elbow and looked about him. The room had a disconcerting property of seeming to expand in the direction in which he was looking, although he was not conscious of any actual movement of its walls or floor. He looked around and then back at the bed in which he lay.

It had never really occurred to him as an important fact—although he had always been aware of it—that he had been raised under conditions that were deliberately spartan and archaic. It had always seemed only natural to him that the books he read should be heavy things of actual paper, that there should be no moving walkways in his home, or that the furniture there should be uniformly of solid, material construction, with physical legs that supported it upon the floor, rather than devices that appeared to float in midair, and to appear out of that same air or dissolve back into it at the touch of a control.

This was the first time he had ever awakened in a force bed. He knew what it was, of course, but he was totally unprepared for the comfort of it. To the eye, he seemed to lie half-immersed in a white cloud perhaps twenty centimeters thick, which floated in the air above the floor of the room. The white cloud-stuff wrapped him in warmth against the cooler air, and that portion of it which was underneath him became firm enough to support him in whatever position he took. Right now the elbow on which he leaned was upheld as if by a warm cupped hand, although to his eye it was merely buried to the depth of half his forearm in the thick mist.

He sat up, swinging his legs over the side of the bed—and with that movement, memory came back completely, like a silent body blow. He saw the terrace and what had happened there in the eye of his mind, as he had watched it all through the screen of lakeside branches. Overcome, he huddled on the edge of the bed, his face in his hands; and for a moment the universe rocked around him and his mind ran screaming from what it now saw.

But there was no longer any wall to hold it back from him, and after a while he came to some sort of terms with it. He lifted his face from his hands again. The color had gone out of the walls of the room. The sensors in them had read the changes in the temperature and humidity of his skin, as well as half a hundred other tiny signals of his body, and accurately reflected his change in emotion. Now the color of the room was a dull, utilitarian gray, as bleak as a chamber carved from rock.

A terrible feeling of rebellion erupted in him, a fury that such a thing as had happened should have been allowed to take place; and riding the energy wave of that fury, as the wall glowed into the redness of heated iron around him, his training was triggered again, and pushed him to a further action.

Under the force of his will his consciousness gathered itself, focused on the glint of a single point of light from one corner of a float and closed in on that point until it was the only thing he saw. Through that point, as through a doorway, his mind moved with its Exotic training into a discipline that was partly self-hypnosis, partly a freeing of a direct channel from his awareness into his own unconsciousness. His vision moved back and out, away once more from the point of light, and he saw all the room again. Only now, there seemed to be three figures sitting in the available floats: Walter, Malachi and Obadiah.

The men who had raised and tutored him were not really there, of course. He knew that. Even as he spoke to them now, he knew that it was not actually they who answered, but constructs of them, created by his imagination from his countless memories of the attitudes and reactions he had observed in them during their lives together. It was, in fact, his own knowledge of them that was answering him, with their voices, uttering the words that he knew they would say if they could be here with him now. The technique was a discipline that had been instilled against a moment just like this one, a moment in which he would need their help and they would no longer be around to give it. But in that first second as he looked at them, it was not a cry for help he threw at them, but an accusation.

"You didn't have to!" He was half-sobbing. "You let them kill you and leave me alone; and you didn't have to!"

"Oh, Hal!" Pain was strong in Walter's voice. "We had to protect you."

"I didn't ask you to protect me! I don't want to be protected. I wanted you alive! And you let them shoot you!"

"Boy," said Malachi, gruffly, "you were prepared for this day. We taught you that something like what happened could happen, and what you must do if it did."

Hal did not answer. Now that he had opened the door to his grief it took possession of him utterly. He huddled on the edge of the bed, facing them, weeping.

"I didn't know . . . ," he sobbed.

"Child," said Obadiah, "you've been taught how to handle pain. Don't fight it. Accept it. Pain alters nothing for him who is beyond such things."

"But I'm not beyond it." Hal was rocking in his misery, rhythmically rocking on the edge of the bed, backward and forward.

"Obadiah is right, Hal," said Walter, softly. "You were taught; and you know how to handle this moment."

"You don't care, none of you . . . you don't understand!" Hal rocked back and forth.

"Of course we understand." Walter's voice sounded the note of the suffering in him, evoked by the suffering in Hal. "We were the only family you had; and now it seems to you you've got no one. You feel as if everything's been taken away. But it's not like that. You still have a family—an enormous family, made up of everyone else in the human race."

Hal shook his head—back and forth, back and forth—as he rocked.

"But you do," said Walter. "Yes, I know. Right now you think there's no one on the fourteen worlds who could take the place of those you've lost. But there will be. You'll find all things in people. You'll find those who hate you and those who love you—and those you'll love. I know you can't believe that, now; but it will be."

"And there's more than love," said Malachi, suddenly. "You'll find that out. In the end you may have to do without love to get done what you have to do."

"That will come," said Obadiah, "if God wills. But there's no reason the child should have to face that test, yet. Leave it to the future, Malachi."

"The future is here," growled Malachi. "He won't survive the forces against him by sitting on a bed and crying. Boy, straighten up—" The command was harsh, but the tone in which it was uttered was not. "Try to take hold. You have to plan what to do. The dead are dead. The living owe their concern to the living, even if the living are themselves."

"Hal," said Walter, still gently, but insistently. "Malachi is right. Obadiah is right. By clinging to your grief, now, you only put off the moment when you have to think of more important things."

"No," said Hal, shaking his head. "No."

He shut his mind against them. It was unthinkable that he should let go any of the grief inside him. To do so, even in the smallest way, threw the earth of certainty upon the doubtless unmarked graves of these three he had loved and still loved. But they continued to talk, saying the things he had heard them say so many times, in the ways he remembered them saying such things; and gradually he began, in spite of himself, to listen.

The shock of what had happened had driven him nearly back into being a very young child again, with all the terrible helplessness of the young. But now, as the familiar voices spoke back and forth around him, he began to come back up to the relative maturity of his sixteen years.

". . . he must hide somewhere," Walter was saying.

"Where?" asked Malachi.

"I'll go to the Exotics," Hal surprised himself by saying. "I could pass for a Maran—couldn't I, Walter?"

"What about that?" Malachi demanded of the InTeacher. "Would your people give him up to the Others?"

"Not willingly," said Walter. "But you're right. If the Others located him there and put pressure on, they couldn't keep him. The Exotics are free of Other control on their own worlds, but their interplanetary connections are vulnerable—and two worlds have to take precedence in importance over one boy."

"He could hide on Harmony or Association," Obadiah said. "The Other People control much of our society, but outside the cities there are those who will never work with the Belial-spawn. Such people of mine would not give him up."

"He'd have to live like an outlaw," Walter said. "He's too young to fight yet."

"I can fight!" said Hal. "Others, or anyone else!"

"Be quiet, boy!" growled Malachi. "They'd have you on toast for break-fast without getting up off their chairs. You're right, Walter. The Friendly Worlds aren't safe for him."

"Then, the Dorsai," said Hal. Malachi's gray thickets of eyebrows frowned at him.

"When you're ready and able to fight, then go to the Dorsai," the old man said. "Until that day, there's nothing they can do for you there."

"Where, then?" said Obadiah. "All other worlds but Earth are already under Other control. They'd only have to sniff him there, and he'd be gone with no one to aid him."

"Still," said Walter. "It has to be one of the other worlds. Earth, here, is also no good. They'll be looking for him as soon as they unravel the full story of his life and our teaching. There're Exotic mixed breeds among them, like that tall man who was there at our death; and they, like me—like all of us trained on Mara or Kultis—know ontogenetics. They're a historic force, the Other People, and they'll know that for any such force there must be a counter-force. They'll have been watching for its appearance among the rest of the race, from the beginning. They'll take no chances of leaving Hal alive once they have his full story."

"Newton, then," said Obadiah. "Let him hide among the laboratories and the ivory towers."

"No," said Malachi. "They're all turtles, there, all clams. They pull back into their shell and pull the shell in after them. He'd stick out like a sore thumb among such people."

"What about Ceta?" said Obadiah.

"That's where the Others are thickest—where the banking and the threads of interstellar trade are pulled," said Malachi, irritably. "Are you mad, Obadiah? Anyway, all of these unspecialized worlds, as well as old Venus and

Mars, are places where much of the machinery of society is under the control of the Others. One slip and it'd be over for our boy."

"Yes," said Walter slowly. "But Obadiah, you said all worlds but the Dorsai, the Exotics, the Friendlies and Earth were already under Others' control. There's one exception. The world they can't be bothered with, because there's no real society there for them to control. Coby."

"The mining world?" Hal stared at Walter. "But there's nothing there for me to do but work in the mines."

"Yes," said Walter.

Hal continued to stare at the InTeacher.

"But . . ." Words failed him. Mara, Kultis, the Friendly Worlds of Harmony and Association, and the Dorsai were all places to which he had longed to go. Any beyond these, any of the Younger Worlds, were unknown, interesting places. But Coby . . .

"It's like sending me to prison!" he said.

"Walter," Malachi was looking at the InTeacher, "I think you're right."

He swung to face Hal.

"How old are you now, boy? You're due to turn seventeen in a month or so, aren't you?"

"In two weeks," said Hal, his voice thinning at the sudden surge of old memories, of early birthday parties and all the years of his growing up.

"Seventeen—" said Malachi, looking again at Walter and at Obadiah. "Three years in the mines and he'd be almost twenty—"

"Three years!" The cry broke from Hal.

"Yes, three years," said Walter softly. "Among the nameless and lost people there, you can do a better job of becoming nameless and lost, yourself, than you can do on any other world. Three years will bury you completely."

"And he'll come out different," said Obadiah.

"But I don't want to be different!"

"You must be," said Malachi to him. "That is, at least, if you're to survive."

"But, three years!" said Hal again. "That's nearly a fifth of my life so far. It's an eternity."

"Yes," said Walter; and Hal looked at him hopelessly. Walter, the gentlest of his three tutors, was the least likely to be moved once he had come to a decision. "And it's because it'll be an eternity for you, Hal, that it'll be so useful. With all we tried to do for you, we've still raised you off in a corner, away from ordinary people. There was no choice for us, but still you're crippled by that. You're like a hothouse plant that can wither if it's suddenly set out in the weather."

"Hothouse plant?" Hal appealed to Malachi, to Obadiah. "Is that all I am? Malachi, you said I was as good as an average Dorsai my age, in my training. Obadiah, you said—"

"God help you, child," said Obadiah, harshly. "In what you are and in what we tried to make of you, you're a credit to us all. But the ways of the worlds are some of the things you do not know; and it's with those ways that you'll have to live and struggle before God brings you at last to your accomplishment and your rest. Your way cannot be in corners and byways anymore—and I should have realized that when I suggested Newton as a place for you to go. You have to go out among your fellow men and women from now on and begin to learn from them."

"They won't want to teach me," said Hal. "Why should they?"

"It's not for them to teach, but for you to learn," said Obadiah.

"Learn!" said Hal. "That's all you ever said to me, all of you—learn this! Learn that! Isn't it time I was doing something more than learning?"

"There is nothing more than learning," said Walter; and in the InTeacher's voice Hal heard the absolute commitment of the three facing him that he should go to Coby. It was not something that he could argue against successfully. He was not being faced with an opinion by three other people, but by the calculation that was part of the pattern trained in him. That calculation had surveyed the options open to him and decided that his most secure future for the upcoming years lay on Coby.

Still, he was crushed by that decision. He was young and the thirteen other inhabited worlds of mankind glittered with promise like tempting jewels. As he had said, going into the mines would be like going to prison, and the three years—to him—would indeed be an eternity.

Chapter

> > **3** < <

Hal did not know at what point the shades of his tutors left him. Simply, after a while, the floats were empty and he was alone once more. His mind had wandered from his need for them, and they had gone, back into the land of his memories, like the flames of blown-out candles.

But he felt better. Even with the dreary prospect of Coby facing him, he felt better now. Purpose had come back to life in him; and the evocation of the attitudes and certainties of his dead tutors had given him a certain amount of strength. Also, though he was not consciously aware of this, the basic vitality of his youth was lifting his spirits whether he wanted them lifted or not. He had too much sheer physical energy to do nothing but sit and mourn, in spite of the severity of the emotional wound the deaths had dealt him.

He dressed, examined the controls of his room and ordered in some food. He was eating this when his annunciator chimed.

He keyed the screen on his bedside table-surface; and the bright and cheerful face of the young woman from the Transit Point took shape in it.

"Hal Mayne?" she said. "I'm Ajela, Special Assistant to Tam Olyn."

There was a split second before the second name she had mentioned registered on him. Tam Olyn was the Director of the Encyclopedia—had been its Director for eighty-odd years. He had originally been a top-level interplanetary newsman; but he had abandoned that as suddenly as a man might turn from the world into the seclusion of a monastery, to step in, almost at the moment of his entrance there, to being the supreme authority of the Encyclopedia. Hal had learned all about the man in his studies; but he had never thought that he might someday be talking directly to one of the Director's close assistants.

"I'm honored to meet you," he said automatically to the screen.

"Can I drop in on you?" Ajela asked. "There's something we should talk about."

Caution laid its hand on him.

"I'm just here temporarily," he said. "I'll be going out to one of the Younger Worlds as soon as I can get passage."

"Of course," she said. "But meanwhile, if you wouldn't mind talking to me . . ."

"Oh, no. No, of course not." He was aware that he fumbled, and he felt embarrassment kindle in him. "Come along right now, if you want."

"Thank you."

The screen lost its image, returning to a uniform pearl grey without depth.

Hastily, he finished his meal and pushed his emptied utensils down the disposal slot. They had hardly disappeared when the annunciator chimed again.

"May I come in?" asked the voice of Ajela, from the blank screen.

"Certainly. Come along—" He went to the door but it opened before he could reach it, and she stepped through.

She was wearing a loose saffron robe that tied at the waist and reached to her knees. In spite of her youth, she was clearly an Exotic; and she seemed to have the Exotic ability to make everything about her seem as if it could never have been otherwise. So the saffron robe seemed to him in that first moment in which he really looked at her, as if it were the only thing she should ever wear. Her impact on him was so profound that he almost drew back defensively. He might, indeed, have been even more wary of her than he was; but the open, smiling face and disregard of pretense reassured his prickly young male fear of making the wrong move, suddenly finding himself face-to-face with a startlingly beautiful woman—he, who had had so little normal acquaintance with women of any age until now.

"You're all right now?" she asked him.

"Fine," he said. "I—thank you."

"I'm sorry," she said. "If we could have warned you, we would have. But the way it is with the Transit Point, if we warn people, we'd never know . . . it's all right if I sit down?"

"Oh, of course!" He backed away and they sat down in facing floats.

"What wouldn't you know?" he asked, his unquenchable curiosity rising even above his feelings of social awkwardness.

"We'd never be sure that they weren't imagining what they said they heard."

Hal shook his head.

"There wasn't any imagination in what I heard," he said.

"No." She was looking closely at him. "I don't believe there was. What exactly did you hear?"

He looked at her closely, cautiously.

His mind was now almost completely recovered from the unsureness he had felt on first talking to her.

"I'd like to know more of what this is all about," he said.

"Of course you would," she said warmly. "All right, I'll tell you. The fact is, early in the building of the Final Encyclopedia they discovered by accident that someone stepping into the Transit Point for the first time might hear voices. Not voices speaking to them—" She stopped to gaze closely at him. "Just voices, as if they were overhearing them. Mark Torre, in his old age, was the first to hear them. But only Tam Olyn, the first time he stepped into the Encyclopedia, heard them so plainly that he collapsed—the way you did."

Hal stared at her. All his training had ingrained in him the principle of going cautiously, the more unknown or strange the territory. What Ajela had just said was so full of unknown possibilities that he felt a danger in showing any reaction at all before he had had time to understand the matter. He waited, hoping she would simply talk on. But she did not. She only waited in her turn.

"Tam Olyn," he said at last.

"Yes."

"Just Tam Olyn and me? In all these years?"

"In all these years," she said. Her voice had a note in it he could not interpret, a note that was almost sad, for no reason that he could understand. She watched him, he thought, with an odd sympathy.

"I think," he said carefully, "you ought to tell me all about this; and then give me a chance to think about it."

She nodded.

"All right," she said. "Mark Torre conceived of the Encyclopedia—you know that. He was Earth-born, no Exotic, but the Exotics found his conception so in agreement with ontogenetics and our other theories of human and historical evolution that we ended by financing the building of this—" She gestured at the structure around them.

Hal nodded, waited.

"As I said, it was in his late years Mark Torre first heard the voices at the Transit Point." She looked at him with a seriousness that was almost severity. "He theorized then that what he'd heard was just the first evidence of the first small use by any individual of the potential of the Encyclopedia. It was as if someone who'd had no knowledge of what to listen for had suddenly tuned in to all the radio noise of the universe. Sorting out the useful information from that roar of noise, Torre said, would take experience."

Again she paused, almost frowning at him. Hal nodded again, to show his appreciation of the importance of what she was saying.

"I see," he said.

"This idea," she went on, "is what meshed with some of our theories on the Exotics, because it seemed to say that using the Encyclopedia the way Mark Torre dreamed of it being used—as a new sort of tool for the human mind—called for some special ability, an ability not yet to be found in all of the human race. Torre died without making any sense out of what he heard. But he was convinced someone would eventually. After him, Tam took charge here; but Tam's lived in the Encyclopedia all these years without learning how to handle or use what he hears."

"Not at all?" Hal could not help interrupting.

"Not at all," Ajela said, firmly.

"But, like Mark Torre, he's been certain that sooner or later someone would come along who could; and when that finally happens the Encyclopedia is at last going to be put to use as what it was built to be, a tool to unravel the inner universe of the race—that inner universe that's been a dark and fearful mystery since people first started to be conscious of the fact they could think."

Hal sat looking at her.

"And now," he said, "you—and Tam Olyn—you think I might be the one to use it?"

She frowned at him.

"Why are you so cautious . . . so fearful?" she asked.

He could not tell her. The implication he thought he heard in her voice was one of cowardice. He bristled instinctively.

"I'm not fearful," he said, sharply. "Just careful. I was always taught to be like that."

She reacted instantly.

"I'm sorry," she said with unexpected softness; and her eyes made him feel as if he had made a most unjustified inference from what she had said. "Believe me, neither Tam nor I are trying to push you into anything. If you stop and think, you'll realize that what Mark Torre and Tam were thinking was something that never could be forced on anyone in any case. It'd be as impossible to force that as it'd be impossible to force someone to produce great art. A thing that'd be as great and new as that couldn't ever be forced into existence. It can only come out of some person willing to give her or his life to it."

These last words of hers echoed with a particular power in his mind. In his heart he had never yet been able to delude himself that he was adult, in any ordinary social sense. Even though he was taller than most men already and had already packed into his sixteen years more learning than a normal person would have had pushed upon him by twice that time, secretly, and inwardly, he had never been able to convince himself that he was grown up yet. Because of this he had been very conscious of the fact that she was probably a year or two older than he was, and had suspected her of being contemptuous of him, of looking down on him because of it. In a way, the capability of his three tutors had so overshadowed him that they had kept him feeling like a child beyond his years.

But now, for the first time in talking to her, he began to be conscious also of an independence and a strength that he had never felt before. He found himself looking on her and thinking of her, and all the rest of them in this Encyclopedia, with possibly the exception of Tam Olyn, as potential equals, rather than superiors; and, thinking this, he found himself—although the thought did not surface as such in his conscious mind—beginning to fall in love with Ajela.

"I told you, though," he said to her, suddenly conscious of the silence between them, "I'm on my way out. So it doesn't matter whether I heard anything or not."

She sat looking at him penetratingly for a long, silent moment.

"At least," she said at last, "you can take the time to come and talk to Tam Olyn. You and he have something very rare in common."

The point she made was not only effective, but flattering. He was aware she had intended it to be that, but he could not help responding. Tam Olyn was a fabulous name. For his own to be matched with it was ego-building.

For just that moment his private grief and loss were forgotten and he thought only that he was being invited to meet Tam Olyn face to face.

"Of course. I'll be honored to talk to him," he said.

"Good!" Ajela got to her feet.

He stared up at her.

"You mean—right now?"

"Why not?"

"No reason not—of course." He got up, in his turn.

"He wants very much to talk to you," she said. She turned, but not toward the door. Instead, she stepped to the bedside table-surface and the panel of controls there. Her fingers tapped out some code or other.

"We'll go right over," she said.

He was not aware of any feeling of the room's movement; but after a moment's wait she turned toward the door, walked across and opened it, and instead of the corridor he had expected to see, he found himself looking into another, much larger room. Another space, in fact, was a better word for it; it seemed to be not so much a room as a forest glade with comfortable, heavily-padded chair-floats scattered up and down its grassy floor along the banks of a small stream that murmured away out of sight between the trunks of a pine forest at the near end of the room and flowed from the base of a small waterfall at the other. A summer midday sky seemed to be overhead.

Behind a desk by the stream, down a little distance from the waterfall, sat the room's single occupant. He looked up as Hal and Ajela approached, pushing aside some time-yellowed and brittle-looking papers that he had been examining on his desk. To Hal's private surprise, he was not the frail-looking centenarian Hal had expected. He was aged—no doubt about it—but he looked more like an eighty-year-old in remarkably good physical condition than someone of his actual years. It was only when they came forward, and Hal met the eyes of the Director of the Final Encyclopedia for the first time, that he felt the full impact of the man's age. The dark gray eyes sunken in wrinkles chilled him with a sense of experience that went beyond any length of years that Hal could imagine living.

"Sit down," Tam said. His voice was hoarse and old and deep.

Hal walked forward and took a float directly in front of Tam Olyn. Ajela, however, did not sit down. She continued walking forward, and turned to stand beside and partly behind the back of the padded chair in which he sat. With one arm she leaned on the top of the float back, the other dropped so that the tips of her fingers rested lightly on Tam's shoulder, as lightly as the lighting of a butterfly. She looked out over Tam's head at Hal, but spoke to the older man.

"Tam," she said, "this is Hal Mayne."

Her voice had a different tone in it that touched Hal for a moment almost with jealousy and with a certain longing.

"Yes," said Tam.

His voice was indeed old. It was hoarse and dry. All his hundred and twenty-plus years echoed in it. His eyes continued to hold Hal's.

"When I first met Mark Torre, after hearing the voices," Tam said slowly, "he wanted to touch my hand. Let me have your hand, Hal Mayne."

Hal got up and extended his hand over the desk. The light, dry fingers of the old man, like twigs covered in thin leather, took it and held it for a second—then let it go.

"Sit down," said Tam, sinking back into his seat.

Hal sat.

"Mark Torre felt nothing when he touched me," Tam said, half to himself, "and I felt nothing now. It doesn't transfer . . . only, now I know why Mark hoped to feel something when he touched me. I've come to want it, too."

He drew a slow breath through his nostrils.

"Well," he said, "that's it. There's nothing to feel. But you did hear the voices?"

"Yes," said Hal.

He found himself awed. It was not just the ancientness of Tam Olyn that touched him so strongly. There was something beyond that, something that must have been there all of Tam Olyn's life—an elemental force for either good or evil, directed these last eighty-odd years to one purpose only. That time, that distance, that fixity of purpose towered over everything Hal had ever experienced like a mountain over someone standing at the foot of it.

"Yes. I didn't doubt you," Tam was saying, now. "I just wanted the pleasure of hearing you tell me. Did Ajela tell you how rare you are?"

"She mentioned that you and Mark Torre were the only ones who'd heard the voices," Hal answered.

"That's right," Tam Olyn said. "You're one of three. Mark, myself . . . and now you."

"I . . . ," Hal fumbled as he had fumbled earlier with Ajela, "I'm honored."

"Honored?" There was a dark, angry flash in the eyes set so deeply beneath the age-heavy brow. "The word 'honored' doesn't begin to describe it. Believe me, who used to make my living from words."

Ajela's fingertips pressed down a little, lightly upon the shoulder they touched. The dark flash passed and was gone.

"But you don't understand, of course," Tam said, less harshly. "You think you understand, but you don't. Think of my lifetime and Mark Torre's. Think of the more than a century it took to build this, all around us. Then think deeper than that. Think of all the lifetime of the human race, from the time it began to walk on two legs and dream of things it wanted. Then, you might start to understand what it means to the human race for you to hear the voices at the Transit Point the way you did."

A strange echo came to Hal's mind as he sat under the attack of these words—and it was a curiously comforting echo. Abruptly, it seemed to him he heard in Tam Olyn's voice the trace of an element of another, loved harshness of expression—which had been Obadiah's. He stared at Tam. His studies had always told him that the other was pure Earthman—full-spectrum Earth stock; but what Hal had thought he had heard just now was the hard ring of Friendly thinking—of pure faith, unself-sparing and uncompromising. How could the Director of the Final Encyclopedia have come to acquire some of the thoughtways of a Faith-holder?

"I suppose I can't appreciate it as much as you do," Hal said. "But I can believe it's a greater thing than I can imagine—to have done it."

"Yes. Good," said Tam, nodding. "Good."

He leaned forward over his desk.

"Ajela tells me your clearance request states that you're simply passing through," he said. "We'd like you to stay."

"I can't," answered Hal, automatically. "I've got to go on, as soon as I can find a ship."

"To where?" The commanding old voice, the ancient eyes held him pinned. Hal hesitated. But if it was not safe to speak to Tam Olyn, who could he speak to?

"To Coby."

"Coby? And you're going to do what, on Coby?"

"I'm going to work there," Hal said, "in the mines—for a while."

"A while?"

"A few years."

Tam sat looking at him.

"Do you understand you could be here instead, with all it means to have heard the voices, and following to whatever great discovery they might lead you to?" he demanded. "You realize that?"

"Yes."

"But you're going to go to Coby to do mining, anyway?"

"Yes," said Hal, miserably.

"Will you tell me why?"

"No," said Hal, feeling the hand of trained caution on him again, "I . . . can't."

There was another long moment in which Tam merely sat watching him.

"I assume," Tam said at the end of that time, "you've understood all I've told you. You know the importance of what hearing the voices implies. Ajela and I, here and now, probably know more about you—thanks to the records of the Encyclopedia—than anyone alive, except your three tutors. I assume they agreed to this business of your going to Coby?"

"Yes. They—" Hal hesitated. "It was their idea, their decision."

"I see." Another long pause. "I also assume there're reasons, for your own good, to make you go; and it's these you aren't free to tell me."

"I'm sorry," said Hal. "That's right. I can't."

There rose once again in his mind the remembered image of his three tutors and the still-semi-obscured memory of what he had watched on the terrace only the day before. A pressure grew in his chest until it threatened to choke him. It was rage, a rage against the people who had killed those whom he loved. There would be no peace for him, anywhere, until he had found the tall man, and everyone connected with him who had brought Walter, Malachi, and Obadiah to their deaths. Something hard and old and cold had been waked in him by their slaying. He was going to Coby only to grow strong, so that in the end he could bring retribution to that tall man and the others. There was no way he could stay here at the Final Encyclopedia or anywhere else. If he were to be held prisoner here, he knew, he would find some way to break loose and go to Coby.

He became aware that Tam was talking again.

"Well then," said Tam, "I'll respect the privacy of your reasons. But I'll ask you one thing in return—remember. Remember our need of you here. This—"

He gestured at everything around him.

"—this is the most precious thing ever produced by the human race. But it needs someone to direct it. It had Mark Torre in the beginning. It's had me since. But now I'm old, too old. Understand—I'm not offering you the Directorship. You'd only qualify for that later on, if you showed you could do the job, and after a great deal of time and work. But there isn't any other prospect but you; and past indications are there isn't likely to be, in the time I've got left."

He stopped. Hal did not know what to say, so he said nothing.

"Have you any conception of what it's like to have a tool like the Encyclopedia at your fingertips?" Tam said suddenly. "You know scholars use it as a reference work; and the overwhelming majority of people think it's nothing more than that—a large library, nothing else. But that use is like using a human being for a beast of burden when he or she could be a doctor, a scientist, or an artist! The Encyclopedia's not here just to make available what's already known. It's been built at all this great cost and labor for something more, something far more important."

He paused and stared at Hal, the deep lines of his face deeper with emotion that could be either anger or anguish.

"Its real purpose—its only true purpose—" he went on, "is to explore the unknown. For that it needs a Director who understands what that means, who won't lose sight of that purpose. You can be that person; and without you, all the potential value of the Encyclopedia to the human race can be lost."

Hal had not planned to argue; but his instincts and training led him to question instinctively.

"If it's that important," he said, "what's wrong with waiting however long it takes? Inside the force-panels nothing can touch the Encyclopedia. So why not just keep on waiting until someone else who can hear the voices comes along, someone who's free?"

"There're no denotations in reality, only connotations," said Tam harshly. The command in his dark eyes held Hal almost physically in his seat. "Since time began, people have given words arbitrary definitions. They created logical structures from those same definitions, and thought that they'd proved something, in terms of the real universe. Safe physically doesn't mean totally safe. There're non-material ways in which the Encyclopedia is vulnerable to destruction; and one of them's an attack on the minds directing it. Marvelous as it is, it's still only a tool, needing the human intellect to put it to work. Take that human intellect from it and it's useless."

"But that's not going to happen," said Hal.

"It's not?" Tam's voice grew even harsher. "Look around you at the fourteen worlds. Do you know the Old Norse legends, the term 'Ragnarok'? It means the end of the world. The doom of Gods and Men."

"I know," said Hal. "First came the Frost Giants and Fimbulwinter, then Ragnarok—the last great battle between Gods and Giants."

"Yes," said Tam. "But you don't know that Ragnarok—or Armageddon, the real Armageddon, if you like that word better—is on us now?"

"No," said Hal; but the words in the old, hoarse voice jarred him deeply, and he felt his heart pumping strongly in his chest.

"Then take my word for it. It is. Hundreds of thousands—millions of years it's taken us to build our way up from the animal level to where we could spread out among the stars. Unlimited space. Space for everyone. Space for each individual to emigrate to, to settle down on and raise those of the same mind as himself or herself. And we did it. We paid the cost and some survived. Some even matured and flowered, until we had a few special Splinter Cultures, like the Exotics, the Dorsai, and the Friendlies. Some didn't. But so far we've never been tested as a whole race, a whole race inhabiting more than one world. The only enemies we met were natural forces and each other, so we've built up worlds; and we've built this Encyclopedia."

A sudden coughing interrupted him. For a little while his voice had strengthened and cleared as he spoke until it nearly lost its hoarseness and sounded young again. But then it had hoarsened rapidly once more, and now the coughing took him. Ajela massaged his neck with the fingertips of both her hands until the fit stopped and he lay back in the chair breathing deeply.

"And now," he went on, slowly and throatily after a long moment, "the work of all our centuries has borne its fruit—just before the frost. The peak of the harvest season is on us and the unpicked fruit will rot on the trees. We've found out the Splinter Cultures can't survive on their own. Only full-spectrum humans survive. Now, the most specialized of our Splinter Cultures are dying—most people can't see it even yet—and there's a general social breakdown preparing us for the end. Where the physical laws of the universe have tried and failed to defeat us, we've done it to ourselves. The pattern of life's become fouled and sterile; and there's a new virus spreading among us. The crossbreeds among the Splinter Cultures are a sickness to our whole race as they try to turn it into a mechanism for their own personal survival. Everywhere, everywhere—the season of our times is going downhill into a winter-death."

He stopped and stared fiercely at Hal for a moment.

"Well? Do you believe me?" he demanded.

"I suppose so," said Hal.

The fierceness that had come into Tam's face relaxed.

"You," he went on, looking at Hal, "of all people, have to understand this. We're dying. The race is dying. Look, and you have to see it! The people on all the fourteen worlds don't realize it yet because it's coming too slowly, and because they're blinded by the limited focus of their attitudes toward time and history. They look only as far as their own lifetime. No, they don't even look that far. They only look at how things are for their own generation. But to us, up here, looking down at the original Earth and all the long pattern of the centuries, the beginnings of decay and death are plain to see. The Others are going to win. You realize that? They'll end up owning the rest of the race, as if all other humans were cattle—and from that day on there'll be no one left to fight them. The race as a whole will start to die, because it'll have stopped growing—stopped going forward."

Tam paused again.

"There's only one hope. One faint hope. Because even if we could kill off all the Others now, this moment, it wouldn't stop what's coming. The race'd only find some other disease to die of. The cure has to be a cure of the spirit— a breaking out into some new, vaster area for all of us to explore and grow in. Only the Encyclopedia can make that possible. And maybe only you can make it possible for the Encyclopedia, and push back the shadows that are falling, falling in now over all of us."

His voice had run down in strength toward the end of his words until it was almost inaudible to Hal. He stopped talking; and this time he did not start again. He sat still behind his desk, looking down at the top of it. Ajela stood silently behind him, soothingly massaging his neck; and Hal sat still. It seemed to Hal, although the little stream ran unchanged beside them, the pseudo-sky overhead was still as blue and the appearance of the pine forest around them was still as green and lovely, that a coldness had crept into the room they occupied, and that all the colors and softnesses in it had become dulled and hardened and old.

"In any case," Ajela said, into the new silence, "I can show Hal around the Encyclopedia during the time he's got before he has to go."

"Yes." Tam lifted his eyes to look at the two of them once more. "Show him around. Give him a chance to see as much as he can, while he can."

Chapter

> >**4** < <

Back in Hal's room, Ajela played with the control bank; and a lean-faced man with grizzled hair appeared on the screen.

"Ajela!" he said.

"Jerry," she told him, "this is Hal Mayne, who just came in yesterday. He wants to go out to Coby as soon as he can. What have you got as possibilities?"

"I'll look." The screen went blank.

"A friend of yours?" Hal asked.

She smiled.

"There're less than fifteen hundred of us on permanent staff, here," she said. "Everybody knows everybody."

The screen lit up again with the face of Jerry.

"There's a liner outbound to New Earth, due to hit orbit here in thirty-two hours, eighteen minutes," he said. "Hal Mayne?"

"Yes?" Hal moved up to where he could be seen on Jerry's screen.

"From New Earth in two days you can transship by cargo ship to Coby itself. That should put you on Coby in about nine days, subjective time. Will that do you?"

"That's fine," said Hal.

"You've got your credit papers on file, here?"

"Yes."

"All right," said Jerry. "I can just go ahead and book it for you, if you want."

Hal felt a touch of embarrassment.

"I don't want any special favors—" he was beginning.

"What favors?" Jerry grinned. "This is my job, handling traffic for our visiting scholars."

"Oh, I see. Thanks," said Hal.

"You're welcome." Jerry broke the connection.

Hal turned back to Ajela.

"Thank you for doing the calling, though," he said. "I don't know your command codes here at all."

"Neither does anyone who's non-permanent personnel. You could have found out from the Assistance Operator, but this saves time. You do think you'd like to have me show you around the Encyclopedia?"

"Yes. Absolutely—" Hal hesitated. "Could I actually work with the Encyclopedia?"

"Certainly. But why don't you leave that until last? After you've seen something of it, working with it will make more sense to you. We could go back to the Transit Point and start from there."

"No." He did not want to hear the voices again—at least, not for a while. "Can we get some lunch first?"

"Then suppose I take you first to the Academic control center—I mean after the dining room, of course."

They left their table, walked out of the dining room, down what seemed like a short corridor, and entered through a dilated aperture into a room perhaps half the size of the dining room. Its walls were banked with control consoles; and in midair in the center of the room floated what looked like a mass of red, glowing cords, making a tangle that was perhaps a meter thick, from top to bottom, and two meters wide by three long. Ajela led him up to it. The cords, he saw from close-up, were unreal—visual projections.

"What is it?" he asked.

"The neural pathways of the Encyclopedia currently being activated as people work with them." She smiled sympathetically at him. "It doesn't seem to make much sense, does it?"

He shook his head.

"It takes a great deal of time to learn to recognize patterns in it," she said. "The technicians that work with it get very good. But, actually only Tam can look at it and tell you at a glance everything that's being done with it."

"How about you?" he asked.

"I can recognize the gross patterns—that's about all," she said. "I'll need ten more years to begin to qualify myself for even the beginning technician level."

He looked at her with a touch of suspicion.

"You're exaggerating," he said. "It won't take you that long."

She laughed, and he felt gratified.

"Well, maybe not."

"I'd guess you must be pretty close to being level with a beginning technician right now," he said. "You're pulling that Exotic trick of talking yourself down. You wouldn't have gone from nowhere to becoming Tam's special assistant in six years, if you weren't unusual."

She looked at him, suddenly sober.

"Plainly," she said, "you're a little unusual yourself. But, of course, you'd have to be."

"I would? Why?"

"To hear the voices at the Transit Point."

"Oh," he said. "That."

She took him up close to the glowing, airborne mass of red lines, and began to trace individual ones, explaining how one was clearly a tap from the Encyclopedia's memory-area of history over to the area of art, which meant that a certain scholar from Indonesia had found a connection to a new sidelight on the work he was doing; and how another line showed that the Encyclopedia itself was projecting related points to the research another person was doing—in effect, suggesting avenues of exploration.

"Is this all just what Tam called 'library' use of the Encyclopedia?" Hal asked.

"Yes." Ajela nodded.

"Can you show me what the other kind would look like in these neural pathways?" he asked.

She shook her head.

"No. The Encyclopedia's still waiting for someone who can do that."

"What makes Tam so sure it's possible?"

She looked gravely at him.

"He's Tam Olyn. And he's sure."

Hal reserved judgment on the question. She took him next to the mechanical heart of the Encyclopedia, the room containing the controls for the solar power it stored and used, to run the sphere and to drive the force-panels that protected it. The panels actually used little of the power. Like the phase-shift from which they were derived, they were almost non-physical. Where the phase-shift drive did not actually move a spaceship as much as it changed the description of its location, the protective panels in effect set up an indescribably thin barrier of no-space. Just as a spaceship under phase-drive at the moment of shift was theoretically spread out evenly throughout the universe and immediately reassembled at some other designated spot than that from which it started, so any solid object attempting to pass the curtain of no-space in the panels became theoretically spread out throughout the universe, without hope of reassembling.

"You know about this?" Ajela asked Hal as they stood in the mechanicals control room.

"A little," he said. "I learned, the way everybody does, how the shift was developed from the Heisenberg Uncertainty Principle."

"Not everybody," she said. He frowned at her.

"Oh?"

She smiled. "You'd be surprised what percentage of the total race has no idea of how space vessels move."

"I suppose," he said, a little wistfully. "But anyway, the force-panels don't seem that hard to understand. Essentially, all they do is what a spaceship does, if a one-in-a-million chance goes wrong. It's just that after things are spread out they're never reassembled."

"Yes," she said, slowly. "People talk about phase-shift errors as if they were something romantic—a universe of lost ships. But it's not romantic."

He gazed closely at her.

"Why does that make you so sad?" he asked, deeply moved to see her cheerfulness gone.

She stared at him for a second.

"You're sensitive," she said.

Before he could react to that statement, however, she had gone on.

"But shouldn't I be sad?" she asked. "People have died. To them there was nothing romantic about it. People have been destroyed or lost forever, who might have changed the course of the race if they'd lived. How about Donal Graeme, who brought the fourteen worlds to the closest thing to a unified political whole that they'd ever known—just seventy years or so ago? He was only in his thirties when he left the Dorsai for Mara, and never got there."

Hal shrugged. He knew the bit of history she referred to. But in spite of the sensitivity she had just accused him of having, he could not work up much sympathy for Donal Graeme, who after all had had nearly a third of a normal lifetime before he was lost. He became aware that Ajela was staring at him.

"Oh, I forgot!" she said. "You were almost lost that way. It was just luck you were found. I'm sorry. I didn't think when I brought the subject up."

It was like her, he thought—already he was thinking of ways in which she was like, although he had only known her a matter of hours—to put the kindest possible interpretation on his indifference to what moved her deeply.

"I don't remember any of it," he said. "I was under two years old when they found me. As far as I'm concerned, it could just as well have happened to someone else."

"Haven't you ever been tempted to try and establish who your parents were?"

Internally, he winced. He had been tempted, hundreds of times. He had woven a thousand fantasies in which by chance he discovered them, still alive somewhere.

He shrugged again.

"How'd you like to go down to the Archives?" she asked. "I can show you the facsimiles of all the art of the race from the paleolithic cave paintings of the Dordogne, up until now; and every weapon and artifact and machine that was ever made."

"All right," he said; and with an effort hauled himself off thoughts of his unknown parents. "Thanks."

They went to the Archives, which were in another room-area just under the actual metal skin of the Encyclopedia. All the permanent rooms made a layer of ten to twenty meters thick just inside that skin. With the force-panels outside it, that location was as safe as anywhere within the sphere itself; and this arrangement left the great hollow interior free for the movable rooms to shift about it.

As Ajela explained, the rooms were in reality always in motion, being shuttled about to make way for the purposeful movement of other rooms as they were directed into proximity with one another. In the gravityless center of the sphere, with each room having its own interior gravity, this motion was all but unnoticeable, said Ajela; though in fact Hal had already come to be conscious of it—not the movement itself, but the changes in direction. He supposed that long familiarity with the process had made permanent personnel like Ajela so used to it that they did not notice it anymore.

He let her talk on, although the facts she was now telling him were some he had learned years ago from Walter the InTeacher. He was aware that she was talking to put him at his ease, as much as to inform him.

The Archives, when they came to them, inhabited a very large room made to seem enormous, by illusion. It had to be large to appear to hold the life-size, and apparently solid, three-dimensional images of objects as large as Earth's Roman Colosseum, or the Symphonie des Flambeaux which Newton had built.

He had not expected to be deeply moved by what he would see there, most of which he assumed he had seen in image form before. But as it turned out, he was to betray himself into emotion, after all.

"What would you like to see first?" she asked him.

Unthinkingly, his head still full of the idea of testing the usefulness of the Encyclopedia, he mentioned the first thing he could think of that legitimately could be here, but almost certainly would not.

"How about the headstone on Robert Louis Stevenson's grave?" he asked.

She touched the studs on her bank of controls, and almost within arm's length of him the transparent air resolved itself into an upright block of gray granite with words cut upon it.

His breath caught. It was an image copy only, his eyes told him, but so true to actuality it startled him. He reached out to the edge of the imaged stone and his fingers reported a cold smoothness, the very feel of the stone itself. He, with all the response to poetry that had always been in him, had always echoed internally to this before all other epitaphs, the one that Stevenson had written for himself when he should be laid in a churchyard.

He tried to read the lines of letters cut in the stone, but they blurred in his vision. It did not matter. He knew them without seeing them:

Under the wide and starry sky,
Dig the grave and let me lie.
Glad did I live and gladly die,
And I laid me down with a will.

This be the verse you grave for me:
Here he lies where he longed to be;
Home is the sailor, home from the sea,
And the hunter home from the hill.

The untouchable words woke again in him the memory of the three who had died on the terrace, and kindled a pain inside him so keen that he thought for a second or two he would not be able to bear it. He turned away from the stone and Ajela; and stood, looking at nothing, until he felt her hand on his shoulder.

"I'm sorry," she said. "But you asked . . ."

Her voice was soft, and her touch on his shoulder so light he could barely sense it; but together they made a rope by which he was able to haul himself once more back up from the bitter ache of the personal loss.

"Look," she said, "I've got something else for you. Look!"

Reluctantly, he turned and found himself looking at a bronze sculpture no more than seven inches in height. It was the sculpture of a unicorn standing on a little patch of ground, with tight-petalled roses growing near his feet. His neck was arched, his tail in an elegant circle, his mane flying and his head uptilted roguishly. There was a look in his eye and a twist to his mouth that chortled at the universe.

It was *The Laughing Unicorn*, by Darlene Coltrain. He was unconquerable, sly, a dandy—and he was beautiful. Life and joy bubbled up and fountained in every direction from him.

It was impossible for pain and such joy to occupy the same place; and after a moment the pain began to recede from Hal. He smiled at the unicorn in spite of himself; and could almost convince himself that the unicorn smiled back.

"Do you have the originals of any of these facsimiles?" he asked Ajela.

"Some," she said. "There's the problem of available storage space—let alone that you can't buy things like this with credit. What we do have are those that have been donated to us."

"That one?" he asked, pointing at *The Laughing Unicorn*.

"I think . . . yes, I think that's one we do," she said.

"Could I see it? I'd like to actually handle it."

She hesitated, then slowly but plainly shook her head.

"I'm sorry," she said. "No one touches the originals but the archivists—and Tam."

She smiled at him.

"If you ever get to be Director, you can keep him on your desk, if you want."

Ridiculously, inexpressibly, he longed to own the small statuette; to take it with him for comfort when he went out alone between the stars and into the mines on Coby. But of course that was impossible. Even if he did own the original himself, it was too valuable to be carried in an ordinary traveller's luggage. Its loss or theft would be a tragedy to a great many people besides himself.

He lost himself after that in looking at a number of other facsimiles of art, all sorts of works, books and other artifacts that Ajela summoned up with her control bank. In an odd way, a barrier had gone down between the two of them with the emotions that had just been evoked in him, first by the Robert Louis Stevenson gravestone and then by *The Laughing Unicorn*. By the time they were done, it was time for another meal. This time they ate in another dining room—this one imaged and decorated to give the appearance of a beer hall, full of music, loud talk, and the younger inhabitants of the Encyclopedia—although few of these were as young as Ajela, and none as young as Hal. But he had learned that when he remembered to act soberly and trade on his height he could occasionally be taken for two or three years older than he actually was. No one, at least, among those that stopped by the booth where they sat, showed any awareness that he was two years younger than she.

But the food and drink hit him like a powerful drug, after the large events of the last two days. An hour or so in the dining room, and he could barely keep his eyes open. Ajela showed him how to code for his own room on the booth's control bank, and led him down another short corridor outside the dining room to a dilating aperture that proved, indeed, to be the door to his own quarters.

"You think there'll be time for me to work with the Encyclopedia tomorrow?" he asked as she left.

"Easily," she said.

He slept heavily, woke feeling happy, then remembered the deaths on the terrace—and grief rushed in on him again. Again he watched through the screen of the bush at the edge of the pond and saw what happened. The pain was unendurable. It was all too close. He felt he had to escape, the way a drowning man might feel, who had to escape from underwater up to where there was air and light. He clutched frantically for something other to cling to, and fastened on the recollection that today he would have a chance to work with the Encyclopedia itself. He clung to this prospect, filling his mind with it and with what he had done the day before when Ajela had taken him around.

Still thinking of these things he got up, ordered breakfast, and an hour later Ajela called to see if he was awake yet. Finding him up, she came to his room.

"Most people work with the Encyclopedia in their rooms," she told him. "But if you like I can add a carrel to this room, or set one up for you elsewhere."

"Carrel," he echoed. He had assumed for some years now that there were no words worth knowing he did not know, but this was new to him.

"A study-room."

She touched the controls on his desk and a three-dimensional image formed in the open center of his quarters. It showed something not much larger than a closet, holding a single chair-float and a fixed desk surface with a pad of control keys. The walls were colorless and flat; but as she touched the controls in Hal's room again, they dissolved into star-filled space, so that float and desk seemed now to be adrift between the stars. Hal's breath caught in his throat.

"I can have the carrel attached to my room here?" he asked.

"Yes," she said.

"Then I think that's what I'd like."

"All right." She touched the control. The light shimmer of the wall opposite the door that was the entrance to his room moved back to reveal another door. As he watched, it opened and he saw beyond it the small room she had described as a carrel. He went to and into it, like a bee drawn to a flower blossom. Ajela followed him and spent some twenty minutes teaching him how to call up from the Encyclopedia whatever information he might want. At last she turned to leave him.

"You'll make better use of the resources of the Encyclopedia," she said, "if you've got a specific line of inquiry or investigation to follow. You'll find it'll pay you to think a bit before you start and be sure you're after information that needs to be developed from the sources it'll give you, rather than just a question that can be simply answered."

"I understand," he said, excitement moving in him.

But once she had gone and he was alone again, the excitement hesitated and the grief in him, together with the cold ancient fury toward Bleys Ahrens he had felt earlier, threatened to wake in him once more. Resolutely he shoved them back down inside him. He pressed the control set in the arm of his chair that sealed the room about him and set its walls to an apparent transparency that left him seemingly afloat in space between the stars. His mind hunted almost desperately, knowing that he must find something to occupy it or else it would go back to the estate again, to the lake and the terrace. The words of Malachi's evoked image came back to him.

". . . the concerns of the living, must be with the living, even if the living are themselves. . . ."

He made a powerful effort to think only of the here and now. What would he want if he were simply here at the Final Encyclopedia in this moment and nothing at all had happened back at his home? Reaching out, his mind snatched again at the dreams built up from his reading. He had asked to see the gravestone of Robert Louis Stevenson yesterday. Perhaps he should simply ask for whatever else the Encyclopedia had to tell him about Stevenson that he had never known before? But his mind shied away from that idea. The image of Stevenson was now tied in his mind to the image of a gravestone, and he did not want to think of gravestones.

He flung his mind wide. The Three Musketeers? D'Artagnan? What about Nigel Loring, the fictional hero of two of the historical novels by the inventor of Sherlock Holmes, Conan Doyle—the novels *Sir Nigel* and *The White Company.*

The idea of Sir Nigel, the small but indomitable hero of those two novels of the days of men in iron and leather, welcomed his imagination like a haven. Nigel Loring was a character who had always glowed with an unusual light and color in his imagination. Perhaps Conan Doyle had even started a third novel about him, and never finished it? No, not likely. If that had been true he would almost undoubtedly have run across some word of it before now. He pressed the query key of the keypad on the arm of his chair and spoke aloud to the Encyclopedia.

"List for me all that Conan Doyle ever wrote about the character Nigel Loring, who appears in the novels *The White Company* and *Sir Nigel* by Conan Doyle."

A hard copy coiled up out of the void into existence and dropped in his lap. At the same time a soft bell note chimed and a voice replied to him in pleasant female tones.

"Data from sources delivered in hard copy. Would you also like biographical details about the historical individual who is antecedent?"

Hal frowned, puzzled.

"I'm not asking for data on Conan Doyle," he said.

"That's understood. The historical individual referred to was the actual Nigel Loring, knight, of the fourteenth century A.D." Hal stared at the stars. The words he had just heard echoed in his head and a bubble of excitement formed within him. Almost fearful that it would turn out there had been some mistake, he spoke again.

"You're telling me there actually was someone named Nigel Loring in England in the fourteenth century?"

"Yes. Do you want biographical details on this person?"

"Yes, please. All possible details—" he added hastily, "and will you list references to the real Nigel Loring in documents of the time and after. I want copies of these last, if you can give them to me."

Another coil of hard copy emerged from the desktop, including paper sections and pictures. Hal ignored the hard copy but picked up the second half of the delivery and went quickly through it. There were an amazing number of things, running from excerpts from the *Chronicles* of Jean Froissart; an account list of presents given by Edward, the Black Prince of England, to courtiers in his train; and ending with an image of a stall in a chapel. With the image of the chapel stall was a printed description identifying it, which Hal found the most fascinating of all the material.

The stall, he read, still existed. Nigel Loring had been one of the charter members of the Order of the Garter. The chapel was St. George's Chapel, in the English palace of Windsor. The existing chapel now, he learned, was not, however, the original chapel. The original chapel had been built by Edward III and its rebuilding was begun by Edward IV and probably finished in the reign of Henry VIII. Work had gone on at night with many hundreds of candles burning at the time in order to get it ready at Henry's express order for one of his marriages.

For a moment the terrace and its happenings were forgotten. The actual historical Nigel Loring and Doyle's fictional character slid together in Hal's mind. It seemed to him that he reached across time to touch the actual human being who had been Nigel Loring. For a moment it was possible to believe that all the people in the books he had read might have been as alive and touchable as any real person, if only he knew where and how to reach out for them. Fascinated, he pulled another character out of his mind almost at random, and spoke to the Encyclopedia.

"Tell me," he asked, "was the character Bellarion, in the novel *Bellarion* by Rafael Sabatini, also inspired by a real historical person of the same name?"

"No," answered the Final Encyclopedia.

Hal sighed, his imagination brought back to the practical Earth. It would have been too good to be true to have had Bellarion also an actual character in history.

". . . however," the Encyclopedia went on, "Sabatini's Bellarion draws strongly upon the military genius of the actual fourteenth-century condottiere, Sir John Hawkwood, from whom Conan Doyle also drew to some extent in the writing of the books that contain the character of Sir Nigel. It is generally accepted that John Hawkwood was, in part, a model for both fictional characters. Would you like excerpts of the critical writings reaching this conclusion?"

"Yes—NO!" Hal shouted aloud. He sat back, nearly quivering with excitement.

John Hawkwood was someone about whom he knew. Hawkwood had caught his imagination early, not only from what Hal had read about him, but because Malachi Nasuno had spoken of him, referring to him as the first modern general. Cletus Grahame also had cited Hawkwood's campaigns a number of times in his multi-volumed work on strategy and tactics—that same Cletus Grahame who had been the great-grandfather of Donal Graeme, of whom Ajela had spoken. Donal Graeme had ended up enforcing a peace on all the fourteen worlds. In Hal's mind, suddenly, a line led obviously from Donal to Cletus Grahame and back through the warrior elements of western history to Hawkwood.

Hawkwood had come out from the village of Sible Hedingham in the rural England of the early fourteenth century, had fought his way up through the beginnings of the Hundred Years' War in France and ended as Captain General of Florence, Italy. He had died at last in his bed at a probable age of over eighty, after a life of frequent hand-to-hand armed combat. He had been called "the first of the modern generals" by others before Malachi; and he had introduced longbowmen from England into the Italian warfare of the fourteenth century with remarkable results.

Hal had been fascinated by him on first discovery. Not merely because of the clangor and color of Hawkwood's life, as seen from nearly a thousand years later, but because in the Englishman's lifetime, going from Sible Hedingham in his youth to Florence in his later years, he had effectively travelled from the society of the deep Middle Ages into the beginnings of the modern era. The flag that had been flying over Hal's terrace, and that Walter the InTeacher had lowered to warn him, the flag of a hawk flying out of a wood, had been made by Hal himself with a device out of his imagination after a thorough search through the books in the library of the estate had failed to have any information on Hawkwood's coat of arms—on sudden impulse Hal spoke again to the Encyclopedia.

"What was the coat of arms borne by Sir John Hawkwood?"

There was a brief pause.

"Sir John Hawkwood's arms were: argent, on a chevron sable three escallops of the field."

The screen showed a shield with a silver background, crossed by a thick V-shaped black band, called a "chevron," point upwards in the middle of the ground, and with three silver cockleshells spaced out upon the black chevron.

Why the cockles? Hal wondered. The only connection he could think of to cockleshells was St. James of Compostela, in Spain. Could Hawkwood at the time have been in Compostela? Or might the cockles in the arms mean something else? He queried the Final Encyclopedia.

"The cockleshells are common to many coats of arms," answered the Encyclopedia. "I can furnish you with details if you like. They appear, for example, on some of the oldest arms, such as those of the Graemes, and on the arms borne by many of the septs of the Graeme family, such as the well-known arms of Dundee and Dunbar. Do you wish details, a full report on cockles as a device on coats of arms during past centuries?"

"No," said Hal.

He sat back, thinking. Something in the deepest depths of his mind had been triggered by this discovery that the real Hawkwood lay in some manner behind the fictional characters of Doyle's Nigel Loring and Sabatini's Bellarion, something that continued backward to tie into this business of the cockleshells and Hawkwood. The cockleshells and Hawkwood somehow fitted together; they linked and evoked something. He could feel the mental chemistry of their interaction like a stirring in his unconscious; it was a sensation which he knew, it was the sort of deep excitement that came on just before he began to envision a poem. The chain of logic that ran from these things to whatever was now building in his creative unconscious was not one his conscious mind could see or follow, but experience had taught him the futility of trying. He felt its workings there, now, as someone might feel conflicting winds blowing upon him in the absolute darkness of night. It was a pressure, a fever, an imperative. Something about this search and discovery had touched on a thing that was infinitely more compelling, was much larger, than what he had sat down here with the expectation of discovering, as an ocean is larger than a grain of sand on one of its shores. It reached out to touch him like a call, like a trumpet note reaching out, reaching all the way through him to summon him to a thing more important than anything he had felt in all his sixteen years before.

The sensation was powerful. It was almost with relief that he found the lines of a poem beginning to stir in his head, forming out of the mists of his discovery, strange, archaic-sounding lines. . . . His fingers groped automatically for the keypad that was on the arm of his chair, not to summon the Encyclopedia back for another question or command but simply to resolve the poetic images forming inside him into words. Those words, as he pressed the keys, began to take visible shape, glowing like golden fire against the starscape before him.

À OUTRANCE
Within the ruined chapel, the full knight
Woke from the coffin of his last-night's bed;
And clashing mailed feet on the broken stones—

His fingers paused on the keys. A chill, damp wind seemed suddenly to blow clear through him. He shook off the momentary paralysis and wrote on. . . .

Strode to the shattered lintel and looked out.

A fog lay holding all the empty land
A cloak of cloudy and uncertainness,
That hid the earth; in that enfoliate mist
Moved voices wandered from a dream of death.

It was a wind of Time itself, the thought came to him unexpectedly, that he felt now blowing through him, blowing through flesh and bones alike. It was the sound of that wind he heard and was now rendering into verse. He wrote . . .

A warhorse, cropping by the chapel wall,
Raised maul-head, dripping thistles on the stones;
And struck his hooves; and jingled all his gear.
"Peace . . . ," said the Knight. "Be still. Today, we rest."

"The mist is hiding all the battlefield.
"The wind whips on the wave-packs of the sea.
"Our foe is bound by this no less than we.
"Rest," said the Knight. "We do not fight today."

The warhorse stamped again. And struck his hooves.
Ringing on cobbled dampness of the stones.
Crying—"Ride! Ride! Ride!" And the Knight mounted him,
Slowly. And rode him slowly out to war.

. . . The chime of the room phone catapulted him out of his thoughts. He had been sitting, he realized, for some time with the written poem before him, his thought ranging on journeys across great distances. He reached out reflexively to the control keys.

"Who is it?"

"It's Ajela." From behind the void and the glowing lines of his poem, her voice came clearly and warmly, bringing back with it all of the reality he had abandoned during his recent ranging. "It's lunchtime—if you're interested."

"Oh. Of course," he said, touching the keypad. The lines of verse vanished, to be replaced by the image of her face, occulting the imaged stars.

"Well," she said, smiling at him, "did you have a useful session with the Encyclopedia?"

"Yes," he said. "Very much."

"And where would you like to eat?"

"Anyplace," he said—and hastily amended himself. "Anyplace quiet."

She laughed.

"The quietest place is probably right where you are now."

"—any quiet place except my room, then."

"All right. We'll go back to the dining room I took you to the first time. But I'll arrange for a table away from other people where no one will be sent to sit near us," she said. "Meet you at the entrance there in five minutes."

By the time he figured out the controls to move his room close to the dining room, and got to the dining-room entrance, Ajela was already there and waiting for him. As he came down the short length of corridor that was now between his room's front door and the entrance to the dining room, he was aware suddenly that this was probably the last time he would see her before he left. The two days just past had done a good deal to shift her in his mind from the category of someone belonging to the Encyclopedia, and therefore beyond his understanding, into someone he knew—and for whom he felt.

The result was that his perceptions were now sharpened. As far back as he could remember, his tutors had trained him to observe; as he met her now, spoke to her, and was led by her to a table in one deserted corner of the room, he saw her as perhaps he should have seen her from the start.

It was as if his vision of her had focused. He noticed now how straight she stood and how she walked with something like an air of command—certainly with an air of firmness and decision that was almost alien in an Exotic—as she led the way to their table. She was dressed in green today, a light green tunic that came down to mid-thigh, hugging her body tightly, over an ankle-length skirt that was slit all the way up the sides, revealing tight trousers of a darker green with the parting of the slits at each stride.

The tunic's green was that of young spring grass. There was a straightness to her shoulders, seen against the distant pearl-grey of the light-wall at the far end of the dining room. Her bright blonde hair was gathered into a ponytail by a polished wooden barrette that showed the grain of the wood. The ponytail danced against the shoulders of her tunic as she strode, echoing in its movements the undulations of her skirt. She reached their table, sat down, and he took the float opposite her.

She asked him again about his morning with the Encyclopedia as they decided what to eat, and he answered briefly, not wanting to go into details of how what he had learned had struck so deep a chord of response within him. Watching her now, he saw in the faint narrowing of her eyes that she had noticed this self-restraint.

"I don't mean to pry," she said. "If you'd rather not talk about it—"

"No—no, it's not that," he answered quickly. "It's just that my mind's everywhere at once."

She flashed her sudden smile at him.

"No need to apologize," she said. "I was just mentioning it. As for the way you feel—the Encyclopedia affects a lot of scholars that way."

He shook his head, slowly.

"I'm no scholar," he answered.

"Don't be so sure," she said gently. "Well, have you thought about whether you still want to go ahead and leave, the way you planned, in just a few hours?"

He hesitated. He could not admit that he would prefer to stay, without seeming to invite her to argue for his staying. He understood himself, starkly and suddenly. His problem was a reluctance to tell her he must leave, that there was no choice for him but to leave. Caught between answers, neither of which he wanted to give, he was silent.

"You've got reasons to go. I understand that," she said, after a moment. She sat watching him. "Would you like to tell me about them? Would you like to talk about it, at all?"

He shook his head.

"I see," she said. Her voice had gentled. "Do you mind, anyway, my telling you Tam's side of it?"

"Of course not," he replied.

Their plates, with the food they had ordered, were just rising to the surface of the table. She looked down at hers for a moment, and then looked back up at him levelly.

"You've seen Tam," she said as they began to eat, and the gentleness in her voice gave way to a certainty that echoed the authority of her walk. "You see his age. One year, several years, might not seem so much to you; but he's old. He's very old. He has to think about what will happen to the Encyclopedia if there's no one to take charge of it after . . . he steps down as Director."

He was watching her eyes, fascinated, as she spoke. They were a bluish green that seemed to have depths without end and reflected the color of her clothing.

He said, after a second, since she had paused as if waiting response from him, "Someone else would take over the Encyclopedia, wouldn't they?"

She shook her head.

"No one person. There's a Board of Directors who'll step in, and stay in. The Board was scheduled to take over after Mark Torre's death. Then Mark found Tam and changed that part of the plan. But now, if Tam dies without a successor, the Board's going to take over, and from then on the Encyclopedia will be run by committee."

"And that's something you don't want to happen?"

"Of course I don't!" Her voice tightened. "Tam's worked all his life to point the Encyclopedia toward what it really should do, rather than let it turn into a committee-run library! What would you think I'd want?"

Her eyes were now full green, as green as the rare tinge that can color the wood flames of an open campfire. He waited a second more to let her hear the echo of her words in her ears before he answered.

"You should want whatever it is you want," he said, echoing what he had been taught and believed in. Her eyes met his for a second more, burningly, then dropped their gaze to her plate. When she spoke again, the volume of her voice had also dropped.

"I . . . you don't understand," she said slowly. "This is very hard for me—"

"But I do understand," he answered. "I told you, one of my tutors was an Exotic. Walter the InTeacher."

What she had meant, he knew from Walter's teachings, was that it was difficult for her to plead with him to stay at the Encyclopedia, much as she plainly wanted to. As an Exotic, she would have been conditioned from childhood never to try to influence other people. This, because of the Exotic belief that participation in the historical process, even in the smallest degree, destroyed the clear-sightedness of a separate and dispassionate observer; and the Exotics' main reason for existence was to chart the movements of history, separately and dispassionately. They dreamed only of an end to which those movements could lead. But she was, he thought, as she had more or less admitted already, a strange Exotic.

"Actually," he told her, "you argue better for my staying here when you don't argue, than you could if you used words."

He smiled, to invite her to smile back, and was relieved when she did. What he said had been said clumsily; but all the same, it was a truth she was too intelligent not to see. If she had argued, he would have had someone besides himself to marshal his own arguments against. This way, he was left to debate with his own desires; which, she might have guessed, could make an opponent far harder for him to conquer than she was.

But his conscience sank its teeth into him, now. He was, he knew, leading her on to hope—which was an unfair thing to do. He must not give in and stay here. But, because she was an Exotic and because he knew what that meant as far as her beliefs were concerned, he could think of no way to explain this to her that would not either wound or baffle her. He did not, he thought almost desperately, know enough about her—enough about her as the unique individual she was—to talk to her. And there was no time to learn that much about her.

"You're from—where? Mara? Kultis?" he asked, striking out at random. "How did you happen to end up here?"

She smiled, unexpectedly.

"Oh, I was a freak," she said.

"A freak?" Privately he had sometimes called himself that. But he could not imagine applying it to someone like her.

"Well, say I was one of the freaks, then," she answered. "We called ourselves that. Did you ever hear of a Maran Exotic called Padma?"

"Padma . . ." He frowned.

The name had a strange echo of familiarity, as if he had indeed heard Walter or one of his other tutors mention it, but nothing more. His memory, like the rest of him, had been trained to a fine point. If he had been told of such a man, he should be able to remember it. But nowhere, searching his memory now, could he find any clear reference to someone called Padma.

"He's very old now," she said. "But he's been an OutBond, from either Mara or Kultis, at one time or another, to every important Culture on the fourteen worlds. He goes clear back to the time of Donal Graeme. In fact—that's why I'm here."

"He's that old?" Hal stared at her. "He must be older than Tam."

She sobered, suddenly. The smile left her face and went out of her voice as well.

"No. He's younger—but just by a few years." She shook her head. "Even when he was a very young man, he had an ageless look, they say. And he was brilliant, even then—even among his own generation on the Exotics. But you're almost right. When I got here, I found out even Tam had thought Padma was older than he was. But it's not true. There's been no one Tam's age; and no one like him—ever. Even Padma."

He looked at her half-skeptically.

"There are fourteen worlds," he said.

"I know," she said. "But the Final Encyclopedia's got no record of anyone else much more than a hundred and eighteen years old just now. Tam's a hundred and twenty-four. It's his will that keeps him going."

He could hear in her voice an appeal to him to understand Tam. He wanted to tell her that he would try, but once more he did not trust himself to put the assurance into words he could trust her to believe.

"But you were telling me how you got here," he said, instead. "You were saying you were one of the freaks. What did you mean? And what's Padma got to do with it?"

"It was his conscience created us—me, and the others," she said. "It all goes back long ago to something that happened between the Exotics and Donal Graeme, back when Donal was alive and Padma was still young. Later, on reflection, Padma began to feel that Sayona the Bond had led the Exotics—including Padma—into being too sure of themselves to notice something important—that Donal had something they should have been aware of and made use of; something critical, Padma said, to the search we've been engaged in for three centuries now."

She paused and looked steadily at him. "Those are Padma's own words," she went on, "to an Assembly of both the Exotic worlds forty years ago. Padma came finally to think that Donal might have been a prototype of the very thing we'd been searching for, the evolved form of human being we've always believed the race will finally produce."

Hal frowned at her, reaching out to understand. Donal he knew of through history and the tales of Malachi. But the thought of Donal had always disturbed him, in spite of Donal's triumphs. Ian and Kensie, Donal's uncles; and Eachan Khan, Donal's grim, war-crippled father, had caught more at his imagination, among the Graemes of Foralie on the Dorsai. But the uneasy feeling that he should recognize the name continued to nag at him on a low level of consciousness.

"Padma," Ajela was going on, "felt we Exotics had to look for what we might have missed seeing in Donal; and because Padma was enormously *respected*—if you had an Exotic teacher, you know what the word *respected* means on Mara and Kultis—and because he suggested a way that had never been tried, it was agreed he could make an experiment. I—and some others like me—were the elements of the experiment. He chose fifty of the brightest Exotic children he could find and arranged to have us brought up under special conditions."

Hal frowned again at her.

"Special conditions?"

"Padma's theory was that something in our own Exotic society was inhibiting the kind of personal development that had made someone like Donal Graeme possible. Whatever else was true about him, no one could deny Donal had abilities no Exotic had ever achieved. That pointed to a blindness somewhere in our picture of ourselves, Padma said."

She was carried away now on the flood of what she was telling him. Her eyes were blue-green and depthless once more.

"So," she went on, "he got a general agreement to let him experiment with the fifty of us—Padma's Children, they called us, then—and he saw to it we were exposed, from as soon as we were able to understand, not only to the elements of our own Culture, but to those in the Dorsai and the Friendly Cultures which our Exotic thinking had always automatically rejected. You know how our family structure on Mara and Kultis is much looser than on the Dorsai or the Friendlies. As children, we treat all adults almost equally as parents or near relatives. No one forced the fifty of us in any particular direction, but we were given more freedom to bond emotionally to individuals, to indulge in romantic, rather than logical thinking. You see—a romantic attitude was the one common element permitted Dorsai and Friendly children, which we on the Exotics had always been steered away from."

He sat, studying her as she talked. He did not yet see where her words were

headed, but he could feel strongly across the short physical distance separating them that what she was saying was not only something of intense importance to her, but something that it was difficult for her to say to him. He
nodded now, to encourage her to go on; and she did.

"To make the story short," she said, "we were set free to fall in love with
things we ordinarily would've been told were unproductive subjects for such
attention; and in my case what I fell in love with, when I was barely old
enough to learn about it, was the story of Tam Olyn—the brilliant, grim,
interstellar newsman who tried and almost succeeded in a personal vendetta
to destroy the Friendly Culture, only to change his mind suddenly and completely, to come back to Earth and take on all the responsibility of the Final
Encyclopedia, where he'd been the only person besides Mark Torre to hear
the voices at the Transit Point."

Her face was animated now. The feeling in her reached and caught up Hal
as music might have caught him up.

"This man, who still controls the Final Encyclopedia," she went on ani-
matedly, "holding it in trust all these years for the race, and refusing to let
any other person or power control it. By the time I was nine I knew I had
to come here; and by the time I was eleven, they let me come—on Tam's
personal responsibility."

She smiled suddenly.

"It seemed," she said, "Tam was intrigued by someone only my age who
could be so set on getting here; and I found out later, partly he hoped I might
hear the voices, as you and he did. But I didn't."

She stopped speaking, suddenly, with her last three words. The smile
went. She had hardly touched the small salad she had ordered; but Hal recognized with surprise that his own plate was utterly empty—and yet he could
not remember eating as he listened to her.

"So it's because of Tam you're still here?" he said, finally, when it seemed
she would not go on. She had started to poke at her salad, but when he spoke
she put her fork down and looked levelly across the table at him.

"I came because of him, yes," she said. "But since then I've come to see
what he sees in the Encyclopedia—what you should see in it. Now, even if
there weren't any Tam Olyn, I'd still be here."

She glanced down at her salad and pushed the transparent bowl that held
it away from her. Then she looked back at him, again.

"It's the hope of the race," she said to him. "Their one hope. I don't believe any longer that the answer can lie with our Exotics, or anyone else. It's
here—here! No place else. And only Tam's been able to keep it alive. He
needs you."

The tone of her voice on her last words tore at him. He looked at her and
knew finally that he could not give her a flat no, not here, not now. He took
a deep, unhappy breath.

"Let me think about it—a little longer," he said. Suddenly, he felt a desperate need to get away from her before he made her some promise that was

neither true nor possible to keep. He pushed his float back from the table, still unable to keep his eyes off her face. He would tell her later, he told himself, call her from his room, and tell her that eventually he would be back. Even with their phone screens on, there would be a psychic distance between them that would lessen the terrible power of persuasion he felt coming at him from her now, and make it possible for him to reassure her he would someday return.

"I'll go back to my room and think about it, now," he said.

"All right," she said without moving. "But remember, you heard the voices. You have to understand; because there're only the three of us who do. You, Tam and I. Remember what you risk if you leave, now. If you go, and while you're gone Tam reaches the point where he can't go on being Director any longer, by the time you come back the Board will be in charge; and they won't want to give up control. If you go now, you may lose your chance here, forever!"

He nodded and stood up. Slowly, she stood up on the other side of the table and together, not saying anything more to each other, they went out of the dining room. At its entrance, Ajela touched a control pad set in the wall, and the same short corridor formed with a door at the end that would be the entrance to his own quarters.

"Thank you," he said, hardly looking at her. "I'll call you—as soon as I've got something to tell you."

After a moment more he met her eyes with his own. Her naked gaze seemed to go through him effortlessly.

"I'll wait for you to call," she said.

He went down the corridor, still feeling her standing watching him from behind, as he had felt the piercing strength of her gaze. Not until the door of his room closed behind him did he feel free of her. He dropped into a float opposite his bed.

There was an empty loneliness and a longing in him. What he needed desperately, he told himself, was some point outside the situation that now held him, where he could stand and look at it—and at her expectations and Tam's. Of course, she would see no sense in his going. From her standpoint, the Encyclopedia was so much beyond Coby in what it had to offer him that any comparison of the two was ridiculous. All Coby had to offer was someplace to hide.

The Encyclopedia offered him not only that, but the shield of the force-panels, the protection of those who belonged to the single institution that the Others probably would never be able to control, and quite possibly would have no interest in controlling. In fact, as long as he stayed and worked with the Final Encyclopedia, here, what sort of threat did he pose to the Others? It would be only out in their territory, on the younger worlds, that he posed a possible threat to them. Even if they discovered him here, it might well be that they would simply decide to leave him alone.

Meanwhile, there was all that the Encyclopedia had to offer him. Walter the InTeacher had been fond of saying that the pursuit of knowledge was the greatest adventure ever discovered by the human race. The degree to which Ajela had touched Hal just now had almost swept him away beyond the power of any personal choice. To be able to work with the Encyclopedia as he had done for a short while was like having the Universe handed to him for a plaything. It was more than that—

It was, thought Hal suddenly, like being able to play God.

On Coby he would be a stranger among strangers—and probably among strangers who were the sweepings of the fourteen worlds, for who would go and work in the mines of Coby if he could be someplace else? Here, he already knew Ajela . . . and Tam.

And her last words had struck him forcefully. She was right in the fact that if he went now and Tam died or stopped being Director, Hal's own chances at that post with the Encyclopedia could be lost forever. His mind shied from the responsibility of the prospect. But it was a great and almost unheard-of thing, to be someone who could be considered as a successor to the Director of the Encyclopedia. Tam seemed a crusty sort of individual— age might have something to do with that, or it might be his natural pattern—but Ajela obviously found him to be someone she could love; and, in fact, Hal had found himself warming to the old man, also, even during their brief meeting.

It might also be his resemblance to Obadiah. Perhaps Hal was deliberately making himself see Obadiah in the Director, and this was giving him a greater feeling of closeness to Tam than the situation actually justified. But it really did not matter whether Tam and he were close or not. The overwhelmingly important thing was the Encyclopedia itself and that it have a continuity of Directors; and if Hal were indeed a serious possibility to take control from Tam's hands eventually, then . . .

Hal's mind drifted into a dark, but comfortable dream of the Encyclopedia, as it might be after he had been here some years and was finally in control as Director. Ajela could probably be brought to agree to stay on with him, in something like the relationship that she had with Tam—of course she could, for the Encyclopedia's sake, if nothing else. And, if they should really agree well together . . .

He looked at the chronometer on his wrist. The ring that was set to local time showed a little less than an hour and a half before his ship was scheduled to lift from its docking, just under the metal and force-panel skin of the Encyclopedia. His mind still caught in his dark dream, he got up and went across the room, to find the travel bag with which he had come to the Encyclopedia. He was holding it in his hands before he realized what he was doing.

He laughed.

He was on his way to Coby.

The recognition came like a dull, but expected, shock. Abruptly, then, he realized; it was not the dead hands of Walter, Malachi and Obadiah reaching out to control him against his will. It was not even the calculation of his training that had implemented its decision by some sort of conditioned lever upon his will. It was simply that he, for reasons he could not clearly enunciate, knew that he had to go; and, far from weakening that certainty, what he had heard from Ajela and experienced in his earlier work with the Encyclopedia that morning had confirmed it.

Heavily, he began to do what little gathering of papers and possessions was necessary. He had been deluding not only Ajela, but himself, by pretending that the question of his staying was still open.

He had not been able to face Ajela with that truth over the lunch table. She would not have pressed him for reasons, he knew, being an Exotic; but she would have—and still did—deserve some. Only, he would not be able to give her any. So he would simply sneak out of the Encyclopedia, after all, as he had, in effect, sneaked in; and he would send both her and Tam a message afterwards, once he was irrevocably on his way among the stars.

He finished up, coded the number of his exit port into the room control, and stepped out the dilated entrance into a short corridor that took him down and through another entrance, past another screen from which an elderly woman perfunctorily scanned his papers, and into the port chamber.

There was a forty-minute wait before he could board the ship. But five minutes later he was in his compartment, and forty minutes after that, the ship sealed and lifted. An annunciator woke over his head.

"First phase-shift in two hours," it said. "First phase-shift in two hours. There will be a meal service immediately after the shift. All portside compartments, first seating; all starboardside compartments, second seating."

He was in a portside compartment; but he was not hungry—although in two hours, knowing himself, he would probably be starving, as usual. He sat down on that one of the two fixed seats in the compartment that was below the bed folded up against the bulkhead.

Once they had phase-shifted, there would be no direct communication possible with the Encyclopedia. At once, they would be light-years distant; and a message physically carried by a ship inbound to Earth would be the quickest way of getting in touch. He did not feel up to talking face-to-face with Ajela, in any case; but something in him rebelled at waiting to tell her until he was well away. She would be looking at the time and thinking that he had decided against going, and was working with the Encyclopedia—and she would hear from him about dinnertime.

He roused himself, stepped across to the tiny desk against the wall of his compartment opposite the bed, sat down on the other seat, and coded a call to the ship's communications center. The screen lit up with a heavy man in ship's whites.

"I'd like to send a message back to the Encyclopedia," he said.

"Certainly. Want the message privacy coded? And written or spoken?"

"Spoken," he said. "Never mind the privacy code. It's to Ajela, Special Assistant to the Director. 'Ajela. I'm sorry. I had to go.' "

His own voice repeated itself back at him from the screen.

"*Ajela. I'm sorry. I had to go.*"

"That's all?" asked the shipman.

"Yes. Sign it—my name's Hal Mayne—" He checked himself. "Wait, add on . . . 'I'll see you both again, as soon as I can.' "

"*Ajela. I'm sorry. I had to go. I'll see you both again, as soon as I can. Hal Mayne.*" The screen gave his words back to him once more.

"All right? Or did you want that last sentence as a P.S.?" asked the shipman.

"No, that's fine. Thank you."

Hal broke the connection and got up from the seat. He pulled the bed down into position and stretched out on it. He lay on his back, looking at the ceiling and bulkheads of his compartment, which showed the same flat brown color everywhere he looked. A faint vibration through the fabric of the ship around them was the only sign that they were under way; it would be the only sensation of movement to be felt—and not even that during phase-shift—until they went into docking mode in New Earth orbit.

There had never been any possible decision except that he should go on to Coby. But it had taken the Encyclopedia to help him see the inevitability of it; and even then the recognition had come in through the back door of his mind. It had been the poem that had told him, its images speaking from his unconscious, as surely as the images of Walter, Malachi and Obadiah had spoken from it on his first night in the great sphere. He was the knight and was summoned in one direction only.

The poem had been no more than a codification of that oceanic feeling he had touched when he worked with the Encyclopedia. Blindly, there, he had felt something, some great effort, that rang its particular call trumpet-like, reading itself back through him. For a little while, unknowing, he had touched what could be—and it was so large in promise that it dwarfed all other things. But the way to it did not lie through a dusty scholar's cell, or even by way of Tam's desk in the Encyclopedia. At least, not yet. There were things within him that would have to grow to match in size what he had felt in the Encyclopedia; and some deep-buried instinct had come to tell him clearly that these would not grow in a sterile, protected environment. It was out among the materials of which the race was made that he must find the particular strength he would need to use the mighty lever that was the Encyclopedia. And, once he had found it, he would be back—whether he was wanted or not.

The faint vibration of the ship thrummed all through him as he lay. He felt caught, like someone apart, suspended between all worlds, waiting.

Chapter

> > 5 < <

As *the spaceship* to New Earth pulled away from Earth orbit preparatory to its first phase-shift into interstellar space, the awareness of his utter loneliness moved in on Hal all at once. In the Final Encyclopedia, thanks to Tam and Ajela, he had not felt completely alone; and until he had gotten to the Final Encyclopedia the anesthesia of shock and his training had held the realities of his new orphan's status at a numb distance from his emotions. But now, unexpectedly, a full appreciation of it flooded him.

That first night on shipboard he dreamed a vivid, colorful dream in which it turned out that the events on the terrace and the deaths of Malachi, Obadiah, and Walter had been nothing but a nightmare from which he had just awakened. He felt foolish, but inexpressibly relieved to discover that the three of them were still alive and all was well.

Then he awoke to reality, and lay in the darkness, listening to the faint breathing of the ventilating system of the ship, echoing out through the grille on the near wall of his stateroom. Emptiness and desolation filled him. He pulled the bedcovers over his head like a very young child, and lay there, cold in his misery, until at some unknown, later time he fell asleep again, to other dreams he did not remember on awakening.

But from then on the awareness of his isolation and vulnerability was always with him. He was able to push it into a back corner of his mind, but there it settled, as if in some dark corner, where Bleys and the rest of the Others seemed also to crouch, waiting. He realized now that he had made a serious mistake in not asking that this passage from the Encyclopedia be booked for him under a false name.

The situation was not completely irreparable, of course. Once he got to New Earth, he could cancel the reservations made under the name of Hal Mayne, and then make new reservations to Coby under an alias. At most, then, this ship's records would show Hal Mayne only as going no farther than New Earth. But the record of his having been outbound from Old Earth aboard this ship would remain, for the Others to find.

A cooler part of his mind told him that even travelling under his real name as he was now, the passenger record would not be easy for Bleys to run down. It was not that ship's records were not kept and that the Others could not eventually get access to them all. It was simply that, given the mass of interstellar shipping and the complexity of individual records on fourteen worlds, it became a statistical nightmare to search through all of these in an attempt to trace or locate a single individual.

Nonetheless, he made up his mind to be as inconspicuous as possible until he reached Coby and, once there, to lose himself under a completely false identity. Being inconspicuous would mean, of course, that he should restrict his contacts with other people aboard, as much as possible; but that was a small hardship. At this moment he felt no great desire to make the acquaintances of his fellow passengers, or those who staffed the ship.

It was a prudent decision, but in making it he had not considered how much such solitary behavior would leave him to his own thoughts and feelings during the days that followed. At times he would find himself unexpectedly immersed in grief, an unbearable grief that would mutate gradually into an icy, compelling rage, that in its own strange way seemed familiar, although he could not recall having felt anything like it before. It made him shiver, thinking of Bleys and the Others, and all their kind. A desire to destroy them and everything connected with them would seize him so powerfully that he could think of nothing else.

As ye have done to me and mine . . .

The words seemed to arise out of some ancient part of him like a stained and weathered carving on the stone of his soul. He would follow the advice of the ghosts of Malachi, Obadiah, and Walter to hide until he was strong enough to fight back against those who had done this; and then he would destroy them as they had destroyed all those he had ever loved. Just as Ajela had reminded him that Tam Olyn had once set out to destroy the entire Friendly Culture. Tam had changed and turned back from what he had started to accomplish, but Hal would never do so.

Walter's teaching had warned against letting destructive emotions grow and take charge of him; and he had been trained in ways to control them. But he found now that in the worst moments of his grief, the rage was the only thing that could push it from him—and at such times the grief seemed too great to be borne.

Still, in all, the trip to New Earth was not that long in actual subjective, shipboard time. Most of the passengers on board were bound beyond that world, to Freiland, which was now the richer and more commercially active of the two worlds under the star of Sirius. But the ships stopped at New Earth first, because New Earth was the major transshipment point for that solar system; and, like Hal, all those who were going on to other destinations would be making their change to other vessels there, rather than at Freiland.

Hal had hoped to find at least one other person aboard who was going to Coby, or who had known that planet firsthand, so that he could ask what the life there was actually like for miners. But none of the other transshipping passengers were bound in his direction—he had asked the purser to check the ship's list to make sure. In the end, when he took the jitney down to New Earth City for the three days he must wait for his vessel to Coby, he was as much alone and knew as little as he had when he had gone on board.

But New Earth City itself caught his attention, even driving the memory of the events on the terrace and the Encyclopedia temporarily into the background of his thoughts. It was a space-base city, which meant it had its primary commercial activity in off-world shipping. The sky was busy with passenger and cargo jitneys going to and from parking orbit; the streets were equally full of a multitude of shipping agents. He had no trouble finding passage under a different name on a ship headed for Coby, after he had cancelled his original reservations.

The city, itself, lay in the uplands of the north temperate zone of that world, in mid-continent, at the confluence of the two large rivers that together with their tributaries provided a watershed for nearly one-third of the continent's landmass. Hal remembered from his geography studies that the city was supposed to be very cold in winter. But now it was mid-summer, the air dusty and windy with the odor unique to vegetation of that latitude on the planet. He sat in sidewalk restaurants, drinking the local fruit and vegetable juices and watching the people who passed.

In spite of his training, the romantic part of him had always clung to the thought that there would be markedly noticeable differences to be seen in the people on the younger inhabited planets. But New Earth was an unspecialized world and the majority of the people on it looked as much like full-spectrum humans as those of Earth. They looked the same, essentially; they talked the same; and, with slight variations in cut and style, they wore the same sort of clothes. Only occasionally did he see an individual who dressed and acted as if he or she clearly belonged to one of the true Splinter Cultures—Friendly, Exotic, or Dorsai—and these stood out sharply from those about them.

Nonetheless, it was a strange and foreign place, New Earth City—the sunlight, the smells, the activity, all had differences about them that caught at his imagination and compelled it. He could see no signs of the decay Tam Olyn had spoken of, the approach of an Armageddon, an end to present civilization, or even to the human race itself. Dismissing the puzzle at last from his mind, he turned to a more immediate question. He tried telling those he met that he was a University-level student from Earth on a thesis-trip, testing his ability to pass for someone in his late teens or early twenties, and was gratified when no one questioned this.

Part of him, he had found out long since, was a chameleon; an imaginative actor who could be seduced by an infinite number of roles. He had three days, local time, to pass before his new transport to Coby would be leaving orbit; and, even in three days, he came close to being strongly tempted to stay where he was for a month or two, learning to fit in with what he saw around him and experiencing New Earth living from within its society.

But the thought that Bleys might already have set—no matter how idly— a search in progress for him, plus the pull of that same amorphous, oceanic purpose in him which had set him unthinkingly to packing as the time approached to board the jitney to the New Earth–bound ship; these sent him up to the ship to Coby in time; and a few hours later, he was once more between the stars, heading toward the first phase-shift that would bring him eventually to work in the mines of that airless world.

The ship he travelled on now was not a passenger liner, like the one on which he had left Earth orbit, but a cargo vessel that carried a small complement of passengers in accommodations comparable to those of the ship's officers. The only other passengers were three commercial representatives who spent all their time gambling with gravityless shotballs in the lounge. The officers and crew were indifferent to conversation with the passengers. They had their own professional clubbishness, and except at meals he never saw them; and so, at the end of five days, they came to Coby.

—Not just to an orbit around Coby, however. At the mining world, it developed, spaceships did not park in orbit and wait for jitneys from the surface. They not only went down like military craft, directly to the surface, they went one step further. They descended below the world's surface. Everything built on Coby had been built underground, and as the ship Hal was on gingerly nudged its way close to the Moon-like landscape of the planet, that landscape developed a crack before them from which light shone upward. Barely hovering, it seemed, on its maneuvering powerways, the ship slid into an opening, as the jitney from Earth had slipped into the opening of the port of the Final Encyclopedia.

The moment they were inside, the opening closed again behind them. With pressure barriers, there had been minimal loss of air; but for a world that needed to make all its air and water out of crustal chemicals, even small losses would be important, Hal thought. But then he forgot problems having to do with the crustal extraction of chemicals; for the place into which they had come was another matter entirely than the entry port of the Encyclopedia.

This was like nothing so much as a full-sized surface military or commercial spaceport, hollowed out of the solid stuff of the world, with a spacepad of remarkable dimensions, its edges thick with fitting yards. In the viewing screen of his room, from which Hal was watching their landing, spaceships could be seen lying in the cradles of those yards and being fitted with the metal parts and fabrications that Coby could supply more cheaply than any of the other worlds.

It had been ironic, Obadiah had said once, harshly, that the human race had been so slow to realize how favored was the planet of its birth. Not only in terms of air, water, climate, and the wealth of its ecology—but in the availability of its metals. The first people settling on the younger worlds had been quick to discover that the metals they needed were neither so available in the quantity that Earth had accustomed them to, nor so cheaply easy to extract from the rocky mantle of their planets. On twelve of the fourteen worlds, the human race had metal-hungry societies; and on a few of those worlds, like both of the Friendly planets and on the Dorsai, that poverty was so great that they could not have existed in a modern interstellar community if they had not been able to buy much of what they needed for their technological life off-planet. The fourteen worlds could only remain one community if they could trade together; and the one currency they had in common was professional skills, packaged in the minds and bodies of their own people. So the worlds had specialized.

Physicians and specialists in the soft sciences came from schools on the Exotics. Statisticians from the Friendlies. Professional military from the Dorsai. An individual working on a world other than his or her own earned not only a personal income in that planet's local currency, but interstellar credit for the world that had raised and trained her or him. And on the basis of that interstellar credit metal-poor worlds like New Earth bought what they needed from Coby. . . .

Their cargo spaceship was already settling onto the field below; and with the other passengers, Hal left the ship. He found immigration officials waiting at the foot of the landing stair; but the checks made were brief and simple.

"Visa?" The heavy-bodied, gray-haired official who greeted him took the visa he had purchased on New Earth, under the name of Tad Thornhill, from Hal's hand. "Visiting or staying?"

"Staying," Hal said. "I want to look for a job here."

The woman ran the papers through the transverse slot of her desk and passed them back to Hal. Endless repetitions of the same words had worn her voice to a near-monotone.

"Check the directory in the Terminal for the nearest Assignment Office outside of the port area," she said. "If you change your mind or for any reason stay in the port area, you must register and leave Coby again within eight days, or face deportation. If you leave the port area, you may only return on pass from your work superiors. Next!"

Hal moved on and the commercial representatives behind him took his place.

Inside the Terminal building, the directory—when he queried its console—printed on its screen the words: *Halla Station Assignment Office, Halla Station: Tube Line C: report for job interview at destination.* It also extruded a small hard-copy card with the same information printed on it.

Hal took the card and tucked it into his bag. The port area looked interesting, especially the fitting yards. He thought of trying to get a job there, rather than in the mines. But a little more thought brought back to mind the fact that he was here to become invisible to the Others; and in a port area, pinned down by job-required identification and security observation, would not be the best place to hide.

In fact, he thought, remembering the lessons that had been drilled into him, he would undoubtedly minimize the danger of being traced here by the Others if he got out of the port area as fast as possible. He went searching for, and found the subway-like station that was the terminal of Tube C, took passage in one of the long, silver cars that floated there in their magnetic rings, and an hour and a half later got out two thousand kilometers away, at Halla Station Terminal.

The Assignment Office was in one corner of the Terminal, four desks in
an open area. Three had no one at them. One had a man interviewing another man, who by his appearance and the travel bag on the floor beside his
chair was a job applicant like Hal. Hal waited until the other applicant had
finished and been sent out through a rear door in the Terminal. Then he
came up to the desk, handed his papers to the interviewer and sat down without waiting to be asked.

The man behind the desk did not seem to resent Hal's not waiting for an
invitation. He scanned the papers, made out in the name of Tad Thornhill,
ran them through the slot on his desk and then looked over at Hal. He was
in his early thirties, a short, slim individual with a narrow, white face and a
shock of red hair—the sort of face that might have been friendly, if it had
not been for an expression of indifference that seemed to have worn lines
in it.

"You're sure you want to work in the mines?" he asked.

"I wouldn't be here if I didn't," Hal said.

The interviewer rattled busily away at the keys of his console and a hard-
copy document emerged from his desktop.

"Sign here, and here. If you change your mind in less than a week, you
will be charged for food and lodging and any other expenses incurred by you.
Do you understand?"

"Yes." Hal reached out to put his thumbprint in the signature area. The
interviewer blocked the motion with his own hand.

"Are you aware that the society here on Coby is different from what you
may have encountered on any of the other worlds? That, in particular, the
process of laws is different?"

"I've read about it," said Hal.

"On Coby," went on the interviewer, as if Hal had not spoken, "you are
immune to off-world deportation by reason of legal papers of any kind orig-
inating other than on this planet. However, all legal power here is vested in
the management of the Company you work for and in the Planetary Con-
sortium of Companies to which the Company you will work for belongs. The
legal authority to whom you will be directly responsible for your actions is
the Company Judge-Advocate, who combines in himself the duties of criminal investigator, prosecutor, judge and jury. If you are cited by him, you are
presumed guilty until you can prove your innocence. You will be held wholly
at his disposal for whatever length of time he desires, and you are liable to
questioning by any means he wishes to use in an effort to elicit whatever information he needs. His judgment on your case is final, not subject to re-
view and may include the death penalty, by any process he may specify; and
the Company is under no obligation to notify anyone of your death. Do you
understand all this?"

Hal stared at the man. He had read all this before as part of his studies,
everything that the interviewer had just told him. But it was an entirely dif-

ferent matter to sit here and have these statements presented to him as
present and inescapable realities. A cool breeze seemed to breathe on the
back of his neck.

"I understand," he said.

"Very good. You'll remember then," said the interviewer, "that what you
may have been accustomed to as personal rights no longer exist for you once
you have put your thumbprint on this contract. I have offered you terms for
a minimum work commitment of one standard Coby year at apprentice
wages. There are no shorter work commitments. Do you wish to contract
for a longer term?"

"No," said Hal. "But I can renew my contract at the end of a year without losing anything, can't I?"

"Yes." The interviewer took his guarding hand away from the signature
area. "Your thumbprint here, please."

Hal looked at the man. There is a unique human being within each sane
member of the human race, Walter the InTeacher used to say. Try, and you
can reach him, or her. He thought of trying to make the effort now, but he
could find nothing in the man before him to touch.

He reached out, put his thumbprint on the contract and signed.

"This is your copy," said the interviewer, detaching it from his desk and
passing it to him. "Go out the door to the rear and follow the signs in the
corridor to the office of the Holding Area."

Hal followed the directions. They led him down a well-lighted tunnel
about four meters wide to a much wider entrance in the right wall of the
tunnel. Turning in at the entrance, he saw what appeared to be an enclosed
office to his right, and a considerably larger enclosed area to his left, through
the doorless entrance of which came the sound of music and voices. Straight
ahead, but farther on, he could see what seemed to be a double row of large
cages made of floor-to-ceiling metal bars, but with their doors, for the most
part, standing open.

He assumed that the office on the right was the one he had been directed
to in the Holding Area; but curiosity led him toward the doorway of the place
opposite, with the noisy interior. He automatically approached its doorway
from an angle, out of training, and stopped about three meters away to look
in; but he need not have been cautious. None of those inside were paying
any attention to anything outside.

Apparently, it was simply a recreation place. It was well-filled with people, but with only one woman visible, and the rest men. There was a bar and
most of those there seemed to be drinking out of silvery metal mugs that must
have held at least half a liter. On any other world, such mugs would have
been expensive items indeed—perhaps here they were simply a cheap way
to cut down on breakage.

Hal turned back to the office, knocked on its door when he could find no
annunciator stud, and—when he heard nothing—let himself in.

Within was a wall-to-wall, waist-high counter dividing the room crosswise, with two desks behind it. Only one desk was occupied, and the man at it was middle-aged, balding and heavyset. He had the look of someone who did little but sit at desks. He glanced up at Hal.

"We don't knock here," he said. He extended his hand without getting up. "Papers."

Hal leaned over the counter and managed to pass them over without taking his feet off the floor. The man behind the counter accepted them and ran them through the slot in his desk.

"All right," he said, handing them back—Hal had to stretch himself across the counter once more to retrieve them—"find yourself a bunk out back. Roll call and assignments at eight-thirty in the morning. My name's Jennison—but you call me Superintendent."

"Thank you," said Hal, reflexively, and for the first time Jennison lifted his gaze from his desk and actually looked at him.

"How old are you?" he asked.

"Twenty," said Hal.

"Sure." Jennison nodded.

"Is there anyplace I could get something to eat?" Hal asked.

"I'll sell you a package meal," Jennison said. "Got credit?"

"You just saw my papers."

Jennison punched his keypad and looked into the screen on his desk.

"All right," he said. "I've debited you the cost of one package meal." He swivelled his float around and touched the wall behind him, which opened to show a food storage locker. He took a white, sealed package from the locker and tossed it to Hal.

"Thanks," said Hal.

"You'll get out of that habit," said Jennison.

"What habit?" asked Hal.

Jennison snorted a short laugh and went back to his work without answering.

Hal took his package and his bag out of the office and went into the back area, among the cages. He found that each cage held two double-decker bunks on each side, sleeping space for eight individuals. The bunks stood against the side walls of the cage, a little distance back from the wall of bars; and beyond them each cell ended in the solid wall of the rock excavated to make this area. The first few cages he came to had two or three occupants in each, all of them sleeping heavily. He continued on back until he could see that there was no cage without at least one person in it.

He finally chose a cage in which the only occupant was a man sitting on one of the bottom bunks toward the back. The cage door was open and Hal came in, a little hesitantly. The man, a leathery-looking individual in his late thirties or early forties, had been carving on a piece of what looked like grey metal, but which must have been quite soft. Now, the knife and the metal bar hung motionless in his hands as he watched Hal enter. His face was expressionless.

"Hello," said Hal. "I'm Tad Thornhill. I just signed a contract for work, here."

The other did not say anything. Hal gestured toward the bottom bunk opposite the one on which the man sat.

"Is this taken?" he asked.

The man stared at him a second longer, still without expression, then he spoke.

"That one?" he said. His voice was hoarse, as if disuse had left it rusty. "No, that doesn't belong to anybody."

"I'll take it then." Hal tossed his bag to the head end of the bunk, in the corner against the back wall. He sat down, and began to open the sealed meal package. "I haven't eaten since I left the ship."

The other man again said nothing, but went back to his carving. Hal spread the package open and saw through the transparent seal that it was some kind of stew with a baked vegetable that looked like a potato in its skin, some bread, and a small bar of what looked like chocolate, but certainly must be synthetic. He could feel the package heating automatically in his hands, now that the outer seal had been broken. He waited the customary sixty seconds, broke the transparent inner seal, and began eating. The food was tasteless and without much texture, but the heat of it was good, and it filled his empty stomach. He suddenly realized he had forgotten to ask Jennison for something to drink.

He looked across at the other man, busy shaping his piece of soft metal into something that looked like a statuette of a man.

"Is there anything to drink around here?" he asked.

"Beer and liquors up in the canteen, front, if you've got the credit," said the other without looking up.

"I mean something like fruit juice, coffee, water—something like that," said Hal.

The other looked at him and jerked his knife up and to his right, pointing chest-high on the wall just beyond them. Rising, Hal found an aperture in the wall, and a stud beside it. He looked about for something to use as a cup, found nothing and finally ended up folding a crude cup out of the outer shell of the meal package. He pressed the stud, and water fountained up in a small arc. He caught it in his jury-rigged cup and drank. It tasted strongly of iron.

He sat down again, finished his meal with the help of several more cupfuls of the water, then bundled the package and containers in his hands and looked around him.

"Throw it under the bunk," said the man across from him.

Hal stared; but the other was bent over his carving and paying no attention. Reluctantly, for it was hard for him to believe that the advice was correct, he finally did as the man had suggested. Then he lay down on the bunk, with his bag prudently between his head and the wall of bars that separated him from the next cages, and gazed at the dark underside of the bunk above him.

He was about to drop off to sleep when the sound of footsteps made him open his eyes again and look toward his feet. A short, somewhat heavy man was just entering the door of the cage. This newcomer stopped just inside the door and stared at Hal.

"He asked me if that bunk was anybody's," said the man doing the carving. "I told him no, it wasn't anybody's."

The other man laughed and climbed up into the top bunk next to the one below which the carver sat. He thrashed around momentarily, but ended up on his side, looking down into the cage, and lay there with his eyes open.

Hal closed his eyes again, and tried to sleep; but with the arrival of the second man, his mind had started to work. He made himself lie still and willed his arms, legs, and body to relax, but still he did not sleep. The powerful feelings of grief and loneliness began to take him over once more. He felt naked in his isolation. This place was entirely different from the Final Encyclopedia, where he had at least found intelligent, responsible people like those with whom he had grown up; and where he had even found those who could be friends, like Ajela and Tam. Here, he felt almost as if he had been locked into a cage with wild animals, unpredictable and dangerous.

He lay watching as other men came into the cage from time to time, and took bunks. Out of the habits of his training, he kept automatic count, and even though his eyes were half-closed, he knew after a while that all the other bunks had been filled. By this time there was a good deal of low-voiced conversation amongst the other occupants of the cage, and from the cages on either side of them. Hal tried to pay no attention. He made, in fact, an effort to block the voices out; and he was beginning at last to think that he might be on the verge of drifting off to sleep when his outer leg was sharply poked.

"You!" He recognized the rusty voice of the man on the lower bunk opposite and opened his eyes. "Sit up and talk for a minute. Where you from?"

"Earth," said Hal. "Old Earth." Effortfully, he pulled himself up and swung his legs over the edge to sit on the side of the bunk.

"Old Earth, is it? This is the first time you've been on Coby?"

"Yes," said Hal. Something about this conversation was wrong. There was a falseness about the other man's tone that triggered off all the alertness that Malachi had trained into him. Hal could feel his heartbeat accelerating, but he forced himself to yawn.

"How d'you like it here?"

The carver had shifted his position to the head of his bed, so that he now sat with his back braced against one of the upright posts at the end of his bunk, the darkness of the solid rock wall half a meter behind him. He continued to carve.

"I don't know. I haven't seen much of it, here," Hal said. He turned, himself, so as to face more directly the man and the end wall behind him. He did not want to make enemies in this new environment, but the feeling of uneasiness was strong, and he wished the other would come to the point of this sudden impulse to make conversation.

"Well, you've got a lot to see. A lot," said the carver. "If you've never been here before, and haven't seen much, I take it you've never been down in a mine, either."

"No," said Hal. "I haven't."

He was conscious that the conversation had died in the other bunks. The rest of the men in the cage must either be asleep, or listening. Hal felt the concentration of attention upon him. Like a wild animal, or like a very young child, he was paying less attention to what the man was saying to him, than he was to how the other was saying it—the tone of voice, the way the man sat, and all the other nonverbal signals he was broadcasting.

". . . you're in for something you'll never forget, first time you go down in a mine," the carver was saying. "Everybody thinks we just punch buttons down there, nowadays. Hell, no, we don't punch buttons. On Coby we don't just punch buttons. You'll see."

"What do you mean?" Hal asked.

"You'll see—" said the carver. One of the other occupants of the room, in an upper bunk near the door, unexpectedly began to whistle, and the carver raised his voice. "Most of the time you're working in a stope so tight you can't stand up in it, carving out the ore, and the heat from the rock gas your torch's boiling off as it cuts builds up until it could cook you."

"But that sort of work's easily done by machines," said Hal, remembering part of his studies. "All it needs—"

"Not on Coby," said the carver. "On Coby, you'n me are cheaper than machines. You'll see. They hang a man here for being late to work too many times."

Hal stared at the other. He could not believe what he had just heard.

"That's right, you think about it," said the carver, whittling away. "You think all that they told you about the Judge-Advocate can't be true? Listen, he can pull your fingernails out, or anything else, to make you talk. It's legal here; and they do it just on general principles in case you've got something to tell them they don't know about, once you're arrested. Three days under arrest and I've seen a man age twenty years—"

It all happened very quickly. Later on, Hal was to guess that the uneasy animal/child part of him must have caught some slight sound that warned him; but at the time all he knew was that something made him glance around suddenly, toward the entrance end of the cage. In that instant, he saw the faces of all the other occupants looking over the edges of their bunks, watching avidly; and, almost upon him from the entrance, coming swiftly, a tall, rawboned man in his forties, with a wedge-shaped face twisted with insane fury, one of the metal mugs held high in one hand, sweeping toward the back of Hal's head.

Hal reacted as instinctively as he might have put out a hand to keep himself from falling. From a time before he could remember, he had exercised under the direction of Malachi; and his exercises had long since lost all conscious connection with the real purpose for which they had originally been designed. They were simply physical games that made him feel good, the way swimming or running did. But now, when there was no time for thought, his body responded automatically.

There was a suddenness of action; no blurring—everything very clear and very fast. He had risen, turned and caught hold of the oncoming man before he had hardly realized it himself, levering and carrying the heavy attacking body forward into the air on its own momentum, to smash against the rock wall. The man struck with a heavy, sodden sound and collapsed at the foot of the wall, to lie there without any motion whatsoever.

Again, with no conscious time lag, Hal found himself turned back and watching all the others in the cage, wire-taut, balanced and waiting. But the rest lay as they had been, motionless, some still with the avid look not yet gone from their faces. But, as he watched, it faded where it still existed, leaving them all looking at him, dull-faced and stupid with astonishment.

Hal continued to stand, motionless, where he was. He felt nothing, but he would have reacted at the slightest movement from any of them; and each of them there seemed to understand this. They breathed through open mouths without sound, watching him . . . and the moment stretched out, and stretched out, as some of the tension in the cage began to trickle away like sands from a broken hourglass.

Gradually, the man on the bottom bunk farthest from Hal on his right slowly put one leg out and lowered a foot to the floor, slowly followed it with the second, and gradually stood up. Carefully, he backed away until he had passed out through the door of the cage. Then he turned and walked away swiftly. Hal stayed as he was, without moving, while, one by one, the others cautiously departed in turn. He was left at last alone, with the motionless figure on the floor.

The occupants of the other cages around him were utterly silent. He looked right and left and everyone he saw was looking away from him. He turned to stare down again at the body lying huddled against the wall. For the first time it occurred to him that the man might be dead. He had been flung headfirst against a stone wall—it could be that his neck had broken.

All emotion in Hal was still lost in wariness and tension, but now, gradually, his mind was beginning to work again. If the man who had attacked him was dead . . . Hal had only been defending himself. But if the others who had been in the cage should all testify that he had been the aggressor . . .

Plainly, he understood now that they all must have known that the man was coming, and that he would be likely to attack anyone using his bunk. He had been drunk, drugged or paranoid, possibly all three; and they had all been waiting for his return and probable attack on Hal. Perhaps, thought

Hal emptily, they were all friends of his. Possibly they had even sent word to him that some stranger had taken his place—since obviously the carver had deliberately lied to Hal and even tried to set him up to be hit from behind, by moving so that Hal would have to turn his back to the cage entrance.

If the others should now all swear that Hal had picked a fight and killed this man deliberately . . . no, it was impossible. Justice, even here, could not be that unreasonably blind.

But the thought again of the right of the Judge-Advocate to use any means he wished to extract answers from someone under arrest returned to him, prickling the skin on the back of his neck.

Could he get back to the port, and off-planet? Not without using his visa as Tad Thornhill, and the moment he did that, he would undoubtedly be arrested.

Common sense came suddenly like a cooling draft of air into his fevered mind. He squatted down and put his fingers on the neck of the man on the floor, feeling for the left carotid artery. It pulsed strongly against his fingertips; and when he put his hand over the other's mouth, he could feel the stir of breath against his palm. A deep sigh came out of him. The attacker had only been knocked out, after all. Hal's knees weakened with relief.

But, on the heels of that relief came a strong urge to get out of this place enclosing him. He turned quickly, and went out the door and up between the row of cages. The people in them had begun talking after their immediate moment of silence following the attack. But they stopped talking again now, as he passed, and this time their eyes watched him as he went by. When he reached the front of the area the canteen was still as noisy as ever, but the office was now dark, and looked as if it had been locked for the night. He hesitated, then walked on and out into the corridor, turning down it in the opposite direction to that from which he had come.

This way, the corridor seemed to run on forever in a straight line ahead of him, and there was nobody within sight in it, as far as his eye could see. He picked up speed as he went along until his long legs were swinging him forward at a rate of nearly seven kilometers an hour.

He had no idea yet where he was going, or why he was going there. He was driven only by an instinct to get away; and he was still charged to the teeth with the adrenalin his body had released in him under his instinct to defend himself. Even now, there was no fury in him, only a steady, sick feeling; and the sole relief from that feeling was to keep striding on, kilometer after kilometer, forcing his body into a mode that would make it forget the fight-or-flight reaction.

Time went by, and, little by little, the sick feeling began to fade. He was left with only a dullness, an empty sort of feeling such as might come after recovery from a hard blow in the solar plexus. He felt hollow inside. His mind brought him no solutions to the situation in which he now supposed he was. Whether his attacker had been insane or not, he had to assume that the others in the cage might well be his friends and would lie about what had happened, if only to protect themselves. They might even be waiting to revenge themselves on Hal when he got back—and there were six of them, not counting whoever else there might be in the other cages who might also know them and want to help them. Nor, probably, could he look for any protection from Jennison, who had given a strong impression of holding himself apart from Hal and everyone else in the Holding Area.

But there was no safe place to go to, except off-Coby. He had been warned that he could not return to the port area without the permission of his superiors. But they might not yet know at the port that he had signed a contract, and he could buy passage on some outbound ship. Otherwise—in this owned and artificial environment, there would be no such thing as existence outside of the social order. And there was no other place for him to go that he knew of, although presumably this corridor led to somewhere else on Coby.

Probably the best thing he could do was to keep on walking. This corridor had to lead someplace. Once there, with authorities who might be at least neutral about what had happened back at Halla Station Holding Area, he could plead his case and perhaps get a fair hearing. . . .

He stopped suddenly, his nerves wire-tight. As he strained to listen, he could now pick up a faint noise coming from ahead of him; and his eyes, now that he tried to see as far as possible down the corridor ahead, seemed to make out something like a dancing dot. He held still, closed his eyes for three counted seconds and then slowly opened them again, comparing the first moment of sight with the last thing he had seen before closing his eyelids. There was no doubt that the dot was there.

Something was coming his way, making a faint humming noise as it did so. Even in his present state, a corner of Hal's mind paused to puzzle over the sound, for it was like no noise he had heard before; but at the same time it had a ring of familiarity that he could not pin down.

In any case, there was nothing he could do but wait for its coming. The dot was expanding at a rate that implied it was coming faster than he could run from it. Hal stood where he was; and, after a little, the puzzle of the sound was solved, for as it came closer, it changed; and he both identified it and realized why he had not been able to earlier.

What he was hearing was simply the sound of an air-cushion vehicle moving toward him. But by some freak of acoustics in the long, straight tunnel, the breathy whisper of the underjets was changed and amplified into a resonance that from a distance rang like a musical humming. The tunnel was acting like the pipe of a flute or the drone on a bagpipe. Now, however, as the vehicle came closer, the humming note began to be lost in the normal, breathy sound of the downward air-rush of the jets, and the total noise became identifiable for what it was.

At the same time, the vehicle itself was growing large enough to be recognized. As with sound, vision was evidently subject to tricks played on it by a corridor of this sort. The still, horizontal layers of air about him, extended into the distance, seemed to have an effect something like that of the heated air of the daytime desert. Even though the vehicle and its rider was now close enough to be seen for what they were—a simple four-place open truck and driver—still their outlines seemed to waver and change as if Hal was looking at a mirage. On impulse he started to walk again, toward the oncoming vehicle, and the outlines began to firm up.

Hal and the truck drew together. As they got close enough that the distortions of air in the corridor no longer bent the truck and its operator into odd shapes, the driver was revealed to be a man at least in his sixties, wearing a gray coverall and a gray cap. Below the cap his face was a remarkably young face grown old. At first glance it looked ancient, but then something almost boyish would glint out from among the lines and leathery skin. Truck and Hal came level, and the driver brought the vehicle to a stop.

Hal also stopped; and looked warily back at the man.

"What are you doing here?" the driver spoke in a half-shout; and his voice was the battered remnant of a tenor.

"Walking," said Hal.

"Walking!" The driver stared at Hal. "How long?"

"I don't know," said Hal. He had to make an effort to remember. "An hour, maybe two."

"An hour! Two hours!" The driver was still in a half-shout, still staring at him. "You know you're nearly twenty kilometers from Halla Station? That's where you're from, aren't you—Halla Station?"

Hal nodded.

"Then where d'you think you're walking to?"

"The next station," said Hal.

"Next station's a hundred and twenty kilometers!"

Hal said nothing. The driver considered him for a few seconds more.

"You'd better get in. I'll take you back to Halla Station. Get in, now!"

Hal considered. A hundred and twenty kilometers without food, and above all without water, was something he could not hope to walk. He went slowly around the rear end of the truck and came up to find the driver trying to lever a large package out of the front seat beside him, into the back part of the vehicle.

Hal pushed it over for him and climbed up into the open seat. The driver started up again.

"I'm Hans Sosyetr," the driver said. "Who're you?"

"Tad Thornhill," said Hal.

"Just got here, didn't you? Brand-new, aren't you?"

"Yes," said Hal.

They drove along for a little while in silence.

"How old are you?" asked the driver.

"Twenty," said Hal—and remembered he was no longer on Earth—"standard years."

"You aren't twenty," said the driver.

Hal said nothing.

"You aren't nineteen. You aren't eighteen. How the hell old are you really?"

"Twenty," said Hal.

Hans Sosyetr snorted. They drove along in silence for a way. The truck breathed steadily under them.

"What happened?" Sosyetr said. "Some damn thing happened, don't tell me it didn't. You were at the Holding Area and something happened. So what was it?"

"I almost killed a man," said Hal. The sick feeling returned to his stomach as the whole moment came alive for him briefly, once more.

"Did you kill him?"

"No," said Hal. "He was just knocked out."

"What happened?"

"I looked around and saw him starting to hit me with one of those metal mugs from the canteen," Hal said. He was surprised that he was answering this man so freely; but there was now an exhausted feeling coming over him, and, besides, Hans Sosyetr's age and direct questions seemed to make it hard not to answer the older man.

"So?"

"I threw him against a wall. It knocked him out."

"So you started to walk to Moon Transfer?"

"Moon Transfer?" Hal looked at him. "Is that the name of the next station?"

"What else? So you started to walk there. Why? Somebody chasing you?"

"No. They all got up and went out of the cage after it happened. They backed out and went away."

"Backed away?" Sosyetr looked over at him. "Who was this kip you threw against the wall?"

"I don't know," said Hal.

"What's he look like?"

"...bout my height," said Hal. "No, maybe a little taller. And heavier, of ...irty or forty standard years. Dark face, wide at the top and

..." said Sosyetr. "Bigger and older than ...wall. How'd you manage to do a thing

...side with caution.

... lucky."

...r ran into. Why don't you tell me the

...l of caution inside him unexpectedly dis-
...e urge to explain the whole thing to some-
...g the older man about everything that had

happened, from the time he stepped into the cage and asked the man carving metal if the bunk was empty.

"So," said Sosyetr, when he was done. "Why'd you leave? Why'd you start walking out that way?"

"Those others in the cage had to be friends of whoever it was I threw against the wall," said Hal.

"Friends? In a Holding Area? And I thought you said they ran like rabbits."

"I didn't say they all ran like rabbits. . . . The point is, if they are his friends, they might swear I started it."

"Swear? Who to?"

"The Judge-Advocate."

"What's the Judge-Advocate to do with all this?"

Hal turned his head to stare at the old face beside him. "I hurt a man pretty badly. I could have killed him."

"So? In a Holding Area? They haul people out of there every morning."

Hal continued to stare. After a moment he managed to get his voice to work.

"You mean—nobody cares?"

Sosyetr laughed, a laugh high in his throat.

"Nobody important. What those kips do, or what happens to them, is their own business. Once they get on a payroll, if they make trouble, Judge-Advocate might take an interest."

He looked over at Hal.

"Judge-Advocate's pretty important. About the only law you're likely to have anything to do with is Mine Personnel Manager, or maybe Company police."

Hal sat, gradually absorbing this new information. There was a hard core forming in him now around the wariness that the attack in the cage had woken in him.

"If there's no law to speak of in a Holding Area," he said, "it was a good thing I left. There'd be nothing to keep his friends from doing anything they want to me."

Sosyetr laughed again.

"Don't sound to me like friends—or that they'd much want to do anything to you, the way you say they ran off."

"I told you," said Hal. "They didn't run."

"Seven of them, and they left? If they went then, I don't think much to worry about when you go back."

"No," said Hal. "I'm not going back. Not tonight, anyway."

Sosyetr blew a breath out, gustily.

"All right," he said. "You wait while I unload this stuff in maybe give me a hand unloading, and I'll sign for you to Guest House until morning. You can give me a debit t wages. You want to be back at the Holding Area for job assignment at eight-thirty A.M., though."

Hal looked at the older man with abrupt astonishment and gratitude, but Sosyetr was scowling at the front of the truck with his head cocked on one side as if listening for some noise in the underjets that should not have been there. Hal sat back in his truck seat, a sense of relief making him feel limp. Out of the wariness in him, out of what he had just learned from Sosyetr, from the attack of the man with the metal mug, and from the behavior of the other seven men in the cage, a new awareness was just beginning to be born in him.

For the moment, he was only aware of this as a general feeling. But, in a strange way, as it grew and began to come to focus in him, the images of Malachi, Walter, and Obadiah seemed to move back a little. Time and experience were already beginning to come between him and his recent memories of them—when he had as yet not really come to accept the fact that they were gone. A sadness too deep for expression moved in him, and held its place there all the rest of the silent ride with Sosyetr into Halla Station.

Chapter

> > 6 < <

The Guest House in Halla Station proved to be a form of barracks for those who were not employees of local Companies or offices. Hal learned, somewhat grimly, that the Guest House had been open to him all the time, since he had credit to pay for it. The Holding Area was only for job seekers, or former miners rehiring who had no credit. Everything at the Area, including the beer in the canteen, was free. This also included the package of food Jennison had charged him for. The Holding Area, in short, was for the Coby version of indigents—or those who knew no better, like himself.

"Hell," said Sosyetr, as they sat over a late meal in the clean and comfortable meal room of the Guest House, "didn't you ever think to ask the interviewer at Halla Station what you could buy?"

"No," said Hal. "I just took for granted he'd tell me whatever I needed to know. I was stupid."

"Sure," said Sosyetr, nodding. "You were stupid, all right. Stupidest twenty-year-old I ever met."

Hal looked up quickly from the chunk of processed meat he was cutting. But if there had been a grin on the older man's face, he had been too slow to surprise it.

He finished eating—Sosyetr had already finished a much smaller meal and was sitting with a cup of Coby coffee, watching him—and pushed the plate aside.

"Sost," he said, for the other had said this was the version he preferred to hear of a last name most people mispronounced—and he was not partial to Hans—"what happens from the time I report for job assignment to roll call?"

This time he did see Sost grin.

"Going to ask some questions now?"

"From now on," said Hal.

Sost nodded.

"All right," he said. He drank from his coffee cup and set it down again. "You'll show up there tomorrow morning and everybody who can stand on their feet'll be out in front of the office. Agent'll call the roll, mark off anyone not there, and hand out assignments on the basis of the work orders he got since roll call the morning before. That's about it."

"Then what? What if I'm called for a work assignment?"

"Then you get travel papers with directions and travel passes credited against your new job; and you take off for whatever Company needed you enough to hire you."

"And when I get there?"

"You'll be assigned to a team on one of the shifts—unless the team cap-tain throws you back. If that happens, they'll bounce you around until they find a team that'll take you."

"What if no one wants me?"

"You?" Sost looked at him. "Not likely. But if they did, the Company'd give you a week's wages and dump you at the nearest Holding Area. You get to start all over again."

He got up to get himself another cup of coffee from the wall dispenser and sat back down at the table they were sharing.

"Sost," said Hal, "what are the things that make you think I'm younger than twenty?"

Sost stared at him for a long moment.

"You want to know what to look out for?" he said at last. "I'll tell you. The first thing is, keep your mouth shut. Sure, I know your voice changed four–five years ago; but every time you say something you talk like a kid. Hell, you think like a kid. So don't talk, if you can help it."

Hal nodded.

"All right," he said. "I won't."

"And take your time," said Sost. "Don't start talking to everyone you meet like he was an old friend. I don't mean act suspicious all the time, either. Just—hold back a little. Wait a bit. Don't go jumping around with your body, either. You get a little older, you won't have that kind of energy to waste. Sit still when you sit. But the big thing is—watch that talking. Just get in the habit of not doing it."

"You talk a fair amount," Hal said.

"There you go," Sost said. "That's just the sort of thing a kid would say. That's just the wrong thing. What's it change things for you, what I do? As far as me talking, I know what to say. I can make noise with my mouth all day long and not give anything away I don't want to. You, you give every-thing you've got away, every time you open your lips."

Hal nodded.

"All right," he said.

"That's better," said Sost. "Now, what're you planning to do tomorrow?"

"Wait and see," said Hal.

"All right." Sost nodded, in his turn. "Good for you. You're learning. But I mean, what're you going to do about those kips back at the Holding Area?"

Hal shrugged.

"That's even better. You'll do," said Sost. He got up. "I'm folding up. That's another difference. You grow up, and you know there's a next day com-ing. You don't forget it."

After the older man had left, Hal sat for a little while, enjoying the clean smells and the privacy of the dining room, in which he was now alone. Then he went to bed behind a locked door in the comfortable room his credit had been able to provide for him.

A knocking at his door seemed to wake him the minute he had closed his eyes. He got up, unlocked and opened the door, and found Sost dressed and waiting.

"What time is it?" Hal asked thickly.

"Seven-thirty," Sost said. "Or don't you want breakfast?"

They had breakfast in the same meal room and Sost drove him out to the Holding Area.

"I'll wait," said Sost, parking the truck when they got there just at the 8:30 roll-call time. "You're a natural to get assigned today. But if you don't, I can give you a lift back to the Guest House before I go on."

Hal started to get out of the truck to join the men standing before the office.

"Sit still," said Sost, under his breath. "What the hell, you can hear from here, can't you? What'd I tell you last night about jumping?"

Hal settled back in his seat in the truck. He sat silently with Sost, waiting with the standing crowd for Jennison to put in an appearance. He had time to study the others who were waiting; and he found himself looking for the man who had attacked him. But the wedge-shaped face and long body did not seem to be there. Perhaps the other man had been hurt more badly than Hal had thought. . . . The thought chilled him, but after Sost's words the night before, he did not say anything to the older man.

He started to get out of the truck again.

"Sit still, I said," growled Sost softly.

"I've got to get my bag—if it's still there."

"After."

Hal sank back in his seat. He went back to searching the crowd for faces he could recognize. He picked out the man who had been doing the carving, but was not able to identify certainly any of the others from the cage. He gradually became aware that none of those in the crowd were meeting his eyes. In fact, the carver had turned away when Hal had started watching him.

Experimentally, he picked out a man he was sure he had never seen before and stared only at him. The man, apparently casually, first turned away from Hal's gaze; then, when Hal continued to watch, the other moved deeper into the crowd, stepping behind other, taller individuals and using them as screens until they moved, until he had been herded by Hal's unrelenting watch to the far edge of the crowd.

The door opened finally, and Jennison appeared. It was almost a quarter to nine. He was carrying a hard-copy printout in his hand, and without looking at the crowd, he began to read off names. Hal's was the third to be read. When Jennison had finished, he looked up and saw the truck with the two of them in it.

"Sost!" he called, and waved. Sost waved back. Jennison turned and went back into the office.

"You know him?" Hal asked.

"No," said Sost. "Looks like he knows me, though. Lots do."

The crowd before the office was beginning to disintegrate slowly as disappointed members of it began to break off toward the cages or the canteen and those whose names had been called moved up to cluster just outside the door.

"No hurry," Sost said, as Hal again started to get out of the truck. "Let the others go in first. Now's a good time to get that bag of yours."

"If it's still there," said Hal again, glumly.

Sost laughed, but said nothing.

Hal got out of the truck and, tensing instinctively, approached the men, who were still in a loose gathering before the office. They parted unobtrusively to let him through, with none of them looking directly at him in the process. Beyond them, the corridor between the rows of cages was empty, and the cages themselves were deserted except for a heavily-inert body here and there on a bunk. He went to the cage he had been in the night before, stepped inside, and looked for the bunk he had occupied.

His bag was there, just where he had left it. He took it back to the truck. There were still a number of men waiting before the office door and, as he came through the space before the building, one came out and another entered. Hal climbed back into the truck.

"It was there, all right," he said. "I can't believe it."

Sost chuckled, this time quietly.

"Who of them'd take it?" he asked.

Hal looked curiously at the older man; but playing his new game of speaking as little as possible, he waited, instead of asking what the other had meant. Either Sost would tell him before he left, or the answer would emerge otherwise.

He sat comfortably with Sost until the last man had come out of the office, then got down from the truck and crossed the space to the office door, himself. He stepped in and found Jennison in position at his desk behind the counter. But this time Jennison got up, smiling, and came to the other side of the counter.

"Here's your assignment papers," Jennison said, handing them over. "You're hired by the Yow Dee Mine, Templar Mining Company. You ought to be there in two hours by tube. I gave you a good assignment."

Hal did not answer immediately. He had not liked Jennison on first encounter. He liked him no more now; and he was certain that the apparent generosity and friendliness must tie in with some advantage Jennison was hoping to gain from him. The thing would be to try and find out what that advantage was. "Such situations," Walter had told him once, "always develop into bargaining sessions. And the first secret of successful bargaining is to make the other party do the proposing."

"You charged me for a meal, last night," Hal said, picking up the assignment papers.

"That's right, I did," said Jennison. He leaned on the counter and continued to smile. "Officially, of course, I shouldn't have done it. If I'd known more about you, I wouldn't have. But in a job like this, you take what you can. I wouldn't do it again; but now the credit's entered with central book-keeping, it'd be a little awkward to fix it without upsetting the accountants at Headquarters. And I get along by getting along with people. Now, I did you a big favor with the mine I assigned you to—ask your friend Sost about that if you don't believe me. Why don't you do me the small favor of for-getting that small charge to your credit? Maybe someday we can do a little business, and I can knock the amount of it off a price."

"And maybe we won't do any business," said Hal.

Jennison laughed.

"On Coby everybody does business with everybody. As I say, ask your friend Sost."

"Maybe I'm different," said Hal.

He had chosen the words at random; but his senses, stretched to their greatest alertness, suddenly convinced him that he had triggered a reaction from Jennison with that last answer. Of course, Jennison could be inter-preting what he had just said as a threat. . . . Hal suddenly remembered that he had come here to Coby to hide, and he was abruptly conscious of the dan-ger of insisting too much on any difference he might have. He spoke again quickly.

"Anyway, I don't expect to come through here again."

"There's always a chance," said Jennison. "I don't know myself what might bring us to talking again; but I always like to part friends with everybody. All right?"

"I don't make friends that easily."

Jennison showed a trace of impatience.

"I'm just pointing out I may be able to do you some good, someday!" he said. "You'll maybe find out you want to do business with me, after all. It'll work a lot better then if we're already—all right, not friends, then—but at least friendly."

Hal watched the man closely. Jennison was sounding sincere. Hal could check with Sost, but he was beginning to be strongly convinced that the agent must have some specific stock-in-trade which the events here had con-vinced him he might be able to sell to Hal, someday; and he was trying to pave the way for that sale, in advance.

Hal put the assignment papers safely in an inside jacket pocket.

"What happened to that man who jumped me last night?" he asked.

"Who?" Jennison raised an eyebrow, turned about and ran his eye down a list of what seemed to be names on a printout on his desk. " . . . Khef? Oh, yes, Khef. He's all right. In the infirmary. Slight concussion; probably be back here in a day or two—though they say they may want to hold him for some psychiatrics."

Hal turned and went out the door. He had to struggle against a lifetime of training to keep from saying good-bye; but he managed it.

Outside, the space between the canteen and the office was now empty.

Things seemed to be going full blast once more in the canteen. He walked over and got in the truck with Sost.

"What does 'psychiatrics' mean here?" he asked.

"Head-tests. For crazies." Sost looked at him. "What's your assignment?"

"Yow Dee Mine," said Hal. "Jennison seemed to think he'd done me a particular favor."

Sost whistled briefly.

"Could be," he said. "It's a good mine. Honest management. Good team leaders—or used to be good team leaders, last I heard, anyway."

Sost raised the truck from the ground on its air jets and turned it back toward Halla Station.

"What are team leaders?" Hal asked.

"Six to ten men to a team. One man leads them. You'll be taking the tube. I'll run you over to it."

"You mean, working down in the mine, they work in teams?"

Sost nodded.

"What's the procedure when I get there? Are they going to stick me on a team—do I go right down the mine and to work? Or is there some sort of training I'll have to get first?"

"Your team leader'll train you—all the training you'll get," said Sost. "But they don't just stick you on. Like I say, the team captain can turn you down if he wants to. They don't do it too much, though. A team captain that hard to please wears out the patience of management, pretty fast. Probably they'll send you down on your first shift the day after you get there, but if they want to, they can tell you to suit up, hand you a torch and walk you right out of the hiring yard into the skip."

"Skip? That's what you called the others back at the Holding Area, wasn't it?"

"No—kip. A kip—that's what you're going to be—is the last man joined onto the team. He's got to run all the errands for the rest of them. A skip—that's the car you go down into the mine in. Like an elevator."

"Oh," said Hal. He continued to ask questions, however, until Sost dropped him off at the tube platform.

"Just do what it says on your travel orders," said Sost, finally. "I got to get to work. So long."

He turned the truck about abruptly and began to drive off.

"Wait!" Hal called after him. "When am I going to run into you again? How do I find you?"

"Just ask anybody!" Sost called back without turning his head. He lifted one hand briefly in farewell and drove around a corner out of sight of the platform and the tube tunnel.

It was some twenty minutes later that the train Hal was waiting for came through and he got on board. The mine that he had been assigned to was south of Halla Station but back towards the port city, almost half the distance Hal had originally come out. The tube car he was riding was almost

empty of other passengers, and none of these showed any eagerness to so-
cialize, which relieved him of the need to discourage conversation. He was
free to sit by himself and think; and he did.

He was feeling curiously empty and lonely. Once again, he had met someone he liked, only to leave him behind. Except that, in the case of Sost, he
still had the other's advice for a companion. Though it was not easy advice
to follow. Hal would not have thought of himself as someone who jumped
around physically and talked too much. His own self-image was of someone
almost too quiet and almost too silent. But if he had struck Sost as being
overactive and talkative, he must be doing more moving about and talking
than he should, or else the older man would not have chosen those charac-
teristics to pick on.

But advice alone was a cold companion. He thought now that he seemed
fated to end up alone in the universe. Maybe it was necessary for things to
happen that way to him now that his life had turned out the way it had. Certainly, if he was going to become invisible to the Others who might be looking for him, he probably could not afford the risk of having friends. He had
been brought up, particularly by Walter the InTeacher, to reach out automatically and make connection with all other human beings around him.
But now he would have to practice, not merely at not making friends, but
rebuffing anyone who might try to make a friend of him.

To turn himself into a close-lipped solitary individual was one way to make
sure nobody else would care much to be close to him. The ghosts of Walter,
Malachi, and Obadiah had been right. His first imperative was to survive—
by any means possible—until he was old enough and strong enough to defend himself against Bleys Ahrens and Dahno.

In any case, whatever method he chose to survive, one thing was sure.
From now on, he could not afford the luxury of letting things happen to him.
He would have to take control of his life and steer it the way he wanted it
to go. To leave it any longer to circumstance and the will of others was a
certain invitation to disaster. He had no idea yet how to go about taking such
control, but he would learn.

It came to him, riding the strong wave of loneliness and unhappiness in
him, that this was evidently what adulthood was meant to be—the taking
on of the necessity of doing things he had no idea of how to do, and carrying the responsibility alone because now there was no one else to trust with
it. He would have to become, he thought, like an armed ship belonging to
no nation, travelling always alone, and running out his weapons at the first
sight of any other vessel that ventured close to him.

But he had to do it. Sitting on the soft train seat, soothed by the minute
vibrations of the car he was in, as it flew through endless tunnels in the planetary crust of Coby, he drifted off toward sleep, telling himself that he must
find out how to do it, some way. . . .

He woke shortly before he got to his destination, and was reasonably alert
by the time the car slowed for his stop. He roused himself to get up and step

down onto the station platform, and went on into the station, to the area where, as at Halla Station, a single interviewer sat at one of several available desks.

"Papers," said the interviewer as he came up, automatically extending a hand.

Hal made no move to produce his papers.

"Where's the Guest House?" he asked.

The interviewer's arm slowly sank back onto the desktop. He looked at Hal for a long moment, uncertainly.

"Guest House?" he answered at last. "Out the back door and two streets to your right. You'll see the sign."

Hal went toward the door, feeling the eyes of the interviewer following him. The man would have no way of knowing whether or not Hal was a new employee under assignment; and plainly he was not sure enough of himself to check and find out. Sost's advice had been good.

Hal found the Guest House and walked inside to its lobby, which was identical in every way with the lobby of the Guest House in Halla Station. But there was a short young woman behind the registration counter instead of the elderly man he had encountered at the Guest House at Halla Station. Hal put down his bag and signed in, passing his credit and employment papers over.

"I've been hired by the Yow Dee Mine," he said to her. "Is there some way I can get a ride out to it, if it's some ways to go?"

The Guest House manager had brown hair and a cheerful, acorn-shaped face.

"You won't want to wait in the terminal until all the other hires are in, and then ride out in Company transportation, will you?" she asked. "No, I thought not. You're all to be added to teams on the day shift, so they won't be holding showup until this evening, after dinner. You might as well be comfortable here until then; and our on-duty maintenance worker'll run you out for a small charge."

"Thanks," said Hal, gratefully; and was immediately angry with himself for not succeeding in being more taciturn and unsociable. But it was hard to adjust all at once.

Later, the maintenancer—a girl younger than he was—drove him out to the mine. Its main area was a very large cave-space holding the pithead, a number of structures built of what looked like concrete, including the offices and the bunkhouse—the maintenancer pointed out and named them for him—clustered around three sides of an open space that looked to be half recreation area, half marshalling yard, in which a number of people were already gathered.

"Looks like they're all ready to start your show up," the maintenancer said, as Hal got down from the small duty truck in which she had run him out. "On the side over at the left there, those six you see, they're the other kips like you."

Hal took his bag and walked over. He was conscious that a number of the men in the crowd of miners standing around—he could see no women—turned to look at him as he came. He made it a point to ignore this and go straight to the six people the maintenancer had pointed out. One of these was a lean, brown-haired, snub-nosed woman in her early twenties, wearing the same sort of hard-finish work jacket and slacks that a number of the men in the watching crowd also wore. She gazed at Hal, frowning a little.

He had barely joined these others when a tall, rawboned miner, at least in his fifties, came over from the watching crowd, took Hal roughly by the elbow and turned him around, so that they were face-to-face.

"You just in from Halla Station?"

The man had some of the rhythms of someone from one of the Friendly Worlds in his voice, although nothing else about him looked as if he came from the same Splinter Culture that had produced Obadiah.

"Yes," said Hal, looking directly back, almost on a level, into his face. The other released him and went back into the crowd without saying anything more.

There was a stir among those watching and faces turned to the door of what the maintenancer had pointed out as the Management Office. A very erect, thick-stomached man with wavy gray hair and an impatient face came out of the door there and stood at the top of the three steps that led down into the walled area.

"All right, team leaders," he called, his dry, harsh baritone carrying out over the other sounds of the crowd. "Where are you? Who's short?"

The general crowd moved back, leaving four men standing each a little apart from the other. One was the rawboned fifty-year-old who had spoken to Hal. The others were between that age and thirty; one, a lean, dark man in his forties; one who looked like a somewhat younger version of Sost—a burly blond-headed individual in his thirties; and a short, very wide-bodied and powerful-looking individual with a round head and jet-black hair who could have been any age between thirty and sixty.

"All right. Who's got priority for first assignment?" called the man on the steps. "You—Beson, isn't it?"

"Me," said the lean, dark man.

"All right." The man on the steps looked at a piece of printout in his hand. "Tonina Wayle!"

With a satisfied look on her face, the one woman among the kips, who had been continuing to watch Hal, crossed over to Beson. Several of the men from the crowd behind the four team leaders greeted her as if she was an old acquaintance.

"Next? Charlei?" The burly, Sost-like man nodded. "You draw Morgan Amdur. Morgan Amdur, which one are you?"

The man next to Hal stepped forward a little.

"All right," said the burly man, dryly. The man next to Hal crossed over. "Anyo Yuan. Step out there!"

The man farthest from Hal among the kips took a pace forward.

"John, he's yours."

"All right," said the wide-bodied leader with the black hair. Anyo Yuan, who was evidently as new to this as Hal, hesitated, looking around him uncertainly.

"Go on over to John Heikkila, Yuan," said the man on the step. "Tad Thornhill."

Hal stepped forward.

"Will, he's yours. Thornhill, your leader is Will Nanne—"

"Don't want him!" The words from the tall, rawboned man were loud enough to echo from the walls of the surrounding buildings. Hal felt the sick drop of stomach that comes with the sudden fall of a fast elevator.

Chapter

> > 7 < <

"*Cause or peremptory?*" the grey-haired man was demanding.

"I hear he's a troublemaker." Once more, Will Nanne's voice was painfully clear over all the open area.

"All right," said the man on the steps. "Thornhill, you step back. Wallace Carter?"

The smallest of the kips stepped out as Hal retreated.

"Yours, Charlei."

"All right."

"Johannes Hevelius."

"Yours, Beson."

"He'll do."

The other two crossed over. Hal was left standing nakedly alone.

"All right. Last call on Thornhill. You're all still short at least one worker. Will Nanne, you don't want him?"

"No."

"Beson?"

"Not for me."

"Charlei?"

"Not for me."

"John? Last chance."

The powerful, short man turned and walked with a rolling gait over to Will Nanne.

"Tell me what you heard about him," he said.

Nanne leaned down and spoke quietly in Heikkila's ear. The shorter man listened, nodded, and turned to the man on the step.

"I'll take him."

Hal moved slowly across the flat surface of the space toward John Heikkila. The powerful-looking leader who had claimed him was talking to Anyo Yuan. Hal stood waiting until the conversation was done, and then Heikkila turned and saw him.

"You come with me," he said.

He led Hal, not toward the bunkhouse, to which everyone else was now moving—the man on the steps having gone back into the Management Office—but in the opposite direction, across to an empty far corner of the enclosure. Then he stopped and turned to face Hal. He looked at Hal in silence for a moment.

"You like to fight?" he said. His voice was tenor-toned, but hard.

"No," said Hal. He was torn between his desire to sound convincing to

Heikkila and his attempt to maintain the tight-lipped taciturn image Sost had urged on him.

"That's not what I hear. Will tells me you put a man in the infirmary down at Halla Station Holding Area, yesterday."

"He tried to hit me with a metal mug when I wasn't looking," said Hal. "It was just an accident he ended up in the hospital."

Heikkila stared at him coldly for an extended moment.

"You think you could put me in the infirmary?"

Hal stared at him, suddenly weary with a weariness much older than his years. The other was standing with his face barely eight inches from Hal's. The black hair of his round head came barely to Hal's eye-level; but his great chest and arms seemed to blot out half the scene behind him. He would carry nearly as much weight again as Hal, in experienced adult bone and muscle; and there was a dangerousness about the way he stood that marked plain upon him the fact that he was something more than a merely ordinarily competent fighter. Someone like this—again, the knowledge, like the answer, came from a time older than Hal's years, older than the lessons of Malachi— would have to be killed, killed quickly, by someone as light and young as Hal if there was to be any hope of stopping him at all. He was waiting now for assurance that Hal would know better than to pick a fight with him. Hal did—but he could not lie in answering. Not if he was to work and live with this man from now on.

"If you came for me the way that man at the Holding Station did," Hal said heavily, "I'd have to try. But I don't want to fight—anybody."

Heikkila continued to stare harshly. Slowly, then, the harshness went and something a little like puzzlement came into the round face.

"It's a good thing, then," he said slowly, at last. "Because there's no fighting on my team. We don't have time to fight. We don't have time for anything but getting the ore out. You understand me?"

Hal nodded. Unexpectedly, he found he wanted to be on this man's team rather than that of any other leader he had seen there.

"If you'll give me a chance," he told Heikkila, "you'll see I'm telling the truth. I'm not a troublemaker."

Heikkila watched him for a second more.

"You calling Will Nanne a liar?"

"I don't know what he heard," said Hal. "But whatever it was he can't have heard it as it happened."

"That so?" Heikkila still stared at him; but the last of the dangerousness Hal had felt like a living presence in the team leader was gone. "Damn if I understand. How big was this kip you laid out?"

"About my height," said Hal, "but older."

"Oh. Real old?"

"Not real old . . . ," said Hal—and then suddenly realized he might be implying too much in an opposite direction. "But he came at me without any warning, from behind. I was just trying to save myself. He hit a wall."

"You're saying he put himself in the infirmary?"

"Yes . . . in a way."

Heikkila nodded.

"Damn," he said, again. He studied Hal. "How old are you?"

"Twenty."

"Twenty!" Heikkila snorted.

"—next year," said Hal, desperately.

"Sure," said Heikkila. "Sure you are."

He sighed gustily, from the depths of his wide chest.

"All right, come on with me, then," he said. "But it's rough working in the mines. You better know that."

He turned and led the way across the open space toward the bunkhouse.

"That woman, the first one to get picked. She's been a miner, before, hasn't she?" asked Hal, catching up with him.

"Sure," said Heikkila. "Right here at the Yow Dee."

"If she can do it," Hal said, thinking of her relative smallness, "I can."

Heikkila snorted again. It was almost a laugh.

"You think so?" he said. "Well, you just worry about showing me you're willing to work, or you'll be off my team after the first shift. My team bids top quota at this mine. You make it through the first shift and I'll give you two weeks to toughen in. If you don't do it by then—out!"

As they got close to the bunkhouse, Hal found himself at last identifying something that had bothered him from first landing on Coby. Because the habitable area of the planet was underground, there was no real outdoors. Odors and sunlight and a dozen other small, natural signals did not intrude their differences here to remind him that he was no longer on Earth. In spite of this, an unrelenting sense of alienness had been with him from the first moment of his leaving the ship. Now, suddenly, he realized the cause of it.

There were almost no shadows. Here in this open space, a thousand sources of illumination in the cave roof far overhead gave a light that came from all angles and did not change. Even where there were shadows, these, too, were permanent. Here, there would be neither night nor day. It occurred to him suddenly that it might be almost a relief to go down into the mine and get away from this upper area where time seemed forever at a standstill.

They had reached the bunkhouse. He followed John Heikkila in, through a lounge area into a narrow corridor, with lines of doors in each wall, some open but most closed, entrances to what seemed to be a series of single-person rooms. They continued along to the end of the corridor before John stopped and let them both into a room which was half again as large as the ones Hal had glimpsed through open doors as they walked down the corridor. This room held not only a bed, a couple of comfortable chair-floats and a small writing desk, as the other rooms had, but also a large, business-style desk; and it was at this desk that Heikkila now sat down, extended one square, thick hand, and said the word that Hal was coming to hear even in his sleep.

"Papers."

Hal got them out and passed them over. The leader passed them through the transverse slot in his desk, fingered some code on his pad of keys beside the slot, and returned the papers to Hal. A hard copy of a single printed page came up through the slot and he handed this also to Hal.

"You're hired as kip," said John. "One-fiftieth team share and an open charge against all necessary equipment, supplies and living expenses."

He held out his hand to Hal, who gripped it automatically. "I'm John," he said. "You're Tad. Welcome to the team."

"John . . . ," said Hal. He looked at the hard copy in his hand.

"I don't understand," he said. "Doesn't the mine management hire me—"

"We bid and subcontract here, team by team, just like most of the honest mines do," said John, looking up at him. "You work for the team. I work for the team. The only difference between you and me is I'm leader—I do all the paperwork and make all the decisions. And I get the biggest share."

He got to his feet.

"We're on day shift for the rest of this two-week," he said. "Another pair of three-days. Better set your caller for four-thirty, if you want to make breakfast by five hundred hours and lineup by five-thirty with all your equipment. Come on, I'll show you your place."

He got up from the desk, and led the way out into the hall and down to one of the doors. Opening it, he revealed a room in which everything was neat and ready for occupancy.

"Bunkhouse maintenance takes care of ordinary cleanup," he said. "You make an unusual mess, you settle it with them; whether you clean up yourself, or pay them extra out of your own account. Better settle it yourself, because if they come to me with it, it's going to cost you even more."

Hal nodded. He laid his bag down on the bed. The sheets, he saw, were synthetic.

John looked at him. The team leader's dark brown eyes were as bleak as an arctic night; and there was no way to tell if there had ever been any emotion in them or not.

"Better get some sleep," John said. He went out, closing the door behind him.

Hal put his travel bag in the small closet and stretched out on top of the bed's coverings.

He felt in him a desperate need for time to sort out in his own mind what had happened to him. Evidently, the leader called Will Nanne had gotten word of what had happened at the Holding Area of Halla Station; and if that was so, this world of mines must be an incredible whispering gallery. How could word travel so fast? And why?

He puzzled over it, but found himself drifting off to sleep in spite of the questions in his mind. He was just about lost to slumber when it occurred to him that it might be one of Jennison's sources of income, selling information on the men he assigned to the team leaders at the mines he assigned them to. But Jennison had seemed to want to be on Hal's side, the last time Hal had talked to him—the assignment man had flatly said that he expected them to do some business together in the future. If so, why would he pass on a report that had come very close to costing Hal the job he, Jennison, had assigned him to?

Sost had said that if Hal was not hired, he would be sent back to the nearest Holding Area to be processed again. In this case, would the Holding Area have been Halla Station again? And if so, could Jennison have set the whole thing up to impress Hal with his power to produce or withhold good jobs?

Hal was dropping into sleep with this question, too, unanswered, when a knock at the door jarred him into instant, wary wakefulness.

"Thornhill?" said a woman's voice through the panel. "You in there? Can I come in?"

He got up and opened the door. Tonina Wayle was standing outside; and as if she assumed that the opened door was an invitation, she walked in, closed it firmly behind her and sat on the float closest to his bed.

"Thought I'd say a word or two to you," she said.

She stared at him, almost the way John had, for a second without saying anything more. Then she spoke again.

"You're from Old Earth, aren't you?"

"You can tell?" he said. She laughed, surprising him; for the laugh was not unkindly.

"I can guess—now," she said. "Maybe a lot of the others couldn't. Give you another two weeks here and nobody'll be able to guess."

She sobered, suddenly.

"You've never been in a mine before, have you?" she asked.

"No."

"Well, you're not starting too badly. John Heikkila's one of the best. I'm on Beson McSweeney's team now, so I won't say anything one way or another between them; but you can be proud of being on John's."

"That story," said Hal, "of what I did to that man who jumped me down at the Holding Area—it was an accident he got hurt, actually. I told Heikkila—John—that, but I don't know if he believed me."

"If it's the truth, he'll end up believing it," said Tonina. She ran her eyes over him. "I don't find it too easy to believe, myself. How—"

"I'm twenty," said Hal, quickly. "I just look young for my age."

Tonina shrugged.

"Well, as I say, you'll get a fair shake from John. He wants production, but so does any other leader," she said. "Did he tell you what you'd be doing?"

"No," said Hal.

"I thought not," she said. "There's none better, but he's been in the mines so long he forgets there're people who don't know. Well, he won't expect much of you your first shift tomorrow, anyway, so there's no need to worry."

"What do I do?"

"You'll be mucking out behind the men with torches," she said. "They'll be cutting ore from the rock face, and it'll be up to you to get what they cut out sorted and back into the carts."

She paused and looked at him.

"You don't even follow that much, do you?" she said. "When you and your team go down into the mine, the skip'll take you to the level your team's working on. After you leave the skip you'll ride the carts—they're like a train without tracks to run on, a train with cars that look like open metal bins. They'll each carry two men at once. You'll ride the carts back through the levels—tunnels to you—until you come to the end of the one where your team's bid to work on a section of the vein. The vein's the way the ore with the metal in it runs through the rock. It never runs level, so you're nearly always working on what's called a stope, that's sort of like a step up or a step down to get at the ore, and you cut out what's there until you have to go on and make another stope."

He nodded, fascinated.

"But what's 'mucking out'?" he asked.

"The top men in the team'll be carving rock—working ahead in the stope with laser torches—"

She laughed at the look on his face.

"Yes, real laser torches, right out of three hundred years ago. Here on Coby's the only place on all the worlds where miners cost less than equipment; and a laser's the only safe type of torch for anyone to use for cutting. You'll be behind the top men, gathering up the ore they've cut out of the rock. Just be damn sure you do two things. Keep the gloves of your suit on, no matter how you sweat inside your suit. You start handling a rock barehanded and get burned, you'll know it. And be God damn sure you don't take your helmet off, ever!"

Her last word came with a vehemence that startled him.

"All right," he said. "I won't."

"You'll see the lead people, and maybe some of the others, throwing their helmets back from time to time. But don't you do it. They know when it's safe, because they know what they've just been cutting. You don't. I don't care how miserable it gets inside that headpiece, you keep it on. Otherwise you'll see them take theirs off, you'll take yours off, and then all of a sudden they've got theirs back on; but by then it's too late for you. You'll've inhaled some of the hot gases the torches boil out when they cut the rock; and it's too late."

"I see," said Hal.

"You better." She got to her feet. "Well, I've got to turn in myself. We work a twenty-hour day here, three days on, three days off; and on a three-day stint you better learn to sleep any time you can. You can catch up on your threes-off. I guess John'll keep an eye on you, this first day at least, about taking off your helmet. But nobody can watch you all the time; so you better get in the habit of taking care of yourself."

She went toward the door. Hal stood up.

"Wait—" he said. All his resolution about being taciturn and reserved had slipped away from him. She had been the first person to show anything like kindness to him at this mine, and he felt he could not let her go without knowing her better. "Uh—you used to work at this mine before, John Heikkila said."

"Yes," she replied, with the door half open.

"You must have liked it here, or you wouldn't have come back."

"Wrong," she said, and almost grinned. "The other way around. They liked me here. That meant better shares in a team; and people I could trust, down in the mine, when I worked with them."

"Why'd you leave?"

The humor went out of her face suddenly.

"I left to go down to the main infirmary with someone," she said.

"Your husband?"

"Husband?" For a moment she looked startled. "No, my brother."

"Oh," said Hal. Some inner part of his emotional sensitivities was beginning to fly warning signals, but he blundered on. "Did your brother work here before you did?"

"No. I got him the job." She hesitated. "He was my younger brother. He was bound to go working in the mines after knowing I was. He was about your age when I first got him in here."

She looked at him grimly, again.

"Your real age," she said.

"And he's working in some other mine now?"

Her face was wiped clean of expression.

"He's dead."

"Oh." Hal felt the way someone teetering on the edge of a precipice might feel, hearing the ground break suddenly under his feet. He stammered, lamely, "I'm sorry."

"He took his damn helmet off. I'd told him a million times not to!"

She turned and went out, the door closing hard behind her.

He stood for a long moment, then slowly turned and began undressing for bed.

He woke to the sound of his alarm in the morning, dressed and stumbled down the hall, following the foot traffic there, until it led him to the dining hall. The room was a place of long tables, loaded with eggs, fried vegetables, breads and what must certainly be processed meats in the forms of sausages and steaks. Evidently people simply took whatever seat was vacant, as they came in. It was not a time of conversation but of stoking up. Grateful for the silence, he surrounded an excellent and gargantuan meal, wistfully realizing even as he finally pushed his plate away from him, that—even with this—he would probably be starving again long before the lunch break came.

Something seemed to have happened overnight. This morning was all business, and the feeling he had had earlier of being shunned by everyone there no longer seemed to hold. No one paid any particular attention to him but no one avoided him, either. As he was leaving the dining hall, John Heikkila came and found him.

"You come with me," John said.

He led Hal off into the crowd of men who were heading for the far end of the bunkhouse. They emerged into a room filled with racks from which hung what looked like heavy cloth coveralls with boots, gloves and helmets, each helmet containing a wide transverse window for vision. John took him to the end of one rack, glanced at him, selected one of the coveralls and threw it at him.

"This is yours from now on," he said. "Come to me when we get off shift and I'll show you how to check it for leaks. You got to check after every shift. Now get it on, and come along with the rest on our team."

Hal obeyed. With the coverall on, it was not as easy to pick out the people he recognized, among the identically-clad figures around him. But John's wide, short shape was unmistakable. Hal followed it; and ended moving in a mass of bodies out through a farther tunnel that echoed and roared to the sound of their thick-soled boots, until they came to an open area where the walls were naked rock. In the center of the floor of the area was the large mouth of a steeply-inclined shaft, surrounded by machinery. As Hal watched, there was a puff of what looked like white dust from the hole; and a second later, the cage of some sort of elevator rose through the opening until its floor stood level with that of the stone underfoot around it.

"Everybody in!" said John, his voice booming out with metallic echoes through the speaker valve of his helmet. They crowded clumsily into the cage. There was room for all of them, but they ended up pressed tightly together. Within the enclosed confines of his own suit, Hal could hear the loud sound of his own breathing; as if he panted, except that he had no reason to pant.

"You, Thornhill, stand clear of the side of the skip!"

It was John's voice again, booming out. Obediently, Hal pressed inward upon the bodies about him, and away from the metal bars that separated him from the roughly-cut rock walls of the inclined shaft.

"All right. All down!" boomed John.

The cage dropped suddenly, and kept dropping. Hal pressed against the bodies around him as he almost became airborne. He was already beginning to sweat inside his suit; but, curiously, there was an unexpected feeling of satisfaction in him.

He was being dropped rapidly into the deep rock of Coby. There was no longer any choice about what he was doing. He was committed. He was, in fact, a miner; one of the miners who surrounded him. Their work was the work he would be doing. He could imagine it coming, in time, to be second nature to him; and even now he seemed to feel the beginnings of a familiarity with it.

He had achieved at last what he had begun when he had run from Ahrens and Dahno; and from what had happened on the terrace. He had hidden himself from the Others and taken charge of his own life. No one but he had brought himself to this point. No one but he would be directing himself from now on. He would be all by himself, apart and isolated from those around him, which was a sad and lonely thought. But at the same moment, for the first time, his survival and his future would be in his own hands alone. From this moment forward there was no going back. One way or another he would survive—and grow—and finally return to bring retribution to Bleys and the Others.

The realization was cold but strongly attractive. There was almost a feeling of triumph in him. The hidden, oceanic purpose that he felt at times, hidden deep in his mind, seemed content.

Chapter

> > 8 < <

The skip dropped swiftly between the close, rough-cut rock walls, its interior lights illuminating the brown of their igneous rock, shot through with the occasional flicker of white that was the gold-bearing quartz. It was gold and sometimes silver that they dug for at the Yow Dee Mine, according to the information in Hal's employment papers. He tried to watch the swiftly-passing rock to get a glimpse of whether the quartz he was seeing was indeed visibly veined with gold; but the skip was going down too quickly. He found himself up against the bars of the cage and, remembering John Heikkila's orders to stand away from these, stepped guiltily back.

He felt a hard jab in the center of his spine.

"Who in hell you think you're standing on, kip?"

He turned clumsily in his protective suit and found himself looking through his face shield at another face shield and the features of a lean, big-nosed man in not more than his early twenties, slightly shorter than Hal himself, with straight black hair and an angry expression.

"I'm sorry," he said. "I was just—"

"Sorry don't make it. Just stay off my foot."

Hal had not stepped on any foot. The years of exercises had trained him to be aware at all times of the balance of his own body and the character of what he supported himself on. If he had felt a foot beneath his own, he would have shifted clear of it instinctively before his weight had fully come down upon it. He stared into the other face, baffled; and stopped himself just before he protested that the other had imagined being stepped on.

"I will," he said.

The man growled something at him that was lost in its passage through the speaker valve of his suit and the pickups of Hal's. Hal backed a few inches toward the bars and the other turned away.

The skip's floor began to press up against their feet as its descent slowed. It came to a stop, and the gates by which they had entered it swung open. Following the other miners, the last one out because he had been farthest from the gates, Hal stepped from the overhead gloom of the skip shaft into a large, brilliantly-lit, high-ceilinged chamber that seemed to be the terminal for a number of trains of small cars, each train pointing through one of the many openings in the circular wall of the chamber. The crowd that had filled the skip was now breaking up into smaller groups, each heading toward a different train of waiting cars, in a general mutter of conversation, from which he was sharply conscious of being apart. Some of the cars were already filled with miners from what must be previous skip-loads. With some relief, Hal saw that the black-haired individual who had complained about being stepped on in the skip was headed toward a partly-loaded train beside which Will Nanne waited.

Hal woke suddenly to the fact that he was being left alone by the skip. He looked for John Heikkila and located him, finally, heading with a contingent of miners toward a string of six cars. Hal hurried to catch up.

By the time he did, the others were already climbing into the cars. These were little more than open metal boxes on soft-tired wheels, their four sides sloping outward from above those wheels; wheels, sides and all painted green. Hal was the last to board of the twelve miners who apparently made up the Heikkila team, with the exception of John himself, who had stood frowning by the head car as everyone else climbed in.

"Come on, Tad!" he called, now. "Work-time's counting."

Hal climbed into the next to the last car, which he had to himself, the other miners in John's team having filled the first four cars, with the exception of a space for John in the first car. John, seeing Hal in, climbed in himself, and with a chorus of metallic clankings the train of cars jerked into movement without any command from John that Hal could make out.

They trundled into one of the openings, which turned out to be the end of a tunnel. Here, the sounds of their travel picked up, echoing into a roar cast back by the close rock walls. The floor of the car Hal in bumped and jibed under him. The tunnel floor was plainly level, but not smooth, as the floor of the larger, terminal chamber had been; and the cars were without springs. Hal, who had sat down unthinkingly in his car, hastily moved to imitate the other miners in the cars ahead, whom he now saw were squatting, knees under their chins. This was a more comfortable, if less balanced way to travel, and he found that it paid to cross his arms and press his hands against the sides of the car to brace himself.

All the same, the ride was fascinating. Now that they were well into the tunnel, the train of cars was picking up speed. They swayed and lurched thunderously along between rocky walls, here less than two meters apart, their way illuminated every ten meters or so by what looked like thousand-year lights stuck to the naked rock of the ceiling, another two meters overhead. Once more, Hal searched the rock to see if he could see any signs of visible gold in the quartz veining. But here, he was not even able to discover any streaks of the quartz itself. He strained his eyes through the window of his suit—and suddenly became aware that in the cars ahead of him all the others had the hoods of their suits thrown back.

He hesitated, remembering Tonina's warning about taking off his helmet, then reminded himself she had been talking about not exposing himself to possibly lethal gases when the other miners were using their torches. Here in the tunnel it ought to be safe, since all the others had theirs off. He threw his own headgear back and peered at the passing rock. But it still appeared as he had seen it through the window of the suit. There was no veining of quartz visible in the granite of the rock.

But it was a relief to have the hood off. The air blowing past his face with the movement of their passage was cold and damp with a faintly musty, acidic smell. He began to have some notion of what it was going to be like to work and sweat sealed in his suit, if this was the way he felt after only a matter of minutes in it, with no exertion.

But there was an eeriness, a magic to being underground like this, rolling through the tunnelled rock at a speed that seemed to threaten to scrape them against the walls on curves. He thought of the story of Peer Gynt in the hall of the Mountain King, from the long poem by Henrik Ibsen; and the music Edvard Grieg had written for that scene thundered and pounded in his memory over the hum of the tires on the rock and the metallic clanking and creaking of the connected cars as they fled down the tunnel.

The cars of the train turned off abruptly into a narrower tunnel. They clanked along another short distance at reduced speed, then came out into a slightly enlarged area where a ramp led from the level they were on to another level about a meter or so higher, like one step of a giant stair. The cars rolled up the ramp, straight ahead for a few feet, then up another ramp, and so continued, mounting or descending ramps at small intervals until they stopped so suddenly that Hal was thrown against the front end of his car.

Ahead of the front car they seemed to have come to a solid wall of granite; but since everyone in the cars ahead was getting out, Hal could not be sure at first glance. He climbed out himself and went forward to discover that the front car had come to a stop with its front wheels almost touching a meter-high rise of rock. It was another of the giant stairsteps, but this time there was no ramp rising to it, and the space at its top barely gave standing room before it reached a wall of stone scored up and down and crosswise until it looked as if someone had made a clumsy attempt at a vertical chessboard.

In an untidy pile at the foot of the step were various tools, which the other members of the team were already taking up. Hal watched curiously. Most of the tools were stubby, thick-bodied devices like handguns with thick, short barrels, which Hal guessed to be the torches Tonina Wayle had spoken of; and what seemed to be an equal number of prosthetic-like apparatuses, fitted onto a left-handed glove with the fingers ending in five long, metal spines which curved inward until their points almost touched.

These made no sense. Then, Hal saw those who had put them on beginning to manipulate them. The spines spread open and closed, apparently independently of any action by the gloved fingers. In some cases their needle-sharp points glowed cherry red for a second, then white, then dulled back to ordinary metal color. Each of the miners who put these on tested them several times, looking like creatures half-human, half-insect, groping at thin air; then climbed up onto the step of rock and faced the scored wall.

The rest of the team, except for the six now on the ledge and John Heikkila, had gone back past Hal about ten meters down the tunnel and were sitting down with their helmets thrown back. John, standing by the front car below the ledge, looked about and saw Hal.

"All right, kip!" he said. "Over here!"

Hal went forward to him, wondering.

"Put your helmet on. Keep it on."

In spite of himself, Hal glanced back at the six other team members who were sitting with their backs to the rock and talking, farther back in the tunnel. He put the helmet on and John's voice came to him through the earphones of his head-covering with the slight unnaturalness of sounds heard over the phone circuits between the two closed suits.

"You don't know anything about this, do you, Thornhill?"

"No," said Hal.

"All right. Your job's to muck out while the torchers are working." John reached up and closed his own helmet over his head. Up on the ledge, the six torchbearers had had their helmets closed for some time. They were standing looking down at John and Hal, obviously waiting.

"Ordinarily, I'd be up there with the first shift with the torches," John said. "But I'll stay down here with you until you get the hang of it. Now, the blocks are going to come off the ledge as they cut them out, until the ledge gets wide enough so they can't sling them all the way back off the edge. When that happens, we'll cut a ramp and you'll be going up to work right behind the torchers. But for now, the blocks'll be coming off the stope to you, and you want to keep your feet out from under. You understand?" He paused.

Hal nodded.

"Yes," he said.

"All right. The other thing to look out for is that the blocks'll still be hot when they come. So don't try to handle them except with tongs. These are tongs. . . ."

He picked up a couple of the spined devices.

"Hold out your hands."

Hal did, and John pushed one of the devices onto the end of each of Hal's gloves. There was a hand-shaped indentation in the end of each device, Hal discovered, into which his suit glove fitted; thumb, forefinger, middle finger, and the last two fingers as a unit—each slipped into one of the four indentations. Experimentally, he flexed the fingers of his right hand and the four claw-like extensions spread and closed in response.

"Waldos," he said.

"No, they're tongs," said John. "Now you use them to pick up the blocks. Watch me. All right, Torchers, get moving!"

He was fitting a pair of the devices onto the gloves of his own suit as he spoke. He barely had them on before the hiss and crackle of the torches burning into the rock exploded up on the ledge; and a moment or two later one of the torchers kicked a block of granite about the size of a grapefruit back over the edge to fall almost at Hal's feet. Easily, John scooped it up in the four pincers of his tongs. He held it out before Hal.

"Don't touch it," he said. "Just look at it. See the vein in it?"

Hal looked. He could see a line of quartz streaking through the piece of granite.

"Is there gold in that?" he asked, fascinated.

"You're damn right," said John, "and probably some silver, but you can't see traces of that. Look, you see the color in the quartz, there?"

Hal squinted at the quartz, uncertain as to what he should be looking for.

"I think so," he said. John tossed the block into the first car.

"You'll learn," he said.

Several more chunks of rock carved from the wall had landed at their feet while they had been talking. John scooped them up, showed them momentarily to Hal and then tossed them into the car. The next one, however, he again held out to Hal for more extended examination.

"See?" he said. "No veining. Those you ditch."

With a flip of his tongs, he threw the last block over against the wall of the tunnel.

"That's sorting," he said, continuing to work steadily now, for now the blocks were coming in a continuous stream off the ledge. "It'll take you a while to learn it, but you'll get it. The team gets paid only for the good ore it brings back. Any dead rock just takes up space in the cars and cuts our production for the day. But don't sweat it to begin with. Just do the best you can for now. The quicker you learn, though, the better off the team's going to be and the more the rest of us are going to like you. Now, you try it with some of these blocks."

Hal tried it. It took no great skill to learn to use the tongs, though it was a little tricky at first, getting a good grip on the blocks without the feeling in his fingers to guide him; and the waldo controls into which his gloves fitted were so responsive that he overcontrolled at first. But within a dozen minutes he was picking up the blocks with fair skill and dropping them into the cars. Sorting, however, was another matter. Whenever he paused to examine the blocks closely, John snapped at him to keep going.

While he was learning, John kept helping him. But Hal picked up speed in handling the blocks swiftly, although he was very aware that he was still rejecting only about one block in ten, whereas John was rejecting more like one in five. Still, the team leader seemed satisfied with just his handling ability; and gradually he let Hal take over more and more of the work until finally he himself was only standing and watching.

"All right," he said at last. "Just keep doing it that way. But take a break now and we'll change crews."

He turned and called up at the crew on the ledge.

"Change!"

The torches hissed and crackled down into silence. Those on the ledge dropped off it and those who had been seated back in the tunnel came forward, pulling their helmets into place and taking the torches from the first workers, climbing up on the ledge to take their place. This time, John was among the torchers, his own helmet pulled into position. He paused for a second, looking over his shoulder, down at Hal.

"Keep your helmet on, until I tell you to take it off," he said. "You hear that?"

"Yes," said Hal.

"All right!" John turned to face the wall and the rest of his crew turned with him. "Let's go!"

So the workshift began. At first Hal sweated over the prospect of handling the stream of blocks without John to back him up. But if there was anything at all in which life had supplied him with experience, it was the process of learning anything new. He quickly became practiced at seizing the blocks firmly with the tongs, so that they did not slip from his grasp or skitter out of reach when he tried to lift them into the cars; and after a while even his choice of the ore-filled blocks, as opposed to those that should be discarded, seemed to improve.

As the shift wore on, the torchers themselves picked up speed. Hal had to struggle anew to not let the blocks coming off the ledge get ahead of him. He succeeded, becoming faster himself. But as he did, the unaccustomed use of the muscles involved in bending and lifting began to build up on him.

Fortunately, he had a chance to stop and catch his breath every fifteen minutes or so when the crews changed. But even with these breaks, as the first half of the shift wore on he began to tire and slow. The lunch break came just in time to save him from getting badly behind the torchers, but food and rest revived him. He started out the second half of the shift keeping up almost easily; but this burst of strength turned out to be temporary. He tired more quickly now than he had in the morning; and to his deep embarrassment the blocks finally got ahead of him to the point where even by working right through a break time, he was losing ground to the torchers.

Sweating, gasping for air inside his suit, he looked longingly every so often at the miners at the rock wall, whom he could see occasionally throwing back their helmets for a brief breath of fresher air. A hundred times he was tempted to lift his own helmet for a second, but the discipline worked into him in his early years helped him to fight off the temptation. Nonetheless, he was literally staggering on his feet, when he finally felt a hand on his shoulder and turned to see John standing beside him.

Chapter

> > **9** < <

"Go *take a* break," said John. He gave Hal a light shove away from the blocks with which Hal had been working and bent to the task of handling the blocks himself.

On rubbery legs, Hal walked back down the tunnel and slid down the wall into a sitting position on the tunnel floor. He lifted his helmet and breathed more deeply than he could ever remember breathing in his life before.

He had thought John was merely taking over for him. But now he saw not only John, but all the current torchers, knocking back their helmets and coming down off the ledge, which was already too deep to be properly called only a ledge. As he watched, they were joined by the resting crew of torchers and the whole team together began to cut a ramp to the ledge.

They had almost completed this when a train of five empty cars rolled in to join them, with only one passenger aboard; a great, spiderous old man with his helmet thrown back to show oriental features, and tongs at the end of both the long arms depending from his massive, bowed shoulders. This new train braked to a halt beside their own and the old man hopped out. John went over to speak to him; and Hal, too far away to make out what was being said, saw the old man listening with his face at right angle to John's, nodding occasionally and twitching the tongs at the ends of his arms as if impatient to have the conversation over. John finished finally and turned away. The old man took one step to the chunks of rejected rock lying along the base of the rock wall where Hal had thrown them, and attacked them with both sets of tongs.

Attack was the proper word. Hal had thought that John was fast and experienced with the tongs; but this old man was unbelievable. He faced the wall, using both arms at once, and slung the chunks of dead rock behind him without looking. Not only did they all land in the empty car just behind him, but when the car was full, he seemed to know it by instinct and moved on, still without turning to look, to begin filling the car next in line. Hal watched him, fascinated.

"All right, Tad. Let's go."

Hal looked up to see John standing over him and scrambled hastily to his feet, ready to go back to work. Then he realized that the cutting of the ramp was completed but the torchers had not gone back up on the higher level to resume work, themselves. Instead, everyone was climbing into the cars of their own train, perching on top of the ore there.

"Are we through?" Hal said, unable to believe it.

"We're through," said John. "Get aboard."

Lost in his fog of effort, it had not registered on Hal that all the cars of their train were now filled with ore. He glanced once more at the old man and saw that the other had almost finished picking up, in minutes, the rejected rock that Hal had worked a full shift to accumulate.

"What's he doing?" asked Hal, dazedly, as he turned toward the last car of their own train.

"Slag-loading," said John. "Cleanup. He'll take the dead rock for a last sort, in case anything worthwhile's been missed, and pile it at the minehead for pickup and dumping topside on the surface. Get in there, now."

"I can't believe the shift's over," said Hal. He climbed into the last car.

"It's over," said John. He went up and got into the lead car. Hal did not see what controls he used, but as soon as John was aboard the train started moving, backing and filling several times to make the tight turn in the narrow space that would allow it to head back the way they had come.

They hummed and clanked through the tunnels. Perched on the ore in his own half-filled car, Hal abandoned himself to the luxury of being through with the day's work. He felt worn out, but not uncomfortable. In fact, there was a half-pleasant exhausted warmth to his body, now that the labor was done with and he had had some small time to rest. It had been explained to him by Malachi Nasuno within the past year that his immature muscles could not yet be expected to deliver the power that an equal weight of them could provide once he had stopped growing; but that, on the other hand, his recovery rate from exertion would be correspondingly faster than that of an equivalent, older individual—and the older the other individual, the greater Hal's advantage. As he rode the swaying car now, he could feel strength being reborn in him; and this, together with the satisfaction of having gotten through the shift without trouble, left him feeling more secure and comfortable than he had felt at any time since he had left his home on Earth.

It seemed to him that there was now a bond of identity with the other miners riding the ore train back to the skip. He was suddenly close to them. The dark colors and the enclosing walls of the tunnels made one family of them all. For the first time since he had left Earth, he had a sensation of being accepted and belonging somewhere in the universe.

He was still in the warm grasp of this feeling when they reached the terminus room and the bottom of the skip. Other trains, also loaded with ore, were already there, or just pulling in ahead of theirs. They stopped and everyone in Hal's team piled off the loaded cars—Hal following suit. Only John stayed aboard, and when they were all off, he put the train in motion again, driving it off through a tunnel opening beyond the skip.

"What do we do now?" Hal asked one of the other team members, for they were making no move to go toward the skip, which was standing open and waiting at the bottom of its shaft.

"Wait for John," said the team member, a short, lean man in his mid-twenties with a piratical black mustache drooping its ends around the corners of his lips.

Hal nodded. He stood waiting with the rest; and after three or four minutes, John came walking back out of the tunnel into which he had driven the train and rejoined them.

"Half ton over quota," he said, holding a printed slip before tucking it into a chest pocket of his suit. There was a mutter of approval from the other team members.

"Hey, with a new kip! Good!" The miner Hal had spoken to punched Hal's shoulder in friendly fashion—or rather, tried to, for Hal reflexively swayed away from the fist, riding the blow so that the man's gloved knuckles barely touched him. The other did not seem to notice that his punch had not landed.

"Let's ride up!" said John, and led the way toward the skip, which was half full of men from other teams ready to go up as John led his own people on to it.

"Watch it!" a voice called almost in Hal's ear as he stepped aboard. "Watch your feet. We got a new kip with big boots and no manners."

Hal turned and found himself looking across only inches of space into the face of the lean, big-nosed young miner who had complained about his foot being stepped on by Hal on the way down.

"What's the matter with you, Neif?" said the black-mustached miner from Hal's team. "It's his first day."

"I'm not talking to you, Davies." The miner called Neif glanced at Hal's team member. "Let him answer for himself, if he thinks he belongs down in a mine."

The skip closed its door and started upwards with a jerk.

"I didn't touch your foot," said Hal to Neif.

Neif pushed his face close.

"I'm a liar, am I?"

"What's going on over there?" the voice of John Heikkila reached them through the mass of packed bodies. Hal looked away from Neif and said nothing.

The skip rose. When they reached the top and the gates opened, Hal stepped out quickly and moved away from the bodies behind him. In spite of the close-packed ride to the minehead, some of the warmth and identity with his team members while riding the ore cars back to the terminus had now gone from him.

"This way," he heard John's voice in his ear. "We slip these suits, and I'll show you how to check yours for leaks."

Hal followed him back to the room where he had first been given the suit. There, at John's direction, he took it off and watched as John hooked up to the suit a small hose hanging from the wall below a vernier-shaped scale. John sealed the coveralls, tightened the hose about a valve near the suit's belt level and squeezed the tube. The coveralls inflated.

"Fine," said John after a second, deflating the suit. "No leaks. Never forget to do that after every shift. You won't get a second chance. The first time you inhale hot gases downstairs is it."

"I'll remember," said Hal. "Now what—"

"Dinner in forty minutes," John answered without waiting for the question to be finished. "Why don't you go outside—oh, here's someone looking for you."

The someone was Tonina. John went off and Tonina came forward to stand and look Hal up and down.

"How'd you get back before we did?" Hal asked. "I didn't even see you in the skip this morning."

"The shifts are staggered," she said, "so the slag loaders can have a regular round for cleanup. Beson and the rest of us went down before you, so we came back up before you."

"Oh," said Hal. She had led off and he was automatically following her. "Where are we going?"

"Outside," she said. "I want a look at you under the high lights."

They emerged through a door into the open staging area with its flat and dusty surface bright under the ceiling lights far overhead in the general cavern. What looked to Hal to be most of the other miners not on shift were milling around, talking in groups and obviously waiting for the dinner hour.

"Now stop," said Tonina, once they were well out under the ceiling lights, which had the apparent brightness of the noonday sun on Earth. She squinted up at him. "You look good. All right! I heard you did fine down there."

"I did?" said Hal. "But I kept falling behind. The shift ended just in time or John would have had to have helped me."

"That's still good," said Tonina. "You worked clear through your first shift down. Almost nobody new to the mines does that. It doesn't matter what kind of shape they were in when they got here, either. You use a different set of muscles on the tongs and everybody gets wrung out to start with."

"Hey, you—big-foot kip!" said a voice Hal had come to recognize. He turned to see Neif bearing down on them. Now, out of his suit, the other man was less impressive. He was a good half a head shorter than Hal and he looked lean, but Hal's training told him that the other would probably outweigh him by a good twenty percent more of mature bone and muscle. In the open V-neck of his loose shirt, his neck and chest area showed a deep tan that could only have been achieved here by the use of special tanning lamps. His shoulders were square and broad, his waist narrow, and his eyes very dark.

"I want a couple more words with you," he said.

"Get away from him, Neif," said Tonina. "He's brand-new. Pay no attention to him, Tad."

"You stay out of this, Tonina," said Neif. "I'm talking to you, kip. I don't like my foot tramped on and I don't like being called a liar."

There was a sick feeling in Hal. Other miners, attracted by the raised voices, had begun to drift into a circle around them.

"Don't tell me what to do, Neif!" Tonina shoved herself between the two of them, facing Neif. "You ought to know better than to take off on someone new. Where's John? John! John Heikkila, this bastard here's trying to be a big man by taking off on your kip!"

Her voice carried.

"What is it?" said John, a moment later, shoving through the crowd to join them. "What's your problem, Neif?"

"None of your business," said Neif. "This kip of yours rode my foot all the way down in the skip today, then called me a liar when I told him not to do it."

John looked at Hal. Hal shook his head.

Hal's feeling of sickness increased. He was here to be inconspicuous and with every moment this business with Neif was making him more conspicuous. It seemed to him as if everyone at the mine was becoming involved.

"I wasn't on his foot," he said, "but it's all right—"

"You say you weren't on his foot. All right. Then there's no problem," said John. He stood facing Neif like a human tank. But Neif's face twisted.

"You're not my leader. If this kip can't take care of himself, what's he doing here?"

"Go crawl in a hole!" Tonina broke in, fiercely. "You heard he had a rep and you want to get a piece of it, that's all."

Neif ignored her. He was looking at John.

"I said, you're not my leader."

"Sure," said John. He looked around at the crowd. "Will?"

Will was standing in the front rank to John's left.

"What about it?" Will said to John, without moving. "We heard he's a troublemaker. You knew that when you took him on. If he isn't, let him stand up for himself. If that rep's true, he maybe engineered this fight himself to show off."

"It's all right," said Hal, hastily. "John, it's all right. I didn't step on his foot, but if he thinks I did, I'm sorry—"

"Sorry, hell!" said Neif. "You think you can call me a liar and just walk away. Either stand up for yourself or get out of the mine."

"John!" said Tonina.

John shrugged and stepped back. The circle of people around them were moving back until Hal and Neif were at the center of a large open space. Tonina waited for a moment longer, then she, too, stepped back.

Hal stood looking at Neif, feeling despair now. The light was very bright and the air was dry and hot about him. The surrounding miners seemed faraway and alien. He was as isolated in his own mind as if he stood in the midst of a pack of wolves. He stared at the face of Neif and saw no reasonableness there.

Let him, he thought suddenly to himself. I'll let him do what he wants. That's the only way out of this mess. If he beats me up, then maybe they'll forget that reputation business. . . .

He could see Neif beginning to step toward him, the other man's right shoulder dropping as his fist clenched. Hal's body cried out to move into any one of a dozen defensive postures from his training, but he held it prisoner with his mind. He only put up his fists in what he hoped was a clumsy and amateurish fashion.

Neif came toward him. I will stand still, Hal told himself. He forced himself to stand without moving as Neif stepped close.

. . . Hal was confused. Something was wrong, but he could not immediately remember what it was. He was on the ground and certain of only one thing, and that was that he had been attacked. He saw a figure of a man over him, stepping toward him and shifting his body weight in a way that announced a kick was coming.

Instinctively his own body reacted, gathering itself up, somersaulting backward to roll on and up once more onto its feet, facing the attacker. He was remembering now that this was the man called Neif; and that he had intended to let the other do what he wanted; but his mind was still fogged and strange and he could not remember why he should do that.

At the same time, Neif was coming on again, after a slight, startled pause at seeing Hal move so swiftly from a helpless position on the ground to his feet and ready to react. Neif came in swiftly, swinging his right fist for Hal's Adam's apple.

Shaky and weak, but automatically responding, Hal turned his body sideways to let the fist go by and made one sweeping step forward and around the other as Neif staggered, off-balance from his unsuccessful punch. He stood, facing the back of the other man. Automatically, without conscious thought, Hal pumped two short, twisting blows with right-and left-hand fists into the kidney areas of the back before him. Neif dropped.

Hal took a step away and stood looking down at the other. His head was clearing rapidly now, and as it did the feeling of sickness came back on him.

It was no use. He could not make himself simply stand there and take whatever punishment Neif wanted to hand out. He simply could not make himself do it. That first blow that had made him momentarily unconscious had awakened a primitive fear and instinct for survival within him. But the other man was down now, and unmoving. Maybe that would be the end of it.

He started to move away . . . and Neif stirred. His arms tensed, pulled his hands back alongside his body, and then pushed him up on one knee, facing away from Hal. He rose uncertainly to his feet and turned around. He came toward Hal.

If I could just knock him out, Hal thought. . . .

But his head was still not completely clear and Neif was almost on top of him. Hal raised his two arms, trapped the arm that was attempting to hit him, and, turning, knelt, so that Neif cartwheeled over Hal's right shoulder to land heavily on his back. Again, he lay still for a moment, the breath knocked out of him. But once more, after a few seconds, he began to stir, to turn and climb to his feet.

Hal's head was almost clear now and bleakly he faced the impossibility of what he had been thinking of doing. There was no way just to knock Neif out, harmlessly. That was the stuff of romantic adventures found in the bound volumes of the library that Walter the InTeacher had made available to him—not the reality of what Malachi had taught him. Only in fiction could someone be hit so cleverly with fists or club that he was knocked briefly unconscious, but otherwise put into no danger of real damage. In real life the same impact that would render one person only unconscious could kill another of the same weight, size and general physical condition.

No, the only blows he knew that he could be sure would put Neif down to stay were all killing blows. Someone with the experience of Malachi Nasuno might have risked using one of them with just the right amount of force to only stun, but Hal was neither strong enough nor skilled enough to risk it.

He felt despair. Neif was coming at him again, a crazy expression around his eyes. Once more Hal faded away before the other's attack, caught him, led him off balance and threw him. Once more, after a second, Neif struggled back to his feet and attacked again. Hal threw him once more; and still, again, Neif climbed back to his feet and came on. Hal threw him.

The man was plainly in superb physical condition from his hard work in the mines; and also he was obviously not going to give up until he was stopped. The internal sickness came again to fill Hal completely. The crowd watching seemed very far away. The world about him was a place of rock and light; dry, dusty and empty except for the unending necessity to deal with this attacker who would not lie down, would not leave him alone, and who forced him to continue handing out punishment.

Please, make him stay down! . . . the prayer repeated itself, over and over in Hal, as Neif continued to climb back to his feet and come again. In his mind, long ago, Hal had stopped reacting; in his mind, he was trying to leave himself open for Neif to do anything the other man wanted to do to him. But the fear still with him overrode and ignored his mind; and refused to let the other man close.

In his imagination Hal saw the other lying still—too still—on the ground; and inside himself he shuddered away from the image. This could not go on. With a sudden spasm of desperate self-control, Hal succeeded in forcing himself to stand still with his arms down; and Neif finally reached him, grappled with him, and pulled him to the stony floor on which they fought.

But the miner was a man with his strength almost gone. Nothing was truly left in him but the blind will to keep fighting as long as he was alive. Neif's fingers fumbled up Hal's cheeks to gouge at his eyes, but Hal dodged them— and was suddenly filled with hope born of inspiration.

Lying on the ground with the other man on top of him, he slid his hands up to hold the other's shoulders, and under the pretense of trying to push him away, pressed his thumbs into the carotid arteries on each side of Neif's neck. In the same moment Neif's fingers finally found Hal's eye sockets.

Desperately Hal bowed his head on his neck so that most of the pressure was taken by his cheekbones. His mind counted slowly as Neif continued to try to sink his fingers into Hal's eye sockets . . . one thousand . . . one thousand one . . . one thousand two . . . he pressed his face as close as possible to Neif's dusty hair and continued counting as he held the pressure on the other's arteries.

As he counted one thousand forty-three, Neif's fingers began to relax and at one thousand sixty they fell away entirely; and the miner lay motionless. Hal crawled out from under the other man's body and looked down. Neif continued to lie still.

Hal turned and walked, stumblingly, away from the motionless man toward the wall of bodies between himself and the bunkhouse. He could see Tonina directly ahead of him, her face for some reason in focus where the faces around her were featureless blurs. The surface on which he walked seemed constructed rather of pillows than of the hard rock and packed dust.

A sudden, swelling murmur went through the crowd. They were looking past him. He stopped and turned exhaustedly to look.

Neif was up on one elbow, looking around him. He was obviously conscious again; but, just as Hal had lost orientation after absorbing the other's first blow, so Neif's temporarily blood-starved brain cells were for the moment confused, and he would not be sure just why he was lying where he was.

Hal turned away again and plodded on toward the ring of faces and Tonina. He reached them; and, as he did so, the ring broke up, the miners in it streaming past him to surround Neif, help him to his feet and assist him to his room. Tonina was suddenly before Hal and she caught him strongly around the waist with one arm, as he tripped and almost fell.

"It's all right," she said. "It's all right. It's over now. I'll take you in. Where are you hurt?"

He stared down at her. He was suddenly conscious of the aching of his eyes and jaw, and the bruises and scrapes of the hard rock on which he and Neif had wrestled. But he wanted to tell her that there was nothing really wrong with him, nothing but exhaustion; that outside of that first blow, Neif had done nothing to him. But the sickness in him mounted, and his throat was clenched as tightly shut against it as if a pipe wrench had been tightened upon it. He could only stare at her.

"Lean on me," she said.

She turned and half-led, half-carried him toward the bunkhouse. Her arm around his waist was incredibly strong—stronger by far, a portion of his mind thought bitterly, than his own. He let himself be taken away in silence and brought to his own room, dropped on his bed and undressed. Lying on the bed, he began to shiver violently and uncontrollably.

Tonina wrapped the bedcover tightly around him and turned its controls to heat, but he still shivered. Hastily, she shrugged out of her own outer clothes and slipped in under the blanket with him. She put her hard, strong arms around him and held his trembling body to her, warming it with her own body heat.

Gradually, his shuddering ceased. Warmth was born in him again and flooded out through all his limbs. He lay relaxed. He still breathed deeply and tremblingly for a while longer, but finally even that slowed. Instinctively, his arms closed around Tonina, drawing her even more closely to him, running his hands over her body.

For a moment she tensed and resisted him. Then the tightness went out of her and she let him pull her to him.

In the night he woke to find Tonina asleep beside him. His bruises ached, and there was no comfort for him. He had been dreaming of that last evening on Earth, and there was a purpose in him that he could not see clearly, but which pushed at him with a cold and hard determination.

It took him a long while to get back to sleep.

Chapter

> > 10 < <

A *month and* a half later, Sost showed up unexpectedly at the mine with a delivery, pulling into the staging area just as dinner was ending for the teams that ate with John Heikkila's. Hal wandered comfortably out of the door of the dining hall and saw a familiar-looking truck shape before the office building and an even more familiar human shape getting out of it.

Hal started toward the truck, picking up speed as he went. Sost, however, disappeared into the office building carrying a large package before Hal got there, and Hal stood waiting until the older man came out again.

"Hey there," said Sost when he emerged, as casually as if they had parted fifteen minutes before. He rambled down the steps and came up to offer Hal a square, thick hand. "How's the Yow Dee been doing for you?"

"I like it here," said Hal, taking the hand. "Come on over to the canteen and sit down."

"Won't refuse," said Sost.

The canteen was half full of off-shift miners. Hal looked around for Tonina or anyone from his team, but saw none of them.

"Here," said Hal, finding them seats at an empty table with six places. "What would you like? There's only food-drinks and coffee, because of the mine regulations."

"Coffee's fine," said Sost, taking a seat.

Hal got them both coffee—or what was called coffee on Coby—and brought it back to their table in copper mugs with ceramic rims at the top so that lips would not be burned on the hot metal when the cups were filled.

"I didn't know you came way over here," he said to Sost.

"I'm liable to end up anywhere," Sost said, drinking from his own cup. "Like it here, do you?"

Just then Tonina came in the door.

"Tonina!" he called. She looked around, saw him, and Sost, and headed toward them. "Yes, it's a good mine. . . . Tonina, sit down. I'd like you to meet Sost. Do you want something to drink?"

"Not right now," she said, joining them at the table. She and Sost looked at each other.

"I've heard the name," she said.

"I get around," said Sost. "I met the boy, here, just outside his Holding Station. Stupidest twenty-year-old I ever saw; and I told him so. We ended up getting on real well."

"Ah," said Tonina. She relaxed. Hal had noticed before how quick she was to tense up in any unusual situation. Normally she did not relax this quickly. "He's getting brighter every day."

"Don't say?" said Sost, drinking coffee.

"I do say," Tonina said. "He's rating right at the top among the muckers-out and he's only been here a little over a month."

"Six weeks," said Hal.

"I remember you now," Tonina said to Sost, "you used to come in regularly to the old Trid Mine. Nearly two years ago. I got started there. You remember Alf Sumejari, the head cook. . . ."

They talked about people whose names were unknown to Hal. But he did not feel uncomfortable at being left out of the conversation. He sat listening comfortably, and when John Heikkila walked through the entrance a few minutes later he called the team leader over to join them.

"He's doing all right," John told Sost, whom he had evidently met before.

"About time then, isn't it?" said Sost.

"I'll be the judge of that," said John. "Are you going to be coming in here regularly, then?"

"Not on a regular schedule," Sost said. "But I'll be working this territory generally for quite a while. There'll be things to bring me to the Yow Dee."

He pushed his empty coffee mug away from him and stood up. John and Tonina were also getting to their feet and Hal scrambled to his. He had the sudden, sharp feeling that something he had not understood had gone on about him.

"You're leaving right away?" he said to Sost. "I thought we could take a few hours—"

"Got to keep schedule," said Sost. He nodded at John and Tonina. "See you in Port, sometime."

He went out the door. John and Tonina were already moving away in different directions into the room. Hal looked after them for a second, then followed Sost out.

"But when'll I see you again?" he asked Sost as the older man climbed into his truck.

"Anytime. Not too long," said Sost.

He powered up the truck on its fans, turned it on its axis and drove out of the staging area. Hal looked after him for several moments, then turned back to the canteen. He wanted to hear what John and Tonina thought of Sost. But as he got there, John came out and went across toward the office; and a second later Tonina also came out and went toward the bunkhouse.

Hal started to follow her, then read in the set of her back and shoulders that she was not in a mood for company. His steps slowed. He felt a little sadness. Since that first night following his fight she had never really let him within arm's length of her, although in all other ways she had been as warmly friendly as ever.

He watched her go. Walter the InTeacher had coached him in the Exotic way of empathy, and he could feel deep in Tonina an old unhappiness that she had long ago given up any hope of conquering. She had simply lived with it until it had reached the point where she was all but unaware that it was still there. Still, he could feel how much of everything she did was directed by that ancient pain and the mechanisms she had developed to bury it. She would not have been willing to be helped with it now, even if Hal had known how to help her; and he did not. All he could do was feel the entombed ache in her and ache in sympathy with it.

By the next day, however, his empathic sense found something else to oc-cupy it as he rode down in the skip with the rest of the team. He could not miss noticing a difference in all of them toward him, today. But it was not an unfriendly difference. Hal shrugged internally; and, since it seemed to be harmless, he put it out of his mind.

When they got to the vein on which they were currently digging, he fit-ted himself automatically with a pair of tongs on each glove and turned around to the ledge, only to come within inches of bumping into Will Nanne. Hal had not exchanged a word with the other team leader since the day of his arrival; and he stopped, surprised and wary at seeing him here now, in the area of the Heikkila team.

"Well," said Will. Like Hal and the rest of them at the moment, the hel-met of his suit was thrown back; and his face was as unsmiling as ever. "You been here nearly two months now, haven't you?"

"About a month and a half, actually," said Hal.

"Time enough," said Will. "I need another torcher on my team. Want to shift over, and I'll train you?"

"Torcher?"

Hal stared at him. He had been having daydreams of the day when John Heikkila might offer him a chance to try working with a torch; and only a small part of that daydream was concerned with the larger percentage of the team's profits that would be coming to him if he became a torcher. The large part had had to do with the dream of being, in his own eyes as well as in the eyes of the other workers, a full-fledged miner.

For a moment he was strongly tempted; and then the whole weight of the friendships he had made with John and the rest of the team rejected the offer, even as he was voicing his incredulity.

"You don't want *me?*"

"I don't say it twice," Will said. "I've offered you a job. Take it or leave it."

"But you don't like me!" said Hal.

"Didn't. Do now," said Will. "Well, how about it? Work-time's counting. I can't stand around here all shift waiting for you to make up your mind. Coming with me, or not?"

Hal took a deep breath.

"I can't," he said. "Thanks anyway. I'm sorry."

"You mean you won't."

"I mean I won't. But thanks for offering me the job—"

A strange thing was happening to Will Nanne's grim face. It was not changing, but laughter was coming out of it. Hal stared at the man, bewildered, and suddenly began to realize that there was merriment all around him. He looked again at Will, at the closed lips and scowling features with the snorts of laughter coming from the long nose. He looked around and saw the rest of his own team in a circle about him, not getting ready for work at all, their helmets all thrown back, and laughing.

John was one of them, standing almost at Hal's right elbow. But when he saw Hal's eyes on him, he sobered in turn and became almost as sour-faced as Will.

"All right, damn it!" he said. "I guess I got to give you a chance to try torching if everybody's going to be coming around here trying to hire you away from the team. Come on, everyone, let's get to work. Time's counting. Better luck next time, Will."

"I expect you'll be over to steal one of my team next," grumped Will; and turning, he went off, still snorting softly to himself.

Hal looked at John and grinned. He was beginning to understand.

"What're you looking so pleased about?" said John. "For two profit points, I'd fire you now and give you no place to go but with Will. How do I know you haven't been talking to him about changing teams, before this, behind my back?"

Hal only grinned more widely.

"All right," John said, turning away. "Let's see how happy you are after a shift of torching. Come on up on the ledge."

Hal followed him up to join the other torchers. They stood facing the wall, in front of about a body's width of rock apiece. John took a position at the left end of the line next to the stope wall.

"Put your helmet on," said John. "No. Put it on, *then* pick up your torch. Always do it that way. Now . . . ," his voice came filtered through the suit mechanism, "watch me. Don't try to do any torching to start with, just watch how I do it. Don't knock your helmet back until you see me take mine off. When you see me put mine back on, put yours back on—and keep watching at all times. You understand?"

"Yes," said Hal, hearing his own voice hollow with excitement inside the helmet.

He obeyed. The wall before him—before each of them—was scored vertically and horizontally by earlier torch cuts; and its surface was a mosaic of different depths of rock, marking the planes where torch cuts had parted a surface chunk from the granite beneath. His eyes were on John.

John raised his torch to the wall, with its muzzle less than a hand's length from the rock. A slim golden pencil of visible light that was the guide for the cutting beam, which could not be seen, reached out and into the face of the stope before him—and a wave of heat that was like a body blow struck Hal, even through the protection of his suit, as the rock was vaporized in an incredibly thin section by the moving, invisible beam.

As he had grown more expert at mucking-out, there had been more and more occasions when Hal had been caught up with his own work and could simply stand for a moment and watch the torchers; and he had come to the conclusion that their work must be very easy compared to his own. In fact, he had puzzled over why it made sense to have two teams working alternate periods, when it would have seemed to have been more practical to simply work a single crew of six or seven men straight through the shift. He now discovered one reason why. The sudden heat blow from the outburst of hot gases from the vaporized rock was breathtaking, even inside the protective suit; and his first experience of it now explained why the torchers worked in spurts, cutting for a few minutes, then pausing, then cutting again.

It was some moments before he could manage to observe two more new things. One was the fact that John seemed to be cutting in a peculiar pattern that moved his torch about strangely on the face of rock before him, as if the areas to be cut were marked in some complicated sequence; and the other was that he shut his torch off each time before beginning to cut a new chunk. He had barely absorbed these facts when John stopped working abruptly; and simply stood, a mechanical-looking figure in his suit, facing the wall. Hal stared at him, not understanding, then became aware that the hiss and crackle of the torches to his right were also giving way to silence. He looked and saw that all the others of the current crew had stopped cutting, except the miner at the far end of the face. Then that man also shut his torch off.

Hal's glove twitched upward to knock back his helmet and give himself some air as he had seen the current crew do so many times. Then he realized that no one else had yet touched their helmets. He checked his movement and stood, gasping in the closed suit, watching John until John reached up and lifted back his own helmet. Hal imitated him and, looking around, taking deep breaths, saw the other torchers opening up as well.

For a few seconds, he breathed air that was only warm; then he saw John putting his helmet back on and followed suit. The torches took up their hiss and crackle again; and once more Hal watched and sweated under the momentary heat-blows before another helmetless break came. It seemed to last only seconds before they were buttoned up and at work again.

Before it came to be time for the other crew to replace them at the rock wall, Hal was soaked in sweat and as enervated as if he had worked a full half-shift at mucking-out, although he had done nothing but watch. But, as he became more accustomed to the heat-blows and the noise, his observation of the way the work went had been improving. He saw that a chunk would be carved out, wherever possible, by undercutting a projecting piece of rock; and then taking out as many other chunks as possible by cutting vertically down to the horizontal undercut. Where there was no way of undercutting, the torcher made slanting cuts into the face of the rock, until these intersected behind the chunk.

At the first touch of the cutting beam, there would be an explosion of gases from the vaporized rock; and for a moment the seeing was, not exactly foggy, but distorted; as if he was looking at the rock wall through the updrafts of heated gas and air. In the moment following the heat-blow and the distortion, the view of the rock became solid again; but for a few seconds after that a sort of silver mist seemed to cling to the face of the rock, before vanishing.

It was not until the second time the crew including John and Hal attacked the wall that Hal put the sight of the silver mist together with the pattern of the torchers in knocking back their helmets. It was never until that haze had completely gone that any of them cracked their suits open. Hal's mind, galloping ahead with that observation, deduced that the silver mist must be some of the gasified rock, boiled out from the surface of the face despite being chilled there by the liquefied gas coolant projected around the cutting beam from its reservoir in the heavy body of the torch. Until the mist evaporated, there would be danger of breathing some of the vaporized material in the atmosphere before the stope wall.

As work wore on, Hal began to pick up more understanding of the pattern in which John was cutting into the rock face. The pattern seemed to be designed to keep him cutting always at the greatest possible distance from where the man on his right was cutting on his own section. Looking down along the face, Hal saw that the same patterning seemed to be at work to keep the others of the crew cutting at as close to maximum distance from each other as possible.

The lunch break finally came. John sat down to eat with his back to the tunnel wall beside Hal.

"Well," he said, tearing into a sandwich with his teeth, "how about it? You ready to try it?"

Hal nodded.

"If you think I can."

"Good," said John. "At least, you're not so all-fired sure you can just stand up there and do it. Now, I'll tell you what. Pay no attention to how fast the others are cutting. You cut only when I tell you to, and where I tell you to. Got that?"

"Yes," said Hal.

"All right." John finished his sandwich and got back to his feet. "Let's go, crew!"

He, Hal and the others returned to the face. Davies, who had taken over the mucking-out temporarily while Hal tried out with the torch, winked at Hal as Hal passed. Hal took the wink for encouragement and felt warmed by it.

At the face, guided by John's voice and pointing finger, Hal slowly began to choose and excavate pieces of the rock. He did not do well, in his own estimation. He found himself taking a dozen cuts to loosen a piece of rock that John might have taken out in three. But, gradually, as he worked, he began to get a little more efficient and economical in the use of the torch, although the patterns in which John directed his work remained beyond him.

As the shift wore toward its end, the heat seemed to sap the strength out of him; it became enormous effort just to lift the torch and concentrate on the cuts John indicated he was to make. His cuts became clumsier; and, for the first time, he began to realize the danger of losing precise control of the torch, which, waved around carelessly in its *on* mode, could slice through suits, human flesh and bone with a great deal more ease than it could through rock—and the rock offered it no resistance.

Through the window of his helmet, as he continued cutting, he was aware of John watching him closely. John must know that exhaustion was making him uncertain; and at any minute now the team leader would be taking the torch away from him. Something in Hal surged in rebellion. At the next chance he had to knock back his helmet, he deliberately drew a deep breath and let it out in slow, controlled fashion as he had been taught, both by Malachi and by Walter . . . and his mind smoothed out.

He had been letting himself become frantic because he could feel his strength dwindling. That was not the way he had been taught to handle situations like this. There were techniques for operating on only a remaining portion of his strength.

The answer was to concentrate what strength remained on what was essential, and close out his attention on anything unnecessary. It was something like controlled tunnel vision, making the most of what was available over the smallest possible area. Having breathed himself back into self-control, he closed up his suit, addressed the rock face again and let his mind spiral inward, his vision close in . . . until all he saw was the rock before his torch and John's directing hands, until all he heard was John's voice.

The heat became distant and unimportant. The fatigue ceased to exist except as an abstract phenomenon. The stope, the mine itself, the very fact that he was underground, became things unimportant and apart. Even the relief periods were brief, unimportant moments before he was back at the face of rock again. The real universe was restricted to that rock face, the torch, and John's directions.

His grip on the torch steadied. His cuts regained their precision and certainty. In this smaller universe, his present strength and attention was enough and to spare to get the job done. He worked. . . .

Suddenly, they had all stopped and put back their helmets; and they were not starting again. John and the other torchers were turning away from the rock face. Baffled, Hal opened up his perceptions; and staggered physically as the larger world came back into existence about him, a bone-weariness exploding all through him.

He was conscious of John catching his arm and holding him up, guiding him back from the ledge and down the ramp cut the day before to the level below. His legs were wobbly and the torch he had unthinkingly carried back from the rock face—when he should have left it there for the next day's first crew—seemed to weigh several tons. He laid it against the face of the rise in which the ramp was cut; then, overwhelmed, slid down into a sitting position himself with his back to the rise.

Everybody was gathering around him. In the crowd, strangely, were Tonina and Will Nanne, who had left them hours ago.

"Well," said Will's harsh voice. "He did it. I wouldn't have believed it if I hadn't seen it myself."

"All right," said John, looking down at Hal. "I suppose you'll do. I hope you understand the whole team's going to have to carry you and lose production until you learn enough to do a fair shift of work?"

"Oh, leave him alone!" said Tonina. "Can't you let him be now that he's won the job?"

"I have?" Hal said, foggily.

"Well, you still got to throw a Port party for the team," said Davies.

Escorted back to the skip by them all, with Tonina on one side of him and John on the other, acting as bumpers to bounce him back on course when he staggered out of the direct line of march, Hal felt a sense of triumph beginning to rise within him and a deep feeling of affection for those around him. He was one of them at last. They were like family, and he felt for each of them as if each was a brother or a sister.

"Port party tonight," said an unfamiliar voice in the crowded skip. Evidently the whole mining camp had been in on the plans for his trial as a torcher.

"Wait until you make leader, if you ever do," said Tonina in his ear. "Then you have to get the whole crowd of underground workers at the mine drunk."

As they had left the rock face, Hal had felt that he had hardly the strength left to do anything but fall on his bed and sleep the clock around. But once back in the bunkhouse, showered and dressed for Port, he found himself coming back to life. In the end, as they boarded the subway in a group—the team, Tonina, and Will Nanne, who was evidently entitled to share in the party because of having been one of the actors in the traditional drama in which Hal had been offered his chance to try out as a torcher—Hal found himself feeling as well as ever, except for a slight sensation as if he had lost so much weight he might float off the ground, with any encouragement at all.

Chapter

> > 11 < <

Hal, himself, had not been back to the main Coby spaceport since he had come in to this world; but he had come to know that nearly all the miners headed there in their off-time, particularly on the day and a half off they had between their six-and-a-half-day work weeks. The six and a half days came about because every three working days there were twelve extra hours off between work periods in which the slag loaders did general cleanup and maintenance or other administrative work was carried on down in the mine. Every third week, the extra half day of weekend holiday was cancelled as each shift made a move forward of that many hours into a new work-time slot.

He had been puzzled that the shifts should need to change at all on this world where there was no sun and no natural day or nighttime hours. But he came to learn that a number of the miners had living partners or other personal arrangements in Port, where for administrative purposes day and night were strictly set and held. Certainly, everyone else but he seemed to know their way around Port when their group got there, heading off in one specific direction by unanimous agreement.

"Where are we going?" he asked John.

"The Grotto," said John. They were walking together in the back of the crowd; and now John took Hal by the elbow and slowed him down until they had fallen several meters behind everyone else. Even Tonina, seeing John holding Hal's arm, had gone on ahead. ". . . You've got the credit for this, haven't you?"

"Yes," said Hal.

"All right," said John. "If you find yourself getting in too deep, remember I can advance you what you need to make up the difference. You'll have to pay me back as soon as possible, though, or I'll take it out of your profit share, some every week until it's paid back."

"No, I've really got all the funds I need," Hal said.

"All right."

John let go of him and moved back up into the crowd ahead. Hal, stretching his own legs to catch up also, felt a twinge of guilt. John, in spite of handling Hal's papers, obviously did not know that Hal had brought in with him probably more in the way of a credit balance than a team leader in the mines could earn in twenty years in the mines—and a good chunk of that amount was in interstellar credits.

Remembering his credit balance started Hal on a new train of thought. The Others were unlikely to trace him here; but that did not mean that they could not, or would not. He might one day have to run for it again; and if he did, it would not help if they had located his funds under his own name and tied them up so that he could not use them to get away. What he needed was interstellar credit hidden away, untraceable to any official eye, but quickly available to him in an emergency. He filed the thought to be acted on as soon as possible.

Meanwhile they had reached their destination; they all poured through an arched entrance in the frontage wall of one of the Port blocks of construction. Above the arch, the name GROTTO floated in blue flames.

Within, it was so dark that at first he could see nothing and stumbled as he went forward, before he realized he was walking on some soft surface. As his vision adjusted, he saw that this was a thick carpet of something looking very much like grass and that the illusion overhead was of a night sky with the moon hidden behind clouds.

He followed the others forward, and passed with them through a light curtain into a scene of bright moonlight, seeming so brilliant after the short period of near-darkness that he was startled. The illusion of a moon shone down on the appearance of a tiny bay on the shore of a tropical sea, with actual tables and chair-floats intermingled with rocks or ground features that also gave sitting or table space. A surf spoke gently on the sandy beach before them all. Soft, spice-perfumed air blew around them; and a full moon surrounded by innumerable stars was overhead in a now-cloudless sky.

The place had evidently been alerted to their coming, for while there were other patrons, a large section of the beach shore with its seating and serving arrangements was empty. Into this area, the team poured and settled itself. A thin, blond man in his mid-forties, perhaps, got up from one of the tables where he was sitting with one of the other customers and came over to the table to which Hal had been steered, and at which he had been joined by John, Tonina and Will Nanne.

"You're the host, I take it?" he said, smiling at Hal. His teeth were white and even, but he was one of those individuals who actually do better not to smile.

"That's right," said Hal.

"Could I have your credit number?"

Hal passed over his identity card. The other touched it to his wrist monitor, took it away and glanced at the dial of the monitor, then handed it back.

"Enjoy yourselves," he said. He smiled at Hal again and went away. About Hal, drinks and other consumables ordered by the rest of them were rising to the tops of the table surfaces.

Hal looked at the others at his table. Tonina had a tall yellow drink in a narrow goblet. Will Nanne and John had steins of what appeared to be— and smelled like—beer. Hal spelled out beer on the tabletop waiter, picked the same brand that John and Will had ordered, and got a glass just like theirs.

"That'll do for me," said John. "The next one's with Will."

Hal stared at him.

"You got to have one drink with everyone else her before you settle down to your own drinking," said John, a little grimly. "That's the way it's done."

"Oh," said Hal. It did not require any effort to do the sum in his head. Twelve crew members meant twelve drinks. Will Nanne made that figure thirteen, and if they expected him to drink with Tonina as well, that would make fourteen. He felt uneasy for a moment.

However, there was no acceptable alternative. He put aside his uneasiness, lifted his glass of beer and drank. It was a lightly carbonated brew that did not seem too strong, and it went down easier than he had expected.

"You'd better slow down," said Tonina. "At that speed you won't make it to the third table."

His head felt perfectly clear, and his always-hungry stomach did not feel at all overfilled by the one beer. But she undoubtedly knew what she was talking about. He drank the beer with Will Nanne more slowly. After all, no one had said anything about a time limit in which he had to do all this. Will's beer also went down comfortably. Hal decided he rather liked beer. The only time he had tasted it before was when he had been six years old, at a picnic at which Malachi had been drinking some; and at that time he had decided it was bitter, unattractive stuff. But there was a lot of food value in beer, he remembered now. Perhaps that was what made it taste better to him in these, his years of greater appetite.

He looked from his second empty glass to Tonina.

"Why don't you save me for last?" she said.

"All right," said Hal. He was feeling somewhat carefree. "Which table do I take first?"

"Doesn't matter," said Will. "Take the first one you come to."

Hal got up and, on second thought, chose first a table of three team members, one of which was Davies.

He found it enjoyable drinking with Davies and the others—although all the drinks they had ordered were strong enough to burn his throat. He was a little surprised when they reminded him that, having drunk with each of them, it was now time for him to move on.

He moved on.

He had not enjoyed himself so much in a long time. At the next table, the drinks were all different again. These also burned his throat, but they did not seem as strong as the drinks had at the table where Davies had sat. Once more he lost track of what he was supposed to be doing and had to be reminded to move on. At some indefinite time later, he found himself being piloted back to his original table by people who went along on either side of him. He dropped into his chair and grinned at John, Will and Tonina.

Everyone else in their group, it seemed, was now gathered in a circle around the table, watching him. Tonina had scarcely touched her drink in all this time. Its level was lowered only slightly from what it had been when it had risen through the delivery slot in the table. She pushed it at him.

"You might as well just drink this," she said.

There was an explosion of protest from around the table.

"No fair! Cheat! He's got to drink a full one each time. . . ."

"What do you want?" Tonina suddenly flared at them. "He shouldn't even be conscious, after what you've been feeding him! You want to kill him?"

"All right," said John. "All right . . . there's not enough gone from that glass to matter."

The protests died down. Tonina pushed the glass over in front of Hal. He reached out carefully, closed his hand around it and lifted it to his lips. It was warm, after all this time, and sweeter than he would have preferred; with a thick, lemony taste. But there seemed hardly any alcohol in it at all, as far as his taste buds could tell in their present numb condition. He decided that a thing worth doing was worth doing well and drained it before he put the glass back on the table.

The wall of people around him exploded in noise. He was slapped on the back, shoulder-punched in friendly fashion, congratulated . . . and without warning, his stomach seemed to come loose within him and float upward, queasily.

He kept the grin on his face and tried to order the stomach to stay put. But the physical controls he had learned from Walter and Malachi had deserted him. His stomach surged rebelliously. . . .

"Excuse me. . . ." He pushed himself to his feet, turned from the table and looked around with rising panic.

"Help him!" said Tonina, sharply over the chatter of voices. The voices died. Everyone was turning to look at Hal.

"What'd you order, anyway?" somebody asked her. But Hal did not stay to hear the answer. Davies had him by the arm and was piloting him away from the table.

"This way," Davies said.

Somehow he made it to the restroom with Davies' help; and there it seemed that not only everything he had drunk tonight, but everything he had eaten and drunk for the past two weeks, came up. A little later, alone, haggard and wan, he made his unsteady way back to his original table.

"Feel better now?" asked Tonina, when he sat down.

"A little," he said. He stared at her. "Did you give me something to make me sick?"

"I gave you what I ordered for myself," said Tonina, "and a good thing, too. You'd be in the hospital right now, if I hadn't. What made you think you could drink like that?"

"I was doing all right," said Hal, feebly.

"All right! Most of the alcohol hadn't hit your bloodstream yet. Thirty minutes and they'd have been giving you oxygen, at the rate you drank it. Don't you realize the only way to handle that much drink is to take it so slowly that you metabolize most of it as you go?"

She sounded like Malachi.

"I know that," he said. "I thought I was going slow."

"Hah!"

"All the same," said Will, heavily, "that's not the way it's supposed to be done. He's supposed—"

"Why?" Tonina turned fiercely on the other team leader. "What more do you want? He drank everything the team gave him first. I was only along as an extra. And I told you. I only gave him what I ordered for myself. If he hadn't drunk it, I would have. Want me to order one right now and drink it to make you happy?"

"No need for that," said John, as Tonina's hand shot out to the buttons of the table waiter. "Will, she's right. He had a drink with everyone on the team, first, and you as well."

"You forget what he is," said Tonina. "For God's sake, you forget what he is! Look at him. Twelve large drinks in less than three hours and he's still not only conscious but halfway sensible. How many grown men do you know who can do that?"

"Not the point . . . ," protested Hal, weakly. But Tonina ignored him and the others were not listening either. Sitting in the chair, he felt intolerably tired. His eyes closed in spite of anything he could do. . . .

He woke some time later to find himself sitting at the table alone. He felt as if his bones would creak when he moved; his body in general felt dried out and his mind was dulled. But in a sense he felt better than when he had dropped off to sleep. Looking around, he saw that about half the team had left the Grotto, along with Will Nanne. John and Tonina sat with Davies and a couple of the other team members at a table down near the edge of the illusory ocean.

Hal got up to join them, changed his mind and detoured to the restroom again. There was a water fountain there, and after he had drunk what seemed like several gallons of water he felt better. He went out again, found their table and sat down with them.

"Well! Back from the dead?" said Tonina. He smiled, embarrassed.

"Come on," she said, standing up, "I'll steer you home."

"Hey, he doesn't want to go yet," protested Davies.

"I don't want to go yet," said Hal.

She stared at him.

"Well, I'm going," she said, after a moment. "I've got to get back. I missed half a shift as it is. Will one of you see him safe home and not try to kill him with drink in the meantime?"

"I'll see him back," said John.

"All right, then." She looked at Hal. "We'll see how you feel about this staying when it comes time for you to go on shift, tomorrow."

Hal felt uncomfortable; but, stubbornly, he was determined not to go. He watched her leave.

"How do you feel?" Davies asked him.

"Dry," said Hal.

"Beer," said Davies. "That's what's good for that—beer."

"Take it easy," said John.

"I'm not forcing him!" said Davies. "You know he'll feel better with some beer in him."

John sat back, and Davies coded for a beer from the table waiter.

Hal took it, feeling nowhere near as enthusiastic about it as he had felt about the beers earlier. Nonetheless, it was cold, wet and not too unpleasant to swallow. After he had gotten it down, Davies insisted that he have another.

As he drank the second one, Hal noticed that their original party had been dwindling rapidly since he had woken up. Only two others were left at another table besides Davies, John and himself; and Davies was showing signs of becoming silent and drowsy. The two others moved over to sit and talk with them for a while; and while they talked Davies dozed off in his chair. Then the others finished their drinks and headed off, on their way back to the mine and their rooms in the bunkhouse.

Hal was coming alive again, whether it was the two fresh beers or his own physical ability to bounce back. At the same time, even he could see the sense in going back to their beds, now. But instead of suggesting this, John turned back from watching the two who were just leaving as they walked from the room, then glanced at the still-slumbering Davies. He looked at Hal.

"What did happen at that Holding Station when you first got here?" he asked heavily.

"I came in and the man in charge there—his name was Jennison—" said Hal, "told me to find myself a bed. So, I went looking. . . ."

He ran through the events at the Holding Station, step-by-step, exactly as they had happened. John listened, without saying anything, sitting back in his seat, one heavy hand holding his beer glass, his eyelids half down over his eyes.

". . . That was it," said Hal, finally, when he had finished and John still had not said anything. "That's all there was to it. They all seemed to think I'd done something unusual in stopping that man who tried to brain me; and then word of it must have got to your mine and Will Nanne before I showed up. I didn't know then how fast word gets around here."

"It wasn't unusual?" John said, not moving, his eyelids still down over his eyes. "A grown man, big as you or bigger, heavier than you, and you just tossed him against a wall and laid him out, like that?"

"I . . ." Hal hesitated. "I had an . . . uncle who taught me a few things. I thought it was playing, mostly, when I was growing up, and I learned how to do them without really thinking. When he came at me, I just acted without thinking."

"And when you had that little go with Neif? You weren't thinking then, either?"

"I was kind of out on my feet after he hit me hard at first. Things just came to me."

"Sure," said John. "You see me?"

Hal nodded.

John reached out his hand and laid it palm-up on the table. He closed his fingers. He did not close them dramatically or with any great emotion, but the thick fingers, the wide palm, came together with an impression of power that was unmistakable.

"When I was fourteen," he said, as if talking to himself, "I was as tall as I am now. I never grew a centimeter after that. But even then I could pick up two grown men at once and carry them around."

Hal watched him across the table, unable to look away.

"When I came here . . . ," said John, and for a moment Hal thought he had stopped talking, "when I came here, six standard years ago, I was in my twenties; and I hadn't settled down, yet. When you're like I was, then, some people can smell you, a kilometer off, and they came looking for you. I was in a Holding Station, when I first came here; and somebody had to try me and it happened. I broke his back. It was him started it, but I was the one broke his back. When I came to my first mine, my first job, they had me tabbed as somebody who was always like that—a gunfighter."

He stopped talking again. This time he did not go on.

"Is that why you took me on?" said Hal, at last.

John drew a deep breath and let it out.

"Time we were getting back," he said. "Wake him up there."

Hal got up himself, reached over and shook Davies gently by the shoulder. The other miner opened his eyes.

"Oh?" Davies said. "Time to go?"

He sat up, took hold of the edge of the table and pulled himself upright.

"I guess I'm late," said a familiar voice. Hal looked up and saw Sost standing at the end of the table. "All over, is it?"

"Sit down," said John. "We can last for one more drink."

"Not for me," said Sost. "Why don't I take you all home? Talk on the way."

"Fair enough," said John, getting to his feet. Hal also stood up. He turned and found a face with an unprepossessing smile at his elbow.

"Come back again," said the proprietor of the Grotto. "It was our pleasure to have you."

"He'll want a bill," said John. "Itemized."

"I'm afraid that'll take a few minutes. . . ."

"It shouldn't," said John.

The proprietor went off and came back in a few seconds with a hard copy, which he handed to Hal. John took it and looked it over.

"Close enough," he said. "We'll check it, of course."

"I'm sure you'll find it the way it should be."

"Sure. See you again," said John.

He turned the hard copy back to Hal and led the way out.

"It's been a pleasure for us, serving you," said the proprietor behind them, as they went.

Outside, Sost's truck was waiting in the street before the Grotto. A Port marshal, with a green sash around his waist, was standing beside it.

"Are you the operator?" he said to Sost, as Sost started to get into the control seat. "I'll have to summon you for leaving this vehicle here."

"Send the summons to Amma Wong, then, sonny," said Sost. He looked around behind him. "Everybody in?"

John and Davies had climbed into the empty bed of the truck in back and stretched out, closing their eyes. Hal, who was beginning to feel hungry and very much awake, climbed into the other front seat beside Sost.

"Amma Wong?" the marshal was standing absolutely still, his narrow, middle-aged face blank of expression. Sost reached into an inside shirt pocket, brought out a wallet, flipped it open and showed it to the marshal, then put it away again before Hal could see what Sost had shown the man.

The marshal stepped back. Sost lifted the truck on its fans and drove off.

"Who's Amma Wong?" asked Hal, as they turned the corner of the block onto one of the arterial roads.

"Director of Freight Handling at the Port here," said Sost.

"You know her?"

"I work for her."

"Oh," said Hal, not much wiser than he had been before his first question. His stomach once more reminded him of its existence. "Could we stop and pick up something to eat?"

"Hungry?" Sost looked sideways at him. "Once I park the truck on the freight car, you can get something to eat from the machine on the subway train."

Hal stared at him.

"You're taking us all the way back to the mine?" he said. "You're going to put the truck and all on the subway?"

"Right," Sost nodded.

They drove along in silence for a minute or two.

"Thought you'd have gone home with Tonina," said Sost.

"She left early," said Hal. "What made you think I'd leave early when it's my party?"

Sost chuckled.

"Drinkingest twenty-year-old I ever saw," he said, half to himself. He looked at Hal. "Thought she wanted to talk to you privately about something."

"She did?" Hal stared back at him. "But she didn't say anything to me. When did she tell you she wanted to talk to me privately?"

"Saw her in Port, here, last week."

"Last week?" Hal shook his head. He had not thought Tonina had been in Port in any of the weeks recently. "What did she want to talk to me about?"

"Didn't say," answered Sost.

Chapter

> > 12 < <

Hal woke the next morning to the alarm of his chronometer and only by the sternest exercise of will got himself out of bed. By the time he was showered and dressed for work, however, he felt a great deal better.

He was digging into breakfast in the cookhall, when he became aware of Davies, across the table staring at him. Davies' face was pale and his eyes were red.

Hal slowed down in the face of that stare and finally stopped completely.

"What is it?" he asked Davies.

"I never," said Davies, "in my life, saw a man with a hangover eat like that."

Hal felt embarrassed, as he usually did when people paid attention to his appetite.

"I'm hungry this morning," he said. It was his usual excuse when the matter came up—hungry this morning, this noon, or this evening.

"How do you feel?" demanded Davies.

Hal stopped to consider himself.

"Sort of washed out," he said. Actually, there was a curious feeling in him, a sort of feeling of satisfied exhaustion as if he had just finished casting out a gang of inner devils.

"How about your head—your headache?"

"I don't have a headache," Hal said.

Davies continued to stare at him.

"And you're really hungry."

"I guess I am," said Hal.

By this time the rest of the miners within earshot, most of them fellow team members, were listening. Hal had the uncomfortable feeling that once more he had done something to mark himself as different from the rest of them.

He forgot the matter, however, as the day's work started. He was still a complete beginner with the cutting torch and it took all his efforts to do a full shift of work. In the days and weeks that followed that began to improve. It came slowly, but eventually he could cut in patterns that meshed efficiently with those of his neighbors on either hand at the rock face, and still keep up with the rest of them.

Some days before he reached that point, however, Tonina had rapped on his door late after one shift was over and drawn him out for a walk on the staging area; now, between shifts, deserted.

Under the high, eternal ceiling lights of the cavern they paced back and forth together and she looked at him strangely.

"I'm leaving the Yow Dee," she said. "Moving to Port. I was going to tell you about it, the night you made torcher, but I didn't get a chance to talk to you."

"Sost said you might have wanted to talk to me."

"He did?" Her voice was sharp. "What did he say?"

"Just that he didn't know why. I thought," Hal said, "I shouldn't just go asking, that you'd tell me yourself if you really wanted to."

"Yes," her voice and eyes softened. "You would think like that."

They walked a little more in silence.

"I'm getting married," she said. "I almost got married a couple of months ago. That's why I came to the Yow Dee here. I wasn't sure. Now I am. I'm marrying a man named Blue Ennerson. He's in Headquarters, at Port."

"Headquarters?" Hal said.

She smiled a little.

"Yow Dee and about three dozen other mines and Port businesses are all part of one Company," she said. "The Headquarters for that Company's in Port. Blue's Section Chief of the Record Section."

"Oh," said Hal. He felt inadequate, and not only because of his youth. He had learned that most women miners, who were a minority among the other mine workers, tended to marry upwards, into staff or management. Tonina was evidently going to be one such.

"I'm leaving tomorrow," she said.

"Tomorrow?"

"I didn't have a chance to tell you before this. You were either working, eating or sleeping, since you've become torcher."

"Yes."

There was a bleakness in him. He felt he should say something, but had no idea what was said on occasions like this. Eventually, they went back to their rooms; and before he was up the next morning she was gone.

He had expected that the mine would be hollow and empty without her, and it was—at first. But as the months wore on, the buried, unclear purpose in him grew, producing a restlessness he couldn't really define.

In its way, the mine had become something like a home; and the other team members, although they changed frequently as some left and new workers joined, became, almost, the family he had imagined them, the day he made torcher.

At the same time, he was becoming skilled at his work. In less than a year, he was offered a chance to compete for the position of leader, in voting among the miners to form a new team. To his own surprise, he won; and it was exactly as Tonina had predicted. He found he was expected to make the whole mine drunk. This time he did not have to drink with everyone else; but he did have to foot the bill.

Happily, there were still the funds he had brought to Coby, to draw upon. The next time he had seen Sost after the night in Port, he had asked the older man's advice on a way to hide his funds; and it had ended as a scheme whereby he transferred them, in installments over a period of months, to Sost himself, who set them up in an account under his own name.

"You're going to have to trust me," said Sost, bluntly. "But then, you're going to have to trust somebody if you really want to hide those credits. If you find somebody else you feel safer with, just let me know and we'll make the shift. Won't hurt my feelings."

"I don't think I'm likely to find anyone else," said Hal.

It was a true prediction. As a team leader, he was set a little at arm's length, necessarily, from the others on his team. Also, he was thrown more in the company of the other leaders like John and Will. He found that he welcomed the privacy this gave him as he continued to grow up.

And he was, indeed, continuing to grow up. The pretense that he had been twenty when he came had to contend with the fact that he continued growing physically, in all ways. Not only did he put on weight and muscle; in the next two and a half years his height shot up, until by the time he was nearly nineteen he was over two meters in height and evidently still growing.

Still, he looked young. He was still, in spite of his height, in the thinness of youth. The width of his shoulders and the mine-developed strength of his long arms did not make up for the youngness of his face and a certain innocence that also seemed to be an inescapable part of him.

He had not been challenged physically again since his first fight with Neif. The miners on his team, the staff, the business people, the inhabitants of the entertainment places he frequented in Port, all seemed to like him and get on well with him. But he made few casual friends and no more close friends. His regular visits to Port usually were in the company of John, Sost, or one or two of his own team members, when they were in the company of anyone he knew at all. Word about Tonina came to him from time to time, but he had not seen her since she had left the Yow Dee to get married.

But he continued to feel a restless dissatisfaction, as of something nagging at him. Sometimes he woke from his dreams angry, for reasons he could not trace. More and more, he had fallen into the habit of prowling about in solitary fashion, walking for hours in the streets and corridors of Port, dropping in on drinking establishments as the whim took him.

These particular establishments began to seem more and more alike as he got to know them. They all catered to the hunger of the Coby-dwellers for sight of an open sky, for a world with atmosphere and with the growing things of a planetary surface. Whatever else their interior was like, it would almost always offer the illusions of sky and a natural body of water, plus growing plants, real or illusory.

Away from their work the Coby miners were lonely and nostalgic individuals. He had been sitting in one of the bars one time when a miner there passed out, leaving unattended the stubby stringed instrument on which he had been playing; and Hal had discovered for himself the usefulness of such a tool.

Walter the InTeacher had taught him the basics of music and given him a nodding acquaintance with several instruments, including the classic Spanish guitar. It had not been hard to retune the stubby device in the bar to a more familiar mode and play it. He discovered that the miners would listen to him as long as he wanted to sing, provided the songs were ballad-like and simple.

After that, with Sost's help, he managed to buy a real guitar to carry around on his bar expeditions. In a sense, that purchase marked his trading of the making of individual friends for the making of friends with a general audience, wherever he went—and this was a change that was becoming necessary.

The reason was that as he grew up it became harder for him to talk on the ordinary level of what passed for conversation among the miners, particularly on their times-off. He had begun to find that whenever he talked he had a tendency to make the others around him uncomfortable. They were not interested in the same topics that he was, or in the questions to which his mind naturally drifted. The singing became something he could hide behind and still be social.

More than that. Once fully launched, he began almost without thinking to start putting much of the classical poetry he knew by heart to music. Much of it was singable—or could be made singable with a little surgery on the words and lines. From there it was only a short step further to start writing poetry again himself, in forms that could be sung.

It was an illusion, he told himself, to think that great art could not find its expression in the simplest of materials. The most complex feelings and thoughts were, in the end, only human feelings and thoughts, and as such, by definition could be rendered in the commonest and most familiar of terms, and still carry the overburden of their theme.

"Your songs are always different," said a hostess in one of the bars to him, one evening.

He read the message she hardly knew she was giving him. She, too, found him different enough to be attractive from a distance, but too different for comfort, up close. Hostesses like herself were only to be found in the luxury bars and the demand for them among the customers anywhere far exceeded the supply. But they flocked around Hal. Flocked . . . and went away again. Wistfully, he watched them go. He would have given far more than they dreamed to find even one of them with whom he could discover again the closeness he had experienced with Tonina after his fight with Neif. But it was never there. He did not know what was missing and, as far as he could discover, the hostesses did not know either—or perhaps they knew, but could not tell him.

He knew he was growing more and more apart from those around him, with the exception of John and Sost; but he could not discover what to do about it. Occasionally he remembered Malachi, Walter and Obadiah and felt that he ought to be away and doing something about what had happened to them, but what to do remained a question.

Then Neif came back into all their lives.

Neif had left the Yow Dee shortly after losing the fight with Hal. He had evidently worked at a number of mines before drifting back to the Yow Dee, where he found a spot on the team of someone who had not been a leader when Hal had first come there. The shift his team was on was one nearly eight hours at variance with the shift Hal's was on, and Hal hardly saw him. Then, without any hint of any such thing being in the wind, marshals from the Headquarters of the Company that owned the Yow Dee mine showed up and arrested Neif on charges of stealing pocket gold.

Pocket gold was the gold occasionally found in the mines in size larger than that of the tracing in the veins. In effect, pocket gold was any small nugget. The charge against Neif was that he had been doing this for some time.

In all these years, Hal had forgotten how different the legal pattern was on Coby. It was a shock to find himself being herded out of the bunkhouse without warning, the morning after the arrest, by what seemed to be a small army of Company marshals equipped not with sidearms, but with cone rifles.

"What's going on?" he asked the first person he had a chance to speak to, one of his own team members.

"They're going to shoot him," said the miner, a heavyset, dark man looking stupid with sleep and shock.

"They can't. . . ." Hal's voice stopped in his throat. Now that they were outside, they could see Neif being brought from the office building and positioned with his back to the slag pile on the far side of the staging area.

Neif's hands were not tied, but he moved awkwardly as if in a daze. He was left where he had been placed by the two marshals who had brought him out. Three other marshals with cone rifles formed a line facing him and about ten meters from him, and put their rifles to their shoulders with the unanimity of people who were used to working together.

Something like an earthquake of emotion moved suddenly in Hal. He opened his mouth to cry out; and at the same time started to plunge forward. But neither shout nor plunge was finished.

From behind, two arms like hawsers folded about him and the powerful hand of one of those arms closed about his throat, cutting off his voice. There was nothing amateurish about the actions of those arms and that hand. He stamped backwards with his right heel to break an ankle of whoever was holding him and free himself; but his heel found nothing, and in almost the same second, the fingers at his throat pressed on a nerve. He found himself fading into unconsciousness.

He came to, it seemed, only a second later. He was still held—but now held upright—by the powerful arms. Neif lay still, facedown on the ground of the staging area. The marshals were bringing up a closed truck for the body, and the crowd was melting away, back into the bunkhouse. He turned furiously and saw facing him not only John, but Sost.

"You just keep your mouth shut," said Sost, before Hal could get a word out, "and come with me."

The years with Malachi had taught Hal when not to stop and ask questions. There was in Sost's expression and voice a difference he had never seen or heard in the truck driver before. He followed without a word, accordingly, as Sost led the way around the end of the cookhouse to where his truck was standing. John had followed them to the truck and stood watching as Sost and Hal climbed into it.

"See you in town," said John, as Sost lifted the truck on its fans.

"With luck, maybe," said Sost. He turned the vehicle and drove off, away from the Yow Dee.

He took the corridor toward the nearest station, but branched off before they reached the station, down a tunnel Hal was not acquainted with. For the first time Hal saw him open up the truck. They hummed down the corridor at a speed that turned its walls into tan blurs; and Hal found himself marvelling that someone as old as Sost could have the reflexes to keep the truck from scraping the nearby walls at that speed.

It was the beginning of a breakneck trip to Port. At more than a hundred kilometers of tunnel distance from the Yow Dee, Sost stopped, put Hal in back, covered him up with some old tarpaulins, and pulled that truck aboard a branch of the subway at the next station they came to. Half an hour later the two of them walked into a small bar in Port, one which attempted to look something like a cross between a rathskeller and a jungle clearing. Tonina was already there, waiting for them at a table.

Hal looked at her searchingly as they sat down with her. The years of her marriage seemed not to have made any real difference in her, as far as his eyes could tell. Somehow, he had expected that they would.

"Thank God!" she said as they sat down. "I was beginning to think you hadn't made it."

"I couldn't risk getting on the subway until I was clear," said Sost. "I had to cover more ground on fans than they'd think I could cover, before we could risk taking the train."

He chuckled.

"Nothing like a reputation for being slow and sure," he said. "Always knew the time would be it'd come in handy."

"Can I ask what all this is about, now?" Hal said.

"Take your drinks, first. Make it look like you're drinking," said Tonina.

She had been coding at the table waiter as they sat down; and three glasses of beer had already risen to the surface of the table some seconds since. Hal and Sost obeyed her.

"You're going to have to get off Coby," she told Hal, once he had raised the glass to his lips and set it down again. "Someone either wants you, or wants you dead. I don't know which, and I don't want to know who; but you're going to have to move fast!"

Hal stared at her. Then his gaze moved to Sost. Even though Hal never explicitly told the older man his name, he had accepted the fact that Sost would have seen it on the credit papers Hal had entrusted to him.

"You told her?" he said.

"Her and thirty-four other people," Sost answered. "Somebody's got to look out for you."

He grinned a little at Hal.

"Don't take it so hard," Sost said. "I didn't let on to anyone, including Tonina, that this Hal Mayne had anything to do with you. But I put the name out in what you might call a sort of spiderweb to catch any questions about him showing up here on Coby."

"Only Sost has that kind of connections," said Tonina, tartly. "You're lucky."

"But that means thirty to forty people who can tell whoever's asking that they've heard the name," said Hal.

"Not before they tell me," answered Sost. "And that gives us the head start we need. As Tonina says, I've been around here long enough to have connections—good connections." He stared for a second directly into Hal's eyes. "You figure Tonina'd tell whoever was interested about Hal Mayne before she'd tell me?"

"No," said Hal, ashamed.

Hal sat, saying nothing. A thousand times in his mind he had imagined the moment in which he would learn that the Others had concluded he was on Coby; but the present scene was one he had never imagined. He had taken for granted that when it came time for him to run again, he would have been the one to have discovered danger close upon him; and he would have some idea of the situation in which he was caught. But now, it seemed everyone else knew more than he did.

"What happened?" he asked at last. "How'd you find out someone was looking for me?"

"An inquiry into the whereabouts of someone named Hal Mayne came into the Record Section of the Company Headquarters where my husband's in charge. It ended up as just one on a list of names sent to him for authorization to release information from Company records, to whoever was inquiring about the names. He recognized your name and checked with me, first. I told him to destroy your records and all record of the inquiry. He's done that. John will destroy all records at the Yow Dee; and no one there will think twice. Miners quit without warning every day."

"What do I owe your husband?" asked Hal. Nearly three years had taught him a great deal of how business was done on Coby.

"Nothing," said Tonina. "He did it because I asked him to."

"Thank you," said Hal. "And thank him for me. I'm sorry I suggested—"

"Never mind that," said Tonina. "Then I got in touch with Sost and Sost looked into it."

She nodded at Sost and Hal looked over at the older man.

"I did a little checking through some friends of mine," Sost said. "The Port marshals are all looking for you, all right; and they mean business. Someone high up's either had his arm twisted or been paid off handsomely."

"But if they can't find my records?"

"Even with no records," said Sost. "It looks like they know, or they've guessed the time you came to Coby. They do know what mines were hiring then. They're doing things at each of those mines—somebody from off-Coby's coaching them, is my guess—that they think'll smoke you out. They don't know what you look like or anything about you; but it figures they know some things about how you'll act when other things happen. That arrest and execution of Neif was aimed at smoking you out."

Hal felt a chill. He remembered the power of the arms holding him from crying out, from trying to do something before the cone rifles could fire.

"That's why you and John were right behind me?" he asked.

Sost nodded.

"Right. I just got there a second before. There wasn't time to explain things to you. We just went after you and did what we had to. Lucky John was handy. I'm not as young as I used to be."

"All right," said Tonina. "Now you know. Let's get down to how we get you off-world. The faster you move, the safer you'll be."

Sost nodded. He reached inside his shirt and came out with three packets of papers, which he dropped on the table before Hal.

"Take your pick," he said. "I've been spending some of that credit of yours. Jennison—you remember Jennison?"

Hal nodded. He had never forgotten the man in charge at the Holding Station. Apparently Jennison had known what he was talking about when he had said that Hal would be doing business with him later.

"This is his main business. Running a Holding Station lets him pick up a lot of things. But papers are the most valuable."

"How does he get them?" Hal asked.

"Sometimes someone comes through with more than one set and needs money. Sometimes somebody dies and the papers don't get turned in. Lots of ways."

"And never mind that," said Tonina. "Hal, Jennison sent you three different sets to look at. Pick the one you can get the most use out of."

"And I'll take the other two back to him," added Sost.

Hal picked up the packets one by one and looked at them. All were identifications and related papers for men in their early twenties. One was a set from New Earth, a set from Newton, and another from Harmony, one of the two Friendly Worlds. He remembered—in fact, his mind had moved back in time; and, evoked by his early training in recall, he seemed to hear the voices of his tutors again as he had conceived them in his room of the Final Encyclopedia. In particular, he heard the voice of Obadiah saying that there were people of his on Harmony who would never give Hal up.

"This one," said Hal.

He looked more closely at the Harmony packet as Sost took the other two back. Its papers were for someone twenty-three years old and named Howard Beloved Immanuelson, a tithing member of the Revealed Church Reborn, with an occupation as a semantic interpreter and a specialty in advising off-world personnel divisions of large companies. In one sense, these particular papers were a fortunate find. It was only in the past thirty years that the two Friendly Worlds had—almost inexplicably—reversed a centuries-old pattern of behavior that held those of their natives who chose work off-world as being less than respectable in religious conviction and fervor.

The only really acceptable work for a church member on other worlds was that of mercenary soldier—and then only if you had been sent out at the orders of your church or district. Three hundred years of starving for the interstellar credit that could be gained only by natives who worked on other worlds had not shaken this attitude. But in the last thirty-odd years those from Harmony and Association were suddenly cropping up on all the other inhabited planets in considerable numbers. They were even going to worlds of other Cultures with the approval of their authorities, to study for such occupations as that of a semantic interpreter. It was a change that had puzzled the Exotic ontogeneticists, Hal remembered Walter the InTeacher telling him. No adequate sociohistorical reason for the sudden change in behavior had yet been established.

It followed therefore that, as Immanuelson, Hal could be expected by fellow-Friendlies to be one of a younger, newer breed, infected with off-world habits and ideas, and not necessarily aware of recent events on Harmony— which could help cover any inconsistencies in his masquerade as the other man. "Off-world," as currently used on the two Friendly planets, meant any world but those of Harmony and Association.

Some work, he now saw, had already been done to adjust the papers to him. Each of the spaces for his identifying thumbprint were blank. He proceeded to press down on each of these sensitized squares in turn and watch the whorls of his thumbprints leap into visible existence on the papers as he took his hand away. He was now officially Howard Immanuelson. There was a strange little emotion involved in acknowledging the change. It was a feeling as if some part of him had been lost. Not the Hal Mayne part that was basic to him; but that part of him that had come into existence on Coby, and was now officially being removed from existence.

He put the papers into an inside pocket.

"Here's your credit," Sost said, passing over another set of papers, "reassigned to your Harmony name. There's still a lot left."

"Can you trust Jennison?" Hal asked, taking the credit papers.

"Wouldn't have dealt with him, otherwise," Sost said. "Don't worry. Freight Handlers has a lock on him."

"Can Freight Handlers be trusted?" Hal said; and stared a little as the other two laughed.

"Sost was Freight Handlers before Freight Handlers was invented," Tonina said. "He may not have the office and the title, but you don't need to worry about Freight Handlers as long as he's here."

"I just kept my hand in," said Sost, "and over the years you get to know people. Now, give me your own papers."

"We'd better destroy them," said Hal, passing them over.

"That's the idea. Now," said Sost, as he tucked the Tad Thornhill papers away. "We'll leave here, you and me. You've got passage on a ship to Harmony, and a ticket to Citadel, there. You know anything about Citadel?"

"I studied about it, once," said Hal. "It's a fair-sized city on the continent they call South Promise, in the low latitudes of the temperate zone."

"That's right; and it's the one city-sized place on Harmony this Immanuelson's work record doesn't show him as having been in. Once there you're on your own." Sost stood up, and Hal and Tonina followed suit. "We'll get you on board with the freight and slip the whole business of outgoing customs. Come on."

Hal turned toward Tonina. She had made him uncertain about trying to touch her; but now he would never see her again. He put his arms around her awkwardly and kissed her; and she held him strongly for a moment.

"Get going," she said, pushing him away.

He went out with Sost. Looking back he saw her still standing upright and motionless by the table, watching them go.

Chapter

> > 13 < <

Hal sat in the jitney taking him down from orbit around Harmony to the city of Citadel. Curiously, in this moment of stepping into a totally new world, it was not his three years on Coby that were beginning to lose reality in his mind, it was the four days of interstellar space travel, with the frequent psychic shocks of the phase-shifts that had brought him here. The trip had had the feel of unreality to it; and now he found it also difficult to think of the Friendly World to which he was rapidly descending as real; although he knew it would be so, for him, soon enough.

Something else was filling his mind and driving out anything else but the years just passed on Coby. For the first time in his life, on the trip from there to here, he had come to a stark understanding of why his three tutors had insisted that he go to the mines and work, instead of hiding on one of the Younger Worlds. Their reason had not been merely a matter of shielding him from the eyes of the Others until he was old enough to protect himself. No, the important factor in their decision had lain in what they had said about his need to grow up, to learn about people before he ventured forth to face his enemies.

Only now, after three years on the mining world, he could realize that he had been—up until the moment of the deaths of Obadiah, Malachi and Walter the InTeacher—a hothouse plant. He had been raised as an unusual boy, by unusual people. He had had no real, day-to-day experience or understanding of ordinary men and women; those who were the rootstock of the race itself—those from among whom the unusual people like himself were occasionally produced, simply to be taken and used by the historic pressures of their time. Until Coby, such ordinary people had been as unknown to him as if they had been creatures from the furthest stars. Their goals had never been his goals, their sorrows his sorrows, their natures his nature. His lack of understanding of these differences had been an unacceptable defect; because now it came home to him, unsparingly, that it was these, not the gifted ones like himself and those who had brought him up, whom he would be fighting for in the years ahead.

It had been necessary that he begin by realizing his place among such ordinary people, that he learn to understand and feel with and for them, before he could be of any use to the race as a whole. For they were the race. In the mines he had come face-to-face with this. He had discovered it in Tonina, in John Heikkila, in Sost—in all of them. He had found unremarkable people there he could care about, and who cared about him—regardless of his abilities. People who, in the end, had made his escape possible when alone, with all his special talents, he would have failed.

The remembrance of that escape now made his eyes burn with regret that he had never told Sost, at least, how much the old man had come to mean to him. The manner of their leave-taking had been almost casual. They had driven Sost's truck out to the ship he was now in, ostensibly to deliver a large but lightly-sealed package, with Hal seated beside Sost and dressed in the gray coveralls of a freight handler. Together, they had carried the package in through the ship's loading entrance to the number-one hold and been met there by the Chief Purser, who had evidently been expecting them.

At his direction Hal had taken off the coveralls, dropped them in a refuse container, and taken leave of Sost. He had followed the Chief to a portside cabin, been ushered in, and left with directions not to leave the cabin until after the first phase-shift. He had obeyed; and, in fact, had stayed close to his cabin through the first third of the trip. The solitary hours had offered an opportunity for him to practice casting himself mentally into the persona of a tithe-payer of the Revealed Church Reborn.

He had the role model of Obadiah to draw on. Growing up with his three tutors, he had come, instinctively, to imitate each of them. To be like Obadiah, he had only to imagine himself as Obadiah—but the trick down on the surface of Harmony would be to carry that bit of imagination in his mind so constantly that even under moments of stress he would not slip out of character.

He also practiced on the one fellow-passenger who seemed to have any inclination to talk with him beyond the barest exchange of civilities; and this passenger proceeded to open his eyes to an unsuspected danger. The other was an Exotic named Amid, a small, erect old man with—for an Exotic—a remarkably wrinkled face. Amid was returning from Ceta where he had been as an OutBond, teaching the history of the Splinter Cultures at the University of Ceta, in the city of the same name as that of the planet and the University.

Like most Exotics, he was as at ease with everyone as the Friendlies and other Harmony-bound passengers were stiff and suspicious. He was also, like many teachers, in love with his subject; and Hal found him full of fascinating historical anecdotes out of the history of Harmony and Association that he would not have thought anyone but one of the native-born Friendlies could have known, and then only if they were from the area or district of the world with which the anecdote dealt.

"Faith," said Amid to him, the third day out of Coby, "in its large sense, is more than just the capacity to believe. What it is, is the concept of a personal identity with a specific, incontrovertible version of reality. True faith is untouchable. By definition, anything that attacks it is not only false but doomed to be exposed as such. Which is why we have martyrs. The ultimate that can be offered against any true Faith-holder to force him to change his beliefs is a threat to destroy him utterly, to cancel out his universe, leaving only nothingness. But for the true Faith-holder, even this threat fails, since he, and that in which he has faith, are one; and, by definition, that in which he has faith is indestructible."

"But why can't someone who merely believes be just as immune to having his personal universe destroyed?" Hal had asked.

"Because merely believing—if you want to define the word separately—implies something to believe in—that is, something apart from the believer. In other words, we have two things in partnership, the believer and his belief. A partnership can be dissolved. Partners can be divorced. But, as I just pointed out, the Faith-holder is his faith. He and it make, not two, but a single thing. Since he and it are one, there's no way to take it from him. That makes him a very powerful opponent. In fact, it makes him an unconquerable opponent; since even death can't touch him in his most important part."

"Yes," said Hal, remembering Obadiah.

"That difference," said Amid, "between the mere believer and the true Faith-holder, is the one thing that has to be grasped, if the peoples of this Culture are to be understood. Paradoxically, it's the hardest distinction for the non-Friendly to grasp—just as the intimate parallel commitments of the Exotic and the Dorsai are also the hardest things for people not of those Cultures to understand. In the case of each Culture, it's a case of an ordinary human capability—for faith, for courage, or for insight—raised to a near-instinctive level of response."

Remembering that conversation, now, as the jitney approached the landing area, Hal made an effort to apply the distinction Amid had been talking about to what he knew of the Friendly character. It was not easy, because all he really knew about what made a Friendly a Friendly had been absorbed directly into his unconscious by observing Obadiah as he had been growing up. In short, he knew, without having to think, what Obadiah would do in almost any situation, once he had been confronted with it, but he had little conscious understanding of why Obadiah would do just that. Hal was, in fact, in a position very like that of someone who could operate a piece of machinery but had no idea of why or how it worked.

As the jitney touched down, he made a mental note to at least not let himself be lulled into complacency by the fact that the people here might seem at first to take him easily for one of themselves. He would have to make a conscious effort to observe and study those around him, in spite of whatever ability he already had to play the role he had adopted. Otherwise, he could end up making a wrong move without ever knowing he had made it; and the results from that wrong move might result in tripping him up without warning.

The passengers left the jitney and found themselves in a closed tunnel that led for some distance before delivering them into a series of rooms where they were sorted out according to the type of personal papers they were carrying. As someone with Harmony papers, Hal was channelled with a couple of dozen other Friendlies into the last room to be reached. Within were a number of desks with Immigration Service officials seated at them.

Hal was a little out of position to be first at the table nearest him. Just ahead of him was a slight, slim, dark-skinned young man. There was a hush-zone around each desk, and Hal stood at such an angle to both his fellow traveller and the official that lip-reading was difficult, so there was no way for him to find out in advance any of the questions he might be asked.

Finally, the man ahead of him was directed onward to a fenced enclosure made of two-meter-high wire mesh and containing physical, straight-backed chairs, watched over by a stocky, middle-aged enlisted man in a black Militia uniform. The dark young man took a chair there, and Hal was beckoned forward to the desk with the official.

"Papers?" said the official, as Hal sat down.

Hal produced them and the official read through them.

"How long has it been since you were on Harmony?" he asked.

Hal took it as a good sign that the other had not addressed him in the canting speech of the ultra-fanatics among the Friendlies. It might indicate that the official was one of the more reasonable sort. In any case, he had his answer ready, having studied the papers he was carrying.

"Four and a half standard years, more or less."

The official shuffled the papers together and handed them back to him.

"Wait over there," he said, nodding to the enclosure.

Hal took the papers, slowly. No one else of the native Friendlies except the dark-skinned young man had been sent to wait. The rest, from other desks, were all being directed ahead, through a farther doorway and out of the room.

"May I ask why?" he said, standing up.

"Anyone off-planet more than three years is checked."

Hal felt grimness as he walked over toward the enclosure. He should have thought of this. Sost should have thought of this. No, it was unfair to blame Sost, who would have had no way of knowing that a special effort should have been made to get Friendly papers that were less than three years off the individual's home world. Naturally, the chances of the papers Jennison dealt in being out of date were likely to be greater rather than lesser.

He took a seat across the enclosure from the dark-skinned man, under the watchful eye of the policeman. It seemed to him that the glance of the dark-skinned man met his own eyes strangely for a fraction of a second; then they were watching nothing, again. It would have been easy to believe that the other man had never glanced at him at all, but one of Hal's earliest teachings by Malachi had been in the art of observation. Now, in his mind, Hal replayed the last few minutes of what he had just seen, and his memory produced, beyond argument, the brief moment in which the other's eyes had met his.

It was something that could mean nothing—or a great deal. Hal sat back on the stiff, upright chair and let his body relax. Time went by—more than a standard hour. At the end of that period the room was empty of his fellow travellers, except for those in the enclosure; and there were now five of these, including himself. The other three were unremarkable-looking individuals, obviously Friendlies, all of them at least twenty years older than Hal and the dark-skinned man.

"All of you now," said the policeman, nasally. "Come. This way."

They were taken out of the enclosure and the room they had been in, down another short corridor to an underground garage and a waiting bus. The bus hissed up on its fans and they slid out through the garage, emerging into the nighttime streets of Citadel. It was raining, and the rain streaked the windows of the bus, blurring the gray shapes of the building fronts they passed under the sparse yellow glow of the street lighting. They drove for a little under half an hour, then entered another interior garage, down below the street level.

From the bus in the garage, they were taken upstairs into what seemed at first sight to be an office building. Their papers were taken from them; and there was another long wait on straight chairs in an outer office, with trips to the water tap in one wall and to the restroom, under the eye of their police guard, as the only distractions. Then, one by one, they were called into interior offices that had only a single desk and a single interviewer behind it. Once more, Hal saw the dark-skinned young man called before him.

When Hal's turn came, he found himself sitting down at the side of a desk, facing a small, balding man with an egg-shaped face, unblinking eyes and an almost lipless mouth. The gray man picked up papers that Hal recognized as his from the desk, and read through them with a speed that made Hal suspect the other of being already familiar with their contents. He laid the papers back down and looked at Hal from a bureaucratic distance.

"Your name?"

"Howard Beloved Immanuelson."

"You're a communicant of the Revealed Church Reborn, born into that Church twenty-three point four standard years ago, in the hamlet of Enterprise?"

"Yes," said Hal.

"Your father and mother were both communicants of that Church?"

"Yes."

"You remain a communicant in good standing of that Church?"

"I am," said Hal, "by the grace of the Lord."

"You have just returned from four years of work off-planet as a semantic interpreter, having been employed by various of the unchurched. . . ."

The questioning continued, covering the facts of Howard Immanuelson's life as set forth in the papers Hal had been carrying. Once these had been exhausted, the interviewer pushed the papers from him and stared at Hal with his unchanging eyes.

"Do you keep regular times of prayer?" he asked.

Hal had been expecting this sort of question.

"As far as I can," he said. "Travelling about as I do among those who do lack the Word, it isn't always easy to keep regular hours of prayer."

"Ease," said the interviewer, "is not the way of the Lord."

"I know," said Hal. "I know as you do that the fact that regular hours of prayer are difficult to keep is no excuse for laxity. So I've become used to inward communication at my usual times of literal prayer."

The gray man's upper lip seemed to curl a little, but it was so thin Hal could not be sure.

"How many daily are your times of prayer—when it's convenient for you to pray, that is?"

Hal thought swiftly. He did not know the sectarian rules of the Revealed Church Reborn. But if it was a church in the North Oldcontinent region where Enterprise was located, then it was probably in the so-called "Old" Tradition, rather than the New. In any case, as the saying went, each Friendly was a sect on his own.

"Seven."

"Seven?" The interviewer kept his tone level and his face expressionless, but Hal suddenly suspected he was talking to one of those who held to the New Tradition, and believed that more than four times of formal prayer a day were arrogant and ostentatious.

"Matins and lauds, prime, terce, sext, none, vespers and compline," said Hal.

He saw the hint of an unmistakable sourness on the face of the man before him as he reeled off the Latin names. It was a risk to do something like this deliberately; but he would be out of character if he did not clash with almost any other Friendly on details of religious dogma or observance. At the same time he did not want to goad anyone like this strongly enough to give the other a personal reason to make the conditions and results of this interview more harsh than they might otherwise be.

"Yes," said the interviewer, harshly. "But for all those gaudy names you pray secretly, like a coward. Perhaps you belong to that anathema, that new cult among our sinful youth, that professes to believe that prayer is unnecessary if you only live with God and His purposes in mind. There's a Great Teacher just arrived here among us who could show you the error of that way. . . ."

The tone of his voice was rising. He broke off abruptly and wiped his lips with a folded white handkerchief.

"Did you have much contact with other churched individuals during your years among the ungodly?" he asked, in a more controlled voice.

"By nature of my work," said Hal, "I had little contact with anyone from the Promised Worlds. My associations, of necessity, were with those people of the planets on which I was working."

"But you met and knew some from Harmony or Association?"

"A few," said Hal. "I don't think I can even remember the names of any."

"Indeed? Perhaps you might remember more than names. Do you recall meeting any of those who style themselves the Children of Wrath, or the Children of God's Wrath?"

"On occasion—" Hal began, but the interviewer broke in.

"I'm not referring merely to those who live in knowledge of, and sometimes admit, that they are deservedly forgotten of God. I'm talking of those who have taken this impious name to themselves as an organization counter to God's churches and God's commandments."

Hal shook his head.

"No," he said. "No, I've never even heard of them."

"Strange," the thin upper lip curled visibly this time, "that so widely travelled a person should be so ignorant of the scourge being visited upon the world of his birth. In all those four years, none of those from Harmony or Association that you met ever mentioned the Children of Wrath?"

"No," said Hal.

"Satan has your tongue, I see." The interviewer pressed one of a bank of studs on his desktop. "Perhaps after you think it over, you may come to a better memory. You can go, now."

Hal got up and reached for his papers, but the gray man opened a drawer of his desk and swept them in. Hal turned to leave, but discovered when he got to the door that that was as far as the freedom of his permission was extended. He was taken in charge by an armed and uniformed police guard and taken elsewhere in the building.

The two of them went down several floors and through a number of corridors to what now began to strongly resemble a jail rather than an office building. Past a couple of heavy, locked doors, they came to a desk behind which another police guard sat; and here all pretense that this was anything but a jail ended. Hal had the personal possessions he was carrying taken from him, he was searched for anything he had not admitted carrying, then taken on by the guard behind the desk, down several more corridors and to a final, heavy metal door that was plainly locked and unlocked only from the outside.

"Could I get something to eat?" asked Hal as the guard opened this door and motioned inside. "I haven't had anything since I landed—"

"Tomorrow's meal comes tomorrow," said the guard. "Inside!"

Hal obeyed, hearing the door crash shut and locked behind him.

The place into which he had been put was a large room or cell, with narrow benches attached to its bare concrete walls. The floor was also bare concrete with an unscreened latrine consisting of a stool, a urinal and a washstand occupying one blank corner. There was nothing else of note in the cell, except a double window with its sill two meters above the floor, in the wall opposite the door, and one fellow-prisoner.

Chapter

> > **14** < <

The other occupant of the room, a man stretched out on one of the benches with his back to the room, was apparently trying to sleep; although this was something of an endeavor in the face of the fact that the room was brightly illuminated by a lighting panel let into the center of its ceiling. Hal recognized the man by the color of his hair and his general shape as the dark-skinned young man who had been in front of him through most of the procedure that had taken place since they had all disembarked from the jitney.

Now, as the door to the cell clanged shut and locked behind Hal, the other came to life, rolled over off the bench onto his feet and walked lightly to the cell door to look out through the small window set in its upper panel. He nodded to himself and, turning back into the room, came soft-footedly to Hal, cupping one hand behind his right ear and pointing at the ceiling warningly.

"These Accursed of the Lord," he said, clearly, taking Hal's arm and leading him toward the corner containing the latrine, "they make these places so, deliberately, to rob us of all decency. Might I ask you, out of kindness, to stand where you are over there and turn your back for a moment. . . . Thank you, brother. I'll do as much for you, whenever you wish. . . ."

He had drawn Hal by this time right into the corner where the latrine stood. He turned on the water taps of the washstand, triggered the cleansing unit of the stool, and drew Hal's head down with his next to the spouting taps. He wiggled the fingers of both of his hands before Hal's face. Covered by the sound of the running water, he whispered directly into Hal's right ear.

"Can you talk with your fingers?"

Hal shook his head and turned to whisper in the ear of the other.

"No. But I read lips and I can learn very quickly. If you'll mouth the words and show me enough finger-motions to start with, we can talk."

The dark-skinned young man nodded. He straightened up; and while they still stood covered by the sound of the water coming from the taps, he formed words with his lips.

"My name is Jason Rowe. What is yours, brother?"

Hal leaned close again to whisper in Jason Rowe's ear.

"Howard Immanuelson." Jason stared at him. Hal went on. "And you don't need to make the words slowly and exaggeratedly. Just move your lips as if you're speaking normally, and I can follow you easily. Just don't forget to look at me when you speak."

Jason nodded in turn. He lifted his right hand with thumb and forefinger spread slightly and the other fingers curled into the palm.

"Yes," he mouthed at Hal.

Hal nodded, imitating the sign with his own thumb and forefinger.

A few minutes later, when Jason shut off the water coming from the taps and they moved off to take flanking benches in another corner of the room, Hal had already learned the signs for *yes, no, I, you, go, stay, sleep, guard* and half the letters of the alphabet. They moved to that corner of the room that was to the right of the door, so that anyone looking through the window of the door would not be able to see what they were doing.

Seated as they were, on the benches at right angles to each other, they came as close as possible to facing each other. They began to talk, at first slowly, as Hal was put to the problem of spelling out most of the words he needed to use. But he gained speed as Jason would guess the word he was after before it was completely spelled and give him the sign for it. Hal's signing vocabulary grew rapidly, to what he could see was the profound, if silent, surprise of Jason. Hal made no attempt to explain. It would hardly help here to air the fact that his mnemonic and communicative skills owed a debt to the skills of the Exotics. Their conversation seemed headed at first in a strange direction and Hal was grateful that he could hide his ignorance of what the other was talking about behind his ignorance of the sign language.

"Brother," Jason asked, as soon as they were seated facing each other, "are you of the faith?"

Hal hesitated only a fraction of a second. On the surface there was no reason why any Friendly should not answer such a question in the affirmative; although what the other might mean specifically could be something very much to be determined.

"Yes," he signed, and waited for enlightenment from Jason.

"I, also," said Jason. "But be of good cheer, brother. I do not think that those holding us here have any idea that we're the very kind they're seeking. This witch-hunt they've swept us up in is just part of a citywide attempt to make themselves look good, in the eyes of one of the Belial-spawn who's come visiting here."

"Visiting?" Hal spelled out.

He had gone tense at the last words of the other; and now, for the first time, there was a touch of cold sickness in the pit of his stomach. The words "Belial-spawn" were words he had heard Obadiah use to describe the Others. It was too far-fetched a supposition to imagine that the Other or Others looking for him on Coby had traced the route of his escape and beaten him here to Citadel. But, assuming that they had indeed traced him, a spaceship piloted by someone more inclined to take risks on his phase-shifts than the paid master of a freighter could indeed have reached the city here a day or two before him.

"So they say," Jason answered him with silently-moving lips.

"When did he get here?"

Jason's eyes watched Hal curiously.

"Then you had heard—and knew that it was a man, rather than a woman?"

"I . . ." Hal took advantage of his ignorance of the sign language to cover up his slip, "assumed they'd probably send a man to a New Tradition city like this."

"Perhaps that was the reason. Anyway, it seems he's been here in Citadel less than twenty standard hours." Jason smiled startlingly and suddenly. "I'm good at getting interrogators to tell me things when they're questioning me. I found out quite a bit. They call him Great Teacher—as the lickspittle way of their kind is; and they'll be planning to fawn on him, offering up some examples of those of the faith as sacrifices to his coming."

"Why should I be of good cheer if that's the situation?" asked Hal. "It doesn't sound good to me."

"Why, because they can't be sure, of course," said Jason. "In the end, unless they're certain, they'll delay showing us to him, because they're all like whipped dogs. They cringe at the very thought of his scorn if they're wrong. So, we'll have time; and with that time we'll escape—"

He looked almost merrily at Hal.

"You don't believe me?" he mouthed. "You can't believe that I'd trust you with the knowledge I was going to escape, just like that? Why do you think I open myself to you like this, brother?"

"I don't know," said Hal.

"Because it happens I knew the Howard Immanuelson whose papers you carry. Oh, not well; but we were advanced students in the same class in Summercity, before he left for Kultis to qualify himself for off-planet work. I also know when it was he went to Coby, and that he died there. But he was of the faith; and all his moving away from Harmony was to launder himself, so that he could come back and be useful to us here. You got aboard at Coby with his papers. Also, you've picked up the finger speech far too swiftly to be other than someone who has used it all his life—you must watch that, brother, while you're here. Be careful of seeming to know too much, too quickly. Even some of the Traitors to God have the wit to put two and two together. Now, tell me. What's your real name, and your purpose in being here?"

Hal's brain galloped.

"I can't," he signalled. "I'm sorry."

Jason looked at him sadly for a long moment.

"Unless you can trust me," he said, "I can't trust you. Unless you can tell me, I can't take you with me when I leave here."

"I'm sorry," signed Hal again. "I don't have the right to tell you."

Jason sighed.

"So be it," he said. He got up and went across the cell, lay down with his back to the room in the position he had been in when Hal had entered. Hal sat watching him for a few minutes, then tried to imitate the other man and stretch out himself. But his success was limited. The width of his shoulders was too great for the narrow bench; and the best he could do, lying down, was balance himself so precariously that a second's relaxation would send him tumbling to the floor.

He gave in, finally, and sat upright on the bench, drawing in his legs until he perched in lotus position with his back to the wall. His knees and a good part of his legs projected outward into thin air; but in this position the center of his mass was closer to the edge of the bench that touched the wall behind him and he could relax without falling off. He dropped his hands on his thighs carelessly and hunched his shoulders a little to make it appear to any observer that his position was unthinking and habitual rather than practised. Then he turned his mind loose to drift. Within seconds, the cell faded about him; and, for all physical intents and purposes, he slept. . . .

The cell door clashed open abruptly, waking them. Hal was on his feet by the time the guard came through the open door and he saw out of the corner of his eye that Jason was also.

"All right," said the man who had entered. He was thin and tall—though not as tall as Hal—with a coldly harsh face, and Captain's lozenges on his black Militia uniform. "Outside!"

They obeyed. Hal's body was still numb from sleep, but his mind, triggered into immediate overdrive, was whirring. He avoided looking at Jason in the interests of keeping up the pretense that they had not talked and still did not know each other; and he noticed that Jason avoided looking at him. Once in the corridor they were herded back the way Hal remembered being brought in.

"Where are we going?" Jason asked.

"Silence!" said the Captain softly, without looking at him and without changing expression, "or I will hang thee by thy wrists for an hour or so after this is over, apostate whelp."

Jason said no more. They were moved along down several corridors, and taken up a freight lift shaft, to what was again very obviously the office section of this establishment. Their guardian brought them to join a gathering of what seemed to be twenty or more prisoners like themselves, waiting outside the open doors of a room with a raised platform at one end, a desk upon it and an open space before it. The flag of the United Sects, a white cross on a black field, hung limply from a flagpole set upright on the stage.

The Captain left them with the other prisoners and stepped a few steps aside to speak to the five other enlisted Militiamen acting as guards. They stood, officer, guards and prisoners alike, and time went by.

Finally, there was the sound of footwear on polished corridor floor, echoing around the bend in the further corridor, and three figures turned the corner and came into sight. Hal's breath hesitated for a second. Two were men in ordinary business suits—almost certainly local officials. But the man between them, tall above them, was Bleys Ahrens.

Bleys ran his glance over all the prisoners as he approached, and his eye paused for a second on Hal, but not for longer than might have been expected from the fact that Hal was noticeably the tallest of the group. Bleys came on and turned into the doorway, shaking his head at the two men accompanying him as he did so.

"Foolish," he was saying to them as he passed within arm's length of Hal. "Foolish, foolish! Did you think I was the sort to be impressed by what you could sweep off the streets, that I was to be amused like some primitive ruler by state executions or public torture-spectacles? This sort of thing only wastes energy. I'll show you how to do things. Bring them in here."

The guards were already moving in response before one of the men with Bleys turned and gestured to the Militia officer. Hal and the others were herded into the room and lined up in three ranks facing the platform on which the two men now stood behind the desk and Bleys himself half-sat, half-lounged, with his weight on the farther edge of that piece of furniture. To even this casual pose he lent an impression of elegant authority.

A coldness had developed in the pit of Hal's stomach with Bleys' appearance; and now that feeling was growing, spreading all through him. Sheltered and protected as he had been all his life, he had grown up without ever knowing the kind of fear that compresses the chest and takes strength from the limbs. Then, all at once, he had encountered death and that kind of fear for the first time; and now the reflex set up by that moment had been triggered by a second encounter with the tall, commanding figure on the platform before him.

He was not afraid of the Friendly authorities who were holding him captive. His mind recognized the fact that they were only human; and he had been deeply instructed in the principle that for any problem involving human interaction there was a practical solution to be found by anyone who would search for it. But the sight of Bleys faced him with a being who had destroyed the very pillars of his personal universe. He felt the paralysis of his fear spreading all through him; and the rational part of him recognized that once it had taken him over completely he would throw himself upon the fate that would follow Bleys' identification of him—just to get it over with.

He reached for help; and the ghosts of three old men came out of his memory in response.

"He is no more than a weed that flourishes for a single summer's day, this man you face," said the harsh voice of Obadiah in his mind. "No more than the rain on the mountainside, blowing for a moment past the rock. God is that rock, and eternal. The rain passes and is as if it never was. Hold to the rock and ignore the rain."

"He can do nothing," said the soft voice of Walter the InTeacher, "that I've not already shown you at one time or another. He's no more than a user of skills developed by other men and women, many of whom could use them far better than he can. Remember that no one's mind and body are ever more than human. Forget the fact he's older and more experienced than you; and concentrate only on a true image of what he is, and what his limits are."

"Fear is just one more weapon," said Malachi, "no more dangerous in itself than a sharpened blade is. Treat it as you would any weapon. When it approaches, turn yourself to let it pass you by, then take and control the hand that guides it at you. The weapon without the hand is only one more thing— in a universe full of things."

Up on the platform, Bleys looked down at them all.

"Pay attention to me, my friends," he said softly to the prisoners. "Look at me."

They looked, Hal with the rest of them. He saw Bleys' lean, aristocratic face and pleasant brown eyes. Then, as he looked at them, those eyes began to expand until they would entirely fill his field of vision.

Reflexively, out of his training under Walter the InTeacher, he took a step back within his own mind, putting what he saw at arm's length—and all at once it was as if he was aware of things on two levels. There was the level on which he stood with the other prisoners, held by Ahrens like animals transfixed by a bright light in darkness; and there was the level in which he was aware of the assault that was being made on his free will by what was hidden behind that bright light, and on which he struggled to resist it.

He thought of rock. In his mind he formed the image of a mountainside, cut and carved into an altar on which an eternal light burned. Rock and light . . . untouchable, eternal.

"I must apologize to you, my friends and brothers," Bleys was saying gently to all of them. "Mistakenly, you've been made to suffer; and that shouldn't be. But it was a natural mistake and small mistakes of your own have contributed to it. Examine your conscience. Is there one of you here who isn't aware of things you know you shouldn't have done. . . ."

Like mist, the beginnings of rain blew upon the light and the altar. But the light continued to burn, and the rock was unchanged. Bleys' voice continued; and the rain thickened, blowing more fiercely upon the rock and the light. On the mountainside the day darkened, but the light burned on through the darkness, showing the rock still there, still unmarked and unmoved. . . .

Bleys was softly showing all of them the way to a worthier and happier life, a way that trusted in what he was telling them. All that they needed to do was to acknowledge the errors of their past and let themselves be guided in the proper path for their future. His words made a warm and friendly shelter away from all storm, its door open and waiting for all of them. But, sadly, Hal must remain behind; alone, out on the mountainside in the icy and violent rain, clinging to the rock so that the wind could not blow him away; and with only the pure but heatless light burning in the darkness to comfort him.

Gradually, he became aware that the wind had ceased growing stronger, that the rain which had been falling ever heavier was now only steady, that the darkness could grow no darker—and that he, the rock and the light were still there, still together. A warmth of a new sort kindled itself inside him and grew until it shouted in triumph. He felt a strength within him that he had never felt before, and with that strength, he stepped back, merging once more the two levels, so that he looked out nakedly through his own eyes again at Bleys Ahrens.

Bleys had finished talking and was stepping down from the platform, headed out of the room. All the prisoners turned to watch him go as if he walked out of the room holding one string to which all of them were attached.

"If you'll come this way, brothers," said one of the guards.

They were led, by this single guard only, down more corridors and into a room with desks, where they were handed back their papers.

Chapter

> > **15** < <

Apparently, they were free to go. They were ushered out of the building and Hal found himself walking down the street with Jason at his side. He looked at the other man and saw him smiling and animated.

"Howard!" Jason said. "Isn't this wonderful? We've got to find the others and tell them about this great man. They'll have to see him for themselves."

Hal looked closely into Jason's eyes.

"What is it, brother?" said Jason. "Is something wrong?"

"No," said Hal. "But maybe we should sit down somewhere and make some plans. Is there anyplace around here where we can talk, away from people?"

Jason looked around. They were in what appeared to Hal to be a semi-industrial section. It seemed about mid-morning, and the rain that had been falling when they had landed the day before was now holding off, although the sky was dark and promised more precipitation.

"This early . . ." Jason hesitated. "There's a small eating place with booths in its back room; and this time of day, the back room ought to be completely empty, anyway."

"Let's go," said Hal.

The eating place did indeed turn out to be small. It was hardly the sort of establishment that Hal would have found himself turning into if he had simply wanted a meal; but its front room held only about six customers at the square tables there and the back room, as Jason had predicted, was empty. They took a booth far back in a corner and ordered coffee.

"What plans did you have in mind to make, Howard?" asked Jason, when the coffee had been brought.

Hal tasted the contents of his cup and set the cup down again on the table between them. Coffee—or rather some imitation of it—was to be found on all the inhabited worlds. But its taste varied widely between any two worlds, and was often markedly different in two widely distant parts of the same world. Hal had spent three years getting used to Coby coffee. He would have to start all over again with Harmony coffee.

"Have you seen this?" he asked, in turn.

From a pocket he brought out a small gold nugget encased in a cube of glass. It was the first piece of pocket gold he had found in the Yow Dee Mine; and, following a Coby custom, he had bought it back from the mine owners and had it encased in transparent plastic, to carry about as a good-luck piece. His fellow team members would have thought him strange if he had not. Now, for the first time, he had a use for it.

Jason bent over the cube.

"Is that real gold?" he asked, with the fascination of anyone not of either Coby or Earth.

"Yes," said Hal. "See the color. . . ."

He reached out across the table and took the back of Jason's neck gently and precisely between the tips of his thumb and middle finger. The skin beneath his fingertips jumped at his touch, then relaxed as he put soft pressure on the nerve endings below it.

"Easy," he said, "just watch the piece of gold. . . . Jason, I want you to rest for a bit. Just close your eyes and lean back against the back of the booth and sleep for a couple of minutes. Then you can open your eyes and listen. I've got something to tell you."

Obediently, Jason closed his eyes and leaned back, resting his head against the hard, dark-dyed wooden panel that was the back of the booth. Hal took his hand from the other's neck and Jason stayed as he was, breathing easily and deeply for about a hundred and fifty heartbeats. Then he opened his eyes, stared at Hal as if puzzled for a second, and then smiled.

"You were going to tell me something," he said.

"Yes," said Hal. "And you're going to listen to me all the way through and then not say anything until you've thought about what I've just told you. Aren't you?"

"Yes, Howard," said Jason.

"Good. Now listen closely." Hal paused. He had never done anything like this before; and there was a danger, in Jason's present unnaturally-receptive state, that some words Hal used might have a greater effect than he had intended them to have. "Because I want you to understand something. Right now you think you're acting normally and doing exactly what you'd ordinarily want to do. But actually, that's not the case. The fact is, a very powerful person has made you an attractive choice on a level where it's very hard for you to refuse him, a choice to let your conscience go to sleep and leave all moral decisions up to someone else. Because you were approached on that particular level, you've no way of judging whether this was a wise decision to make, or not. Do you follow me so far? Nod your head if you do."

Jason nodded. He was concentrating just hard enough to bring a small frown line into being between his eyebrows. But otherwise his face was still relaxed and happy.

"Essentially what you've just been told," Hal said, "is that the man who spoke to you, or people designated by him, will decide not only what's right for you, but what you'll choose to do; and you've agreed that this would be a good thing. Because of that, you've now joined those who've already made that agreement with him; those who were until an hour ago your enemies, in that they were trying to destroy the faith you've held to all your life. . . ."

The slight frown was deepening between Jason's brows and the happiness on his face was being replaced by a strained expression. Hal talked on; and when at last he stopped, Jason was huddled on the other seat, turned as far away from Hal as the close confines of the booth would allow, with his face hidden in his hands.

Hal sat, feeling miserable himself, because the other man was, and tried to drink his coffee. The silence between them continued, until finally Jason heaved a long, shivering sigh and dropped his hands. He turned a face to Hal that looked as if it had not slept for two nights.

"Oh, God!" he said.

Hal looked back at him, but did not try to say anything.

"I'm unclean," said Jason. "Unclean!"

"Nonsense," said Hal. Jason's eyes jumped to his face; and Hal made himself grin at the other. "What's that I seem to remember hearing when I was young—and you must remember hearing—about the sin of pride? What makes you feel you're special in having knuckled under to the persuasion of someone like that?"

"I lacked faith!" said Jason. "I turned and loved that spawn of Belial who spoke to us."

"We all lack faith to some extent," Hal said. "There are probably some men and women so strong in their faith that he wouldn't have been able to touch them. I had a teacher once . . . but the point is, that everyone else in that room gave in to him, just as you did."

"*You* didn't!"

"I've had special training," said Hal. "That's what I was telling you just now, remember? What that man did, he succeeded in doing because he's also had special training. Believe me, someone without training would have had to have been a very remarkable person to resist him. But for someone with training, it was . . . relatively easy."

Jason drew another deep, ragged breath.

"Then I'm ashamed for another reason," he said bleakly.

"Why?" Hal stared at him.

"Because I thought you were a spy, planted on me by the dogs of the Belial-spawn, when they decided to hold me captive. When we heard Howard Immanuelson had died of a lung disease in a Holding Station on Coby, we all assumed his papers had been lost. The thought that someone else of the faith could find them and use them—and his doing it would be so secret that someone like myself wouldn't know—that was stretching coincidence beyond belief. And you were so quick to pick up the finger speech. So I was going to pretend I was taken in by you. I was going to bring you with me to someplace where the other brothers and sisters of the Children of God's Just Wrath could question you; and find out why you were sent and what you knew about us."

He stared burningly at Hal.

"And then you, just now, brought me back from Hell—from where I could never have come back without you. There was no need for you to do that if you had been one of the enemy, one of the Accursed. How could I have doubted that you were of the faith?"

"Quite easily," said Hal. "As far as bringing you back from Hell, all I did was hurry up the process a little. The kind of persuasion that was used on you takes permanently only with people who basically agree with the persuader to begin with. With those who don't, his type of mind-changing gets eaten away gradually by the natural feelings of the individual until over time it wears thin and breaks down. Since you're someone opposed enough to fight him, the only way he could stop you permanently would be to kill you."

"Why didn't he then?" asked Jason. "Why didn't he kill all of us?"

"Because it's to his advantage to pretend that he only opens people's eyes to the right way to live," said Hal, hearing an echo of Walter the InTeacher in the words even as he said them. He had not consciously stopped to think the matter out, but Jason's question had evoked the obvious answer. "Even his convinced followers feel safer if that particular man is always right, always merciful. What he did with us, there, wasn't because we were important, but because the two men with him on the platform were important— to him. There're really only a handful of what you call the Belial-spawn, compared to the trillions of people on the fourteen worlds. Those like him don't have the time, even if they felt like it, to control everyone personally. So, whenever possible they use the same sort of social mechanisms that've been used down the centuries when a few people wanted to command many."

Jason sat watching him for a long moment.

"Who are you, Howard?" he asked at last.

"I'm sorry." Hal hesitated. "I can't tell you that. But I should tell you you've no obligation to call me brother. I'm afraid I lied to you. I'm not of the faith, as you call it. I've got nothing to do with whatever organization you and those with you belong to. But I really am running from those like the man we're talking about."

"Then you're a brother," said Jason, simply. He picked up his own cup of cold coffee and drank deeply from it. "We—those the Accursed call the Children—are of every sect and every possible interpretation of the Idea of God. Your difference from the rest of us isn't any greater than our differences from each other. But I'm glad you told me this; because I'll have to tell the others about you when we reach them."

"Reach them?" asked Hal. He had not been thinking of going anywhere with Jason. The experience they had just had made it clear that the local authorities were under Bleys' control. As far as he had any specific plans at all, they were to continue hiding, but . . . with these people, he could at least do that; and maybe, finally, find some way to oppose Bleys, somehow.

"Can we reach them?" he asked now.

"There's no problem in that," said Jason. "I'll make contact in town here with someone who'll know where the closest band of Warriors is, right now; and we'll join them. Out in the countryside, we of the faith still control. Oh, they chase us, but they can't do more than keep us on the move. It's only here, in the cities, that the Belial-spawn and their minions rule."

He slid to the end of the booth and stood up.

"Come along," he said.

Out in the coldly-damp air of the street, they located a callbox and coded for an autocab. In succession, changing cabs each time, they visited a clothing store, a library and a gymnasium, without Jason recognizing anyone he trusted enough to ask for help. Their fourth try brought them to a small vehicle custom-repair garage in the northern outskirts of Citadel.

The garage itself was a dome-like temporary structure perched in an open field on the city's edge; out where residences gave way to small personal farmplots rented by city dwellers on an annual basis. It occupied an open stretch of stony ground that was its own best demonstration of why it had not been put to personal farming the way the land around it had. Inside the barely-heated dome, the air of which was thick with the faintly banana-like smell of a local tree oil used for lubrication, hanging like an invisible mist over the half-dismantled engines of several surface vehicles, they found a single occupant—a square, short, leathery man in his sixties, engaged in reassembling the rear support fan of an all-terrain four-place cruiser.

"Hilary!" said Jason, as they reached him.

"Jase—" said the worker, barely glancing up at them. "When did you get back?"

"Yesterday," said Jason. "The Accursed put us up overnight in their special hotel. This is Howard Immanuelson. Not of the faith, but one of our allies. From Coby."

"Coby?" Hilary glanced up once more at Hal. "What did you do on Coby?"

"I was a miner," said Hal.

Hilary reached for a cleansing rag, wiped his hands, turned about and offered one of them to Hal.

"Long?" he asked.

"Three years."

Hilary nodded.

"I like people who know how to work," he said. "You two on the run?"

"No," said Jason. "They turned us loose. But we need to get out into the country. Who's close right now?"

Hilary looked down at his hands and wiped them once more on his rag, then threw it into a wastebin.

"Rukh Tamani," he said. "She and her people're passing through, on their way to something. You know Rukh?"

"I know of her," said Jason. "She's a sword of the Lord."

"You might connect up with them. Want me to give you a map?"

"Please," said Jason. "And if you can supply us—"

"Clothes and gear, that's all," said Hilary. "Weapons are getting too risky."

"Can you take us close to her, at all?"

"Oh, I can get you fairly well in." Hilary looked at Hal. "Jase's no problem. But anything I'll be able to give you in the way of clothes is going to fit pretty tight."

"Let's try what you've got," said Jason.

Hilary led them to a partitioned-off corner of his dome. The door they went through let them into a storeroom piled to the ceiling with a jumble of containers and goods of all kinds. Hilary threaded his way among the stacks to a pile of what seemed to be mainly clothing and camping gear, and started pulling out items.

Twenty minutes later, he had them both outfitted with heavy bush clothing including both shoulder and belt packs and camping equipment. As Hilary had predicted, Hal's shirt, jacket and undershirt were tight in the shoulders and short in the sleeves. Otherwise, everything that he had given Hal fitted well enough. The one particular blessing turned out to be the fact that there were bush boots available of the proper length for Hal's feet. They were a little too wide, but extra socks and insoles took care of that.

"Now," Hilary said when the outfitting was complete. "When did you eat last?"

Hunger returned to Hal's consciousness like a body blow. Unconsciously, once it had become obvious in the cell that there was no hope of food soon, he had blocked out his need for it—strongly enough that he had even sat in the coffee place with Jason and not thought of food, when he could have had it for the ordering. As it was, Jason answered before he did.

"We didn't. Not since we got off the ship."

"Then I better feed you, hadn't I?" grunted Hilary. He led them out of the storeroom and into another corner of the dome that had a cot, sink, food-keeper and cooking equipment.

He fed them an enormous meal, mainly of fried vegetables, local mutton and bread, washed down with quantities of a flat, semisweet beer, far removed in flavor from the native Earth product. The heavy intake of food operated on Hal like a sedative; and he reacted, once they had all piled into a battered six-place bush van, by stretching out and falling asleep.

He woke to a rhythmic sound that was the slashing of branch tips against the sides of the van. Looking out the windows on either side, he saw that they were proceeding down a forest track so narrow that bushes on either side barely allowed the van to pass. Jason and Hilary were in mid-conversation in the front seat of the van.

". . . Of course it won't stop them!" Hilary was saying. "But if there's anything at all the Belial-spawn are even a little sensitive to, it's public opinion. If Rukh and her Command can take care of the Core Shaft Tap, it'll be a choice for the Others of either starving Hope, Valleyvale, and the other local cities, or shifting the ship outfitting to the Core Tap center on South Promise. It'll save them trouble to shift. It's a temporary spoke in their wheel, that's all; but what more can we ask?"

"We can ask to win," said Jason.

"God allowed the Belial-spawn to gain control in our cities," said Hilary. "In His time, He'll release us from them. Until then, our job is only to testify for Him by doing all we can to resist them."

Jason sighed.

"Hilary," he said. "Sometimes I forget you're just like the other old folk, when it comes to anything that looks like an act of God's will."

"You haven't lived long enough yet," Hilary said. "To you, everything seems to turn on what's happened in your own few years. Get older and look around the fourteen worlds, and you'll see that the time of Judgment's not that far off. Our race is old and sick in sin. On every world, things are falling into disorder and decay; and the coming among us of these mixed breeds who'd make everyone else into their personal cattle is only one more sign of the approach of Judgment."

"I can't take that attitude," said Jason, shaking his head. "We wouldn't be capable of hope, if hope had no meaning."

"It's got meaning," said Hilary, "in a practical sense. Forcing the spawn to change their plans to another core tap delays them; and who's to know but that very delay may be part of the battle plan of the Lord, as He girds His loins to fight this last and greatest fight?"

The noise of the branches hitting the sides and windows of the van ceased suddenly. They had emerged into an open area overgrown only by tall, straight-limbed conifers—variforms of some Earthly stock—spaced about upon uneven, rocky ground that had hardly any covering beyond patches of green moss and brown, dead needles fallen from the trees. The local sun, for the first time Hal had seen it since he had arrived on Harmony, was breaking through a high-lying mass of white and black clouds, wind-torn here and there to show occasional patches of startling blue and brilliant light. The ground-level breeze blew strongly against the van; and for the first time Hal became aware that their way had been for some time uphill. With that recognition, the realization followed that the plant life and the terrain indicated a considerably higher altitude than that of Citadel.

Hal sat up on the seat.

"You alive back there?" asked Hilary.

"Yes," answered Hal.

"We'll be there in a few minutes, Howard," said Jason. "Let me talk to Rukh about you, first. It'll be her decision as to whether you're allowed to join her group, or not. If she won't have you, I'll come back with you, too; and we'll stay together until Hilary can find a group that'll have us both."

"You'll be on your own, if I have to take you back," said Hilary. "I can't afford to keep you around my place for fear of attracting attention."

"We know that," said Jason.

The van went up and over a rise in the terrain, and nosed down abruptly into a valley-like depression that was like a knife-cut in the slope. Some ten or twenty meters below was the bed of the valley, with a small stream running through it; the stream itself hardly visible because of the thick cluster of small green-needled trees that grew about its moisture. The van slid down the slope of the valley wall on the air-cushion of its fans, plunged in among the trees, and came to a halt at a short distance from the near edge of the stream. From above, Hal had seen nothing of people or shelters; but suddenly they were in the midst of a small encampment.

He took it in at one glance. It was a picture that was to stay in his mind afterwards. Brightly touched by a moment of the sunlight breaking through the ragged clouds overhead, he saw a number of collapsible shelters like bee-hives, the height of a grown man, their olive-colored side panels and tops further camouflaged by tree branches fastened about them. Two men were standing in the stream, apparently washing clothes. A woman approaching middle age, in a black, leather-like jacket, was just coming out of the trees to the left of the van. On a rock in the center of the clearing sat a gray-haired man with a cone rifle half-torn-down for cleaning, its parts lying on a cloth he had spread across his knees. Facing him, and turning now to face the van, was a tall, slim, dark young woman in a somber green bush jacket, its many square pockets bulging with their contents. Below the bush jacket, she wore heavy, dark brown bush pants tucked into the tops of short boots. A gun-belt and sidearm was hooked tightly about her narrow waist, the black hol-ster holding the sidearm with its weather flap clipped firmly down.

She wore nothing on her head. Her black hair was cut short about her ears, and her deeply-bronzed face was narrow and perfect below a wide brow and brilliant, dark eyes. In that single, arrested moment, the repressed poet in Hal woke, and the thought came into his mind that she was like the dark blade of a sword in the sunlight. Then his attention was jerked from her. In a series of flashing motions the disassembled parts of the cone rifle in the hands of the gray-haired man were thrown back together, ending with the hard slap of a new rod of cones into the magazine slot below the barrel. The man was almost as swift as Hal had seen Malachi in similar demonstrations. The movements of this man did not have the smooth, unitary flow of Malachi's—but he was almost as fast.

"All right," said the woman in the bush jacket. "It's Hilary."

The hands of the gray-haired man relaxed on the now-ready weapon; but the weapon itself still lay on the cloth over his knees, pointing in the gen-eral direction of Hal and the other two.

"I brought you a couple of recruits," said Hilary, as cooly as if the man on the rock were holding a stick of candy. He started to walk forward and Jason moved after him. Hal followed.

"This is Jason Rowe," said Hilary. "Maybe you know him. The other's not of the faith, but a friend. He's Howard Immanuelson, a miner from Coby."

By the time he had finished saying this he was within two meters of the woman and the man. He stopped. The woman glanced at Jason, nodded briefly, then turned her brilliant gaze on Hal.

"Immanuelson?" she said. "I'm Rukh Tamani. This is my Lieutenant, James Child-of-God."

Hal found it hard to look away from her, but he turned his gaze on the face of the gray-haired man. He found himself looking into a rectangular, rawboned set of features, clothed in skin gone leathery some years since from sun and weather. Lines radiated from the corners of the eyes of James Child-of-God, deep parentheses had carved themselves about his mouth from nose to chin, and the pale blue eyes he fastened on Hal were like the muzzles of armed rifles.

"If not of the faith," he said now, in a flat tenor voice, "he hath no right here among us."

Since he had left his home, Hal had until this moment encountered no Friendly cast in the mold he knew, the mold of Obadiah. Now, he recognized one at last. But this man was Obadiah with a difference.

Chapter

> > 16 < <

There was a moment of silence. The soft fingers of the breeze came through the trees across the stream, quartering past Rukh Tamani and James Child-of-God, and cooled Hal's left cheek as he stood, still facing them.

"He's not of that special faith that's ours," said Jason. "But he's a hunted enemy of the Belial-spawn and that makes him our ally."

Rukh looked at him.

"And you?"

"I've worked for the faith, these past eight years," Jason said. "I was one of the Warriors in Charity City, even when I was going to college. Columbine and Oliver McKeutcheon both had me in their Commands at different times—"

He turned to nod at Hilary.

"Hilary knows about this. He knows me."

"He's right," said Hilary. "About all he says. I've known him five years or more."

"But you don't know this other," said James Child-of-God.

"He said he was a miner on Coby," said Hilary. "I've shaken hands with him and felt his calluses. He has them where a miner gets them, holding his torch; and the only place on the fourteen worlds they still use torches are in those mines."

"He could be a spy." The voice of James Child-of-God had the flat emotionlessness of someone commenting on statistics.

"He isn't." Jason turned to Rukh Tamani. "Can I talk to you privately about him?"

She looked at him.

"You can talk to us both privately," she said. "Come along, James."

She turned away. James Child-of-God got to his feet, still carrying the cone rifle, and, with Jason, followed her to the edge of the clearing. They stopped there, and stood together, talking.

Hal waited. His eyes met Hilary's briefly; and Hilary gave him the ghost of a smile, which could have been intended as reassurance. Hal smiled back and looked away again.

He was conscious of his old, familiar feeling of nakedness and loneliness. It had come back upon him, as keenly as the sensation of someone thinly dressed stepping into the breath of a chill and strong wind. At the same time, the touch of the actual breeze upon him, the scent of the open air—were all acting powerfully upon his feelings. That part of him that had always lived in and by poetry had come suddenly to life again after having slept these last years in the mine; and everything that in this moment was impinging on his mind and senses was registering itself with a sharpness he had not felt since the deaths of Walter, Obadiah and Malachi. Now, all at once, it was once more with him; and he could not imagine how he had been living these past years without it. . . .

Abruptly he woke to the fact that the conversation at the edge of the clearing had finished. Both Jason and James Child-of-God were walking back toward him. Rukh Tamani still stood alone where she had been, and she called to him, her voice carrying clearly across the distance between them.

"Come here, please."

He walked to her and stopped within arm's length.

"Jason Rowe's told us what he knows about you," she said. Her eyes were penetrating without hardness, brown with an infinity of depths to them. "He believes in you, but he could be wrong. There's nothing in what he told us that proves you aren't the spy that James is afraid you might be."

Hal nodded.

"Have you got any proof you aren't a spy, sent either by the Others or by the Militia to help them trap us?"

"No," he said.

"You understand," she said, "I can't risk my people, even to help someone who deserves help, if there's a danger. There's only one of you, but a number of us; and what we do is important."

"I know that too," he said.

They said nothing for a second.

"You don't ask our help, anyway?" she asked.

"There's no point to it, is there?" he said.

She studied him. Her face was like her eyes—unguarded, but showing no hint of what she was thinking. He found himself thinking how beautiful she was, standing here in the sunlight.

"For those of us who've taken up arms against the Others and their slaves," she said, "other proofs than paper ones can be meaningful. If that weren't so, we wouldn't be out here, fighting. But we not only don't know you or anything about you, but Jason says you refused to tell him who you really are. Is that right?"

"Yes," he said. "That's right."

Once more she watched him for a moment without speaking.

"Do you want to tell me—who you are and how you come to be here?" she said at last. "If you do, and I think what you tell me is true, we might be able to let you stay."

He hesitated. The first and most important principle of all those he had been taught, against the time when he might have to run as he had these last years, was to keep his identity secret. At the same time, something in him—and maybe it was the reawakened poetic response, was urging him strongly to stay in this place, with Rukh and these others, at any cost.

He remembered Obadiah.

"One of those who brought me up," he said, "was a man named Obadiah Testator, from Oldcontinent here on Harmony. He said once, talking about me—*my people would never give you up*. He was talking about people like you, not giving me up to the Others. Can I ask—would you give me up, once you'd accepted me? Can you think of any conditions under which you would?"

She gazed at him.

"You aren't really of Harmony or Association, are you?" she asked.

"No," he answered. "Earth."

"I thought so. That's why you don't understand. There're those on both of our worlds here who might give you up to the Others; but we don't count them among us. God doesn't count them. Once you were accepted here, not even to save the lives of all the others would we give you up, any more than we'd give up any other member of this Command. I'm explaining this to you because you're not one of us; and it's not your fault you need said what shouldn't need to be. What use would it be—all the rest we do—if we were the kind who'd buy safety or victory at the price of even one soul?"

He nodded again, very slowly.

"This Obadiah Testator of yours," she said. "Was he a man strong in his faith?"

"Yes."

"And you knew him well?"

"Yes," said Hal; and after all these years suddenly felt his throat contract remembering Obadiah.

"Then you should understand what I'm saying."

He controlled the reflex in his throat and looked once more into her eyes. They were different than the eyes of Obadiah, but they were also the same. Nor would Obadiah have betrayed him.

"I'll tell you," he said, "if no one but you has to know."

"No one does," said Rukh. "If I'm satisfied, the rest will take my word for you."

"All right, then."

Standing there at the edge of the clearing, he told her everything, from as far back as he could remember, to this moment. When he came to the deaths of Obadiah, Walter and Malachi, his throat tightened again and for a moment he could not talk about it; then he got his voice under control and went on.

"Yes," she said, when he was done, "I see why you didn't want to talk about this. Why did your tutors think the Others would be so determined to destroy you if they knew of you?"

"Walter the InTeacher explained it according to ontogenetics—you know about that Exotic discipline?"

She nodded.

"He said that since some of the Others are of Exotic extraction, they'd understand it, too; and they'd know that according to ontogenetic calculations I could represent a problem to them and what they were after. So to protect themselves, they'd try to destroy me. But if I could survive until I was mature enough to fight back, I could not only protect myself, I might even help stop them."

"I see." Rukh's dark eyes were almost luminous in the sunlight. "If I believe you—and I do—you're also a weapon of the Lord, though in your own way."

She smiled at him.

"We'll keep you. Come along."

She led him back to the little knot of standing men that was James Child-of-God, Hilary and Jason.

"Howard Immanuelson will be one of us from now on," she said to Child-of-God; and turned to face Jason. "And you, of course, if that's what you want."

"I do," said Jason. "Thank you."

"If you know the life of a Warrior, as you say you do, you know there's little to give thanks for." She turned again to Child-of-God. "James, I've just accepted Howard among us because of some things he told me in confidence, things I can't tell you or the others. But I promise you I trust him."

Child-of-God's blue eyes, hard as diamonds, fastened on Hal.

"If it is thee who say so, Rukh," he said; and added, directly to Hal, "Howard, after Rukh, I am in command here. Thou wilt remember that, at all times."

"Yes," said Hal.

"Hilary," said Rukh, "will you stay to dinner?"

"Thanks, Rukh," said Hilary, "but I'm behind with the work in my shop as it is; to say nothing of the fact I've already missed my prayers twice today getting these men out to you."

"There'll be prayers before dinner."

"Twice a day, eh?" said Hilary. "Morning and evening, and that's it? The Lord'll have a heavy account for you people one day, Rukh."

"To each his own way," she said.

"And your way is this new one of letting actions be your prayers, is that it?" Hilary sighed and looked over at Child-of-God. "How does *your* soul feel with only two moments of prayer a day?"

"I pray when God permits," said Child-of-God, nasally. "Six times daily or more, that being my way. But it's speaking to God that matters, not the bended knee or the joined hands—and indeed our Rukh serves the Lord."

His eyes glinted on Hilary.

"Or would you say that was not so?"

"No, I would not say it was not so; and you know I wouldn't say it was not so," said Hilary calmly. "But the time may come when prayer at regular times is completely forgotten on these two worlds of which so much was expected once—and if so, won't we prove to have followed in the way of the Belial-spawn after all?"

"Stay for dinner or not, Hilary," said Rukh. "We'd like to have you. But we live too close to the edge of our lives to argue practices in this camp."

Hilary shrugged.

"Forgive me, Rukh," he said. "I'm getting old; and it's hard when you get old to feel your race turning from God when we had such high hopes in our youth that one day all would acknowledge and live in His way. All right, all right, I won't say any more. But I can't stay to dinner. Thank you, anyway. When do you think you'll be out of my district?"

"In two days. Are there others you plan to bring to us?"

"No. I just wanted to know in case of emergency."

"Two days. We've one more district to sweep for makings. Then we move to supply and prepare ourselves." Rukh turned to Jason. "Jason, you take Howard around the camp and explain how we do things. Introduce him and yourself to the other members of the Command. Then come back to the cook tent. Both of you can give those on meal duty a hand with the serving of dinner. Jason, have you ever managed donkeys?"

"Yes," said Jason.

"You'll be able to help us right away, then, when we break camp and move on. In the next few days, try and teach Howard as much as you can about the animals."

She turned back to Hilary.

"And now, Hilary, we're all going to have to get to work. With luck we'll come past here again before the year's out."

"Good luck," said Hilary.

They embraced.

"And good luck to the rest of you, as well," said Hilary, soberly, sweeping Child-of-God, Jason and Hal with his glance. He turned and walked back to his van, got in and lifted it on its fans. A second later he had spun it end for end and taken it into the trees, on his way back up the slope and out of sight.

Rukh turned away, into conversation with Child-of-God. Hal felt a touch on his elbow. He turned to see Jason.

"Come on, Howard," said Jason, and led him off toward the far edge of the clearing and into the trees beside the stream there.

Chapter

> > **17** < <

In appearance, the men and women of Rukh's command seemed to Hal to be less like guerrilla fighters and more like simple refugees. The strongest impression he received as Jason led him about the confines of the camp was one of extreme poverty. Their beehive-shaped tents were patched and old. Their clothing was likewise patched and mended. Their tools, shelters, and utensils had either the marks of long wear or the unspecific, overall appearance of having been used and used again.

The weapons alone contradicted the refugee appearance, but hardly improved it. If not impoverished fugitives, they were, by all visible signs, at best an impoverished hunting party. There were apparently several dozen of them. Once among the trees, Hal revised his first estimate of their numbers upwards, for the majority of their tents were tucked back in under the greenery in such a way as not to be visible from the edge of the valley cut, above. As Jason led him along upstream to their left, they passed many men and women doing housekeeping tasks, mending, or caring for equipment or clothing.

Those he saw were all ages from late teens to their middle years. There were no children, and no really old individuals; and everyone they passed looked up at them as they went by. Some smiled, but most merely looked; not suspiciously, but with the expressions of those who reserve judgment.

They came, after about a hundred yards, to an area that was not a true opening in the trees, but one sparsely overgrown, so that patches of sunlight struck down between the trees in it, and between trees large patches of sky were visible.

Tethered each beneath a tree, at some little distance from each other, were a number of donkeys cropping the sparse grass and other ground vegetation that the sunlight had encouraged to spring up between the trees. Jason led the way to the nearest animal, patted its head, looked at its teeth and ran his hands over its back and sides.

"In good shape," he said, stepping back. "Rukh's Command won't have been too hard pressed by the Militia, lately."

He looked at Hal.

"Did you ever see donkeys before?"

"Once," said Hal. "They still have them in the Parks, on Earth, to use for camping trips."

"Did you ever have anything to do with one of them on a camping trip?" Jason asked.

Hal shook his head.

"I only saw them—and of course, I read about them when I was growing up. But I understand they're a lot like horses."

Jason laughed.

"For what good that does us," he said.

"I only meant," said Hal, "that since I've had something to do with horses, I might find what I know about them useful with these."

Jason stared at him.

"When were you on Earth long enough to learn about horses?"

Hal felt suddenly uncomfortable.

"I'm sorry," he said. "I ended up telling Rukh more than I'd told you—and I still can't tell you. But I forgot for a moment you didn't know. I've ridden and handled horses."

Jason shook his head slowly, wonderingly.

"You actually did?" he said. "Not variforms—but the original, full-spectrum horses?"

"Yes," said Hal.

He had let it slip his mind that many of Earth's mammals—even the variiforms genetically adapted as much as possible to their destination planet—had not flourished on most of the other worlds. The reasons were still not fully understood; but the indications were that, unlike humans, even the highest orders of animals were less adaptable to different environmental conditions, and particularly to solunar and other cycles that enforced changes on their biorhythms. The larger the animals, the less successful they seemed to be perpetuating their own breed under conditions off-Earth; just as, once, many wild animals were unlikely to breed in zoos on Earth. Horses, unlike the ass family, were almost unknown on other worlds, with the exception of the Dorsai, where for some reason they had flourished.

"Do you know anything about harnesses and loading a pack donkey—I mean a pack animal?" asked Jason.

Hal nodded.

"I used to go off in the mountains by myself," said Hal, "with just a riding horse and a packhorse."

Jason took a deep breath and smiled.

"Rukh'll be glad to hear this," he said. "Take a look at these donkeys, then, and tell me what you think."

Together they examined the whole string of pack beasts. To Hal's eye they were in good, if not remarkable, shape.

"But if they were my animals, back on Earth," he said, when they were done, "I'd be feeding them up on grain, or adding a protein supplement to their diet."

"No chance for that here," said Jason. "These have to live like the rest of the Command—off the country, any way they can."

The light had mellowed toward late afternoon as they made their inspection; and it was just about time for the second of the two meals of the day that would be served in the camp. Jason explained this as he led Hal back toward the main clearing.

"We get up and go to bed with the daylight out here," Jason said as they went. "Breakfast is as soon as it's light enough to see what you're eating; and dinner's just before twilight—that's going to vary, of course, if we move into upper latitudes where the day's going to be sixteen hours long in summer."

"It's spring here now, isn't it?" asked Hal.

"That's right. It's still muddy in the lowlands."

The kitchen area turned out to be a somewhat larger tent under the trees on the far side of the clearing. It was filled with food supplies and some stored-power cooking units. A serving line of supports for cooking containers were set up just outside the tent. Inside, were the cook—a slim, towheaded girl who looked barely into her middle teens—and three assistants at the other end of the age scale, a man and two women in their forties or above. The preparations for the meal were almost done, and food odors were heavy on the twilight-still air. Both Jason and Hal were put to work carrying out the large plastic cooking cans, heavily full with the various cooked foods for the meal; and setting these cans up on the supports of the serving line.

By the time this was done and they had also brought out and set up an equally large container of Harmony-style coffee, the members of the Command had begun to queue for dinner, each one having brought his or her own eating tray.

They went down the line of food cans, served by the three assistants with the aid of Jason and Hal. Hal found himself with a large soup-ladle in his hand, scooping up and delivering what seemed to be a sort of stiff gray-brown porridge, of about the consistency of turkey stuffing. To his right Jason was ladling up what was either a gravy or some kind of sauce that went over what Hal had just served.

When the last of those who had gathered had gone through the line the assistants took their turn, followed by Jason and Hal with trays they had been given from the supply tent. Last of all to help herself was the cook, whose name apparently was Tallah. She took only a dab of the foods she had just made, and carried it back into her supply tent to eat.

Jason and Hal turned aside from the serving line with loaded trays, looking for a comfortable spot of earth to sit on. Most of the other eaters had carried their trays back to their tents or wherever they had come from.

"Howard, come here, please. I'd like to talk to you."

The clear voice of Rukh made him turn. She and Child-of-God were seated with their trays, some twenty yards off at the edge of the clearing. Rukh was seated on the large end of a fallen log and Child-of-God was perched on the stump of it, from which age and weather had separated the upper part. Hal went over to them, and sat down cross-legged on the ground, facing them with his tray on his knees.

"Jason showed you around, did he?" Rukh asked. "Go ahead and eat. We can all talk and eat at the same time."

Hal dug into his own ladleful of the porridge-like food he had been serving. It did taste a little like stuffing—stuffing with nuts in it. He noticed that Child-of-God's tray held only a single item, a liquid stew of mainly green vegetables; and it occurred to him that only in one of the cans at the serving line had he seen anything resembling meat—and that had been only as an occasional grace note of an ingredient.

"Yes," he answered Rukh, "we walked through the camp and had a look at the donkeys. Jason seems to think the fact that I've had something to do with horses on Earth would help me be useful with them."

Rukh's eyebrows went up.

"It will," she said. She looked, as Jason had predicted, pleased, and put her fork down. "As I promised you, I haven't said anything to anyone, including James, of what you told me. Still, James—as second-in-command—needs to know much of what I need to know about your usefulness to us. So I asked him to listen while I ask you some specific questions."

Hal nodded, eating and listening. The food tasted neither as dull nor as strange as he had been afraid it would when he was helping to serve it; and his ever-ready appetite was driving him.

"I notice you aren't carrying anything in the way of a weapon," Rukh said. "Even bearing in mind what you told me, I have to ask if you've got some objection to using weapons?"

"No objection, in principle," Hal said. "But I've got to be honest with you. I've handled a lot of weapons and practiced with them. But I've never faced the possibility of using one. I don't know what'll happen if I do."

"No one knows," said Child-of-God. Hal looked at the other man and found his eyes watching. It was not a stare that those hard blue eyes bent upon him—it was too open to be a stare. Strangely, Child-of-God looked at him with an unwavering, unyielding openness that was first cousin to the nakedness of gaze found in a very young child. "When thou hast faced another under conditions of battle, thou and all else will know. Until then, such things are secrets of God."

"What are the weapons you've practiced with?" asked Rukh.

"Cone rifle, needle rifle, slug-throwers of all kinds, all varieties of power rifles and sidearms, staffs and sticks, knives, ax, sling, spear, bow and crossbow, chain and—" Hal broke off, suddenly self-conscious at the length of the list. "As I said, though, it was just practice. In fact, I used to think it was just one kind of playing, when I was young."

Child-of-God turned his head slowly to look at Rukh. Rukh looked back at him.

"I have reason to believe Howard in this," she said to Child-of-God.

Child-of-God looked back at Hal, then his eyes jumped off to focus on Tallah, who had suddenly appeared at his elbow.

"Give me your tray," Tallah said, holding out her hand, "and I'll fill it for you."

"Thou wilt not," said Child-of-God. "I know thee, and thy attempts to lead me into sin."

"All I was going to do was refill it," said Tallah, "with that mess you try to live on. I don't care if you get a vitamin deficiency and die. Why should I care? We can get another second-in-command anywhere."

"Thou dost not cozen me. I know thy tricks, adding that which I should not eat to my food. I've caught thee in that trick before, Tallah."

"Well, you just die, then!" said Tallah. She was, Hal saw, very angry indeed. "Go ahead and die!"

"Hush," said Rukh to her.

"Why don't you order him to eat?" Tallah turned on her. "He'd eat some decent food if you ordered him."

"Would you, James?" Rukh asked the older man.

"I would not," said Child-of-God.

"He would if you really ordered him."

"Hush, I said," said Rukh. "If it becomes really necessary, James, I may have to order you to eat foods you consider sinful. But for now, at least, you can eat a decent amount of what you will eat. If I refill your tray will you trust me not to put anything in it you wouldn't take yourself?"

"I trust thee, of course," said Child-of-God, harshly. "How could it be otherwise?"

"Good," said Rukh.

She stood up, took the tray from his hand and was halfway to the serving line before he started to his feet and went after her.

"But I need no waiting on—" he called after her. He caught up; and they went to the food container holding his vegetable stew together.

"These Old Prophets!" said Tallah, furiously, turning to Hal. She glared at him for a moment, then broke suddenly into a grin. "You don't understand?"

"I ought to," Hal said. "I have the feeling I ought to know what this is all about, but I don't."

"There aren't many like him left, that's why," said Tallah. "Where did you grow up?"

"Not on Harmony," said Hal.

"That explains it. Association's hardly a comparable world of the Lord. James—now don't you go calling him James to his face!"

"I shouldn't?"

"None of us, except Rukh, call him James to his face. Anyway, he's one of those who still hang on to the old dietary rules most of the sects had when we were so poor everyone ate grass and weeds to stay alive—and when anything not optimum for survival was supposed to be flying directly in the face of the Lord's will. There's no human reason now for him to try to live on that antique diet—as if God wouldn't forgive him one step out of the way, after the way he's fought for the faith all his life, let alone he calls himself one of the Elect."

Hal remembered that the self-designated Elect in any of the sects on Harmony or Association were supposed to be certain of Heaven no matter what they did, simply because they had been specially chosen by God.

"—And we can't, we just can't, get the vegetables he'll eat all the time, on the move as we are. There's no way to give him a full and balanced diet from what we have. Rukh'll just have to end by ordering him to eat."

"Why hasn't she done it before?" Hal tasted his own portion of the vegetable stew that had been the only thing on Child-of-God's tray. It was strange, peppery and odd-flavored, not hard to eat but hardly satisfying.

"Because he'd still blame himself for breaking his dietary laws even if it wasn't his fault he broke them—here they come, and at least she got his tray decently filled."

Tallah went off. Rukh and Child-of-God came and sat down again.

"We've got two tasks," Rukh said to Hal. "In the coming months we'll be trying to do them while dodging the Militia and covering a couple of thousand kilometers of territory. If we get caught by the Militia, I'll expect you to fight; and if we don't, I'll expect you to work like everyone else in the Command; which means as hard as you can from the time you get up in the morning until you fall into your bedsack at night. In return for this, we'll try to feed you and keep you alive and free. This Command, like all those hunted by the slaves of the Others, doesn't have any holidays, or any time off. It spends all its time trying to survive. Do you understand what you're getting into?"

"I think so," said Hal. "In any case, if I were trying to survive out here by myself, it'd be a lot worse for me than what you describe."

"That's true enough." Rukh nodded. "Then, there're two things more. One is, I'll expect you to give instant and unquestioning obedience to any command I give you, or James gives you. Are you capable of that, and agreeable to it?"

"That was one of the first things I learned, growing up," Hal said. "How to obey when necessary."

"All right. One more point. Jason's been with a Command before, and he's also of the faith. You'll notice in the next few weeks that he'll be fitted right in with the rest of us, according to his capacities. You, on the other hand, are a stranger. You don't know our ways. Because of that, you'll find that everyone else in camp outranks you; and one result of that is going to be that almost everyone is going to end up giving you orders at one time or another. Do you think you can obey those orders as quickly and willingly as you can the ones from James and myself?"

"Yes," said Hal.

"You're going to have to, if you plan to stay with us," Rukh said, "and you may find it's not as easy as you think. There'll be times when something like your training with weapons is concerned, when you may be positive you know a good deal more than the person who's telling you what to do. In spite of how you feel then, you're still going to have to obey—or leave. Because without that kind of obedience, our Command can't survive."

"I can do that," said Hal.

"Good. I promise you, in the long run you'll get credit for every real ability you can show us. But we can't take the time or the risk of accepting you as anything but the last in line, and keeping you that way, until we know better."

Rukh went back to her eating.

"Is that all?" asked Hal. His own tray was empty and he had visions of not being able to get back to the serving line in time to refill it.

"That's all," said Rukh. "After you've finished eating, help the cook people to clean up, then look up Jason. He'll have found a tent and equipment for the two of you. Once you're set up in that respect, if it's already dark, you'd probably better turn in, although you're welcome to join whoever's around the campfire. Think before you stay up too late, though. You've got a long day tomorrow, and every day."

"Right. Thanks," said Hal.

He scrambled to his feet and went back to the serving line. There he filled and emptied another trayful of food, then hesitated over taking a third until Tallah saw his uncertainty and told him it was all right to eat as much as he wanted.

". . . For now, anyway," she said. "When the Command's short on rations, you'll know it, everyone'll know it. Right now we're fine. We're in rich country and it's good to see people eat."

"Rich country?" Hal asked.

She laughed.

"This is a district where there're plenty of the faithful, and they've got food and other things they can afford to share with us."

"I see."

"And when you're done, you'd better get busy with these serving cans. Take them down to the stream and wash them. Then you can go."

Hal ate, cleaned the cans and went. It was unmistakably twilight now. He cast about under the trees for Jason, hoping to find him without having to ask. Finally, he was reduced to querying a nearly-bald, but still young-looking, man, who was seated cross-legged in front of one of the tents, putting new cleats on the bottoms of a pair of boots.

The man spat staples out of his mouth, caught them in the palm of his left hand, shifted his hammer to join them, and reached up with his right hand to clasp Hal's.

"Joralmon Troy," he said. "You're Howard Immanuelson?"

"Yes," said Hal, shaking hands.

"Jason Rowe's set a tent up for the two of you back by the beasts. He's either there now, or still feeding and caring for them. You're not of the faith?"

"I'm afraid not," said Hal.

"But you're not a scorner of God?"

"From as far back as I can remember, I was taught never to scorn anything."

"Then that's all right," said Joralmon. "Since God is all things, one who scorns nothing, scorns not Him."

He put boots, hammer and staples aside, just inside the front entrance of his tent.

"Time for evening prayers," he said. "Some pray separately, but there are those of us who gather, night and morning. You're always welcome if you wish to come."

He looked up at Hal, getting to his feet as he spoke. There was an openness and simple directness to his gaze that was a less intense version of what Hal had seen in Child-of-God.

"I don't know if I can, tonight," said Hal.

He went back through the twilit woods toward the area where the donkeys had been tethered. With the shadows growing long all about him the forest seemed vaster, the trees taller, reaching pillar-like up to support the dimming sky. A more chill breath of air wandered among the tree trunks and cooled him as he went.

He found the tent off to one side of the area where the donkeys were tethered, next to a larger one that had its entrance flaps pressed together and sealed. A faint, musty odor came from the sealed tent.

"Howard!"

Jason came around the far side of the tent, smiling.

"What do you think of it?" he said.

Hal looked at the tent. Back on Earth it would have been inconceivable to house himself in such a structure without either replacing it or remaking it completely. It had been a good example of a beehive tent once, of a size to sleep four people, with their packs and possessions for a two-week trip. Now it was shrunken by virtue of the many repairs that had been made in its skin and looked as if its fabric might split from old age at any minute.

"You've done a good job," said Hal.

"It was sheer luck they had one to give us," said Jason. "I was all prepared to start building a lean-to of branches to tuck our bedsacks under—oh, by the way, they had liners for our bedsacks, too. We'll need them at this altitude."

"How high are we?" asked Hal, as he ducked his head to follow Jason into the tent. Within, under the patched fabric with its smells of food and weapon oil, Jason had the bedsacks laid out on opposite sides of the equally-patched floor, with the feet meeting underneath the highest arc-point of the tent's main support rib. Their packs and other equipment were near the heads of the sacks, but stowed prudently away from possible condensation on the tent's inner surface. Jason touched a glow-tube fastened to the main rib above the feet of the bedsacks, and a small, friendly yellow light illuminated the shadowy interior.

"A little over two thousand meters," said Jason. "We'll be going higher when we leave here."

He was obviously warm with happiness and pride over their tent; but trying not to lead Hal deliberately into praise and compliments.

"This is very good," said Hal, looking around him. "How did you do it?"

"The credit's all due the people of this Command," said Jason. "They were able to give us everything. I knew you'd be surprised."

"I am," said Hal.

"Well, now you've seen it," said Jason, "let's go sit by the main fire for a bit and meet people. We have to help the cook crew, but then we'll be getting ready to move on, tomorrow."

They extinguished the glow-tube and left the tent. The campfire to which Rukh and Joralmon had also referred was in a place away from the rest of the camp, on the bank upstream beyond the far edge of the clearing. It was a large fire and it warmed an equally-large dispenser of coffee, Jason explained, which served as a focal point for whoever wished to come by and mingle, after the day's work and prayers were done. When Hal and Jason arrived, there were six men and two women already sitting around drinking coffee and talking with each other; and in the next half hour that number tripled.

The two of them helped themselves to coffee and sat down by the pleasant light and heat of the fire. One by one introductions were exchanged with the others already there, and then the rest went back to the conversations they had been having when Hal and Jason arrived.

"What's in that tent just behind us, here?" Hal asked Jason.

Jason grinned.

"Makings," he said, in a lowered voice.

"Makings?" Hal waited for Jason to explain, but Jason merely continued to grin.

"I don't understand," Hal said. "What do you mean by 'makings'?"

"Makings for an experiment. A—a military weapon," said Jason, still softly. "Not refined yet."

Hal frowned. Jason's tone had been reluctant. He looked at the expression on Jason's face, which struck him as most peculiar. Then he remembered Jason's words about the lack of privacy in the latrine corner of their cell in the city Militia Headquarters.

"I can tell by the smell," he said, "it's organic matter. What kind is it, in that tent?"

"Shh," said Jason, "no need to shout it out. Bodily fluids."

"Bodily fluids? Which? Urine?"

"Shh."

Hal stared at him, but obediently lowered his voice.

"Is there some reason I shouldn't—"

"Not at all!" said Jason, still keeping his own voice down. "But no decent person goes shouting out words like that. It's the only way we can make it;

but there're enough dirty jokes and songs about the process as it is."

Hal changed ground.

"What sort of weapon do you need urine for?" he asked. "All the weapons I've seen around here have been cone rifles or needle guns—except for a few power sidearms like the one Rukh carries."

Jason stared at him.

"How do you know it's a power sidearm that Rukh's carrying? She never unsnaps that holster cover unless she has to use the pistol."

Hal had to stop and think how he did know. The fact that Rukh's sidearm was a power weapon had merely been self-evident until this moment.

"By its weight," he said, after a second. "The way it drags on her weapon belt shows its weight. Among weapons, only a powered one weighs in that proportion to its size."

"Excuse me," said a voice over their heads. They looked up to see a heavy-bodied, thin-limbed man who looked to be about Child-of-God's age, standing over them in heavy jacket and bush trousers. "I'm Morelly Walden. I've been out of camp on an errand and I didn't get to meet you two, yet. Which one of you is Jason Rowe?"

"I am," said Jason as both he and Hal got to their feet and clasped hands in turn with Walden. The other man's rectangular face had few wrinkles, but the skin of it was toughened and dry.

"I knew Columbine, and he mentioned you'd been in his Command once. And you are . . . ?"

"Howard Immanuelson."

"Not from this world? You're from Association?"

"No, as a matter of fact I'm not from either Harmony or Association."

"Ah. Well, welcome, nonetheless."

Walden spoke to Jason about members of Columbine's Command. Others also came from time to time and introduced themselves. Jason was kept busy talking to them, but beyond introducing themselves they did not offer to talk at any length with Hal.

He sat listening and watching the fire. The instinct in animals and small children, Walter the InTeacher had told him—the instinct, in fact, of people of any age—was to first circle any stranger and sniff him out, get used to his intrusion into their cosmos; and then, only when they were ready, to make the first move to communicate themselves. When the other members of Rukh's command began to feel comfortable with his presence, Hal assumed, they would find occasion to talk to him.

Meanwhile, he was content. This morning he had been an isolated stranger, adrift in a strange world. Now, he had a place in it. There was a close feeling around the campfire, the atmosphere like that of a family, that he had not felt since his tutors' deaths, except for that one day in the mine after he had made torcher. A family together at the end of the day. While some of the conversations he heard were purely social, others were discussions of shared responsibilities, or shared problems being discussed by people who had been physically separated by the day's events until now. As more members of the Command drifted in around the fire, more wood was added to it. The flames reached up; and their light enlarged the apparent interior area of the globe of night that enclosed them all. The firelight made a room in the darkness. They were private in the midst of the outdoors, housed by immaterial walls of warmth and familiarity and mutual concerns.

Altogether, the situation and the moment once more woke that same urge to poetry in him that had first come back to life with his first sight of Rukh. But it was not the urge to make poetic images that touched him now. It was the memory of poetry in his past.

It is long, the night of our waiting,
But we have a call to stay. . . .

They were the first two lines of a poem he had written when he had been ten years old and drunk with the image of the great picture Walter the In-Teacher had painted for him; a picture of the centuries-long search of the Exotics for an evolved form of humankind, a better race, grown beyond its present weaknesses and faults. Like most of the poems of extreme youth, what power it possessed had been all in the first couple of lines, and from there it had gone downhill into triteness. Since then, he had learned not to go so fast to the setting down of the first words that came to mind. It took restraint and experience to do deliberately what amateur poets tended to do only unconsciously—carry the poem around in the back of the mind until it was complete and ready to be born.

He lost himself now in just that process—not forcing his mind into any mold, but under the influence of the surrounding darkness and the firelight letting the powerful creative forces of the unconscious drift uncontrolled, forming images and memories, good and bad, recent and distant.

Making mental pictures in the city of the white-red embers glowing beneath the burning logs, he watched armies march and builders build; while Sost and Walter, Malachi and Tonina, mixed and mingled in his thoughts and the ghost of Obadiah stood around the fire, talking with the living bodies with whom Hal shared its warmth.

Now that he stood back and looked at himself, something in him had healed with the three years on Coby; but much else was still either unhealed or unfinished. Somewhere, there was waiting a purpose to his life; but he had let that fact be forgotten, until he had driven into the clearing this afternoon and seen Rukh, Child-of-God, and now these others. There must be a purpose because it was unthinkable that life could be otherwise. . . .

So he continued, sitting, dreaming and thinking, occasionally interrupting himself to reply to an introduction or some brief word from other members of the Command, until he was roused by a touch on his arm. He turned and saw Jason.

"Howard," said Jason. "I'm turning in. You can keep the fire going here as long as you want, even by yourself, but dawn comes early."

Hal nodded, suddenly aware that the gathering had shrunk to only a handful of people. Two pairs of individuals, and one group of three, were deep in private conversations. Otherwise, only he and Jason were left.

"No," he said. "Thanks, but you're right. I'll fold up too."

He got to his feet, and they went off into the dark. Away from the fire, the night at first seemed pitch-black, but gradually their eyes adjusted to show the moonlit woods. Even with this, however, the area held a different appearance at night; and they might have wandered indefinitely in search of their tent, if Jason had not produced and lit a pinhole torch. The beam of the torch picked up eye-level reflectors pinned onto trees to mark out the numbered routes throughout the camp. They followed the route that led back to the clearing; and there Jason picked out what was evidently the line of reflectors that would lead them to the tethering place of the donkeys, and their tent.

The tent itself was a welcome place to step into at last; and Hal recognized, as Jason turned out the glow-tube and he pulled the hood of his own bedsack into place to keep the top of his head warm, that he was ready and overready for sleep. Exhaustion was like a warm bath relaxing all his limbs; and even while thinking this, he was asleep.

He awoke suddenly, holding somebody's throat in the darkness, so that whoever it was could not cry out or breathe. A twist of his thumbs would have broken the neck he held. But swiftly—though it seemed slowly—the odors of the tent, the smell of the camping gear and clothing, brought him back to a realization of where he was. It was Jason he was holding and strangling.

He let go. He got to his feet; and, reaching out in the darkness, found and turned on the glow-tube. Yellow light showed Jason lying on the floor of the tent, breathing now, but otherwise not making a sound, staring up at him with wide-open eyes.

Chapter

> > 18 < <

"*Are you all* right?" asked Hal numbly. "What happened?"

Jason's lips worked without a sound. He lifted a hand and felt his throat. At last his voice came, huskily.

"I woke and heard you breathing," he said. "Then, suddenly, your breathing stopped. I called to you to wake you up, but you didn't answer. I crawled over to see if you were still there, and you were—but you weren't breathing at all. I tried to shake your shoulder to wake you. . . . "

His voice ran down.

"And I woke up and grabbed your throat," said Hal.

Jason nodded, still staring up at him.

"I'm sorry," said Hal. "I don't know why I did that. I wasn't even awake. I'm sorry."

Jason got slowly to his feet. They looked at each other with their faces only a few hand-widths apart in the yellow light of the glow-tube.

"You're dangerous, Howard," said Jason, in an expressionless voice.

"I know," said Hal, unhappily. "I'm sorry."

"No," said Jason, "it's good for this Command to have dangerousness like that on our side, against our enemies. But what made you attack me?"

"I don't know."

"It was because I woke you suddenly, wasn't it?"

"I suppose," said Hal. "But even then . . . I don't usually go around attacking anyone who wakes me suddenly."

"Were you dreaming?"

"I don't remember. . . ." Hal made an effort to remember. "Yes."

"A bad dream?"

"In a way . . . ," said Hal.

"A bad dream. It's not surprising," said Jason. "Many of us know what it's like to have that sort of dream. It's all right. As long as we're both awake now, let's have some coffee."

Hal shivered.

"Yes," he said. "That's a good idea."

Jason turned to a corner of the tent and came up with a temperature-sealed plastic container that looked as if it might hold about a liter of liquid.

"I filled it after dinner—I meant to tell you it was here," he said, almost shyly. He pressed the thumb-stop to jet a stream of dark liquid, steaming in the chill air of the nighttime tent, into a couple of plastic cups. He handed one filled cup to Hal and got back into the warmth of his own bedsack, sitting up with it around him.

Hal imitated him. They looked at each other across the width of the tent.

"Would you want to tell me what the dream was?" Jason asked.

"I don't know if I can," said Hal. "It wasn't very clear. . . ."

"Yes. I know that kind, too," said Jason. He nodded. "Don't try to talk about it, then. Drink the coffee and lie down again. The thread gets broken that way, and the same nightmare doesn't come back. Tomorrow's another day. Think about tomorrow while you're falling asleep."

"All right," said Hal.

Jason finished his cup quickly and lay down again, pulling the hood of his bedsack up close around his head.

"Leave the light on or turn it off, whichever you like," he said. "It won't bother me."

"I'll put it out," said Hal.

He got up, extinguished the glow-tube and crawled back into his bedsack in darkness. He had set his cup to one side of the bedsack and it was still half full. Sitting up, he drank it off, then laid back down himself. The feeling of the dream he had admitted having came back to him. There was nothing he could have told Jason about it that would have made sense out of his murderous response at being wakened, or his earlier unaccountable ceasing to breathe.

. . . He had been riding, armed and armored, on horseback with others. They had ridden out of some trees onto the edge of a vast plain, and halted their horses. Distant in the middle of the otherwise stark emptiness of the plain was a dark, solitary, medieval-looking structure—like a peel tower, narrowing as it reached upward to its crenelated top. There were no other buildings around it, only the tower itself—and it was far off. There was a terrible sense about the tower of waiting, that held them all silent.

"I'll go alone," he had said to the others.

He had gotten down from his horse, passed the reins to the man next to him and started out on foot across the endless distance of the plain, toward the tower. At some time later, he had looked back and seen those who had been with him, still sitting their horses, small under the trees which were themselves shrunken with the distance he had put between himself and them. Then he had turned again and continued on toward the tower, to which he seemed hardly to have progressed a step since he had left the edge of the wood; and without warning something he could not see had come up out of the wasteland behind him and touched him on the shoulder.

And that had been all. The next thing he had known was that he was awake with his hands around Jason's throat. Still holding in his mind the dream-memory of the tower as he had last seen it in his dream, he fell asleep again.

He woke to the feel of his foot being moved. He opened his eyes and saw that it was Jason who had hold of it, through the bedsack. Jason squatted at arm's length from the bottom end of the bedsack, at maximum distance from him; and his gaze was anxious.

"Wasn't I breathing again?" Hal said, and grinned at him.

Jason let go of his foot and grinned back.

"You were breathing, all right. But we're due to help with breakfast. You'll have to hurry."

Hal rolled over, fumbled for and found the bath kit with which Hilary had supplied him, and pulled himself out of the warmth of the bedsack into the chill morning air. He stumbled from the tent toward the nearby stream.

Fifteen minutes later they were walking through the dawn woods toward the cook tent. The light was grayish white and mist was everywhere in wisps between the trees. Sounds came very clearly through the mist, sounds of wood being chopped, people calling back and forth, metal objects clanking against each other. The cold, damp air laved Hal's freshly depilated cheeks and touched deep into his lungs when he drew it in. From dead sleepiness, he was waking powerfully to a sense of being very alive, warm and alive within the protection of his heavy outdoor clothing. He was hollow with hunger.

When they got to the cook shack, however, he and Jason had time only for a hastily-gulped cup of coffee before going to work. But eventually the rest of the Command was fed and they got a chance at their own breakfasts.

"We'll look over the packsaddles, first," Jason said as they sat eating, perched on some boxes in the cook tent, "along with the other gear. Then we'll check out the animals and decide which to load first and which to lead unloaded for rotation. I haven't had a chance to look in the load tent, yet; but Rukh said we've already picked up about three-quarters of as much raw makings as we can carry; and we'll get the rest on our way."

"Our way to where?"

Jason stopped eating for a moment and looked at him.

"No one's said anything?" he said. "Rukh didn't say?"

"No."

"Why don't you go ask her what you're supposed to know, then come back and tell me?" Jason looked uncomfortable. "I don't know what to say and what not."

"I remember you talking in the van to Hilary about the Core Tap—"

"I didn't know you were awake." Jason's face was stricken.

"I'd just waked."

"Yes. Well," said Jason, "why don't you talk to Rukh? That way we'll all know what we can talk about."

"All right," said Hal. "I will."

They finished their breakfast and went back to the donkeys and the load tent. All that day they worked over the packsaddles and other carrying gear and practiced loading and unloading. Ten of the donkeys were required to carry the community equipment of the Command, and whatever personal gear a member of the Command was temporarily unable to carry. That left sixteen others to carry what Jason continued to refer to as "the makings," and act as replacement animals for any of the other donkeys who fell lame or otherwise needed to be rested from their loads. It was ordinary practice, Hal learned, to rotate the loads on the animals, so that each one of them periodically was led unburdened; and this went beyond keeping the animals in the best possible condition. It had its roots in the idea that it was sinful not to allow the beasts, like humans, periodic rest.

The next day the Command packed up and started out; and with that began some weeks of daily travel through the mountains. They made fifteen to eighteen kilometers a day; and each night when they camped, they would be visited by people living in the vicinity, bringing in donations of food or supplies, or more of the raw materials for the potassium nitrate.

The physical demands of this life were entirely different from those the mines had made on Hal, but he adapted quickly. He was still as lean as a stripped sapling and he suspected he was still adding height; but to a great extent he had begun to develop the strength of maturity, while still having the elasticity of youth. Before they were a week on their way, he was completely acclimated to this new life. Even the local coffee was beginning to taste good to him.

Their weeks were all very much alike; high-altitude days full of bright sunshine and wind, with a few small white clouds, the air very clean and light, the water icy cold from the mountain streams and their sleep sudden and sound after days that grew steadily longer as they moved south to meet the advancing summer.

Hal and Jason were up at dawn. They ate, harnessed and packed the donkeys for the day's trek. Two hours later, the Command was on the move, its human members lined out ahead with backpacks containing their immediate personal equipment and followed by Jason at the head of the donkeys carrying the general gear of the Command. At the tail end of the donkey contingent were those animals carrying the makings and the unloaded animals. Last of all came Hal as rearguard on the pack train. It was his job to make sure none of the beasts or people fell behind and got left, meanwhile keeping a wary eye on the donkeys ahead of him to make sure no load had slipped and no animal had gone lame.

It was a duty that called for vigilance rather than activity; and Hal's mind was free. It was the first time he had been able to stop to think since he had run from his home in the Rockies. On Coby the weekday life of the mines and the weekend life in Port had not given him the kind of mental privacy in which he could stand back and take stock. Now, it was amply available. In the solitude of his position at the end of the donkey line, with the long day's walk and the solidity of the mountains all around him, peace flowed into him and he had the chance to think long thoughts.

Now that he could hold it off at arm's length, he recognized that the Coby life had been an artificial one. He had spent the last three years indoors. It had been necessary as a place to hide while he grew up physically; and it had taught him to live, if not be completely comfortable, with strangers. But in a deeper sense, it had been, as planned, only a marking of time while he had grown up. Now, he was like a convict released from prison. He was back out in the universe where things could begin to happen; and he saw matters more in their proper dimensions.

One of the things that he saw most clearly was that it would be easy to underestimate most of the people he was now with. Not Rukh, and not Child-of-God—each of whom radiated power like hot coals inches from the palm of a hand. But most of the rest were so limited in their view of the universe, so steeped in their religious beliefs, and in many ways so unquestioning as to be hardly suspected even of shrewdness.

But there was more to each one of them than those limitations implied. They were, in fact, very like these mountains through which they now trudged, committed to a conflict they did not really understand but which they would pursue while any flicker of life was still in them, in the name of what they believed to be right.

Deep down, there was a great strength in each of them; an innate strength and a search toward something of more meaning than mere survival. This difference in them from the miners of Coby had reawakened Hal to the reasons and purpose his own life should have. He found himself thinking of where he would need to go from this present moment, to what end he should be looking, and planning to meet.

Somewhere in the last few weeks, he had hardened into the resolve to meet the Others head-on as soon as he should be strong enough. Among the complex bundle of attitudes that made him what he was, was one reflex that looked back always to the moment in which Malachi, Obadiah and Walter had died on the terrace; and a feeling, hard and ancient and unsparing, looked also toward Bleys and Dahno and all their kind. But beyond that he felt, without the understanding that would enable him to define it, that oceanic purpose that had always been there behind everything else in him, now developing into something like a powerful commitment only waiting for the hour in which it would be called to action.

Because he could not define it, because it evaded his grasp when he tried to get his mind around it, he drifted off into the area of poetic images, which had always acted as translator for him of those things which his conscious mind could not grasp. As he had used his memories of Walter, Obadiah and Malachi in the Final Encyclopedia to give form to his problem of escape from the Others, so he found himself coming to use the making of poetry to reach the formless images and conclusions in the back of his mind.

As he tramped along, he cut the creative part of himself loose to the great winds of awareness that blew invisibly behind all thoughts; and, line by line as he walked behind the donkeys through the bright-cold of the high mountains, he found himself beginning to reach out and build a poem that put a form and a language to that awareness. Line by line it grew; and just before one of the midday halts, it was done.

No one is so plastic-fine
That he lacks a brown man.
Twisted core of the old-wood roots,
In blind earth moving.

Clever folk with hands of steel
Have built us to a high tower,
Pitched far up from the lonely grass
And the mute stone's crying.

Only, when some more wily fist
Shatters that tower uplifted,
We may yet last in the stone and grass
By a brown man's holding.

The poem sang itself in his head like a repeated melody. It was a song, he thought reasonlessly, to eat up the distance between him and the dark tower of his dream.

With that thought, a vagrant idea came to him of another possible poem waiting to be born about the dark tower of his dream—a poem that charted the path into a new and larger arena of possibilities that was waiting in the back of his mind, somewhere. But it slipped away as he reached for it now. Like his song about the brown man, it bore a relationship to himself and his circumstances in ways he could feel but not yet define. Only, the poem about the tower was massive and touched great forces waiting to be. He forced himself to put aside thinking of it and came back to the brown-man song to see what it had to tell him.

Clearly, it was saying that a stage was now past for him, a step was achieved—before he could think any further into it, he saw Jason standing by the side of the route, holding the halter of one of the donkeys. Hal shooed his own beasts ahead and drew level with Jason and his.

"What's up?" he called.

"A thrown shoe," said Jason. "It must have happened right after we started. We'll have to switch the load to another animal."

Chapter

> > **19** < <

The donkeys were divided into two strings, and the one with the thrown shoe was the first of Jason's string. The path they had been following along the mountain slope was only wide enough for one animal in some places and the whole string was blocked from moving farther until that beast was out of the line.

"Howard, can you take her back?" Jason asked. "I can hold the rest."

Hal came up and began the job of coaxing the donkey off the solid surface of the trail onto the loose rock of the hillside beneath it, so that she could be turned around and led to the rear.

They were moving through a pass in the mountains along the flank of a steep slope, following a path that evidently had not been used since the fall before. It was covered with a winter's debris; twigs and needles and cones from the imported variform conifers that had come to clothe these high-altitude slopes in the temperate zones of Harmony. But it was a route that looked as if it had existed during some years for use in good weather. It took advantage of natural flat areas along the way, winding up and down as it went, but trending always southward.

Below the solid and flat surface of the narrow path, the gray-brown tree-less slope pitched sharply downward for over three hundred meters to a cliff-edge and a vertical drop of as much again to a mountain river, hidden far below. Above the path, the slope became less steep and was consequently treed—sparsely, but enough so that, fifty meters up, vegetation blocked the eye completely from a view of a short stretch of higher horizontal ridge that had been parallelling the path for the last several hundred meters.

At the moment, Rukh's Command was following the outward swell of the mountain's breast. Ahead of Hal and Jason, the slowly-moving line of people disappeared from sight around the curve of it, to their left. Behind them, Hal, as he got the donkey turned, could see back for several kilometers of open mountainside, past a vertical fold in the rock that made a dozen-meters-wide indentation where they had just passed, an indentation that narrowed sharply upward until it became first a cleft, then a narrow chimney, rising to the stony surface of the ridge above. Behind them, also, there were fewer trees and the full slope of the mountainside up to the treed ridge above lay open to the eye. The air was dry and clear, so that distances looked less than they actually were, under a sky with only a few swift-moving, small clouds.

"So . . . so . . . ," soothed Hal, conning the donkey over the loose shale below the path to a point behind the other animals, where he could lead her back up on to it. He reached that point and got her up, turning to find that Jason had ground-hitched the next donkey in line behind the one just taken out. The whole back half of that particular string was now waiting patiently, and Jason was scrambling rapidly along the shale to join him.

"We can put Delilah back in, to replace her—" Jason began as he reached the path beside Hal—and the air was suddenly full of whistlings.

"Down!" shouted Hal, dragging the other man flat on the mountainside below the lip of the path. Sharp-edged pieces of the loose rock that covered the slope stabbed at Hal through his shirt and slacks. Up on the path, several of the loaded donkeys were staggering down onto the slope, or slowly folding at the knees to lie huddled on the path. The whistling ceased, and the abrupt silence was shocking.

"Cone rifles!" Jason's voice was high-pitched and strange. "Militia up there!"

His tense face was staring up at the tree-hidden ridge. He scrambled to the next-to-last donkey in line, which carried their own gear, and wrestled with its load until he could tug free the weapon that had been issued to him. He slid back down to lie flat beside Hal once more.

"That won't do you any good at this range," Hal said. Jason's weapon was an ancient needle gun, inaccurate beyond sixty or seventy meters, and ineffective at less than double that distance.

"I know," panted Jason, still staring up at the hidden ridge. "But maybe they'll come down on us."

"They'd have to lose their heads—" Hal was beginning, out of the lessons he had absorbed as a child, when a crunching of boots in shale to their right brought their heads around. They saw Leiter Wohlen, one of the younger men of the Command, running crouching toward them.

"Seen anything?" he gasped, stopping at last over them.

"Get down!" said Hal—but it was too late. The sound of whistlings filled their ears once more, and Leiter fell, dropping his own needle gun. He started to roll bonelessly away from them down the slope. Hal plunged in pursuit, caught him, and saw that he was undeniably dead. Three cones had torn their way through his chest and one had furrowed across the side of his head. Hal snatched up the fallen gun; and, crouched over to take advantage of the cover of the path above, ran across the slope back the way they had travelled.

"Where are you going?" he heard Jason calling after him. But he had no breath to answer.

He scuttled across the loose scree of the slope until the curve of the mountain began to block the direct line of sight between him and that part of the ridge from which the cones had been sent down upon them. He was back in the indentation, that fold of the mountain rock leading upward to the cleft and the chimney. Safe now from observation by the weapon-holders above, he scrambled back up onto the path, and began to climb directly upward in the cleft.

There were not so many loose stones here. He scrambled upward mostly over bare rock, and he went swiftly, the needle gun bouncing on his back, held there by the strap of its sling across his chest. Sweat sprang out on his face, cooling it so that it felt naked in the dry mountain air. He found himself breathing deeply and steadily. It had been a long time since he had pushed himself physically in just this fashion, and his body felt stiff and awkward. But the early habits of his training lived deeply in him, and he could feel the air being drawn powerfully into his lungs, the hammering of his heart in his chest rapid but steady. He climbed swiftly into the narrow neck of the chimney; and from a scramble on hands and feet up the steep slope, he went to rock climbing.

The chimney was some nine or ten meters in height, narrowing sharply until at the top, just below the upper ridge, it was less than a meter in width. He made himself stop and breathe deeply at the bottom of the climb, willing his heart to slow and refilling his depleted tissues with oxygen for the effort.

The needle gun was the real problem. Ordinary procedure would have been to pull it up after him once he got to the upper ridge. But he had no line to lift it with. He stood for a moment, mentally calculating the distance between the ridge above him and the place farther along it, from which the fire of the cone rifles had come. Unless he was unlucky enough to have one of the Militiamen just above him at this moment, the sound of the weapon falling onto the flat rock of the upper ridge should not carry far enough to attract attention.

He stepped back and down from the base of the chimney to find a place where he could plant his feet firmly, then took the needle gun from his back and checked to make sure that its safety was on. It was, and he took the weapon firmly by the muzzle end of the barrel in both hands, swung it at arm's length, then flung it wheeling upward, until it dropped from sight with a distant crash on the upper ridge.

He stood waiting, listening. But there was no sound of anyone coming to investigate. He began to climb.

It had been over four years since his muscles had done this kind of work, and they were slow to respond to it. He climbed with extreme care, checking and rechecking every handhold and foothold, his eyes on the reddish, weather-smoothed rock only inches before them. Little by little, as he went, the old reflexes came back and the familiar skills. He was soaked with sweat now and his shirt clung to his back and shoulders. He panted heavily as he went. But he was warming to the ascent and something of his earlier pleasure at such conquests of vertical space, arm-reach by arm-reach, woke in him again.

He crawled out at last from the shadow of the chimney into the hot sun of the ledge above him and lay there, panting. After a moment a small breeze came by and chilled him pleasantly. His breathing slowed. He looked around for the needle gun, saw it lying within reach of his left arm and pulled it to him, sitting up.

There was a complete silence around him. He might have been alone in the mountains. For a moment a small finger of panic touched him, the thought that he had taken too much time coming up the chimney and the attackers might already have control of the Command. Then he put the feeling aside. Unprofitable emotion. He could hear the dry voice of Malachi, lecturing now in his memory.

He stood up, lifting the needle rifle with him. His breathing was almost normal again. He began to run, noiselessly, on the carpet of pine needles deep on this upper ledge, in the direction that would place him above the Command, strung out on the lower ridge.

His ears were tuned for any sounds from ahead as he went. After only a short distance, he heard voices and paused to listen. There were three speakers, just beyond a small clump of trees just ahead. He cut to his left up the slope and went on more slowly and even more silently. After a moment he was able to look down into the area beyond the tree clump. He saw three men there with cone rifles, wearing the same black uniforms he had seen on the Militia guards in Citadel.

Automatically, the needle gun in his hands came up into firing position. They were less than twenty meters from him, in clear view, with their backs to him. *Patience,* said the remembered voice of Malachi silently in his ear. He dropped the weapon again to arm's length and continued moving, parallel to the upper ridge and above it.

He passed two more groups of three men with cone rifles before he came to one with four men seated with their rifles, peering down the slope and occasionally firing, while a thin man with the broad white bar of a Captain's chevron sewed slantwise on the left arm of his battle-jacket stood over them, his back, like theirs, to Hal.

There was an air of relaxation and confidence about the Militiamen that made Hal uneasy. He tried to see over the edge of the ridge to the Command below, but could not. Quietly, he turned and climbed higher on the slope and finally was able to see the line of animals and baggage along the path of the lower ridge. No people were visible at all; and he thought that they had sensibly all taken cover below the edge of the ridge, when he remembered the continued firing of the men he had passed and those just below him.

He shaded his eyes against the brightness of the sky—and for the first time was able to make out movement on the mountainside above the lower ridge. A number of those in the Command were working their way from one point of cover to another, up the slope in an attack upon their attackers; and as he watched he focused in on the movement of one slim, dark-clad figure in particular and realized that it was Rukh herself who was leading them.

It was a desperate response on the part of the Command. The Militiamen could sit and take their time about picking off the climbers as they momentarily exposed themselves; while the Command members were not only under extreme difficulty in firing back, but were being exhausted by the climb. Nonetheless they came on, and suddenly Hal realized what Rukh must have in mind.

He looked to his left, along that part of the upper ridge he had not yet observed, and saw that, a short distance beyond, it tilted abruptly downward, as if aiming itself at a joining with the lower ridge, but thinning out to plain mountainside some fifty meters from that meeting. He stared at this part of the mountainside for some moments before he was able to pick out, among the sparse trees of its slope, the movements he was looking for. But at last he found them. Rukh's frontal assault up the slope directly above her was obviously intended primarily to hold the attention of the Militia while she sent another force around the front end of the upper ridge to attack that way.

It was the only response possible to her; and with that thought, Hal turned sharply back to look down at the standing Militiaman with the white chevron on his sleeve. This Captain must be the Militia officer in charge; and he would be ineffective in the extreme if he had set up this ambush without giving some thought to his left flank.

Hal turned and began to move onward, above that left flank. Shortly, he found himself looking down on a wider spot of the ridge, a slight hollow, fenced with not only a natural stand of trees, but by a rough log barricade, facing in the direction up which Rukh's flank attackers would come. In the hollow were more than twenty of the armed Militiamen, waiting.

Hal squatted on the mountainside above the whole scene, the needle gun across his knees. He felt a tightness in his chest. The only hope he had had for the flank attackers had been destroyed by the sight of those twenty black uniforms. He came back to his position above the four men with the standing officer.

Hal thought for a moment, then went back to his position above the first group he had discovered. Below him as he watched, one of the three raised his rifle, fired; then laughed and pointed. One of the others patted him on the shoulder.

Something old and grim moved in Hal. He sank to his knees, rested the barrel of the needle gun on the half-buried boulder behind which he crouched, and fired three bursts. The needles whispered, lightly as the piping of birds on the mountain air. He lay, listening in the silence that had followed their sound; but there was no reaction from the other Militia positions to indicate that anyone there had heard. He got to his feet again and went softly down the slope.

The forms of the three, when he reached them, lay still in the sunlight. He looked at them, feeling an emptiness in his middle body, like that following some heavy blow or wound, the pain of which was still being held at bay by shock. He gathered up the three cone rifles, carefully, so that their metal parts should not knock noisily together, and carried them with him up the mountainside, high enough so that he could see the slopes up which both attacking groups from the Command were working.

Rukh's group was making slow progress, but the group coming up on the flank was moving swiftly. They should be within point-blank range of the Militiamen waiting in the hollow in another five minutes.

Hal sat down, and took the butt plate off one of the cone rifles to get at the tools in the compartment underneath. Cone rifles were designed to be self-cleaning as they were fired, so that something more than filling the barrels with dirt was called for. He unscrewed the locking gate on the magazine tube underneath the barrel and pried off the last of the cones from the rod of them packed in there. Then, keeping the cone he had pried off, he replaced and rescrewed the locking gate.

He picked up the single cone carefully between thumb and middle finger, being careful not to touch the narrow red rim around the wide upper edge of the cone. The red marked the molding of the propellant, triggered by the rifle's mechanism to drive these self-propelled missiles. Setting the cone gently between his close-held knees, so that the rim touched nothing, he unbreached the firing chamber, opened it, and put the cone into the breach—but facing the rear of the chamber instead of forward into the barrel. Gently, he closed the breach upon it. He performed the same operation with one of the other cone rifles.

Closing the breach of the second rifle, he grinned a trifle bitterly, internally. Some of the Command members, at least, would have a great deal to say, if they knew about his wasting two perfectly good military firearms in this fashion—when they were so short of them. And they would be justified.

He got up, picked up his extra weapons, and moved on until he was at a midpoint above the cliff edge occupied by the other two nests of Militiamen, who were continuing to fire over the edge of the ledge on which they sat, unaware of what he had done to the men in the positions to their right. Here, he built himself a rough barricade of the heavier rocks in the immediate area. Then, kneeling behind this barricade, he took aim at the three black-clad figures in the second nest.

The soft piping of the needles that had cut down the three in the first group had not carried to alarm their fellow soldiers. But the heavier whistlings of the cones Hal now fired would carry farther, and Hal hoped none of the Militia would be alerted. And indeed, he could see a few heads turning, even as the three there fell.

They were not looking up at the slope above them, having no immediate reason to suspect the shooting was not by their own men. Perhaps in a second they might think to look up as well as sideways. But in that moment Hal got to his feet; and, swinging the first of the rigged cone rifles around his head, he sent it wheeling to drop into the last manned nest to the right of the one with the Captain, following it with the other rifle among the four men in the other nest, just as the officer was stepping out of it to go in the direction from which he had plainly assumed Hal must be firing.

The first cone rifle hit and the jar set off the reversed cone in its breach. There was the soft *whump* of an explosion and an upward flare of flame as the heat and shock of the reversed cone trying to get out of the breach the wrong way set off the rod of other cones in the magazine—followed by another explosion, which was the second cone rifle, a moment later in the nest from which the officer had just stepped.

For less than a minute, dust and airborne debris hid the scene in both nests, and then the gentle mountain breeze blew it aside to show all the human figures in both nests fallen. Either the shock of the explosion or the shrapnel from the exploding rifles had put them, at least temporarily, out of the fight.

Hal's aim had been to attract the attention of the Militia in the hollow away from the attackers coming up the slope. Following the two explosions there was a moment of appalled silence on the upper ridge and then a babble of shouting voices. Some, at least, of the watchers in the hollow began to run back toward the center of the Militia line. Hastily, Hal went sliding down the slope from the position of his exposed barricade. If he had been seen up there, the small rock shield he had built would have been useful. But since he had not been, there was more safety for him, now, below among the trees and vegetation of the upper slope.

The Militiamen hurrying back from the hollow could not see his descent, but they heard him. Shouts went up—and were echoed unexpectedly by those still in the hollow. The attackers from the Command coming up the ridge had reached the defenders at the tree-trunk barricade.

Lying flat behind a tree on the lower ridge, less than ten meters from the officer who had fallen—and who was now beginning to stir again—outside his nest, Hal traded shots with those Militia who had come back toward him following the explosions.

The cone rifle was warm against his cheek, warm from the sunlight through the trees upon it, as he watched through its sights for movement among the trees before him. The movements became less frequent. The shots coming back at him diminished, and ceased.

He looked about him. Down the slope from him he caught sight of the Militia officer, now on his feet and swaying uncertainly, but moving back into his command nest, where the cone rifles dropped by his men stood waiting him. Evidently, he had been untouched by the flying metal of the rifle and only knocked unconscious by the explosion shock. Hal's rifle muzzle swung automatically to center on the narrow, upright back of the man, and then revulsion took hold. There was no need for any more killing. He got silently to his own feet and half-ran, half-dove down the intervening slope to catch the officer and slam him to the ground.

The other lay still beneath him. Hal rolled off and sat up. He turned the officer over on his back, and saw that he was still conscious. Hal had simply knocked the wind out of him. For a moment the other struggled to get his breath, then gradually breathing returned. Hal stared down at him, puzzled. The thin face below was familiar. For a moment more it baffled him, then memory connected. The man he was looking at had been the one who escorted him, with Jason, to the session with Ahrens. The same one who had threatened to hang Jason by the wrists for several hours if he continued to talk.

The officer stirred. He looked up at the rifle Hal held covering him, and from there to Hal's face; and his own face was transformed suddenly with a lean smile and a sudden glittering of eyes.

"Thou!" he said. "I have found thee—"

"So, thou art here!" interrupted a harsh voice, and Child-of-God walked from the trees at their left into the nest, and halted. For the first time, Hal realized that the shouting and the whistling of cone rifles had diminished. Child-of-God's pale eyes focused on the weapon in Hal's hand.

"And thou, too, hast captured a cone rifle. Good!" His gaze went to the Militia officer and for a moment, as Hal watched, the two gazed at each other, different by twenty years of age, in bone and muscle and clothing, but in all other ways alike as brothers.

"Save thyself trouble," said the officer. "Thou knowest, as I know, that I will tell thee nothing, whatever thou choosest to do to me."

Child-of-God breathed out through his nostrils. His cone rifle's muzzle came around so casually to center on the officer that for a moment Hal did not understand what the movement implied.

"No!" Hal knocked the cone rifle up, off target.

Child-of-God's weathered face came about to stare at him. There was little strong expression to be seen on it at most times; but now Hal thought he read incredulity there.

" 'No'?" echoed Child-of-God. "To me?"

"We don't have to kill him."

Child-of-God continued to stare. Then he took a deep breath.

"Thou art new to us," he said, almost quietly. "Such as these must all be killed, before they kill us. Also, what the apostate says is true—"

"Thou art the apostate—thou, the Abandoned of the Lord!" broke in the Militia officer, harshly. Child-of-God paid no attention. His eyes were still on Hal.

"What the apostate says is true," he repeated slowly. "It's useless to question such as he, who was once of the Elect."

"It is thou who art fallen from the Elect! I am of God and remain of God!"

Still, Child-of-God paid no attention.

"He would tell us nothing, as he says. Perhaps there is another still living, who was never of the Elect. Such we can make speak."

Child-of-God's muzzle swung back toward the officer.

"No, I tell you!" Hal this time caught hold of the rifle barrel; and Child-of-God, his face plainly registering astonishment, turned sharply to him.

"Thou wilt release my weapon now," he began slowly, "or—"

There was only the faintest sound of movement to alert them; but when they turned back, the Militia Captain was dodging between the trees. All in one movement, Child-of-God dropped on one knee, swung up the cone rifle and fired. Bark flew whitely from a tree trunk. Slowly, he lowered the weapon, staring into the pines. He turned back toward Hal.

"Thou has let one of those who has destroyed many go free," he said. "Free, if we do not gain him again, to kill more of our people."

His voice was level but his eyes burned into Hal.

"And, by hindering me, who would have sent him to God's judgment, thou hast made his freedom possible. Decision will have to be made on this."

Chapter

> > 20 < <

Moments later, Rukh and the attackers who had been coming directly up the mountainside at the Militia position emerged on the ridge. The shouting and the whistling of the cones had dwindled and now fell silent. The members of the Command gathered rifles and equipment from the fallen enemy and returned to the ridge below. There were no prisoners. Apparently neither the Militia nor the Commands took prisoners unless there was a need to question them. The officer who had escaped when Hal had distracted Child-of-God's attention was not recaptured. Possibly, thought Hal, some of the other Militia might have made good their escape. The Command had neither the time nor the energy to pursue fugitives.

Fourteen of the donkeys had been killed by the cone-rifle fire or were so badly injured that they had to be destroyed. Their loads were distributed among packs on the backs of the members of the Command. When they were ready to move again, only Rukh and Child-of-God were not carrying packs.

There were some three hours of light left before sunset. Carrying their dead and wounded, they travelled only an hour and a half before making camp; but this was enough to bring them considerably down and out of the mountain pass and into a foothill valley very like that in which they had been camped when Hal and Jason had first joined them. As soon as they had set up their shelters, a burial service was held in the red light of the sunset for those who had been killed, followed by the first food of the day since they had broken camp that morning.

After the meal, Hal went to help Jason stake out and care for the donkeys that still remained to them. He was busy at this when Rukh appeared.

"I want to talk to you," she said to Hal.

She led him away from the camp, up the bank of the small stream by which they had camped, until they were out of earshot of Jason, and therefore of everyone else in camp. As he followed her, he found himself caught up again by the particular awareness she evoked in him; and her difference from everyone else he had ever known. There was a unique quality about her, and it chimed deeply off the metal of his own inner differences. It was not because he and she were alike, he thought now; because they were not. It was that the common factor of individual uniqueness drew them together—or, at least, drew him powerfully to her.

At last she stopped in a small open space by the stream bank and turned to face him. The twilight was still bright enough so that her face appeared to stand out with a strange three-dimensional solidity. It came to him that, if he only had the ability, he would like to carve her in dark metal as she stood now, facing him.

"Howard," she said, "you and this Command are going to have to come to terms."

"The Command?" he said. "Or Child-of-God?"

"James is the Command," she said, "just as much as I am and every working member of it is. The Command can't survive if those in it don't follow orders. No one gave you any order to attack the Militia position on your own, with only a needle gun that would hardly shoot."

"I know," he said, bleakly. "I learned about orders, and the need for obedience to them, so early that I can't remember not knowing it. But the same man who taught me those things also taught me that, when necessary, you do what needs to be done."

"But what made you think you'd have a chance of doing anything, armed like that, and alone?"

"I've told you about myself, how I was raised," he answered. He hesitated, but it needed to be said. "I never fired at a living person in my life before today. But you have to face something, you and the Command. I'm probably better trained for something like we've just been through than anyone here, except you or Child-of-God."

He stopped. She said nothing, only watched him. He saw the black-clad soldiers again in his mind's eye—laughing and firing down on the lower ridge.

"I was operating by reflex, most of the way," he said. "But I didn't try anything I didn't know I could do."

Surprisingly, she nodded.

"All right," she said. "But tell me—how did you feel when it was all over? How do you feel now?"

"Sick," he said, bluntly. "I was numb for a while, after. But now I just feel sick—sick and exhausted. I'd like to go to bed and sleep for a month."

"We'd all like sleep," she said. "But we don't feel the sort of sickness you feel—any of us, except you. Have you asked your friend Jason how he feels?"

"No," he said.

She looked at him silently for a long moment.

"I killed my first enemy when I was thirteen," she said. "I was with my father's Command when it was wiped out by the Militia. I got away, the way that officer got away from you today. You've never been through that sort of thing. We have. Combat skills alone don't put you above anyone in this camp."

He looked down at her, feeling strangely adrift in the universe. She should be carved, he thought, not in metal, but in some dark, eternal rock—and he suddenly remembered the image of the rock on the hillside with which he had fought the attempt of Bleys Ahrens to control him, in the detention center.

"I suppose you're right," he said, at last, emptily. "Yes . . . you're right."

"We're what we have to be—first," she said. "After that we're what we are, naturally. James is what he was born into—and what he has to be now. You've got to understand both aspects of him. There's no other way if you're going to fit in as a member of this Command. You've got to understand him both as he is, and as he has to be—to be my Lieutenant. Can you do that, Howard?"

"Hal," he corrected her without thinking.

"I think," she said, "for all our sakes, I'd better go on calling you Howard."

"All right." He breathed deeply. *There is no anger—there is no sadness— there is no corrosive emotion*, he heard Walter the InTeacher saying, once more, in his mind—*where there is understanding.* "Yes, you're right. I should understand him. So, I will try."

He smiled at her, to reassure her.

"You'll have to succeed," said Rukh. She relaxed. "But, all right, now that that's settled—you did a great deal for us, today. If we hadn't had your attack on the right of the Militia line, neither James' party nor mine might have won through. And if we'd failed, the enemy would only have had to come down at its leisure and kill those of the Command who were still alive. There's that, and the fact you helped get us a number of good cone rifles and supplies. Under the circumstances, I'm going to let you trade that needle gun in for one of the rifles we just got."

He nodded.

"And," she said, "I think it's time you knew as much as the rest of the Command about what we're about to do."

"Jason said to ask you," he said. "I thought it was better to wait until you were ready to tell me, yourself."

"He was right," Rukh said. "Briefly, from the point where we are now, on this side of the mountains, we're committed. Down on the interior plains there's more of us in the Commands than there are Militia available to hold us down. So they settle for watching key points as well as their personnel allows. There's a dozen routes out of these mountains onto the plains. We had a fifty-fifty chance of being challenged, whichever one we took. But now that we've gotten past one of their patrols, we'll be pretty well left alone, as long as they don't know what we're up to."

"Tell me something," said Hal. "I know the lack of heavy technology makes aircraft not easy to come by and expensive as well, out here on the Younger Worlds. But surely these Militia must have some spotter planes— light aircraft—that could find us, or at least help find us, from the air, even after we're down on the plains?"

"They do have," said Rukh. "But they haven't many. They're machines made of wood and cloth that can't take very rough weather—that's to begin with. And the jealousy between Militia outfits means that a unit that has a plane isn't too eager to lend it out to another unit. Fuel isn't easy to come by. Finally, in any case, even if they get one or more craft into the air looking for us, the plains are heavily treed; and we do our travelling under cover

ninety percent of the time. The other ten percent of the time, when there
is no cover, we move in the dark hours when we can't be seen. You must
have noticed that, yourself."

"I have," said Hal.

"What this all adds up to, as I say," Rukh went on, "is that now, once we've
made it past that one patrol, we can expect to be pretty well left alone unless we do something to draw Militia attention to us. Remember, their first
responsibility remains to act as the government police arm, not only in the
countryside but in the cities; and the requirements of the cities in that area
draw off most of their personnel."

"All right," said Hal. "I believe you. What's the Command up to, then?
You were just going to tell me."

She hesitated.

"There's a certain limit to how much information I can give you, even
now," she said, frankly. "The identity of our target, for example, has only been
known to a few—"

"On the way to your camp where I first met you," he said, "I heard Hilary
and Jason saying something about a Core Tap power plant."

She shook her head, a little wearily.

"I remember now," she said. "Jason reported you overhearing that. The
point is, Jason himself shouldn't have known. Hilary's different, but Jason
. . . well, as long as you know that much you might as well hear all the rest
of it."

She took a deep breath.

"We Commands," she said, "are only the spearheads of opposition to
those controlled by the Others. We'll be experimenting with the makings
we've collected. We'll practice making fulminating mercury out of it; then
when we've got the technique worked out, we'll pass the information along
to sympathizers like Hilary, who'll make more fulminating mercury with
which we'll later fuse and explode the fertilizer. A kilogram of that will set
off tons of oil-soaked nitrate fertilizer. We hope to collect the fertilizer itself
from a farming-area storage plant we'll be raiding on the plains; and it should
be enough to destroy the Core Tap the Others are using to power the construction area for interstellar ships on this North Continent."

"Won't any fertilizer storage plant be in the heart of a town?" Hal asked.

"Not quite in the heart of," she answered. "But definitely in town limits.
As a distraction, at the same time we attack the plant we'll rob a metals bank
in the same town. Our people can use any metal we can get away with, if
we can just smuggle it back through the mountains to the coast; but the bank
raid's still only a cover operation for the fertilizer raid, not vice versa. After
we've got the fertilizer, we'll set fire to the storage area, and hope the destruction will hide the fact we've taken some of their supply."

"I see," said Hal, the back of his mind at work with the necessary tactics
of such an operation.

"The local Militia unit," said Rukh, "will only chase us until we're out of their district—unless they suspect what we've really been after. If they do that, they may guess we're up to something bigger than a metals' robbery; in which case they'll put out the word and all the Militia Districts will be actively hunting us instead of just the one with the fertilizer plant. Which may make collecting our explosive in its finished form a little difficult."

"I can see that," he said, quietly.

"But, with a lot of luck, we'll blow up and block the shaft of the Core Tap, then outrun the alarm that'll be raised for us after that, and make it back into the mountains with enough of us still alive to carry on as a separate Command. But if our luck's anything less than good, we won't make it back to the mountains; and if anything goes wrong, we'll be wiped out and fail to wreck the Core Tap."

"Don't your people in this part of the continent depend on the power from that Tap to farm and live?"

"Yes." She looked him in the eye. "But so do the Others depend on it for a spaceship fitting-yard, the only one in this northern hemisphere. If we blow it, they'll have to switch all their plans to use the one on South Continent— which is smaller and logistically less practical."

"You're paying a very high price just to put a spoke in their wheels, aren't you?" he asked.

"All prices are high," she said.

The light that had lingered in the sky was going swiftly, now. Over them, a full moon had been above the horizon for a couple of hours already; but in the brighter sky it had been hardly noticeable. Now, the first breath of a night wind moved about them, chilling them lightly. In the dimness Rukh's face was still perfectly visible, but remote, as if the oncoming dark had emphasized her isolation, not only from him but from everyone else in the universe. Deeply moved, suddenly, for reasons he could not explain to himself, on impulse he put a hand on each of her shoulders and bent forward to look down closely into her face. For a second their eyes were only inches apart, and unthinkingly, his arms went around her and he kissed her.

For a split second he felt her shock and surprise, then a fierce response came, pressing her against him. But a second later she had put her hands on his upper arms and pushed him back from her with a strength that startled him.

She let go of him. In the near-darkness they looked at each other.

"Who are you?" she said, in a hard voice, so low he could hardly hear her.

"You know who I am," he answered. "I've told you."

"No," she spoke in that same low voice, staring at him, "you're more than that."

"If I am," he said—they were like two people trapped by a spell—"I don't know it."

"You know it."

She stared at him for a moment more.

"No," she said, at last, "you really don't know it, do you?"

She stepped back, away from him.

"I can't belong to anyone," she said; and her voice seemed to come almost from a remote distance. "I'm a Warrior of the Lord."

He could think of nothing to say.

"You don't understand?" she said, at last.

He shook his head.

"I'm one of the Elect. Like James," she said. "Don't you know what that means?"

"One of my tutors was an Elect—originally," he said, slowly. "I understand. It means far more than that. It means you're certain of Heaven."

"It means you've been chosen by God. I do what I must, not what I want." Her face was all but lost now in the dimness; and her voice softened. "Forgive me, Hal."

"For what?" he said.

"For whatever I did."

"You didn't do anything." His voice roughened. "It's me."

"Perhaps," she said. "But it's also me. Only—as long as I have the responsibility of this Command, I can't have anything else."

"Yes," he said.

She reached out and touched his forearm. He could feel the pressure of her fingers and he imagined that he could feel the warmth of her hand, even through the rough thickness of his shirt sleeve.

"Come along," she said. "We still have to talk to James, you and I."

"All right," he answered. She turned and they went back through the woods, close together but careful not to touch each other.

They found Child in his own single-person shelter near the center of the camp. He was apparently just ready to go to bed; and in the light of the lamp hanging from the main rib of the shelter, his face looked deeply lined and much older than Hal had seen it appear, before. At their appearance in the entrance, he got up from the sleeping sack he was spreading out.

"I'll come," he said.

He stepped out of the shelter and they backed away to let him emerge. Outside, the pinned-back flap of the entrance spilled just enough light into the night so that they could see each other's faces without making them out in any detail.

"James," said Rukh. "I've talked to Howard, and I think he understands now what we're up against, out here."

Child-of-God looked at Hal, but said nothing. Remembering his promise to try to understand the older man, Hal fought back the instinct to bristle that came at the sight of the dark shadow pools that hid the other's eyes, turning in his direction.

"Also, since he's to be credited with helping us gain a number of cone rifles in good condition, I've promised him one of them."

Child-of-God nodded.

"And I've told him in full what our plans are for the next few weeks."

"Thou art in command," Child said. He had turned to face her as she spoke of the rifles. Now the blur that was his face swung back to Hal. "Howard, I am thy officer. From now on, wilt thou obey?"

"Yes," said Hal.

He was bone weary. The other two must be, also. They said nothing more. He looked from Rukh to Child. They stood at three points of a triangle with space between them.

"If that's all, then," said Hal. "I'll be getting back to my shelter. Good night."

"Good night," said Rukh, from where she stood.

"We are in God's hands," said Child, unmoving.

Hal turned and went. There was no community fire that night, and once he turned his back to the light, the camp was lost in darkness. But it was always laid out the same pattern; and as he moved into the darkness his eyes began to adjust until the moonlight was enough to show him the way. He got back to his shelter and found it with the hanging lamp within on its dimmest setting—a glowworm gleam barely illuminating the cold, curving walls of the shelter, once he was inside.

In his bedsack, Jason slept heavily. Hal undressed in silence, turned off the lamp and crawled into his own sack. He lay on his back staring up into the darkness, trapped between sleep and waking. In his mind's eye he replayed the climb up the chimney, his reconnaissance of the Militia position. He saw again the Militiaman in the first nest being slapped on the back by his comrade, and laughing. He pressed the firing button of the needle gun and saw the three men fall. He threw the rigged cone rifles into the enemy nests. He watched the rifle of Child come around to point at the Militia officer, and again he knocked it aside. . . .

He saw Rukh, turning to face him in the twilight. . . .

He squeezed his eyes shut, willing himself to sleep, but for once his mind and body would not obey. He lay there, and the ghosts of three old men came out of his memory and stood around him in the darkness.

"It was his first time," Malachi said. "He needed her."

"No," said Walter the InTeacher, "our deaths were his first time. And there was no one there for him then."

"When we were killed, it wasn't like this," said Malachi. "This time it was his doing. If he's not to go down and down from here until he drowns, he needs help."

"She cannot help him," said Obadiah. "She is at God's will, herself."

"He'll survive," said Walter. It was one of those rare occasions when the Exotic was the hardest of the three. "He'll survive without anyone if he has to, without anything. That part of him was in my care; and I promise you he will survive this, and worse."

"Unless thou art wrong," said Obadiah, harshly.

"Unless is not permitted," said Walter, softly. "Hal, you're not sleeping only because you're choosing not to sleep. All things, even this, are subject to the mind. What can't be mended has to be put aside until some time when it can, if ever. What did I teach you? Choice is the one thing that can never be taken from you, right down to the moment of the ultimate choice of death. So, if you want to lie awake and suffer, do so; but face the fact that it's something you're choosing to do, not something over which you've got no control."

Hal opened his eyes and made himself breathe out deeply; and found that he was exhaling through teeth clamped tightly together. He made his jaw muscles relax, but still he lay, staring up into darkness.

"I can't," he said at last, aloud.

"You can," said the ghost of Walter, calmly. "This, and more."

It was like trying to unclench a fist held tight so long that it had forgotten any other attitude, coupled with the deep fear of what might happen to the hand, once it was open, unarmored by tension and bone. But at last the knot within him unwound. The walls of the small, close room he had come to occupy in his mind fell apart, and the universe opened up around him once more.

He slept.

Chapter

> > **21** < <

In the morning they moved on, and by afternoon they were into rolling, nearly-level country squared off into farmlands, the fields now showing the green tint of new growth. It was like coming on an oasis after some long trek through a desert; and the sense of sorrow and loss that had held the Command nearly silent since the attack of the Militia began to lift. Even those who had been wounded cheered up, raising themselves on their elbows in their litters, slung between pairs of the remaining donkeys. Looking about, they breathed the warmer air of the lowlands, occasionally laughed softly as they talked with those carrying packs and walking beside them, as if they had just come into a kinder and better land.

In fact, as Hal had learned in his studies, years before, this area of Harmony came close to being a rich spot on the two impoverished Friendly Worlds. Here, the soil was black and thick and the farms produced a surplus which went to feed hungry mouths in large nearby cities; cities of a size that otherwise could be supported only on Harmony's continental coasts, with their access to the food sources of the oceans.

As soon as they reached the farmlands proper, the Command began to disintegrate. The wounded were taken into the homes of local farmers, to be nursed back to health; and both the remaining beasts and the healthy Command members were organized into small units which would make their way openly on foot to the rendezvous, near their target of the fertilizer plant, at a small city several hundred kilometers in from the mountains.

Hal found himself separated from Jason and assigned to a group of ten headed up by Child. They had been chosen, as had the other small units the Command was now divided into, with an eye to giving the appearance of a single large family, with the ages of its members ranging from grandfather to grown grandchildren. The farms of the central North Continent of Harmony were farmed with donkey and human power alone; and the cultural pattern of the farmers was one of large, compound families, in which sons and daughters married and brought their new mates home so that groups of twenty to sixty people living on a single farm were not unusual.

When such families, or portions of them, travelled, they had the appearance of a small clan on the road; and consequently the ten Command members with Child as their family elder were not conspicuous when at last they set out. Dressed in jackets and slacks or skirts of gray, dark blue or black, with white shirts, string ties and black berets, all furnished by local partisan farmers they had encountered, the ten could not be told from ordinary travellers on these interior roads.

With the change of scene, Hal found a change of attitude taking him over. Walking the roads, lifting his beret with the others when they encountered another family group walking in the opposite direction, he discovered that with the change he had both gained and lost something. As the fields and houses had closed about him, the wide-ranging sense of freedom he had sensed in the mountains was gone. He was held close again—not as close as he had felt himself held on Coby, but close enough so that his mind seemed once more on a leash.

The urge to write poetry had once more left him. In its place was an urgency and a responsibility he was not yet able to define. In an odd way, it was as if he had been on vacation when they were in the mountains, and now he was back at work in a universe where the practical aspects of life had to be considered.

The Militia attack in the pass, the intimate moment with Rukh and the encounter with Child that had preceded it had made him look again at what was around him. He had become closer to these people—all of them, even in this short time, than he had to those on Coby—even including Sost and Tonina and John Heikkila. It was not just that they had fought the Militia together. These in the Command had a dedication and a purpose that echoed to some urge to dedication and purpose in him. In the long run, on Coby, he had needed Tonina, Sost and John, but they had no real need of him. It was as if he had taken a step closer to the whole human race, here on Harmony. At the same time he was even more aware of the distance separating him from each of them. He found he wanted Rukh desperately and at the same time he did not see how he could ever have her. Also, he was unhappy about Child-of-God. The older man was cut of the same cloth as Obadiah had been; and Hal had loved Obadiah. He should, he thought, be able to at least like Child. He wanted to like Child; and he found he did not.

It was more than a simple desire in him to like the older man. As Obadiah had, Child personified the very heart and core of the Friendly Splinter Culture. Hal had responded to the Friendlies, as he had also responded to the Exotic and Dorsai Splinter Cultures. Responded to and felt sad for, because Walter had taught him that, in the long run, all three must disappear.

But still he could not bring himself to like or admire Child. Looked at dispassionately, the other seemed to be little more than an opinionated, unyielding individual with no virtues in him beyond his military skills and the fact that chance had placed him in opposition to the Others, and therefore on the same side as Hal himself in the conflict.

And that brought another matter to mind. He could not simply continue to run blindly as one of Rukh's Command, with the hope of always keeping out of the Others' way. There had to be more to life than that. He needed to make some kind of long-range plans. But what plans? He was deep in thought about this for perhaps the hundredth time when an unexpected hail brought him out of it.

It was the end of the third day since they had started out to tramp the road in their small group on their way to rendezvous. They had just topped the crest of a small hill and were headed down into a hollow of land perhaps five kilometers across, filled with the familiar plowed fields and several widely-separated farmhouse complexes surrounded by trees planted for windbreak. Coming toward them up the slope of the road from the nearest of these building clumps was a round-bodied man of close to Child's age, waving and calling to them.

They met him a minute or so later and stopped to talk. His face was rosy with the effort of the fast walk; and he took off his beret, fanning himself with it as he spoke.

"You're Child-of-God and these are the soldiers of the Lord from Rukh Tamani's Command? We just got word you were coming. Will you stop at my farm tonight? It'd be a pleasure under the hand of the Lord to have you; and I've wanted to talk to someone from one of the Commands for some time."

"We thank God who sent thee," said Child. "We will be thy guests."

His harsh voice made his words on the soft, late-afternoon air more like a command than a polite acceptance; but the farmer did not seem offended. He fanned himself twice more and put the beret back on his head.

"Come along," he said; and he led the way down the slope, talking with Child as he went, unquenched by the short, sharp answers he got in reply.

The farm he led them to was clearly one housing a larger than usual family. The living quarters consisted of at least a dozen interconnected buildings. As they walked into the central yard of this complex, enclosed on three sides by the buildings, thin notes of what sounded like some sort of recorder or flute came from the open doorway of the largest building, to which they were heading.

"Forgive me!" said their host.

He darted ahead, into the dark rectangle of the doorway. The sound of the notes cut off abruptly, and in a moment he was back outside, his face rosy again, as he confronted them where they had stopped.

"I'm sorry." He spoke again, this time particularly to Child. "These children—but he's a good boy. He just doesn't realize . . . please excuse it."

"Praise not the Lord with instruments and other idle toys, for He Himself is not idle, neither will He suffer the same before Him," said Child, grimly.

"I know, I know. It's the times . . . things are changing so fast, and they don't understand. But come in, come in!"

They followed him into a large, airy room, dark after the still-bright day outside. As Hal's eyes adjusted, he saw a number of chairs and benches scattered around a room with a highly-polished wooden floor and an enormous fireplace at one end of it. An opening in the end opposite the fireplace showed another room, long rather than wide, with a table running the length of it that looked as if it could seat half a hundred people.

"Sit down, sit down," said their host. "Excuse me, I should introduce myself. My name's Godlun Amjak; and this is my household. Elder Child-of-God, will you do us the honor of speaking to us at evening service in a few minutes?"

"I am no Elder, nor have I ever sought to be. I am a Warrior of God, and that is sufficient," said Child. "Yes, I will speak."

"Thank you."

"Thank thy God and mine, rather."

"Of course, of course. I do. I thank God. You're quite right."

Younger men and women in the customary dress, white above and dark below, were coming shyly into the room, bringing pitchers of cold water and plates of small dark cakes. Child refused cake but accepted the water. They sat for a short time with food and drink, and then were led back through the house and into a rectangular interior courtyard with a stone floor and white-painted walls, unadorned except for the thin black cross as tall as Hal himself, painted on one of the end walls. In front of the cross was a small platform of dark wood and lectern before it; with, however, nothing on the lectern.

The yard was already full of people—obviously the members of the household of Godlun Amjak—standing in two ranked and ordered groups on either side of a central aisle-space. Godlun led the ten from the Command down this aisle to a space which had been left for them in front of the right-hand group and only a few steps from the cross and the lectern. Once they were placed, Godlun mounted the platform and looked down at all of them. The courtyard was deep in shadow from the buildings surrounding it; but in contrast the visible patch of sky above them was still a startlingly-bright blue without clouds.

There was a moment's hush, as if everyone in the courtyard were holding his breath. Then Godlun spoke.

"We are privileged before the Lord," he said, "in that we have as our guests ten Warriors of God, one of whom is an officer, from the Command of Rukh Tamani. These are those who combat the limbs and demons of Satan himself, the Other People, and their minions—those who would teach us to put our faith and our Lord in second place to them. We are further privileged in that the officer of whom I spoke, Child-of-God, will speak to us at this time of worship. It is a great honor for our family and we will remember it as long as the family lasts."

He got down from the platform and looked at Child, who left the first row of worshippers and came to the platform. His lean face looked down at them all; and his voice rang out like clashed iron over their heads.

" '. . . And I saw three unclean spirits like frogs come out of the mouth of the dragon, and out of the mouth of the beast, and out of the mouth of the false prophet.

" 'For they are the spirits of devils, working miracles, which go forth unto the kings of the Earth and of the whole world, to gather them to the battle of that great day of God Almighty. . . .' "

He broke off, looking at them all.

"Ye know that passage from the Book of Revelations?"

"We know." The soft chorus was unanimous from the listeners standing around Hal.

" 'And he gathered them together into a place called in the Hebrew tongue Armageddon.' " He paused again.

"Ye also know," he said, "that that beast and that false prophet, whose coming was foretold in Revelations, are now among us. Think not that to thou, and thou, and thou, their presence maketh a difference; because to one who testifies for the Living God there is never a difference from that which always was and always will be. There is only one day, the Day of the Lord; and what hour of that day it is, is of no matter to ye who are known to Him, or chosen to be His servants. Other than such as ye, there are only those who will be cast out in the final hour. But among those not to be cast out, none of ye need ask—'What is the hour and the moment in which I will testify for my God?' For all who serve the Lord will be called upon to testify and it matters not when."

He paused once more, this time for so long a moment that Hal began to think that he was done and about to step down from the lectern. But he went on.

"Nor does the manner of that testifying matter. Especially wrong is he who hopes that his testimony will be easily given, and he who dreams of a martyr's testimony. It is not the manner of giving but the giving itself, that matters. Remember that for thee, by night or day, waking or sleeping, alone or in the sight of multitudes, when thy testimony is required, only one thing is important and that is whether thou givest it or not. For he who is part of the Living God cannot fail to lift the banner of his faith in that moment; and he who is not will have no strength to do so."

There was a little sigh from the audience, so faint that it was just barely audible to Hal's ears.

"All are doomed who are not of the Lord. But those who testify do not do so only that they may exist eternally. For thy duty to thy God and His works is beyond thyself. If the Lord should come to thee before the moment of thy testifying and say, 'Servant and Warrior of mine art thou. But yet for my purposes, thou shalt be cast out with those others who know me not'— then, only if thou art truly of the faith will you answer correctly—'If it be thy will, Lord, so be it. For that I testify is all I ask . . .' ."

His voice had dropped on the last sentence almost to a whisper, but it was a whisper that reached every wall of the courtyard.

" 'For Thou my Lord hast been with me all my days and will be with me forever, nor can that which Thou art be taken from me—' " and once more, for three words, his voice dropped to that hoarse, penetrating near-whisper—

" '*Even by Thee,* my God. For as Thou art in me, so am I in Thee, forever and ever, beyond all time and universes; for Thou wert before those things and will be after them; and with Thy people may not be slain, but shall live beyond eternity.' "

He stopped speaking, at the last so quietly and so naturally that not only Hal, but the rest of those listening, were unprepared for the fact that he was finished. It was only when he stepped down from the lectern and returned to his place in the front ranks of those standing that they all realized it was over. Godlun went forward, stepped up and turned to face them.

"We will sing *Soldier, Ask Not*," he said.

They began to sing, without accompaniment but with the harmonious blending of voices long used to sounding together, and Hal sang with them; for this—originally a military hymn of the Friendly mercenary forces drafted to fight on other worlds—was one of those he had learned from Obadiah so early that he could not remember a time when he did not know it.

> "*Soldier, ask not—now, or ever,*
> *Where to war your banners go. . . .*"

They sang it to the end, standing there quietly in their ordinary, everyday clothes, with the peaceful walls of their home buildings surrounding them; and when they were done Godlun stepped down from the platform. The evening service was over; and above them the sky, still cloudless, had darkened with the fading of the light to a deep, cobalt blue in which it was still too early to see the pinprick lights of the stars.

"Come with me," Godlun said to Child; and led his guests back inside to seat them in the chairs by the top end of the long dining table. His own seat was one of the two at the very end itself. The other seat remained empty.

"My wife, Meah," he said to Child, in the first chair at his right, once they were all seated. He nodded his head toward the empty chair as if introducing a ghost to the other man.

"May the Lord keep her always," said Child.

"In His hands," said Godlun. "It's sixteen years now since her death. This large house where we all meet was planned by her."

Child nodded again, but said nothing.

"You are not married?" Godlun asked him.

"My wife and I lived under God's blessing for two years and five days," said Child, "before she was killed by Militia."

Godlun stared at him and blinked.

"How terrible!"

"God chose it so."

Godlun turned abruptly to shout back over his shoulder through a farther doorway from which came the noise and odors of a kitchen.

"Come now! Hurry, hurry!"

With that, the adult members of the family flooded in to fill the rest of the seats at the table as far as seats still remained available; and others of them appeared with burdened serving trays from the kitchen.

The meal was remarkable. Hal counted over fifteen separate dishes. Even in comparison with the way they had been fed by the other farm families that had entertained them since they had come down out of the mountains, this was a banquet. Godlun was evidently exerting himself and his resources to the utmost. In particular, there were an unusual number of vegetable dishes prepared in accordance with the strictures that governed what some-one like Child-of-God might allow himself to eat. Hal had never seen the older man dine so heartily; and it had the effect of making him unusually sociable. He answered Godlun's questions at greater and greater length; until, at last, when they had all moved to the large sitting room and the two were sitting together, close to the fireplace, painted by the light of the flames of the blaze there that had been raised against the chill of the spring evening, Child was all but conducting a monologue, with only an occasional question from Godlun thrown in from time to time.

". . . There is no doubt," he was telling the farmer, "that the numbers of the Militia grow daily as the ranks of those seduced by the Belial-spawn increase. This is a fact we must face; and it is as God wills."

"But . . ." Godlun hesitated. "You yourself—you have hope."

"Hope?" In the firelight the time-carved, lean face of Child stared into the round, anxious one of the other man.

"Hope that eventually the Militia and all other hounds of the Belial-spawn must be conquered, and cleansed from our world."

"It's not my duty to hope," said Child. "What is, is what God wills."

"But He can't will that all we've built here over generations, and on Association as well, should be conquered by such as these? That our churches should be closed, our worshipping voices be silenced and all that we've done go down to dust?" said Godlun.

"Knoweth thou the will of the Lord?" asked Child. "It may be just that which is his wish; and if so, who are we to question? Only an hour since did I not hear thee sing with me—*Soldier, ask not, now or ever, where to war your banners go!*"

Godlun shook his head slowly.

"I can't believe He would—"

"Thou art concerned for thy children, and for thy children's children," said Child, less harshly. "But remember that even these are not thine. They are only lent thee for a little while by the Lord; and He will use them as He requires."

"But things aren't that bad," said Godlun. "The Militia are a trouble to us, yes; and it's true that, in the cities, those who fawn on the Others have things their own way. But the core of our land, our people and our religion, continues here in the countryside, untouched. We—"

"In thy small corner, thou wouldst say, there is still peace," interrupted Child. "But look beyond that corner. When thou art wanted, when thy children and thy fields are desired for purposes of the Others, will they not come and take all these, too, from thee, at their whim? Look not merely at the cities of this world, but at all the cities on all worlds. Everywhere the Belial-spawn move almost without check or hindrance. Those of us who are strong in the faith they cannot touch; but almost all others see them once, and ever after pant at their heels, following without question for one pat on the head, one word of praise from these, their new, false and painted idols. The beast and the false prophet of which Revelation speaks are already among us, gathering their forces for Armageddon across the face of all the worlds."

"But God will conquer when Armageddon comes!"

"In His own way."

Godlun shook his head, and looked away, helplessly into the fire.

"I don't believe this," he said, low-voiced, to the flames. "I've heard many say this, but I couldn't believe it; and that was why I had to talk to someone like you. How can you, who've given your life to fighting His enemies, talk as if the final battle might be lost?"

"Man of plows and peace," said Child, almost sadly, "look outward at the universe. The battle you talk of is already lost. The times are already changed. Even if these whom God has cursed were to be swept away tomorrow, still the old ways are already gone, and not by their doing—but by ours. All the centuries since Mankind first had life breathed into him are coming now to their end, and all that has been built is crumbling. Did not I hear the lascivious and idle sound of a musical instrument in thy own house, as I came up? Yet, he who played—whoever that may be—is still beneath thy roof. He was without doubt at worship with the rest of us, an hour since. If thy own household be so fallen into the gutters and alleyways of sin, how canst thou hope for the redemption of the worlds of men, when within thy own walls there is none?"

Godlun raised his head from the flames and stared at Child. The tendons in his throat moved and stood out, but he made only a small sound that was not even a word.

"Nay," said Child, with real gentleness. "Who am I to blame thee? I only show thee what is. For thousands of years the Earth endured as the cradle of God's children, until it came upon evil ways with the luxury of many tools and instruments. Then might the end have come, at that time. But God gave Man one more chance, and opened these further worlds to him. And all went out, each together with those he thought of as his or her own kind, and tried to build again as they thought best, under different suns. But out of all those efforts were made only three peoples which had never been before: we of Faith; those we called the Deniers of God but who call themselves the Exotics; and those of War known as the Dorsai. And, as time hath shown, none of these were God's answer, however much they might be their own; and from their failure has now come these of mixed breeding whom we call the Others, who would make all the worlds their pleasure garden and all other men and women into slaves. Canst thou look at all this and not see that once more we have thrown away the chance given us; so that nothing now remains but for Him to let us reap the harvest we have sowed; and for all who call themselves Mankind to go down finally into darkness and silence, forever?"

Godlun stared at him.

"But you keep fighting!"

"Of course!" said Child. "I am of God, whatever or whoever else is not. I must testify to Him by placing my body against the enemy while that body lasts; and by protecting those that my small strength may protect, until my personal end. What is it to me that all the peoples of all the worlds choose to march toward the nether pit? What they do in their sins is no concern of mine. Mine only is concern for God, and the way of God's people of whom I am one. In the end, all those who march pitward will be forgotten; but I and those like me who have lived their faith will be remembered by the Lord—other than that I want nothing and I need nothing."

Godlun dropped his face into his hands and sat for a moment. When he took his hands away again and raised his head, Hal saw that the skin of his face was drawn and he looked very old.

"It's all right for you," he whispered.

"It is fleshly loves that concern thee," said Child, nearly as softly. "I know, for I remember how it was in the little time I had with my wife; and I remember the children unborn that she and I dreamed of together. It is thy children thou wouldst protect in these dark days to come; and it was thy hope that I could give thee reason to think thou couldst do so. But I have no such hope to give. All that thou lovest will perish. The Others will make a foul garden of the worlds of humankind and there will be none to stop them. Turn thee to God, my brother, for nowhere else shalt thou find comfort."

Chapter

> > **22** < <

Sometime in the depths of that night following the dinner, Hal awoke in the long room that had been given the visitors for a dormitory; and, looking down the double row of mattresses with their sleeping forms, decorated by the lozenges of illumination from the moonlight shining through the uncurtained windows, saw all quiet and still.

He rose on his elbow, troubled by the feeling of uneasiness with which he had wakened, but unable to account for it. Then from a distance came a small, repeated sound that gave his mind no picture of what could be causing it. It came from outside the room, through the open windows at the far end. He got up, walked on unshod feet to the end of the nearest of the open windows and looked out. In the courtyard below him where the service had been held, he saw a man's figure, black in the moonlight, seated on one of the benches with its shoulders hunched. As he watched, the shoulders shook, the right hand of the figure went up to the mouth and the sound came again, recognizable now as coughing. With that recognition, his mind identified the familiar shape of the figure; and he did not have to look back into the room behind him to see what mattress lay under empty covers.

The man down there was Child-of-God. Hal stood watching while two more of the paroxysms of coughing shook the figure, then turned and went back to his own bed. Child-of-God did not come back to the room as long as he lay awake, watching; and after a while, Hal fell asleep once more.

They were on their way the next morning while dawn was still red in the east. Godlun's entire household turned out to see them off and fill their packs with cold foods packaged by the kitchen to see them through until evening and the next family that would put them up for a night. The leave-takings they had been engaged in with members of the family had been as warm as if they had been members of the family itself.

Once on the road, Child took the lead as usual without a word. Watching the older man, Hal could not see anything in the leathery face and swift stride of the older man that might indicate a cause for the moonlit fit of coughing in the courtyard the night before. But he found himself studying Rukh's lieutenant with reawakened interest.

By day, Child showed no sign of weakness or illness. He led them at a steady pace through the next few weeks; and it was not until five days later that Hal, waking in the night, discovered the older man missing once more from the sleeping room assigned to them at that night's farm. Looking outside, Hal once more discovered Child seated like someone waiting out a bout of pain, and occasionally breaking into coughing.

Hal probed the rest of their group with cautious questions; but evidently none of the others had ever heard or seen Child on one of these nighttime excursions; and any suggestion that the Command's First Officer might be ill was met with the lighthearted belief that he was made of metal and leather and no weakness would dare attack him.

They finally reached their rendezvous. It was the Mohler-Beni farm, a large place operated jointly by two separate families, so that a good hundred-and-twenty-odd people were normally in residence and the coming and going of the additional hundred of the reunited Command would not attract as much attention as their activity would on one of the farms of more average size. They were less than thirty kilometers from Masenvale, the small city that held the metals-storage unit and the fertilizer plant that were their targets.

The group containing Hal and Child was the last to arrive. It was at the end of an unusually warm summer day and after they had stowed their gear in one of the large equipment sheds which were being used as barracks for them, the fresh cool of the evening breeze was pleasant as Hal walked with the others to a late meal in the farm's main kitchen.

After the dinner, Rukh collected not only Child, but Hal, and took them off to her private room in the farmhouse—a guest bedroom now cluttered with papers and supplies.

"Howard," Rukh said to Hal, once she had shut the door of the room firmly behind them, "I'm asking you here now, not to discuss plans with James and myself, but to act as a source of information from that early military training of yours."

Hal nodded.

"Come over here to the map, both of you," she said.

They followed her to a table set up in front of an open window, the large-scale local map on it anchored with fist-sized polished stones against the newly-awakened evening breeze. There was a moistness and electricity in the air that promised a thunderstorm.

"James, I've just got word from our friends in Masenvale," she said. "They've promised at least half a dozen fires and the setting off of burglar alarms in four businesses on the south side to divert local police and Militia away from our targets. We're bound to run into some district police forces at the fertilizer plant, but with any luck the fires and alarms, to start with, and after that the raid by the group you'll be with, Howard, on the metals unit, should keep our opposition at the plant from being reinforced until we've loaded up and gone."

She turned to the table.

"Now, look here," she said.

"Here's the Mohler-Beni farm." Rukh put her finger down on the lower half of the map. "Almost due southwest is Masenvale with the fertilizer plant on the outskirts, on a direct line between us, here, and the center of the city, where the metals-storage is located. South-southwest . . . ," her finger traced a line on the map around and beyond the city area, "are the foothills of the

Aldos mountain range, which is the territory we'll be running for, after we've got the fertilizer—"

She broke off, for the sound of heavy air-cushion vehicles had intruded through the open window upon the conversation. She sighed, relaxing a little; and Hal looked at her, sharply. It was not usual for her to show any sign of emotion, even when gaining something like the transport that was now arriving, and which had been critical to the success of her plans.

"The trucks," she said.

They had been sweating out the arrival of these vehicles from farmers in the neighborhood well enough off to own them, and committed enough to the Command to risk them in an endeavor like the one Rukh was to lead tomorrow. The raids on the fertilizer plant and on the metals-storage building would have been literally impossible without transport; and there had been, until this moment, no absolute certainty that enough would be volunteered. Now, judging by the sounds that continued to come in the open window, the trucks had appeared in numbers that would be more than adequate to the needs of the Command. Rukh turned back to her map.

"With those here now, and any luck at all," she said, "we should be into the back roads of the foothills before the Militia can put any force worth worrying about out after us; and once in the foothills, we can leave them to their regular drivers, off-load the donkeys and lose any pursuit without much trouble—"

"What about the drivers, when the Militia catches them?" Hal asked.

Rukh looked levelly at him.

"I said you weren't here to be involved in the discussion, but only to act as an information source," she said. "However—as soon as they let us off, the drivers will split up, each going his own way along the back roads and trails, or even overland. With their trucks empty, there'll be nothing to charge the drivers with; and not even the Militia's going to be heavy-handed about questioning local people unless they've got some evidence. The authorities know how necessary this farm belt is to the survival of North Continent, to say nothing of the rest of Harmony. That's why they've let the people in this mid-plains area go so free of the restrictions they've placed on people elsewhere."

The sound of the incoming trucks outside ceased.

"They are fat here, with the fat that comes from laziness of soul," said Child. "Though there are those of faith among them."

"In any case," said Rukh, "I've answered your question, Howard. Don't interrupt again. Look at the Aldos range, on the map, please, both of you. It runs south and east. I think we can follow along it in reasonable safety until we come to the general vicinity of Ahruma, where the Core Tap is, and the energy complex built around it. We'll have to leave the foothills then for the open plain to reach Ahruma; but it's within striking distance. We should be able to make the run to it in a couple of hours, going in, and in another couple, coming out after we've sabotaged the Tap. For that, of course, we'll need trucks again and reinforcements from the local people there—will you shut that window, Howard? They're getting noisy out there."

Hal moved to shut the window, catching sight as he turned of Child's face, which was stiff and angry, staring at the open window. As Hal's hands touched the hasp fastened to the lower edge of the top-pivoted window, there broke out, over the babble of voices outside, the unexpected wheezy sound of some instrument like a concertina or an accordion. Hal pulled the window closed in the same instant; and, turning, saw Child heading out the door of Rukh's room.

"James—" began Rukh sharply. But her Lieutenant was already gone, the door closing behind him. She gave a short, exasperated breath, then straightened and turned back to Hal.

"While I have the chance," said Hal, swiftly, before she could send him also out of the room, "can I ask you—is he ill?"

She stood, arrested, one hand still on the map.

"Ill?" she said. "James?"

"On the way here I got the idea he might be," Hal said, apologetically. As she stood listening, he told her what he had seen of Child's nocturnal coughing fits. When he was done, she looked at him almost coldly for a few seconds before answering.

"Have you told anyone else about his?" she asked.

"No," said Hal.

Some of the tension went out of the way she stood.

"Good," she said. She considered him for a moment. When she spoke again, her voice was flat.

"He's old," she said, "too old for this sort of life; and he's driven himself beyond his physical limits since he was a boy. There's no stopping him. His only aim is to use himself up in the service of the Lord in the way he thinks best; and we'd be doing him no kindness to interfere with his doing it."

"That coughing's just age?" asked Hal.

Her eyes were level and dark on him.

"That coughing comes from fluid seeping into his lungs when he lies flat too long," she said. "His heart's worn out; and his body's wearing out. There's nothing to be done for him as long as he goes on putting himself through this like a younger man, and he won't consider stopping. Also—we need him. Moreover his life's the Lord's, first; his own, second; and only after that, anyone else's to dictate."

"I see," said Hal. "But—"

He was interrupted by sudden silence outside as the music broke off, followed by the distant, harsh and angry voice of Child, so blurred by distance and the resonances from surrounding structures that it was impossible to make out what he was saying.

"What if the Command gets into a situation where it's dependent upon his being well enough to do what he'd ordinarily do—" Having begun once more, he broke off again, seeing she was not listening to him but to the sounds from outside. He stood watching her, for a moment, like some unseen observer.

"Read all signals," Walter the InTeacher had told him, "not merely what the eyes, the ears and the nose pick up, but what you can read of gestalt patterns of response in those around you. Situations in which you lack experience may be interpretable through observation of those you are with at the time. Learn to read, therefore, at secondhand. Animals and children do this all the time. We all know how to do this, instinctively; but habits and patterns of the mature and conscious mind lead us away from it."

What Hal read now in the attitude of Rukh was an interpretation of the noise outside as a cause of unusual uneasiness—for reasons he himself could not find. But it did not matter that he could not, for in this case it was enough to see the understanding of Rukh.

Abruptly, though there was no difference in Child's voice that Hal could hear, the uneasiness in Rukh changed to alarm—and decision. Without warning she suddenly swung about and headed out the door. He followed.

They came out together into the wide side-yard of the farm, on to a nighttime scene lit by the overhead lights of the buildings surrounding three sides of it. A long row of large, van-type produce trucks were parked along one side of the yard and before these were gathered a number of the younger people of the Command and almost an equal number of young men in local farm clothes, evidently those who had brought the trucks.

They were gathered about one of the truck drivers, who carried an obviously homemade accordion slung by a wide strap over one shoulder. But the accordion was silent; the people there were all silent, except for Child, who addressed them all and had all their eyes upon him. Now that he could see the faces of those here, Hal understood Rukh's reaction, for the expressions of the Command members were embarrassed, and the expressions of the truck drivers ranged from sullenness to open anger.

With the appearance of Rukh, Child fell silent also.

"What's going on here?" she asked.

"Dancing!" he spat out. "As Whores of Babylon—"

"James!" Rukh's voice snapped. He stopped speaking. She looked over the others, her gaze ending at last on the truck drivers who had drawn closer to each other in a ragged group around the man with the musical instrument.

"This is not a holiday," she said, clearly, "or a children's game; no matter what your community here allows you to do. Is that understood by all of you who've volunteered to help us?"

There was a shuffling silence among the truck drivers. The one with the accordion, a broad-chested individual with tightly-curled brown hair, shrugged the strap of it off his shoulder, and—catching the strap with his hand—lowered the instrument until it sat on the ground at his feet.

"All right, then," said Rukh, when there was no further answer. "You drivers go and stand by your individual trucks. Our Command members have already been organized into truck teams. We'll begin counting from this end of the row of vehicles and the Number One team for the fertilizer plant will use that truck; Number Two, the next, and so on until all the teams for the fertilizer plant are assigned to trucks. Then the Number One team for the valuable-metals raid will take the first succeeding truck, and so on, down the line. Teams get together with your drivers now. I want you to know him, and him to know you, by sight."

She started to turn away.

"James, Howard!" she said to them. "Come back upstairs with me and we'll finish what we were doing—"

"Wait a minute!"

It was the voice of the accordionist, interrupting her. She turned back to face the crowd; and the local man, leaving his instrument on the ground, came forward toward her and Hal. The other locals edged after him.

"Him," said the accordionist, when he stood within arm's length of her, looking past her at Hal. "He's the one they're looking for, isn't he? If he is, hadn't we ought to be told about that?"

"What are you talking about?" asked Rukh.

"This one," the accordionist pointed to Hal, meeting Hal's eyes squarely. "Isn't he the one all the fuss is about? And if he is, what's he doing coming along on something like this, when just having him with us can be dangerous?"

"I'll give you one more chance to explain yourself," said Rukh. "This is one of our Command members, Howard Immanuelson. If the Militia are looking for him, they're looking for all of us."

"Not like they're looking for him," said the accordionist. He glanced aside at Child, who had drawn close on the other side of Rukh. "They've got his picture up everywhere; and there's a special officer—one of the Elect, a Militia Captain named Barbage, spending his time doing nothing but heading up the search. He's got the whole district looking for this Immanuelson. Like I say, it's dangerous just having him here with you, let alone taking him along on a raid. For everybody's sakes, he ought to be cleared out of the territory."

"This officer whom thou callest of the Elect—although when was one of God's enemies such?" broke in Child. "Is he taller than I am, with black hair and a way of squeezing his eyes together when he blasphemes in his attempt to use godly speech?"

The accordionist looked at him.

"You know him, then?"

Child looked at Rukh.

"It was the officer who commanded the ambush against us in the pass," said Child. "He saw both Howard and myself."

"But it's Immanuelson he wants," the accordionist said. "Ask anyone around here. What's he wanted for?"

"You don't ask that of the Warriors of the Commands," said Rukh. Her voice was clear and hard.

The other's eyes fell away for a second time from the gaze she bent on him, then raised stubbornly again.

"This isn't just a Command matter," he said. "We all came to help you, not knowing you had him with you. I tell you, he's a risk to all of us, just by being here! If you won't tell us why they want him so much, you ought to get rid of him."

"This Command is my responsibility," Rukh said. "If you join us, you take directions. You don't give them."

She started to turn away once more.

"That's not right!" called out the accordionist; and there was a small mutter from his fellow truck drivers to back him up. She turned back. "This is our district, Captain! We're the ones who have to put up with the Militia after you've gone and your raid's been made. We don't mind that; we even come to help you make it—like this. But when we're part of what you do, we ought to have a say in the way you do it, when you make it risky for us. Why don't we vote on whether he goes or not? Wasn't that the way the Commands always used to operate—just like the mercenary soldiers? They had the right to vote, didn't they, if their leaders wanted to do something the majority of them didn't want?"

For a moment no one said anything in the farmyard.

"The mercenary code," Hal said, hearing his voice sounding strange in the new silence, "only allowed troops to vote down their officers when at least ninety-nine percent of them—"

His words were overridden by a verbal explosion from Child-of-God.

"Ye would vote?"

They all turned to him. He stood, shoulders wide, hands a little raised at his sides and his head jutting forward, staring at the drivers.

"Ye would all vote?" The echoes of his voice cracked off the walls of the buildings surrounding them on three sides. "Ye, with the milk of your farms wet on your lips, the muck of stables thick on your boots, ye would vote on whether one who has fought for the Lord should be kept or sent away?"

He took two steps toward them. They stood without moving, watching him—almost without breathing.

"Who are ye to talk of voting? Howard Immanuelson hath fought by the side of those in this Command, as ye have not. He hath labored with us, walked with us, gone cold and hungry with us, to oppose the Belial-spawn and their minions; while ye have not, only grown up soft and played and danced under their indulgence. What business is it of such as ye that a Warrior of the Lord is being specially searched for in thy district? Ye are the fat and useless sheep on which our enemies feed. We are the wolves of God— and ye would raise your voice to command us?"

He paused. They stood, unmoving; even the man with the accordion seemed to be caught like a fly in the amber of Child's anger.

"I tell ye all now, so that ye may remember, that what ye fear so has no meaning for us," he said. "What is it to us who fight, that this district of thine should be under special search for Howard Immanuelson? What matter if all the districts between these two mountain ranges should be in search for him, or if this continent, this world, and all the worlds at once should be searching for him? Were none but the hundred of our Command opposed by all other humanity, and should they offer us a choice of immediate destruction or all that we wished to gain, if only we would give up one of us— our answer would be the same as if a child in the roadway asked the same question of us, in our full and weaponed power."

He paused again. In his lined face, his eyes were dark as starless space.

"Ye so fear, some of ye, to be in the company of Howard Immanuelson?" he went on, at last. "Then take thy trucks and go. We have no need of such as ye, nor of anything ye have, for we who fight stand in the shadow of the Lord, who is all-sufficient!"

He stopped speaking and this time did not start again. Hal glanced at Rukh, remembering her relief when she had heard the sound of the trucks arriving. But she stood, watching the drivers and saying nothing. Beyond, the other members of the Command also stood and said nothing. Like Child, like Rukh, they waited, their eyes on the truck drivers. At last, one by one, the drivers stirred and began to move away from one another, each of them going to a truck and turning about to wait beside the door on the control side of the cab. Last of all, the man with the accordion dropped his eyes, turned and went to stand by the single vehicle that still lacked someone beside it.

"All right," said Rukh. She spoke dryly; but in the continued stillness her voice seemed to ring almost as loudly as Child's. "Teams, gather at your trucks. Team leaders, brief your drivers on where they're to take you and what's expected of them. James, Howard, come with me."

She led the two of them back to her room and to the interrupted briefing session.

Chapter

> > **23** < <

The metals-storage unit of Masenvale was a windowless concrete box surrounded by a high, static-charged fence and lit at night by floodlights that showed the fortified gatehouse and the heavy locked entrance doors stark against the surrounding darkness. It stood alone, in the warm lowland night following the one on which the trucks had arrived at the Mohler-Beni farm, surrounded by a square, two business blocks from the District Militia Headquarters, in the downtown area of this middle-sized city. The relative darkness inside the windowed gatehouse made the man on guard there invisible to the twelve members of the Command who had been driven to the edge of the square by the man who owned the accordion. He had parked the vehicle around the corner from the square in the shadows between two floating streetlights; and his passengers, Hal among them, had quietly slipped out of the van into the shadows, and were now gathered just behind the corner of a building facing on the square. The driver had remained with the truck, the vehicle facing away from the scene, his motor switch on warm, with his finger on the switch and the idle position only a finger-twitch away.

The metals unit and its surrounding fence slept in the unchanging pattern of light and shadow. Beyond its front gates and the gatehouse, the concrete surface of the square graded back into the darker shadow of the building, behind a corner of which they stood.

Hal felt a loosening of the muscles of his shoulders and the coolness of the night air being pulled deep into his lungs; and recognized the adaptations of the body to the expectation of possible conflict. A calmness and a detachment seemed, for the first time, to have come over him from the same source. He looked about for Jason, caught the eye of the smaller man, and led the way out into the square. Talking in low voices, apparently immersed in their conversation, the two of them started across the square on a slant that would take them past the front of the static-charged fence with its gate and gatehouse, guarding the unit.

As they moved down alongside the fence past the gatehouse, Hal was just able to make out through one of its windows the peaked cap of the single civilian guard seated within at his desk. Hal slowed his step, Jason slowed with him, and eventually they came to a halt just outside the gates themselves, apparently deep in conversation.

They talked on, their voices so low that their words would not have been understandable unless a listener was standing almost within arm's length of them. They stood, centimeters from the fence with its static charge that would be released at any contact to stun, if not kill, whoever had touched

the metal of the fence. Time went on. After a while, the door to the guard-
house opened and the guard stuck his head out.

"You two out there!" he called. "You can't stand there. Move on!"

Hal and Jason ignored him.

"Did you hear me? Move on!"

They continued to ignore him.

Boots thumping loudly on the three steps down from the gatehouse door
to the concrete of the square, the guard came out. The door slammed loudly
behind him. He came up to the fence, careless about touching his side of it;
for any touch from within deactivated the mechanism producing the static
charge.

"Did you hear me?" His voice came loudly at them through the wide openings in the wire mesh, from less than an arm's length away. "Both of you—
move on before I call Militia Headquarters to come pick you up for distur-
bance!"

Still they acted as if he was not there. He stepped right up against the
fence, grabbed the wire and shouted at them; and as he did so, they stepped
away, back along it on their side.

"What's going on here—" the guard began.

He did not finish. There was a distant, twanging noise, a hum in the air,
and a second later a crossbow bolt with a blunt and padded head flickered
into the lights to strike the side of the guard's head with the impact of a black-
jack. The man slumped against the fence and began to sag down it toward
the concrete; and, reaching swiftly through a couple of the wide mesh spaces,
Hal caught and held him, upright but unconscious, against the fence.

With the fence registering an upright and still-living body pressed against
its inner surface, its static charge was quiescent. Reaching through it, past
Hal's straining shoulder muscles, Jason unclipped the picture-crowned identity badge of the guard from the left pocket of his uniform jacket, and carried it over to the sensor plate in the right-hand gatepost. He pressed the
face of the badge against the plate. There was a slight pause and then, recognizing the badge, the gates swung smoothly and quietly open.

Jason dodged through and put his hand against the interior control plate
on the back of the same gatepost. He held it there and the gates stayed open.
Hal let go of the guard, who slid down to lie still at the foot of the fence.

Jason went swiftly to stand at one side of the closed doors of the building,
drawing a handgun from under his shirt as he did so. Hal came around to
pick up the guard, take him into the gatehouse and immobilize him there
with tape and a gag. The other ten Command members flooded smoothly
across the square and through the open gate of the fence—which the last
of them closed behind him.

Hal came out of the gatehouse, carrying the sidearm from the leg holster
of the once more conscious, but trussed and now-undressed, guard. He
handed the clothes to the member of the Command they seemed most likely
to fit and the man who had taken them put them on, pulling the cap low

over his eyes. Tilting his head down to pull his face back into the deep shadow below the visor of the uniform hat, the spurious guard stood directly before the sensor plate to the right of the doors, blocking out its view of anything else, and pressed the doorcall button.

There was a second's wait.

"Jarvy?" said a voice from a speaker panel above the plate.

The uniformed member grunted wordlessly, still holding his head down.

"What?" demanded the speaker panel.

The spurious guard grunted again.

"I can't hear you, Jarvy—what is it?"

The member said nothing, still looking down with his face in shadow.

"Just a minute," said the speaker panel. "There's something wrong with the voice pickup out there—"

The two doors swung open in neat mechanical unison. Framed in the white glare of illumination from the interior of the metals unit stood another guard, peering out into the darkness.

"Jarvy, what—" he began; and then he went down, silenced by hands on his mouth and throat even as he fell under the unified rush of several bodies.

"Where's the metals room?" Jason asked Hal, soft-voiced.

"Straight back," answered Hal, an image of the plan of the unit's interior which Rukh had shown him clear in his memory. He pointed along the hand truck–wide corridor they had just entered. "But the guard-office's to the right. You'd better wait until we clear that."

Jason nodded and fell back. Hal, with two other men and three women of the Command, all armed now with handguns produced from within their clothing, went swiftly and quietly ahead down the corridor and burst in through the first door to their right, which was standing ajar. But inside there was only a single other guard, sitting on a cot at one end of a small room filled with surveillance screens, a power rifle on his knees.

At the sight of them he stared—grasped the rifle as if he would swing it up into firing position, then dropped it as if it had burned his fingers. Going forward before the protection of the handguns those behind him held levelled on the man, Hal picked up the power rifle and found it, not broken open for cleaning as he had expected, but loaded and ready to use.

"What were you going to do with it?" Hal asked the guard.

"Nothing . . ." The guard stared up at him, hopelessly, with frightened eyes.

"How many other people on duty here, now?" Hal loomed over him.

"Just Ham—just Ham and me, and Jarvy on the gate!" said the guard. He was white-faced and shock was losing out to fear.

"How do you unlock the metals room?"

"We can't," said the guard. "Really—we can't. They don't let us. It's a time lock on the door."

Hal looked down at him through a long moment of silence.

"I'm going to ask you again," he said. "This time, forget what they told you to say. How do you open the metals-room door?"

The guard stared up at him.

"You're the man they're looking for so hard, aren't you?" he blurted out.

"Never mind that," said Hal. "The door to the metals room—?"

"I—code KJ9R on the control keyboard—" The guard nodded almost eagerly toward the other side of the room. "The one under the large screen, there. That's the truth, that really opens it."

"We know." Hal smiled at him. "I was just checking. Lie down where you are, now, and we'll tie you up. You won't be hurt."

The other Command members with him converged on the guard; and Hal took the power rifle with him as he went back toward the door. As they began to tie the man up, he stepped to the screen the guard had indicated and keyed in the code the man had given. Rukh had explained to him that the Commands normally had little trouble finding out ahead of time the information they would need for raids on places such as this; but it was the practice to always check such information when that was possible. Holding the power rifle, he went back out to the corridor.

"The metals door ought to be open now," he told a senior member of the Command, a man named Heidrick Falt. "The guard gave me the same code Rukh had."

Falt nodded, his eyes thoughtful upon Hal. Falt had been named group leader for this raid. Rukh's instructions had been to let Hal lead only on the way in. As far as Hal could tell, Falt had not resented that exception to his authority; but it was a relief to hand the Command back to the other man, now.

"Good," said Falt. He had a reedy voice too young for his face and body. "We'll start to load up. You go back and sit with the driver."

"Right." Hal nodded.

He left the building. Outside, the square showed no change. It still seemed to slumber under the same lights and shadows as before; and from the outside the metals unit sat with the same air of impregnability it had seemed to wear earlier. He turned the corner, reached the truck and climbed back into the cab. In the small interior glow of the instrument panel the driver turned a round face toward him in which there was no hint of friendliness.

"Ready to go?" he said.

"A while yet," Hal answered.

For a moment he played with the idea of trying to break through the shell of enmity in which the other had encased himself. Then he put the thought aside. The driver was too tense to be reached at this moment. The concern here was not with how much he might fear and dislike Hal but with whether, as not infrequently happened with local volunteers, his nerve might snap with the waiting, causing him to drive off and leave the raiding party stranded. It was to guard against this that Falt had sent Hal back here. The less said between the two of them right now, the better.

They sat, and the minutes crawled by. The driver shifted position from time to time, sighed, rubbed his nose, looked out of the window then back at the instrument panel, and made a dozen other small movements and sounds. Hal sat still and silent, as he had been taught to do under such conditions, deliberately removing a part of his attention from the present moment and reaching out into the abstract universe of the mind. In the present semi-suspended state of consciousness that resulted, it seemed to him that he could almost feel beside him the presence of Rukh, who would now be at the fertilizer area. He felt her as if she were both there, and here with him at the same moment. It was an eerie but powerful sensation; and a poem began to shape itself about it, in the back of his thoughts.

> And if it should not be you, after all—
> Down the long passage, turning in the hall;
> Or slipping at a distance through the light
> Of streetlamped corners just within my sight;
> I will not then turn back into my room,
> Chilled and disheartened wrapped in angry gloom;
> But warm myself to think the mind should send
> So many shades of you to be my friend. . . .

The poem disturbed him. It was not right, somehow. It was too light and facile, not cast in the way he normally thought or had been taught to think. But at the same time it rang with a sense of something discovered he had not known before. It seemed to echo off things completely removed from his present reality, things half-hidden in corners and cul-de-sacs of personal pain that he had never known and could not now remember—lonelinesses that had no proper part of life as he now knew it. For a moment, something moved far back in his mind; he seemed to feel an echoing, down endless centuries of moments such as this, in all of which he now remembered being isolated and set apart from others. Uneasily, he pushed the memories from him. But they returned, along with barely-registered sensations of pains he did not remember ever feeling, as if he had known them all, and been the one within them all. . . .

The door to the cab opened. Falt looked inside.

"Open the back doors," he said. "We're coming in."

The driver touched a control stud on his instrument panel. Behind them they heard the doors trundle apart. Hal moved back from the cab section into the body of the van to help with the loading of whatever metal the Command had lifted from the unit.

"What are they?" he asked, as heavy, smooth grey ingots began to be passed in to him by those standing on the pavement outside the doors. "What did you bring?"

"High-tin solder," panted Jason, passing in his personal burden. "About forty ingots all told. Not too much to carry, but it ought to convince the authorities this was what we were actually after and the fertilizer warehouse business was the diversion."

Taking and stacking the ingots, Hal put the poem and the ghost memories firmly from him. He was back now in the ordinary universe, where things were as hard and heavy and real as the ingots of solder.

They finished loading and drove off. Falt took over the passenger seat in the cab, but kept Hal there to talk to him as they went.

"I think we ought to head for the foothills, without trying to rendezvous with the rest at the fertilizer warehouse," Falt said. "What do you think?"

"And give up the idea of splitting the metal up among the other trucks, so that if we lose a truck or two, we don't lose it all?"

"That's secondary," said Falt. "You know that. Our whole raid was secondary to the fertilizer raid; and we took longer than Rukh estimated to get things done here. No, the main thing is to get as many of us as possible safely back to the Command. I think the hills are safer."

"A dozen people on foot," Hal said, "won't be able to move very far or fast with all those ingots, once we leave the truck. We've gotten away clear. No one's chasing us; and if the rest of you left those guards tied up right it could be hours before the alarm goes out on what we did. I'd say make the rendezvous."

Falt had been sitting sideways on the seat to look back at Hal, now squatting on the small space of open floor in the cab behind both seats. At Hal's answer, Falt turned his head back to look out the windshield of the truck. They were skimming at good speed above the concrete strip of one of the main routes radiating from the center of the city.

"We must be halfway to the fertilizer warehouse now—isn't that right, driver?" said Hal.

There was a slight pause.

"Almost," said the driver, slowly.

Falt looked over at him.

"You'd rather head for the foothills now?" he asked.

"Yes!" The answer was explosive.

"We don't know what's happened at the fertilizer area," Hal said. "They could need another truck and the help of the extra dozen of us."

Falt blew out a short breath, staring through the windshield again. Then he looked first back at Hal, then at the driver.

"All right," he said. "That's where we'll go."

When they got to the turnoff from the route that was closest to the fertilizer plant, there was a redness to be seen above the skyline of buildings to their left.

"The place could be swarming with Militia already," said the driver.

"Just go there," Falt said.

The driver obeyed. Less than two minutes brought them around the corner of a tall lightless office building and the driver brought the truck to a halt.

Ahead of them was a fenced-in area that looked as if it might encompass several city blocks. Within the fence was one tall, almost windowless cube of a concrete building, and several other long, wide concrete structures with curved roofs like sections of barrels laid lengthwise over the rectangular blocks beneath. One of these was aflame at its far end; and lights and alarm bells within that or other buildings could be heard shrilling in the distance. Beyond two truck-wide gates in the fence, now gaping wide open, the dark shapes of the other van-type trucks the Command had brought stood outlined against the light of the burning structure.

"They're still there," said Hal.

"Go in," said Falt to the driver.

"No," said the driver. "I'm staying here where I can make a run for it. You go in on foot if you want."

Falt drew a sidearm from under his shirt and held the muzzle against the driver's right temple.

"Go in," he said.

The driver started up the truck once more. They drove in. As they got closer to the trucks, a scene of ordered confusion became visible between and about them. Most of the members of the Command were engaged in the carrying of twenty-five-kilogram bags of fertilizer on their shoulders, from a stack of them outside the burning building to the vans of individual trucks. The body of a man lay before the firelit front end of one of the trucks; and in the center of the activity stood Rukh, directing it.

Hal and the others left their truck; and, with Falt, Hal came up to Rukh. The rest of their team went unordered to the necessary business of loading sacks of fertilizer into their own truck.

As he and Falt got close to Rukh, Hal saw her for a moment outlined against the red light of the fire. It was as if she stood darkly untouched in the heart of the flames. Then someone passed beyond her with a sack over her shoulder and the illusion was lost. As they came up, she turned, saw them, and spoke without waiting.

"We've got three wounded," she told Falt. "No one killed; and we've chased off the district police for the moment. They'll be back shortly with help, so I'm going to have you take those three and whatever you've already got loaded and leave for the rendezvous ahead of the rest of us. They're all three in Tallah's truck, right now. Send six of your people to carry them over. How'd you do?"

"No one even hurt," said Falt. "Typical small-city guards. Not like Militia at all. They practically rolled over and put their paws in the air for us."

"Good," said Rukh. "Get moving, then. We've cut alarm communications and some of the local people are helping to contain information on the fact we're here; but I don't estimate more than another fifteen minutes before we've got Militia around our ears. Howard, if for any reason the wounded have to split off from the rest, you're to stay with them."

"Right," said Hal.

Chapter

> > **24** < <

He and Falt went back to the truck. Falt began reassigning members of their team, as they returned laden, to the job of bringing over the three wounded. Once a sufficient number had been sent, he put the rest as they came in to passing over to other trucks as many of the ingots as could be moved before the three casualties were brought. Five minutes later, they were out of the gates and leaving the red glow behind them; the dark ribbon of the route unwinding before the nose of their truck and the dark shapes of the foothills and further mountains rising on the night horizon under the still starlit sky. The new moon had not yet put in its appearance.

Once more Falt took the cab seat beside the driver. Hal went back into the body of the van to look at the wounded. One was Morelly Walden; and in the dim interior of the van with its single small overhead light, the lines and creases in the heavy face appeared deeper; so that he seemed to have aged another ten years at least into the realm of the truly old.

"It's his leg," said Joralmon Troy, looking up from where he sat cross-legged beside Morelly's stretcher, perched on its low, dark pile of fertilizer bags. "When we blew out the door of the warehouse, a big piece got him in the leg and broke it."

"Did they give you anything for the pain?" Hal asked Morelly, reading the deepness of the facial creases.

"No," said Morelly, hoarsely. "No sinful drugs."

Hal hesitated.

"If you like," he said, "there's a way I could massage your forehead and neck to help relieve the pain."

"No," said Morelly, effortfully. "The pain is by God's will. I'll bear it as His Warrior."

Hal touched him gently on the shoulder and went to look at the other two casualties, a woman who had taken a weapon burn in her right shoulder, superficial but painful, and a man who had been needled in the chest. Both these other two were unconscious, under sedation.

"We're low on painkillers," murmured one of the women who was sitting beside the stretchers of these other casualties. "Morelly knows it. He's really not that much of an Old Prophet."

Hal nodded.

"I thought so," he answered in an equally-low voice. He turned and went back toward the cab. All three would have to be carried. That meant that if he and they split off from the others, he would have at least a party of nine under his responsibility. By the time he got to the cab, the route as seen through the windshield had narrowed down until there was room only for four vehicles abreast; and the exits were no longer ramps, but simple turnoffs. Falt had unfolded his copy of Rukh's local map, which had been issued to all the group leaders, and was looking at it in the overhead light of the cab. Ahead, beyond the mountains, the stars were beginning to be lost in a sky paling toward the dawn.

"Look here," said Falt to Hal, as Hal squatted behind his seat. "Standing orders are that any groups with wounded take priority on the safer rendezvous points over any groups without injured. Since we're the only such group—so far, anyway—that moves us from our prearranged point to this one—"

His finger indicated a starred position higher in the foothills than any others marked there.

"We ought to find more than enough donkeys waiting at that point to carry the light load we've got and sling the stretchers between a pair of beasts apiece." He turned from the map to look at the driver. "How long before we get there?"

"Maybe ten, fifteen—" The driver broke off with a grunt. They had just come around a long curve, and he was staring ahead out the windshield. His face had paled, his knuckles gleamed above the steering wheel in the glow from the instrument panel.

Hal and Falt turned to look as he was looking. Ahead—far ahead on the now-straight route—but unmistakable, were lights set up to shine on a barricade closing the road.

"God save us," whispered the driver. "I can't turn back. They've seen us by now. . . ."

"Drive through," said Falt.

"I can't," the driver answered. He was sweating and he had eased off on the thumb-button on the wheel that controlled the throttle. They were slowing gradually, but still approaching the barricade up ahead far too swiftly for anyone's comfort. "They'll have pylons set up beyond the barricade to turn us over if I try it."

He stared at Falt.

"What're they doing out here?" His face turned back over his shoulder to look at Hal. "It's your fault! They don't know anything about the raid—they couldn't! They're out here looking for you—and now they've got us!"

The truck was close enough now so that they could pick out figures in the black uniforms of the Militia on either side of the barricade.

"Go around, then," said Falt.

"The minute I try that, they'll start shooting!" The driver's face was agonized. "God save us! God save us—"

Falt took his sidearm from his shirt again.

"Go around," he said, softly. "It's the only way."

The driver threw a quick glance at the weapon.

"If you shoot me at this speed, we'll all crash," he said bitterly.

Hal put his right hand up with the thumb on one side of the back of the driver's neck, his fingers on the other. He exerted pressure and the driver made a small sound.

"When I snap his spine," said Hal to Falt, "you take the wheel."

"I'll go—I'll go around," husked the driver. Hal released the pressure on the other's neck but kept his fingers in place.

"At the last moment, only," Falt said to the driver. "I'll tell you when to leave the road. Hold steady, now . . . hold steady . . . *now!*"

At the last moment the barricade had seemed to jump at them. The Militia on either side of it had been waving their arms for some time to command the vehicle to a halt.

"Hit it! Up the speed! Hit it—now!" Falt was shouting at the driver.

But the driver had already dug his finger into the throttle button and the truck was off the road and sliding in a tilted curve over the open ground alongside it like a saucer being sailed into a strong wind. Its body rang as power weapons struck the skin of the van with energy bolts that generated explosions of high temperature in the material. The windshield and the window on the driver's side starred suddenly, as if hit by solid birdshot; and the driver cried out, his hands flying up from the wheel. Falt grabbed the wheel and pulled the truck, skittering, back onto the route beyond the barricade and the sharp-pointed pylons anchored in concrete just beyond. His finger pressed down the throttle again, and abruptly they were flying up the route once more, while the barricade, the figures and the pylons behind it dwindled rapidly in the distance.

The driver was huddled against the cab door.

"Where are you hit?" Falt was demanding.

"Oh God!" said the driver. "Oh God—oh God . . ."

"Howard," said Falt, "take a look at this man, find out where he's hit and lift him over the back of the seat, out of my way, if you can."

Hal stood up, holding to the back of the seat before him and bent over the driver, reaching down to pull him back from the door. A fingernail-sized stain was visible high on the left side of the driver's shirt. Pressing the cloth tight against the man's body as he went, Hal felt for and found wetness on the man's back at a roughly opposite point, then ran his hands over the shirt and the upper areas of the driver's pants, as far as he could reach, bending over the driver as he was.

"Are your legs all right?" he asked the driver.

"Oh, God . . ."

Hal put his hand gently once more on the man's neck.

"Yes—yes," the driver almost yelped. "They're all right! My legs are all right!"

"You got a single needle through your left shoulder, high up," Hal told him. "It's nothing serious. Now . . ."

He massaged the back of the other's neck.

"Now, I'm going to help you up over the back of your seat. I want you to do as much as you can to get over, yourself. Come on, now. . . ."

He reached down with both hands and put them under the driver's armpits. He lifted. The driver scrambled upwards with both arms and legs. Abruptly he screamed and tried to slide back down into the seat again; but Hal held him and half-pulled, half-lifted him over the back of the seat by sheer force. The driver screamed again as the back of his knees bumped over the back of the seat.

"My leg! My leg—oh, God!"

But Hal, with the other already on the floor on his back behind the seats, was checking a stain on the outside of the other's left leg, just above the knee.

"Looks like you've got a needle through the leg, too," he said. "Can you bend it?"

The driver tried and did, but screamed a third time.

"Looks like that one could be more serious," said Hal. "The needle's hit something in there."

He felt under the leg.

"And it looks as if it's still in there."

"Oh, God—"

"He's faking," said Falt clearly. "There's no way it could be hurting him that much."

Hal put a hand over the man's mouth.

"You've got a choice," he said quietly in the other's ear. "Now I know and you know how that leg of yours hurts. But we also both know it only hurts when you move it; and that you should move it as little as possible. Neither wound is going to kill you. So, lie still; and either you keep quiet or I'll have to make sure you're quiet because you're unconscious. Do you understand?"

Part of his mind was appalled at what he was saying; but another part nodded in bleak approval at this evidence of how well he had learned his lessons once upon a time. For a moment he could almost imagine the harsh, old bass voice of Malachi Nasuno echoing behind his own. He had spoken the words he had just said as if he had read them off a blackboard in Malachi's mind.

But the results were successful. The driver now lay motionless and silent. Hal stood up, clinging to the back of the seat before him; and saw that Falt was now behind the wheel and holding the truck steady as it fled.

"Pick up the map and navigate," said Falt.

Hal slipped around into the empty seat Falt had vacated. He picked up the map from the cab floor before the seat.

"Are we still on the route?" he asked, glancing ahead through the windshield, for what he looked out on was now a two-lane roadway of crushed gravel.

"No. Two turns off. Local Way Ten—find it there?"

Hal looked.

"Yes," he said. "We turn off Way Ten onto Way One Hundred Twenty-three, and off that onto Demming Road—follow Demming Road to the first path, unnamed, turning off to the right. We make a ninety-degree left turn off that path after one point eight kilometers, and take out over open country. We go on a compass reading of forty-three minutes, twenty-four seconds, for point six of one kilometer, and that brings us to the gathering point."

"All right," said Falt. "Now direct me."

They continued according to the directions Hal had spelled out, as the sky brightened above them and the open woods along the backcountry roads began to emerge into visibility from the solid blackness that had earlier held everything beyond the cast of the truck's lights. Hal glanced back once to check on the driver, who had been silent all this time, and saw him still as he had been, lying on his side with his eyes closed—either unconscious or determined to attract no further attention to himself.

They came to the gathering point finally in the first somber light of the dawn; by then the whole woods was visible around them, although the sun was still hidden behind the mountains to their right. Waiting for them there, shielded from telescopic observation by a tight clump of variform elms, was a pile of packsaddles and related equipment surrounded by fifteen placid donkeys, tethered to the surrounding tree trunks or limbs. There was no one with them. The local farmers were clearly willing to donate their livestock, but only at minimum risk to themselves.

The truck halted. Falt punched the button to open the back doors. He and Hal, with the rest of the team, got out of the truck and began the process of getting the wounded onto their stretchers, once each of these had been slung between two of the donkeys, and loading the remaining animals with the bags of fertilizer as well as the ingots of high-tin solder, which would be cut up and used as payment for equipment the Command would not be able to get by donation along the way.

They were finishing this when a wild voice shouted at them.

"That's right—go off and leave me to die!"

They all looked toward the sound of it. In one of the cab doorways, the driver lay propped on one elbow, the closure of his shirt pulled open halfway by his effort to crawl there, his eyes bloodshot and face contorted. Without a glance at each other, both Falt and Hal walked over to the cab, while the rest of the team turned back to getting the donkey train ready to move out.

"That's right," said the driver in a lower voice, as they came up to him. He glared at them, his face above the floor of the cab on a level with theirs as they stood outside it. "Leave me here, all shot up. Leave me here to die."

"You can drive," said Falt, flatly. "It'll hurt some, but I've seen Command members drive half a day in worse shape than you are."

"And what'll happen when I get home—if I get home?" the driver demanded. "Because if they've got one roadblock up here, they've got a dozen; and now they'll be looking for this truck after we went around them the way you did! Even if I could get past the roadblocks, even if I could get home, could I go to my family, knowing the Militia'll be searching everywhere and what'd happen to my people if I was found at the farm? Do you think I'm the kind to go back and let them in for that?"

"You can't come with us," said Falt. "What else is there for you?"

The driver stared at him for a moment, breathing raggedly.

"There's a place in the mountains I could go," he said, more quietly. "But I can't make it alone."

"I tell you, you can drive, if you want to," said Falt.

"I can drive!" shouted the driver at him. "I can drive on a road. I can drive a little ways like this is, from a road. But I can't take this truck ten kilometers back into the woods when I might get jammed between trees or hung up on a rock, or turned over at any minute—and what'd happen to me then? Could I crawl the rest of the way to the cabin?"

"Some might," said Falt, dryly. But he looked at Hal with a small frown line between his eyes.

"I'll take him to his cabin," said Hal.

"We can't spare you," said Falt.

"No reason why not," Hal said. "There's no pursuit at the moment. You've got more than enough beasts and the rest of the team's in good shape. I can drive him to his place, and still make it to rendezvous not more than a couple of hours behind the rest of you."

Falt hesitated. Hal turned to the driver.

"This cabin of yours," he said. "What's it doing away off like that, by itself?"

"It's a fishing cabin." The driver lowered his eyes. "All right, there's some fishing up here, but not much. It's mainly a place a few of us go just to get away."

"How few of you? How many know about this place?"

The driver's eyes came up again, defiantly.

"Me, my two next brothers and my cousin Joab," he said. "We all live at home together. The Militia couldn't make any of them say anything, anyway. Besides, when I don't come back, they'll think to look for me up there, in a day or two."

"How far from here is it?" he asked. "How long to get there in your truck?"

"Half an hour." The voice of the driver was now eager. "Just half an hour, and no danger of running into Militia, I swear it."

"So you'd swear, would you?" said Falt, looking at him, disgust in the older Command member's voice.

The driver colored and looked down at the floor of the cab.

"I only meant . . ."

Hal looked back at Falt.

"There's no reason I can't take him and meet you all at rendezvous."

Falt sighed hissingly, between closed teeth.

"Take him then." He turned his back on the driver. "Don't take any risks for him. He's not worth it."

He walked away.

"Move back," said Hal to the driver. "Let me in."

Grunting with pain at each movement of his leg, the other pulled back away from the cab doorway. Hal hoisted himself up inside and took the seat behind the controls. He closed the cab doors, switched the motors from warm to idle, and lifted the truck on its travelling cushion of air from the blowers. Turning the vehicle, he waved through the windshield at the rest of the team who were now watching him, and drove off, toward the road. Behind him there was a good deal of scrabbling and grunting, and the driver at last hauled himself up into the empty seat alongside Hal.

"Which way?" asked Hal, as they came to the road.

"Left."

They turned onto the road, headed deeper into the foothills, toward the mountains. Hal followed the monosyllabic directions through several turns and changes of roads; and very shortly they were climbing steeply up a track that was hardly more than a donkey-trail. He had expected them to turn off even from this, but instead the track itself came to an end.

"Where now?" Hal asked, seeing the end of the trail approaching.

"Straight ahead for now. Then I'll tell you."

Hal glanced over at the other man as he followed this latest direction. The driver's face as he stared ahead out the windshield was tight-skinned, his jaws clamped, his eyes hooded and sullen.

"Left now," he said. They went a short distance. "Now, right again, between those two large trees and to the left of that boulder. Slow down. The spring rains make rocks roll down, and we can run right on top of one of those and get hung up or flipped over before we know it."

Hal drove. The directions continued. After a short while they came through an opening in some bushes and into a small depression through which a stream ran—a stream too small for fish of reasonable size, but sufficient to provide drinking and washing water for the rather clumsy log cabin with a single drunken eye of a window in its front wall.

"Here," said the driver.

Hal stopped the truck. He got out and went around to open the other door of the cab and help the driver out. For a Harmonyite who would not curse, he did a good job of expressing his dissatisfaction with the help he was being given.

". . . Careful! Can't you be more careful?" he snapped.

"Want to try it on your own?" Hal asked. "I can leave you just where you are, here, outside the cabin."

The driver became silent. Hal half-carried, half-supported the man in a hopping progress toward the door of the cabin, through it and into the interior—an untidy area of portable camp beds, a woodbox stove, and a large, round table with four chairs, that looked out of place in these surroundings.

"What's the table for—card games?" asked Hal.

The driver flashed a sudden glance that showed a good deal of the whites of the other's eyes; and suddenly Hal realized that by accident he had named the real reason for the existence of the cabin. He aided the driver to one of the camp beds and the driver collapsed on it.

"Is there something clean around here I can fill with water to leave with you?" Hal asked. "And what have you got, a privy somewhere out back? How far is it? By tomorrow you're literally going to have to crawl to get anywhere. You don't have some kind of bucket I can get to put by your bed?"

"There's a water bucket to the left of the stove," said the driver sullenly. "And there's a compression toilet under the canvas ground cloth in the corner. Get my accordion."

"All right. I'll move the toilet over by your cot," said Hal. He did so, went out to fill the bucket and brought it back full with a dipper floating in it, to put it by the bedside. "Now, what about food? Have you got any food here?"

"There's another box on the far side of the stove," said the driver, sullenly. "You can bring that over. It's got boxed stuff that keeps in it. You can get some more blankets, too, from the other beds. It gets cold up here, nights."

"All right," said Hal. He did so. "Have you got any medical supplies up here?"

"Emergency kit's around here someplace," said the driver. "You'll have to look for it."

It took eight to ten minutes of searching before Hal came up with the kit. He took it back to the driver, cleaned and spot-bandaged the needle holes in the man.

"You said the needle's still in my leg," said the other, suddenly fearful as Hal was doing this. "What'll it do? What's going to happen to me?"

Hal had to stop and think back to what Malachi had told him.

"If you left it there indefinitely," he said, "either your body'd build some kind of shielding tissue around it, or it'd work its way out, eventually— maybe a few years from now. Unless it carried some material in with it, like dirty clothing, it probably won't infect; and gun needles generally don't, because their sharpness sends them through things a slug from missile weapons might push ahead of it into the wound it makes. You'll still want to get it taken out of your leg as soon as you can."

He considered the man for a moment.

"You'll be all right for a few days, in any case."

"But I mean—" The driver broke off. The now-strong daylight, coming through the drunken window-eye to push apart the shadows of the cabin's interior, showed his face both crafty and pale. "You're going to leave me something for the pain, aren't you?"

"Sorry," said Hal. "I've got nothing to give you."

"What do you mean?" the driver's voice rose. "I saw you put your stuff into the truck. You've got to have painkillers in that med kit in your pack—I know all you Command people carry them for when you get wounded! You've got some and you can give me some!"

Hal thought of Morelly, with the old lines of his face deepened as he lay on the stretcher.

"We carry that sort of thing not for ourselves," he said, "but for our brothers and sisters in battle when the time comes that they need it. It's not for you, even if you had to have it—which you don't."

He turned and went out the door to the truck. He opened its rear doors and, gathering his equipment, began to pack it and put it on. As he did there was a sound from the door of the cabin. Glancing over, he saw that the driver had managed to pull himself as far as the doorway to stand propped up there.

"I suppose you think I owe you some thanks?" the driver shouted. "Well, I don't! It's all right when our own people want to fight the Militia, but you don't even belong. You with your foreign accent and your pretending to help! What did you do to make them hunt you like that? You made all the trouble. Everybody who got hurt in this got hurt because they were already looking for you! I've got these needles in me because of you—just you. And you think I'm going to thank you? I wouldn't thank you for anything. You know what I say? I say damn on you! Yes, you heard me—I say the damnation in God's name upon you. . . ."

He was still shouting as Hal closed the rear truck doors and turned about, fully outfitted at last in his gear, and went away from stream and cabin into the woods. He heard the driver's shouting continue for some distance after he was obviously out of sight. There was a heaviness and a bitterness in him that would not be gotten rid of; even though he exercised his mind as Walter the InTeacher had taught him, to put aside the anger that had surged up in him at the last words of the man behind him. Walking steadily south through the mountain woods, it occurred to him with a touch of wonder that when he had explained to the other why he could not give painkillers to him, he had thought and spoken unconsciously, for the first time in his life, as a Friendly. The thought suddenly wiped clean from him the heaviness and bitterness triggered by the reactions of the driver; the sadness in him that such as Rukh and Morelly—and Child-of-God—should pay the price of the life they had chosen for someone who understood and valued that price so little.

For a little while, he walked through the morning-lit woods, bemused by this new development within him. He had imitated Obadiah, but until now he had never reacted in his own right as a Friendly. Like the slow but powerful effects of some heavy shock, he felt an understanding of this stern Culture flooding through him—an understanding he had never had before. But even as he realized this, he understood further that he had only begun to grasp that understanding, that he must be content to wait now, to put it aside to be wrestled with at some other opportunity, when the first heavy effects of it would have been absorbed enough to make it possible to stand back and look at the shape of this new comprehension that had just come to him, in detail.

He came finally out into what he had been searching for, an open spot on the mountainside where he could overlook all the foothills and the area beyond where the city of Masenvale sprawled. He glanced down the flank of the earth on which he stood and saw the dished-in, downward swoop of forested slopes that seemed to march to the very edge of the dark oval that was the city. He reached into his pack, took out the field viewer there, and put it to his eye, dialling it into focus on one point, then setting it on automatic adjustment as he swung about to survey the lower area.

With no great difficulty, he picked out the still-smoking fertilizer storage area, then traced the route he and the others had taken in the truck until he came to the point where the barricade still stood. Taking the viewer off automatic to put it on full magnification, he saw that a second row of barricades had been set up on the other side of the pylons they had passed and that the dark-uniformed figures seemed to be keeping a watch now in both directions, instead of merely toward anyone coming out from the city. Beyond this change, the barrier looked as if it had never been encountered—except for a curve of flattened roadside weeds and other small growth that marked the track of the fans of their truck where they had swung out around it; and the addition of a troop carrier truck, that now stood by the far side of the road, looking as if ready to move at a second's notice.

He moved the viewer on, and found the gathering point where he had parted with the rest of the team. The back of his mind, trained early to remember such things, threw up a perfect image of the map he had held to navigate Falt to that point; and he swung the viewer to check the other gathering points that had been marked on it. All but two were now empty of donkeys and equipment; and neither of the teams now loading up in them had Rukh among them.

He began to search forward along the routes he estimated each team would take from the gathering points to the rendezvous deep in the foothills. Once they were under the trees there, of course, he would not be able to see them. He located more than half of the teams, including his own; but was still not able to find the one Rukh was with, although he located the one led by Child. All the teams he could see were close upon the foothills. It looked as if everyone had gotten away safely, he thought; and then a movement on the traffic ways farther down the slope caught his eye as he panned the viewer about.

Focusing in, he located a column of six troop carriers, raising a faint plume of dust along one of the gravel-surfaced Ways as it headed in at an angle to the foothills some kilometers ahead of the rendezvous. Panning the field viewer backwards along the slope, he found three more plumes of dust and focused in on three more columns of carriers. He stood watching them through the viewer. There was no point in their moving in on the foothills in force that way unless the carriers were loaded with armed Militia; and the organization of the pursuit he now saw testified either to the fact that columns and their personnel had been waiting on a standby basis, or that the Militia had been informed of the fertilizer and metals raids ahead of time.

But they could not have been informed ahead of time; not only because of the unlikelihood of anyone connected with Rukh's Command in this effort being a traitor, but because if the Militia had known, they would of course have been set up around the sites of both raids. It would have been far easier to take the members of the Command that way than to pursue them into the foothills.

The only possible conclusion was that they had been on standby—and that the driver had been correct. They had been on standby for the single purpose of capturing Hal; and only one man could set such a large effort in motion for that purpose. Bleys Ahrens must now be sure that he was on Harmony. The tall Other Man must have seen to it that the Militia, planetwide, had been made acquainted with Hal's face; and the Militia officer called Barbage must have recognized Hal and reported seeing him after he had escaped following the ambush of the Command in the pass.

Now Rukh and the rest were being seriously hunted. Because of him. What it amounted to, in the end, was that what the driver had shouted after him had been no more than the literal truth.

Chapter

> > **25** < <

Drawing lines with a stick in the dirt at his feet to echo the estimated paths of travel of the teams, and the Militia truck units in pursuit of them, Hal came to the conclusion that at his best possible speed he could reach the rendezvous only after the rest had arrived there. But that would still be before the Militia would be dangerously close. He put the viewer back into his pack, erased the lines he had drawn in the earth, and took both a line of sight and a compass heading on the position of the rendezvous, ahead of him in the foothills below.

He began his journey.

He had come a long way back toward good general physical condition in his time with the Command; but he was still not in training for what he might once have done in the way of covering the ground, even back as a fifteen-year-old on Earth. Then, even laden with pack and weapon, he might have chosen to run the whole distance—not at any great speed, but at a steady jog that would have eaten up the kilometers between him and his destination.

As it was, he started out at a fast, smooth walk that was the next best way of covering ground in a hurry. He had had little sleep the day before and he had been up all night. The first two kilometers were work; but by the end of that time his body had warmed to the effort and his mind had moved into the necessary state of mild trance in which he could, if necessary, continue moving until he dropped, without really taking conscious note of his fatigue.

This state once achieved, he effectively abandoned the effort of his travel to the automatic machinery of his body and let his mind go off on its own concerns.

Primary among these now was the fact that his presence in the Command was dangerous to it and its members. Treading on the heels of that fact was that Bleys had now located him, and was clearly ready to go to large efforts to lay hands on him. The best assumption from this was that Bleys, at least— and probably the Other Men and Women as a whole—had concluded that he could be dangerous to them. The effort made to find him on Coby might have indicated only something as small as curiosity on Bleys' part. But what was happening now seemed to indicate more than that.

He was conscious of a feeling of being rushed. He had gone to Coby only to hide out until he was grown enough to protect himself; and until he had a chance to make up his mind as to the specifics of what he wanted to do— with regard to the Others, and to his own life. Now, they were threatening to lay their hands on him and he still did not know how he should fight them, let alone conquer them. His conscience stirred and accused him of letting time slip by these four years, of living in a childish illusion of unlimited time available, until it was too late to decide what had needed to be done from the beginning.

The territory he was passing through was open, for the most part, and his speed was undiminished by the need to go around natural obstacles in his path. From time to time he either took advantage of an open space that gave him a view of the land lower down, or climbed a tree that would offer the same prospect. On his first survey of this kind, he had seen only one of the three Militia vehicle columns out in plain view on a Way. The other two he had to search for; but eventually, he found their vehicles parked and the troops inside them presumably on foot, already penetrating into the hills.

The column that had been still in motion on the Way when he looked the first time had been the column farthest forward, the one that had obviously been intended to cut into the foothills ahead of the fleeing Command. At his second look, this column also had parked, at a point short of being level with the rendezvous; and the Militia in it had taken to the woods. The point from which they had done so reassured him that he would reach the rendezvous, himself, at least a couple of hours before they would be far enough into the wood to cross a trail left by any of the teams on their way there. However, any trails they did cross would be impossible to miss. It was not possible to run donkey trains through an open forest without making it clear even to an untrained eye that they had passed.

He was tempted to step up his pace. But his teaching had been to look ahead in instances like this; and it was plain that merely reaching the Command would not mark the end to his working day. He kept, therefore, to the same steady walk, and let his mind go back to the problem of Bleys' pursuit of him and the question of what his own actions should be under the circumstances.

He was still working with this problem when he finally walked into the temporary camp at the rendezvous site. The day had gone while he had been travelling, and there were no more than a couple of hours of sunlight left. He had been holding fatigue at bay until this moment; but the sight of the tents already set up, the sounds of evening activity and the cooking smells that had gone before to draw him into the camp made him suddenly aware of the weariness in his legs and body.

"Howard!" called Joralmon, spotting him as he walked in. "We were beginning to worry about you!"

Joralmon got to his feet from the cone rifle he had disassembled and spread out before his tent on a cloth for cleaning. He came toward Hal, followed by everyone else close enough to hear the words, and free enough to break off what they were doing.

Hal waved them aside.

"Where's Rukh?" he asked. "I need to talk to her."

Hands pointed. Hal went on toward a tent at the far end of the camp, the others falling back as he turned from them, and paused just outside its closed front flap.

"Rukh?" he called. "It's Howard. I've got to talk to you."

"Come in, Howard."

Her voice was clear and strong from within the tent and he pushed his way in to find her seated on a camp chair at a temporary table that had a map spread out upon it, and Child sitting opposite her. They both looked up at him.

"What is it?" asked Rukh, her eyes on his face.

"Three units of Militia are after us," he said. "I saw them from higher up, after I dropped off the driver of our truck at his cabin."

He told them what he had seen, and what he had estimated.

"Two hours before they cut our trail?" Rukh frowned. "But how close are they likely to cut it? How much time from then until they find us?"

"No telling," said Hal.

He leaned over the map, which showed the foothills beyond Masenvale, and pointed with his finger as he talked. "Figuring their travel time through the woods to give them a maximum distance by the time it took me to get here, I drew an arc to cut the trails of our teams, getting here, and the arc cut the closest of the trails almost right here at the rendezvous. But that's looking at the best they'd be able to do. Where they'll really cut one of them depends on the angle to our line of travel, on which they came into the woods. Straight in, at a ninety-degree angle to the Way where they left their vehicles parked, it'd take them two hours to cross one of our trails. At more than ninety degrees, it'd take longer, but then they'd be headed back the way they came, which isn't likely. At a more acute angle, it'd also take them longer, to reach the trail—but they could strike it right on top of us, here."

Rukh picked up a ruler, set its markings to the scale of the map before them, and measured the distance between the points Hal had indicated.

"Perhaps a third more time to cross our trail at this point here," she said, thoughtfully, while Child bent his harsh visage above her moving hands. "A maximum of forty minutes beyond the two hours you figured, Howard. It'll take us at least half an hour to break camp and get on our way; and we won't be ready to travel properly, at that. But there's no choice."

She looked across at Child.

"James?"

He shook his head.

"No choice." He looked grimly at Hal. "Thou hast done well, Howard."

"I just happened to be in the right spot at the right time," Hal said. "If I hadn't driven that truck driver to his cabin, I'd never have had a chance to see what was coming after us."

"Then we move," said Rukh. "James, would you get people started?"

Child rose and went out.

"Howard," said Rukh, "go with him and help."

He stood where he was.

"If I could mention something—" he began.

"Of course." Her dark eyes considered him. "You've been coming as fast as you could all day to bring word to us. Forget trying to help. Get half an hour's rest while the packing's going on. Sleep some if you can."

"That wasn't what I was going to say." He rested one hand on the back of Child's empty camp chair. Suddenly his weariness was overwhelming. "I ought to tell you we ran into a roadblock on our way to the gathering point. It had to have been set up ahead of time. The man who drove us was right in what he said back at the Mohler-Beni farm, when he said I was a danger to you all. The roadblock had been set up to look for me. That's also why these three units were waiting and could be right on top of us after the raid."

She nodded, still looking at him.

"The point is," he said, with effort, "the man was right. As long as I'm with you, I'm drawing all their attention to this Command. Maybe if I leave, I can draw them off."

"Do you know why they'd be hunting you?" she asked.

He shook his head.

"I'm not sure. All I know about the Others, directly, is what I told you of what happened at my home. I'm guessing it's Bleys Ahrens, their Vice-Chairman—one of the two that were there that day my tutors were killed—who wants me. But exactly why is another question. At any rate, I think I ought to leave."

"You heard James at the farm," Rukh said, quietly, "when that man suggested it. The Commands have never abandoned their own people."

"Am I really one of those people?"

She looked at him.

"You've lived and fought with us. What else?" she said. "But if you want a further reason, think a moment. If they want you badly enough to mobilize the Militia across a countryside, do you think they'd simply let go the Command you were associated with—particularly when that Command had just pulled off two raids within their city limits?"

He did not answer.

"Go rest, Howard," she said.

He shook his head.

"I'm all right. I'll just get something to eat."

"Get Tallah to give you something you can carry along and eat as we move," Rukh said. "Then lie down. That's an order."

"All right," he said.

He got bread and bean-paste from Tallah, ate part of it, rewrapped the rest, put it in his pack and lay down. It seemed that he barely blinked his eyes before he was being shaken awake. He looked up groggily into the face of Jason.

"Howard—time to move," Jason said. He offered Hal a steaming cup. "Here, the last of the coffee."

Hal drank the hot liquid gratefully. It was not really coffee, even as Harmony knew it, but a variform of a native plant that had been tamed to make a brewable hot drink. But the sour-gray liquid contained a certain amount of chemical stimulants; and by the time he was on his feet with his pack on his back and his rifle in hand, he was ready to move.

The Command travelled as rapidly as the terrain and the donkeys would permit, in the two hours that remained to them before darkness. When the ground became obscure under their feet, Rukh called a halt; and Hal went forward from his position with the donkeys at the tail of the Command to talk to her.

"Going to camp?" he asked.

"Yes." Her voice came out of the blur that was her face, not more than arm's length from him.

He looked up at the sky, which was overcast, but lightly.

"The moon'll be up later on," he said. "And the clouds may blow clear from time to time. If we could keep moving we could put a much safer distance between us and that Militia unit. In the daytime, without donkeys to slow them up, they'll begin to gain on us."

"We'll be out of their district by noon tomorrow," said Rukh. "No Militia unit ever follows beyond its own district limits unless it's in a running fight. We ought to be able to stay ahead of them until we're in the next district; and while they get a unit after us from the local Militia there, we ought to be able to lose them."

"Maybe," he said. "In any case, if you want to keep going, there's a way."

She did not say anything for a second. Then—

"What?"

"There're ways of reading the ground even when it's as dark as this," he said. "It was part of my training; and I think I can still do it. We could rope the Command together, in effect, with me in the lead; and if the sky clears and the moon comes out, we can keep going the rest of the night. If we stop, and spread out to sleep, we won't get going again until dawn."

There was silence from her still figure and invisible face.

"Even with you to lead," she said, "how's that going to keep the rest of us from stumbling over ground we can't see?"

"At the very least," he said, "I can steer us around things in our way and pick out the the more level surfaces to walk on. It works, believe me. I've done it back on Earth."

Another short silence.

"All right," she said. "How do you want the Command roped together?"

It took a full hour to get everyone lined up and connected. Hal made one last tour up and down the line, reminding each one he passed to keep slack in the line connected to the person just ahead. Then he took the lead and started out.

There was nothing in what he was doing that ordinary training could not have developed in anyone. His ability to see his way was based on a number of things, chief of which was the fact that even woods-wise people like the members of the Command instinctively raised their gaze to the relative brightness of even a heavily-overcast sky when going through the night-dark outdoors, and lost part of the perception they could have maintained by keeping their eyes adjusted to the darkness at ground level.

What he made use of beyond this was a near-hypnotic concentration of attention on the ground just ahead, reinforced by a similar concentration of his ordinary powers of scent, hearing and balance, to read as much as possible of what was underfoot with these senses as well. All this had been honed by field practice during those early years of his. In fact the largest part of his skill in this was owed to that practice alone. The one danger in what he did was that of running into something above ground level that his downcast eyes had not seen; and to protect himself against this he carried a staff vertically before him, its upper end above his head and its lower end at mid-calf height.

In the beginning of that night trek, the progress of the Command was painfully slow. In spite of his warnings, individuals along the line allowed the rope between them and the person ahead to tighten, with the result that when either of them stumbled or fell, the other was occasionally dragged down as well; and the progress of the whole line halted. But gradually, as with any other physical activity, the members of the Command began to pick up the tricks that made this sort of night movement practical. The falls and the inadvertent stops came less often; and their speed increased. The forward movement of the Command became less like a drunken snake dance through the dark, and more of a purposeful travelling.

But their speed of straight-line movement was still nothing to be proud of. Back on Earth, practicing this technique with Malachi in the lead and three trained helpers, plus equally-trained pack animals, Hal and the others had made almost as good time as they might in broad daylight. Here, the donkeys adjusted to the means of travel faster than the humans in the line, not being cursed with human imaginations and the tendency to guess. But overall, improvement was slow. Rukh, directly behind Hal, was one of the quickest to learn the necessity for a slack line, but there were others, like the woman behind her, who continually forgot.

Hal himself passed quickly into a state of concentration that effectively blanked out everything but his immediate task; and as the evening wore on, the intermediary of his conscious mind cut out entirely. He moved through a maze of perception, navigating through the dark without questioning the impulses that sent him one way or another; almost unconscious of the constant stream of warnings and information about the ground under his feet that he uttered as he went, for the benefit of Rukh behind him, so that there was a steady feed of verbal signals being passed rearward from person to person in the line.

With the waxing of the night hours, the thin new moon rose behind the clouds and the night winds freshened. Breaks in the cloud cover began to come more often; and, even when they did not break, the clouds were thin-

ner, permitting more light to reach the ground. To these changes, Hal paid
no conscious attention. He was not even aware of his own ground speed picking up and the progress of the line behind him improving as the illumination of the earth before him improved. He was long past ordinary fatigue,
into adrenalin overdrive. He had forgotten his body entirely; and nearly forgotten his senses, as direct instruments of that body and mind. He lived in
a universe of varying shades of gray and black; and he swam through that
universe, forgetting everything else. Time, the goal toward which he progressed, the reason for progressing, all these were lost to him. Even the
thought of those things he turned aside from, as physical obstacles, was forgotten. He turned right and left as he went without understanding why he
turned; knowing only that this was his purpose—to move in this careful and
intricate fashion, indefinitely.

A jerk on the line connecting him with Rukh eventually stopped him.
He rotated blindly to face her.

"We'll stop now," her voice came strongly to him. "It's light enough to
see by."

He was aware that the available illumination had increased. He had been
able to tell this from the lightening of the shades of grey he saw, the absence
of blackness. But for a moment, looking across little more than a meter of
distance, caught up still in the concentration of his long navigation, he could
not see her. His mind registered her only as one more abstract in varying
shades of gray, reflected illumination. Similarly, what she said made no sense
to him. His mind registered and identified the words, but could not relate
them to the universe in which he was still continuing to feel the way for all
of them.

Then sight and understanding flooded back in on him at once. He saw
the forest floor, the trees and the bushes about them in the stoic, lean light
of pre-dawn; and it finally registered on him that the night, and his task,
were over.

He was conscious of falling; but he did not feel the ground when he struck
it.

He came slowly back to awareness. Someone was shaking him. With a
great effort he opened his eyes and saw it was Rukh.

"Sit up," she said.

He struggled into a sitting position, discovering that, somehow, a tarp had
materialized under him and blankets over him. When he was up he felt something—it was a filled packsack, he saw, on looking—pushed into place behind him, so that he had something to support his back. Rukh put a bowl
of undefined hot food—stew, apparently—in his hands.

"Get this inside you," she told him.

He looked about at trees lit by a late morning light.

"What time is it?" he asked, and was startled to hear his voice come out
as a croak.

"One hour until noon. Eat."

She rose and left him. Still numb in body and brain, he began to eat the stew, using the spoon she had left in the bowl. He could not remember ever tasting anything so delicious; and with each hot bite, life woke more fully in him. The bowl was suddenly empty. He put it aside, got up, folded the blankets and tarp—they were his own, he discovered, as the packsack was his—and stowed them in the pack. But the bowl and spoon were not his. He took them down to the stream by which they had set up camp and washed both items. Around him the rest of the Command was striking their tents or rolling bedsacks, preparatory to getting on their way. He brought the bowl and spoon to Tallah.

"Not the kitchen's," Tallah said, irritably, over her shoulder as she hurried just-packed equipment onto the backs of the kitchen donkeys. "Those're Rukh's."

He took them to Rukh.

"Thank you," he said, handing them back.

"You're welcome. How are you?"

"I'm awake," he said.

"How do you feel?"

"A little stiff—all right, though."

"I'm sending the wounded off with a separate party," Rukh told him, "with as much of the equipment as we can spare, so as to lighten our load as far as we can. They'll leave us by ones and twos along the line of march today; and hopefully the Militia won't notice their trails in their hot pursuit of ours. Morelly's going leaves us one team leader short. I've talked it over with James and decided it's time we started to use that training of yours on an official basis. I want to appoint you a group leader."

He nodded.

"There's more to it than that," she said. "The other leaders are all senior to you and normally the Command'd have to lose James and myself and all the others before you'd find yourself responsible for the Command. But I'd like to tell the rest of the group leaders something of your special training—with your permission—so that I can also tell them that if you had the experience, James and I would consider you as first in line to be his replacement, as Lieutenant, if anything happened to him. Will you agree to that?"

It took his still-fatigued and sleep-numbed brain a few moments to consider the implications of what she had just asked.

"Since it's an open secret that the Militia want me more than ordinarily," he said at last, "there's no reason not to tell them I had special training, and what kinds of training it was. But I'd appreciate it if you didn't tell them the names of my tutors, or anything more than they actually need to know."

"Of course."

There was, for a moment, almost a gentle note in her voice; but it was gone before he could do any more than register it; and in fact if it had not been for his memory's ability to replay anything he had just heard, he would have been unsure that he had heard it at all. Standing this close to her, he could feel the outflow of a dark and vibrant living power from her, like a solid pressure.

"You're a sub-officer from now on, then," she said, "and I'll expect you to come looking for James and myself, whenever we halt, so that we can make use of what you can offer to our planning. For right now, you might note that the Militia are roughly eight kilometers behind us and they're making a kilometer an hour over our best pace. Also, what's chasing us now is the first and second units you saw, combined."

She proceeded to brief him on other details:

Jason and two of the others had been sent off as soon as they had stopped, to climb the side of the mountain they were currently skirting and get enough altitude to check behind them with field viewers for their pursuers.

They had been early enough to witness the smoke plumes rising above the trees from the cooking of a morning meal, barely within viewer range; and make the estimate of the marching time that the Militia would require to catch up with the Command, if it simply stayed where it was. However, the smoke also indicated a force at least double the size of one of the units Hal had seen and described; and later observation, as the Militia broke camp and began to move, had confirmed this fact.

Once the troops were again on the move, it became possible for Jason and the others to make a firm estimate of their rate of march. It was clear that their progress amounted to a strong four kilometers an hour through the open forest. The Command, with its donkeys, was lucky to make three kilometers an hour under the same conditions. In the three hours in which the Militia units had been on the move while the Command was resting, the troops had gained twelve hours of travel time upon them and were now no more than six hours behind them. By twilight, they would catch up—that is if they continued their pursuit at that speed.

"But I think we can shake them about mid-afternoon," said Rukh.

She explained that they were no more than three hours now from the border of another district.

"And they don't pursue into another district?" Hal asked.

"Legally, only when they're in hot pursuit—which these could consider they were," she answered, dryly. "In practice, there's a lot of rivalry between different districts. It goes back to the old sect differences that made us almost into separate countries, once. The Militia of one district don't like the Militia from another coming on their territory. These after us now could keep coming; but the chances are they'll break off and message the Militia of the other district to take up pursuit."

"If they message ahead before we get there, or if they've messaged ahead already," said Hal, "we could be caught between two fires."

"I said there was a lot of rivalry. If they can't catch us themselves, they aren't usually too enthusiastic about the next district doing it and getting all the credit. The odds are they'll follow us over the border, but only as far as they dare before breaking off pursuit. It's only then they'll message the local Militia; and it'll take the locals two or three hours to get a pursuit going."

"I see," said Hal.

"With ordinary luck, we ought to gain eight or nine hours' lead time while they're changing pursuit units." Rukh smiled slightly. "And by that time we ought to be well on our way to the border of the next district south, where the same thing'll happen and we'll pick up that much more of a lead. This is the way the Commands usually lose pursuit by the Militia forces."

Her gaze went past his shoulder, into the camp.

"But we're almost ready to go," she said. "For the moment, you don't have to do anything but travel with the rest of the Command. I'll check with you later in the day to see how your strength's holding up after yesterday. If you're in shape for it, later on, I might have a special duty for you. Meanwhile, be thinking of who you might want in your team. You'll be taking Morelly's people to begin with, but later on there'll be a chance to have the people you want trade off of the other teams onto yours, if everyone concerned agrees."

Hal went to get his pack.

Chapter

> > **26** < <

The rest of the Command, like Hal, had had a long twenty-four hours before settling down to sleep most of the seven hours just past. At the beginning of this new day's march, they moved doggedly and silently, rather than with their usual accustomed easiness. But, like Hal making the walk from the cabin to the rendezvous the day before, they warmed to the travel as they moved along. They were in good condition from their continual trekking; and they had been eating and sleeping much better than they were used to, these last few weeks among the farm families on their way to Masenvale.

So it happened that they picked up speed as they went along; while the Militia units, for all their full night of rest, began to lag in the heat of the afternoon. Reports from scouts sent up tall trees or nearby observation points, with field viewers, reported evidence that their pursuers had taken to stopping for a ten-minute break every hour. At mid-afternoon Rukh sent a runner to call Hal up to the front of the Command to speak with her. He came, and they walked along side by side, a few meters in front of the others for the sake of privacy, Child walking silent on her other side.

"How're you feeling now?" she asked Hal.

"Fine," he said.

Generally speaking, it was the truth. There was a core of fatigue buried in him; but other than that he felt as well as he would have normally, if not a trifle better. A corner of his mind recognized the fact that he was in over-drive once more; but this was nothing like the extreme state of effort he had worked himself into during the night's travel.

"Then I've got a job for you," she said.

He nodded.

"According to the best estimate James and I can make," she said, "we've just crossed the border into the next district. The Militia behind us'll come at least this far. It'd help in our assessment of the situation if we had any idea of what kind of shape they're in, what kind of attitude they've got toward their officers, and how they're feeling about the prospects of catching us. It's a job for you, because you might be able to get close enough to find out those things without being caught."

"I ought to be able to," he said. "It'd be easier if they were stopped; but then their being on the march gives me advantages too."

He checked himself on the verge of saying something more, about the general amateurishness of the Militia, since many of the things he had been about to mention would be equally applicable to the Commands. But it was a fact that, by the standards he had acquired from Malachi, both organizations acted in some ways more like children's clubs out on a hike than military or paramilitary outfits.

"Good," Rukh was saying briskly. "Take whoever you need, but I'd suggest no more than four or five, for the sake of moving swiftly."

"Two," Hal said, "as fail-safe in case I don't get back. One to carry the word if I don't; and one more, in case the one backing me up has some kind of accident. I'll take Jason and Joralmon, if that's all right."

For a moment a faint frown line marked the perfect skin between Rukh's dark eyes.

"They ought, probably, to be from your own team," she said. "But considering this is a tricky business . . . tell their group leaders I said it was all right."

He nodded.

"Wait here while we go on and keep the Militia under observation," she went on. "That'll let you rest as much as possible; and when they get this far, you can take your chances of getting close enough to observe them then, or follow along until your chances improve."

He nodded again.

With Jason and Joralmon he set up an observation post some three hundred meters off the estimated line of march of the Militia, and they took turns observing from a treetop the approach of their pursuers, while the Command went on ahead. The troops were now only a couple of kilometers behind them; and they came on steadily.

It was possible to hear their approach well before they became visible as individuals, seen through the leaves of the forest cover, for they were not moving silently. Sitting in the high, swaying fork of the tall tree he had chosen to observe from, Hal silently checked out in his own mind one particular supposition he had been wanting to test. It had been his guess for some time that the Militia—unless they were in some special units organized specifically for pursuit purposes—were composed mainly of the equivalent of garrison soldiers, who were more comfortable with pavement under their feet than the earth of a forest floor.

As those now approaching became more visible, what he saw confirmed that notion. The soldiers he watched looked hot and uncomfortable, like men unaccustomed to this kind of moving over rough country on foot. Their packs were obviously designed to carry gear and supplies for only a short excursion; and at the same time gave the impression that they had been designed at least as much for parade-ground looks as for practicality in the field. They were plainly marching under orders of silence for the lower ranks; although the noisily-shouted commands and full-voiced conversations of their officers made a mockery of field-level quiet.

Their column drew close, then stopped, a little more than two hundred meters short of being level with the observation post, for what seemed one of their hourly march breaks. The troops dropped to the ground, loosened their pack straps and lay back with the silence rule apparently relaxed for the moment. Hal slipped down from the tree.

"The two of you stay here," he told Jason and Joralmon. "When they start to move again, keep parallel with them but at least this far out and on this side of them. If I don't get back to you in half an hour, or you see some evidence they've got me, get back to Rukh with the information we've already picked up. If I've just been delayed, I'll still catch up with you. But if they've got me, they'll be watching for anyone else and you won't have a chance to get close safely. Understood?"

"Yes, Howard," Jason said; and Joralmon nodded.

Hal went off toward the Militia's stopping spot. When he got there, he found that it was entirely possible for him to prowl up and down their line close enough to clearly overhear even relatively low-voiced conversation. The column had evidently been marching with no point and no flank guards, and nothing resembling sentries had been set up while they were taking their break. It was an incredible behavior that probably stemmed from the fact that the last thing in the world these domestic troops expected was any kind of counterattack from the Commands they chased—which said nothing complimentary about the Commands, themselves.

He moved up and down the length of the resting column, a handful of meters out from them, hidden by the undergrowth that flanked their line; and, since it was clear he could choose whatever he wished to listen to, he ended up squatting behind some bushes less than five meters from the head of the line, where a sort of officers' council was being held.

There were five men there wearing the better-fitted black uniform of the commissioned ranks, but the argument that was going on seemed to be between two of them, only. Both of these wore the tabs of Militia Captains; and one of them was familiar—it was the officer of the Citadel cells and the ambush in the pass, the one that the driver's information had identified with the name of Barbage.

". . . Yes, I say it to thee," Barbage was saying to the other Captain. Barbage was on his feet. The others sat in a row on a log uprooted by some past storm, with the second Commandant at one end of their line. "I have been given commission by authority far above thee, and beyond that by the Great Teacher himself; and if I say to thee, go—thou wilt go!"

The other Captain looked upward and across at Barbage with a tightly-closed jaw. He was a man perhaps five years younger, no more than midway into his thirties; but his face was square and heavy with oncoming middle age, and his neck was thick.

"I've seen your orders," he said. His voice was not hoarse, but thick in his throat—a parade-ground voice. "They don't say anything about pursuing over district borders."

"Thou toy man!" said Barbage; and his voice was harsh with contempt. "What is it to me how such as thee read thy orders? I know the will of those who sent me; and I order thee, that thou pursuest how and where I tell thee to pursue!"

The other Captain had half-risen from the log, his face gone pale.

"You may have orders!" he said, even more thickly. "But you don't out-rank me and there's nothing that says I have to take that sort of language from you. So watch what you say or pick yourself a weapon—I don't care either way."

Barbage's thin upper lip curled slightly.

"Weapon? What Baal's pride is this to think that in the Lord's work thou mightest be worthy of affront? Unlike thee, I have no weapons. Only tools which the Lord has given me for my work. So thou hast something called a weapon, then? No doubt that which I see on thy leg there. Make use of it therefore, since thou didst not like the name I gave thee!"

The Captain flushed.

"You're unarmed," he said shortly.

And indeed, Hal saw, unlike all the rest of the officers and men here, Barbage was wearing only his uniform.

"Oh, let not that stop thee," said Barbage, ironically. "For the true ser-vants of the Lord, tools are ever ready to hand."

He made one long step while the other still stared at him, to end stand-ing beside the most junior of the officers sitting on the log, laid his hand on the young officer's sidearm buttoned-down holster and flicked up the weather flap with his thumbnail. His hand curled around the exposed butt of the power pistol beneath. A twist of the wrist would be all that would be needed to bring the gun out of its breakaway holster, aim and fire it; while the other would have needed to reach for his own buttoned-down holster before he could fire.

From the far end of the log the Captain stared, suddenly white-faced and foolish, at him.

"I meant . . ." The words stumbled on his tongue. "Not like this. A proper meeting with seconds—"

"Alas," said Barbage, "such games are unfamiliar to me. So I will kill thee now to decide whether we continue or turn back, since thou hast not cho-sen to obey my orders—unless thou shouldst kill me first to prove thy right to do as *thou* wishest. That is how thou wouldst do things, with thy weapons, and thy meetings and thy seconds, is it not?"

He paused, but the other did not answer.

"Very well, then," said Barbage. He drew the power pistol from the hol-ster of the junior officer and levelled it at his equal in rank.

"In the Lord's name—" broke out the other, hoarsely. "Have it any way you want. We'll go on then, over the border!"

"I am happy to hear thee decide so," said Barbage. He replaced the pistol in the holster from which he had drawn it and stepped away from the young Force-Leader who owned it. "We will continue until we make contact with the pursuit unit sent out from the next district; at which time I will join them;

and thou, with thy officers and men, mayst go back to thy small games in town. That should be soon. When are the troops from the next district to meet us?"

The other Captain stared at him without answering for a moment.

"It'll take them a few hours," he said, at last.

"Hours?" Barbage walked forward toward him; and the other stood up swiftly, almost as if he expected Barbage to hit him. "Why hours? When didst thou message them to meet us?"

"We . . . generally don't message until we're sure the Children of Wrath are going to cross over into the next district—"

"Thou whimpering fool!" said Barbage, softly. "Hath it not been plain from the beginning that they were fleeing into the next district and beyond?"

"Well, yes. But we might have caught them. . . ."

The other's voice hesitated and ceased.

"Message them *now!*" Barbage's eyes were absolutely unmoving.

"Of course. Of course. Chaims—" He turned sharply to the young Force-Leader whose sidearm Barbage had laid his hand on. "Get a message off to Hlaber District Command and tell them the situation. Say that Captain Barbage, operating here under special orders, needs a pursuit unit out here to take over from us in one hour. Tell them to check with South Promise HQ on his authority to require that sort of special action. Well? Move! *Move!*"

The junior officer jerked to his feet and ran off down the column.

Hal faded back through the greenery until he was safely enough beyond observation to turn and run himself—for the observation point. Jason, sitting at the foot of the tree with Joralmon above him in the observation post, scrambled upright as Hal reached him.

"I've found out what we need to know," Hal said, "and I'm going to be making the best time I can to get the information to the Command. You two follow as fast as you're able to. As we estimated, it's two full pursuit units under Barbage, the Captain who ran the ambush on us in the pass. They've just sent for help from the next district; and Barbage is going to keep this bunch coming until they can be relieved—then he'll switch over and travel with the new unit. Share that information with Joralmon, and both of you come after me as fast as you can."

"Right," said Jason; and Hal, turning on his heel, set out in pursuit of the Command.

The distance before him now was shorter than that he had had to cover the day before. He ran, therefore, at a steady ground-covering pace through the sunlit afternoon woods, his cone rifle clipped vertically to the harness of the light pack on his back, bouncing rhythmically upon his shoulder blades. When he caught up at last with Rukh and the Command, his shirt was dark and sodden with sweat.

"Jason? Joralmon?" Rukh said, as he stopped before her.

"They're fine. They're behind me. I came ahead to get word to you as soon as possible. Barbage—the officer in the pass—is the one running the pursuit. He's got special authority, it seems. . . ."

Hal ran out of breath. Rukh waited while he got it back.

"He's bullying the local Militia officers to keep after us until they can be joined by a unit from the next district—and they've just now sent for that other unit under pressure of Barbage's special authority, to get it out in an hour. There's not going to be the chance to pick up additional lead time and distance the way you told me the Commands usually do."

She nodded slowly, listening, and he gave her, word for word out of that perfect recall of his, exactly the conversation he had overheard at the head of the Militia column.

When he was done, she breathed deeply once and turned to Child, who had come up while Hal was talking.

"You heard, James? They're going to stay right behind us."

"I heard," he said.

"You've been through these foothills before. How far are we from the next district?"

"A day and a half, thirty-six hours if we go on without stopping," he answered. "Up to three full days with normal rest; and thy people are already short of sleep, Rukh."

"If it weren't for the donkeys we could disperse into the mountains and leave them nothing to chase." Her eyes studied the ground, thoughtfully, as if she read an invisible map there. "But if we abandon the donkeys, we also have to abandon the fertilizer and the finished gunpowder we picked up as a primer for it; and with that, over a year's work to sabotage the Core Tap goes down the drain."

She raised her eyes and looked at Child.

"To say nothing of the lives that have been lost to get it this far."

"It is God's will," the older man answered. "Unless it is thy wish to stand and fight."

"This Barbage has taken that into account, it seems," Rukh said. "With two full units, there're too many behind us now to hope to fight and get away from safely. Presumably, the new Militia replacing these are going to be in the same kind of numbers and strength."

She turned and walked a few steps away from both Hal and Child, turned and came back again.

"All right," she said. "We'll try laying a false trail and see if that can't buy us some time. James, we'll need to give up at least a dozen of the spare donkeys. Rope them three abreast so they leave the most noticeable track; and bring up the rear with them. Luckily, our wounded have gotten away already. Now the rest of us will have to do the same thing, taking off one or two at a time without leaving any sign for the Militia to pick up. Howard—"

"Yes?" Hal said.

"With Jason not back, it's going to have to be you sticking with these particular donkeys until everyone else is gone. Once that happens, keep leading them on straight for at least half an hour more. Then hitch and leave them for the Militia to find, and get out yourself without leaving a trail, if you can. Then come join us at the new rendezvous we'll set up."

"There's no way to really hide the sign of the loaded donkeys you'll be peeling off earlier," said Hal.

"I know." Rukh sighed heavily. "We'll just have to gamble Barbage is following too hotly after us to look for signs of anyone leaving our line of march; and that the plain tracks of the dozen beasts in the rear makes too attractive a trail for them to suspect anything."

Chapter

> > **27** < <

From nearby in the shadowed woods, as he sat wrapped in a weather cloak on sentry duty on a cool, cloudless night, and some twenty meters from the winking coals of the burnt-down campfires and dark tents of the Command, Hal heard the sound of coughing. But he did not turn. It was Child, gone off a little from the camp into the night—no longer to hide his now-frequent discomfort, but to find a small amount of privacy in which to live with it.

Under the stupidity of his own numbing accumulation of fatigue, Hal's mind was working—slowly, but effectively. He was employing an Exotic technique in which he had been drilled by Walter. In essence, it was like reading a printed page with a magnifying glass that gave him one letter at a time. Plainly, some kind of decision had to be made. Unable to catch them, Barbage and his unlimitedly available Militia forces had settled for harrying them into the kind of exhaustion that would make their eventual capture certain.

Rukh's trick with the donkeys had won them enough of an initial lead on Barbage and the Militia from the second district, so that the Command had been able to get safely over the border into the third district; and there, luck, or an uncooperative local Militia official, had stretched that lead into enough of an edge so that they had been able to get clear of that district and into a fourth one. By that time they were into a different type of countryside; one that worked to their advantage more than it did to that of their pursuers.

Here, the foothills had spread out and become an open, rolling territory of sandy and stony soil replacing the flat, rich farmland they had left behind them. They were no longer penned closely between the lowlands and the mountains; the mountains were far off, blue on the horizon, and the lowlands were lost beyond the opposite horizon, even further.

In this different land of scrub trees, bushes, and narrow streams, was their eventual goal, the city of Ahruma itself, which enclosed the power plant built over the Core Tap they planned to sabotage. There were farms in this territory, too, but they were poor ones, scattered, small, and served with a meager network of roads. For Militia, it was bad country in which to mount a pursuit; but for a Command, it was even worse country in which to survive. As Rukh had said, without their donkey-loads of potential explosive, the Command could have dispersed and effectively ceased to be. But as long as they held tenaciously to the fertilizer and the gunpowder—and therefore necessarily to the donkeys themselves—they could not lose the troops that followed them.

For that reason, they dared not move into Ahruma as planned and contact local sympathizers there for help and to begin mounting their attack on the power plant. The end result of this situation had been that they were continuing to wander the dry hill country around the city at a distance far enough off not to arouse Militia suspicions as to their true destination.

They had stripped the Command to its essentials—those beasts and people without whom the mission could not be accomplished. Now the attrition of being hounded day and night was beginning to wear down both those on two legs and on four. In the end, if this kept up, Barbage would run them into an exhaustion in which they would be forced to stand and fight; and which would give him an easy victory.

The military answer, Hal's early lessons told him, was to attack the Militia camp at night with a small number of the Command; who would then throw their lives away, but do enough damage to render the troops incapable of further pursuit until they could acquire replacements of men and equipment—buying at least twenty-four hours. In that space of time the rest of the Command could force-march to the outskirts of Ahruma and lose themselves, with what their donkeys carried, in the city with their sympathizers.

But the military answer was one that could coldly calculate a certain percentage of an available force as expendable for the purchase of a tactical advantage to the force as a whole. This was unacceptable, in the case of the Command, whose people were as close as members of the same family; and where the Captain would never order such an action.

So the question of what to do came back to turn upon his own actions. Both Barbage and Rukh were trapped in a situation where they could do little but wait for it to wear down. He, on the other hand, should be able to act. And should if he could. But until now, fogged by the arrears of tiredness, his mind had failed to come up with a workable plan.

The sound of coughing had ceased. A few moments later, his ears caught the faint sounds of Child making his way back to his tent. Hal got to his feet. As a sub-officer, he was supposed to be exempt from sentry, kitchen, and other ordinary duties so that he could keep himself ready and alert to his higher responsibilities. But in actual practice, like most of the Command's other sub-officers, he ended up a good share of the time filling in under emergency conditions for one or the other of the members of his own group. Just now he had taken over the sentry duty of one of the team he had inherited from Morelly, who had begun out of excess of exhaustion to nod off on post. But now the man he had relieved had had an extra two hours of sleep; and it was time to return him to his obligations. Hal got to his feet and went into the camp.

He pushed through the flap of a tent and shook the slumbering man.

"Moh," he said, speaking softly, so as not to wake the three other sleepers in the tent, into the ear visible above the edge of the sleeping sack, "time to go back on duty."

The sleeper grunted, stirred, opened his eyes and began wearily to climb out of his bedsack. Hal stayed with him until he was armed and on post, then went to check on the other two sentries posted about the camp.

The others, both women, were awake and reporting all quiet. The Militia camp was only an estimated twelve kilometers from them; and while a nighttime attack by the clumsier, city-trained enemy was possible, it was unlikely. Still, it paid not to take chances. On impulse, Hal went back into the camp, found the tent where Child slept alone, and let himself through the flap.

He squatted beside the Command's now-slumbering Lieutenant. For a moment he watched the face, aged a dozen years or more by the exhaustion of the last week, further deepened into a mask of wrinkles and bones by its relaxation into unconsciousness.

"Child-of-God . . . ," he said softly.

He had barely breathed the words. But instantly the other was awake and looking up at him, and Hal knew that inside the sack, one bony hand had closed around the butt of a power pistol with a sawed-off barrel, pointing it through the cloth at whoever had roused him.

"Howard?" said Child, equally low-voiced although there was no one at hand to disturb.

"It's close to the end of my watch," Hal said. "I'd like to make a quick run, by myself, to the Militia camp—just to see how tired they look; and, with luck, I might pick up one of their maps of this area. We could do with the chance to check our own maps against theirs. Also, with real luck, I could get a map marked with their rendezvous and supply spots."

Child lay still for a few seconds more.

"Very well," he said. "As soon as thou art off watch, thou canst go."

"That's the thing," Hal said. "I'd like to leave now, to make as much use as possible of the darkness that's left. I could wake Falt early, and I don't think he'd object to going on watch an hour or so before his time."

Child lay still again for several seconds.

"Very well," he said, "provided Falt agrees. If he hath objection, come back to me."

"I will," said Hal.

He got up and went out. Closing the tent flap behind him, he heard Child, awake once more to the irritation in his lungs, cough briefly.

Falt did not, as Hal had known he would not, object. Hal got his cone rifle and a small travelling pack to supplement his sidearm and knife, blackened his hands and face and left. An hour and eighteen minutes later he was crouching down in the darkness on the bank of a creek behind a stand of young variform willows, having crept up to almost within arm's length of a pair of young Militiamen. The pair was apparently on watch by a fire at one end of the camp—a watch that presumably took the place of the sentries he had never known the Militia forces to put out.

". . . soon," one of these was saying as Hal eased into position. They were both about middle height for Harmonyites, black-haired and fresh-faced— no more than in their late teens. "And I'll be glad to get back. I hath little stomach for this sort of plowing through the woods all the time."

"Thou hath, hath thou?" The jeer in the voice of the other was obvious. "It's I *have* little stomach, brickhead! You'll never make a Prophet, Old or Young."

"You won't, either! Anyway, I'm one of the Elect. You aren't!"

"Who says I'm not? And who told you you were?"

"My folks—"

"*Are we on watch?*" Barbage was suddenly on the other side of the fire, shoulders a little hunched, eyes like polished obsidian chips in their reflection of the firelight. "Or are we playing the games that childhood hath still left in us?"

The two were silent, staring at him.

"Answer me!"

"Games," muttered the two, low-voiced.

"And why should we not play games when we are on watch?"

But Hal did not wait to hear the answers of the two as Barbage continued to catechize them. He moved backward, got to his feet, and slipped around the perimeter of the encampment until he was level with the tents of the officers, just a short distance from the fire and easily recognizable by their better cloth and greater size.

There were six of them. Hal slid out of the darkness of the surrounding undergrowth to the back wall of the first in line. With the razor tip of his knife, soundlessly, he made a small slit in the fabric and spread the slit enough to look within. It took a moment for his vision to adjust to the greater darkness within, but when it did he saw a camp chair, a table, and a cot—unoccupied. As the one in effective command of the expedition, Barbage had—as Hal had suspected—taken the first tent in the officers' row.

Hal crept quietly around the side of the tent and looked toward the fire. The rest of the camp slumbered. Barbage, standing, still had his back to his own quarters; and the two he was verbally trouncing would be blinded by the close firelight to something as far away as this tent row, even if all their attention had not been frozen on Barbage.

Softly and swiftly, Hal turned the corner of the tent, lifted its flap, and let himself inside.

He had no time to examine the interior in detail. There was a map in the viewer lying among papers on the table; but to take it would make too obvious his visit. Hal looked about and found what he expected, a map case at the foot of the bed. Opening it, he came up with a full rack of slides for the viewer. Hastily, he took them all to the table, took out the slide already in the viewer and began to check the other slides out in it, one by one.

He found one of the territory roughly three days' march ahead, took it out and replaced it with the original slide, and put the other slides back in the map case. Outside the voice of Barbage ceased speaking. Hal stepped to the tent flap and peered out, his fingers lightly grasping the knife hilt.

But Barbage was still standing, silently staring at the two by the fire. A moment later he began to speak to them again; and in a second Hal was into the woods. Another minute put him safely beyond earshot of the voice; and five minutes later he was well on his way back to the Command.

When he returned, daylight was still a full hour off; and Child, when Hal looked into his tent, was sleeping heavily. Hal went back to his own tent and found his own map viewer. Sitting cross-legged in the darkness while Jason slept undisturbed behind him, he put the stolen slide into it.

The small interior illuminant of the viewer, triggered to life by his finger pressure on its control, made the map leap into white, illuminated relief before him. It showed a stretch of rises and hollows of land, covered with scrub vegetation identical with the area they were now in. To the bottom of its display, a road ran almost horizontally across the map, to intersect with a crossroad near the lower right corner. Marked along the road were three asterisks, with code marks next to them.

The code marks were undecipherable, but a good guess could be made at what they represented. They would give details of the number of trucks and personnel who would be delivering supplies to the points the asterisks marked. It was the delivery of such supplies that allowed the Militia to travel light; and made up for the fact that the Militiamen themselves were, from lack of experience, slow and clumsy compared to the members of the Command. Also, the frequent contact with vehicles at the delivery points allowed for speedy evacuation of sick or hurt men; or any who might, for one reason or another, slow down the pursuit.

Hal mentally photographed the map, took it from the viewer and put it in his pocket. He went to find Falt and pay back the extra hour of watch the other had taken for him.

"You go get some sleep while you can!" Falt said. "James and Rukh are bad enough without you trying to imitate them and sleep less than half an hour out of the day and night together. I'm fine."

"All right," said Hal. He was suddenly unutterably conscious of his own weariness, and of a sort of light-headedness at the same time. "Thanks."

"Just get some sleep," said Falt.

"If you'll wake me as soon as Rukh gets up."

"Oh? All right, then."

Hal went back to his own tent. Crawling into his bedsack, with nothing but his boots and harness removed and his pockets emptied, he lay back in the dark, staring at the darkness under the tent roof, with one forearm flung up across his eyes. He realized suddenly that his forehead felt hot; and anger erupted in him. A number of the Command besides Child were beginning to show signs of minor infections as the unrelieved exhaustion exacted its price; but he had assumed that he, of all of them, should be immune to any such thing. He pushed the emotion aside as unprofitable. It was true he had been on his feet, with only brief naps, for several days now. . . .

He woke suddenly to the awareness that he had been asleep, and that Falt, standing back, was shaking his left foot within the bedsack, to wake him. He blinked into full awareness.

"Have I been jumping on people who wake me?" he asked.

"Not jumping—but you do come awake as if you meant to hit first and open your eyes after," said Falt. "You'll find Rukh by the kitchen setup."

"Right," said Hal, pulling himself out of his bedsack and reaching for the contents of his pocket where he had laid them out earlier. He checked suddenly and looked back up at Falt. "At the kitchen? How long has she been up? A couple of hours? I asked you—"

Falt snorted, turned and went out.

Hal finished redressing and went out himself. Rukh, as Falt had said, was down where the kitchen had been set up on making camp the night before, standing, plate and fork in hand, to finish her early meal. She looked up at Hal as he approached.

"I made a short visit to the Militia camp early this morning—" he began.

"I know," she said, scraping her plate clean and handing it, with the fork, back to Tallah. "James told me he gave you permission. In the future, I'd like you to be a little more specific about why you want to make such a reconnaissance. I've told James to ask you for it."

"I wasn't too sure what I could find out," he said. "As it happened, I was lucky. . . ."

He told her about Barbage and the two young Militiamen on watch.

"So I took advantage of the chance to go right into his tent," he said. "It's what I suspected. Barbage's not like the others. He's serious military. His tent shows it. Anyway, I got one of the maps from his case."

He handed her his viewer with the map already in it.

She put it to her eye and pressed the button for the illuminant. For a long moment she stood studying it without saying a word. Then she lowered the viewer, took out the map slide and handed the viewer back to him, putting the map in her pocket.

"It looks like the country up ahead of us," she said.

He nodded.

"It was in order with the other maps in his map case—I estimated three days' march ahead."

"What good did you think it would do us to have this?"

"For one thing," he said, "it lets us check our own maps against it. No offense to the local people you got ours from, but what we have's a lot more sketchy and less accurate than this, which has to be from breakdowns of regular survey information."

"All right," she said. "But we might have lost you; and you've become valuable to us, Howard. I'm not sure it was worth the risk."

"I thought," he said slowly, "we might consider hijacking some of those supplies they're sending him."

Her dark eyes were hard on him.

"It could cost us six to ten people, attacking one of those supply points. Do you think they send out trucks like that without adequate troops and weapons to protect it?"

"I didn't mean at the supply point," he said. "I thought we could take just a single truck, someplace along the route, since we know ahead of time where they'll be headed for."

She was silent.

"We can easily figure out the route a truck'll have to take to the supply point. The old hands in the Command tell me they don't generally send them out in group convoy, but one at a time."

"That's true," she said, thoughtfully. "Normally, they don't worry about a pursued Command having the time to get down to the roads. Also, it's easier to send out each filled truck as it's ready, than to struggle with a convoy of half a dozen to be unloaded all at once and brought back together."

"If you want . . ." He closed in on her first expression of interest quickly. "I can figure out the details of taking one of them, and you or Child could decide from there. Almost anything they'd be carrying would be something we'd need."

She looked at him soberly.

"How much rest have you had lately?" she asked.

"As much as anyone else."

"Which anyone else? James?"

"Or you," he said, bluntly.

"I'm Captain of this Command, and James is First Officer. Tonight," she said, "you're to be off any duty you're scheduled for. Tonight, you sleep. The next day, if you've slept through, bring me a plan for taking one of the trucks."

"We'll be only one day away from that map by tomorrow," he said.

"There're three supply points marked on it, each one at least a day apart. You're not going to lack time to plan."

There was no reasonable argument against that. He nodded; and was turning away to get something to eat himself, when his mind exploded suddenly with the understanding that had been gnawing its way out of his unconscious into his conscious from the moment in which he had first glimpsed the slide in Barbage's tent.

"Rukh!" He swung back to her. Her eyes stared questioningly at his face. "I knew there was something wrong! We've got to change route, right away!"

"What is it?" She had tensed, reflecting his tension.

"That slide. I knew something was bothering me about it. You said it yourself just now! It shows supply points for the next three to six days. Why would Barbage have arranged deliveries of supplies up to six days ahead along the road we just happen to be parallelling now? He knows we never move in the same line for more than two days at a time. Six days from now we'd be anywhere but close to that road, and his troops are right behind us!"

He saw understanding register on her. She swung about.

"Tallah!" she snapped. "Go find James. Pass the word to get moving under any conditions at all. The Militia've sent units into the woods ahead of us to catch us between them and the troops that're after us."

Chapter

> > **28** < <

A *scant thirty-one* of the Command that had counted over a hundred members when it left the Mohler-Beni farm drove a struggling line of donkeys, of which only two were unloaded, through the dripping woods. The weather of Harmony's North Continent had turned unseasonably cold, here at an altitude four thousand feet higher than the rich farmland through which they had passed only a week and a half before; and three days now of intermittent, icy rain had soaked everything, human or animal, not protected by impermeable coverings, chilling them all to the bone.

They had stripped themselves of anything not immediately necessary. They were down to only a dozen tents, in which they slept three or four together, and a few donkey-loads of the kind of food that could be eaten without cooking, out of the hand, on the march. They were nearly all staggering with exhaustion and most were hot with fever. Some respiratory illness had run wild among them since Masenvale; coughing sounded continually up and down their column as, fiery-eyed and dry-skinned wherever the frequent downpours had not found a crevice in their ancient raingear, they plodded through the underbrush of the high foothills.

None of them looked as skeletally close to death as Child-of-God. Yet he continued to move, holding his place in the column and performing his duties as First Officer. The penetrating harshness of his voice had sunk to a near-whisper; but what he said was what he had always said, without difference or admission of weakness.

Of them all, Hal and Rukh appeared to be in the best shape. But they were both among the younger members of the diminished Command to begin with; and each, in his or her own way, seemed to possess a unique personal strength. Hal burned with fever and coughed with the others, but there was a reserve of energy in him that even he was surprised to find—as if he had uncovered a mechanism by which he could continue to burn himself internally for fuel until the last scrap of his bone and flesh had been consumed.

In the case of Rukh, an inner flame that had nothing to do with a self-consumption of her physical body appeared to promise to keep her going until the richly-yellow orb of Epsilon Eridani, now hidden by the weeping cloud cover overhead, should become cindered and cold. Like all the rest of them, she had lost weight, until she might have been the look-alike grandchild of Obadiah or Child-of-God; but this seemed in no way to have lessened her. That inner flame of hers glowing through her dark skin seemed to shine before them like a lamp in the night; and she was more beautiful than ever in her present leanness and fatigue.

They had escaped being caught by the jaws of the trap Barbage had planned to close upon them—jaws that consisted of his own Militia and those he had sent ahead into the woods three days' march before them, to come back and assist his own unit in encircling them beyond any possibility of escape. But the Command had slipped out to freedom by bare meters of distance rather than kilometers. Since then, Barbage had pursued them with an unyielding steadiness, resupplying and remanning his Militia ranks constantly, so that fresh troops were at all times on their heels.

They were given no chance to rest or reorder themselves; and by ones, twos and threes, individual members had faltered in their weariness, or sickened, and been sent away from the main body to try and make their solitary escape as best they might. With them had gone nearly all the spare equipment and donkeys—everything that could be done without, except the bare means of continuing to flee and the sacks of gunpowder and fertilizer that Rukh refused to give up.

She would not admit that escape from this unending hunt was impossible. It seemed that while the lamp burned eternally in her she could not; and her utter refusal to consider any other end to their situation than the accomplishment of their mission hauled the remaining members of the Command forward as if her will was a rope tying them all physically together. Even Hal, who from his Exotic training had the ability to stand aside from her effect upon them, ended by letting himself be deeply seized and moved by it, almost to the point of forgetting his own life and purpose—the purpose he knew must be there, but which he had yet to see clearly—to join in that which Rukh clearly put before all other goals.

Thinking of this, even through the fog of his fever and aching muscles, there came to him finally on wings of insight, greatly slowed by fatigue, the commonplace realization that the great charismatic power of Others like Bleys Ahrens derived not from any special combination of Dorsai and Exotic influences, but solely from the Culture of the Friendlies, in its utter absorption with the power to convince and convert. It came as a shock to him, for in spite of knowing Obadiah, he had not been unaffected by the common idea that of the three great Splinter Cultures, the Friendlies had the least in practical powers to offer from the special talents developed by their Culture. And—like the final part of a firing mechanism clicking into place to make the whole weapon operative and deadly, it woke in him that in this obvious reason lay the mechanism that had made possible the Others' sudden explosive rise to power behind the scenes on all the worlds except the Dorsai, the Exotics and Earth.

The point that had always puzzled everyone about the achievement of that power had been the repeatedly-acknowledged fact that the Others were so very few. Granted, they had chosen to model their organization on the large criminal networks of centuries past, so that they influenced those with power to gain their ends, rather than holding power themselves. Still—in terms of the few thousand that they were, compared to the billions of ordinary humans on the inhabited worlds, even that concept did not explain how they maintained their control. Those they controlled personally were in such large relative numbers that it would be an overwhelming job for the Others just to keep track of replacements being made in their positions, let alone make a fresh effort to convert to an Others-follower each new official. But, thought Hal now, if they could send forth non-Others as disciples, whose own sparks of talent for making such conversions had been fanned by Other efforts into roaring flames, such control became not merely possible, but reasonable.

If that was the explanation for Other success, then it also explained their concern with controlling Harmony and Association; as well as the reason for those two worlds' sudden explosion of activity into interworld commerce within the last twenty or so standard years—an activity which in earlier centuries the Friendlies had scorned except when necessity drove them to a need for the things that only interstellar credits could buy.

Something within the formless movement of Hal's unconscious seemed to register the importance of the conclusion he had just achieved. But there was no leisure to ponder the matter any further, now. If he lived and had the chance, he could check out his discovery. If not, nothing would be changed. Only, he could not bring himself to believe that he would not survive. Either the idea was simply not possible to him, or else his absorption of the uniquely Dorsai attitude of Malachi had dyed the inability to give up into his very bones and soul beyond any laundering. Like Rukh, with her goal of destroying the Core Tap power station, he could not turn aside from the goal he had chosen; and, since death would be a form of turning-aside, death was also not to be considered.

Up ahead of him, the next man in line came to an unexpected, staggering halt; and, having halted, sank down as if his body had suddenly lost all strength in its muscles. Hal moved up and past him.

"What is it?" Hal asked.

The man merely shook his head, his eyes already closed and his breathing beginning to deepen into the slow, heavy rhythm of sleep. Hal went on up, past donkeys and past other members of the team, men and women slumped down where they had ceased moving, some of them already snoring.

At the head of the column, he found Rukh, still on her feet, helping Tallah off with her pack.

"Why the stop?" asked Hal, and cleared his throat against the hoarseness in his voice.

"They needed a halt—a short one, anyway." Rukh got the pack all the way off and bent to examine a hole rubbed in the back of Tallah's heavy checked green workshirt. "We can pad it," she said, "and change the dressing again. But it's turning into a regular ulcer. You shouldn't be carrying a pack at all, with that."

"Fine," said Tallah. "I'll leave it off, then, and the pack can trot along behind me on its own little legs."

"All right," said Rukh, "go see Falt and get a new dressing put on the sore; then you and he figure out what you want to do about putting a better pad on your pack harness. We'll be up and moving again in ten minutes."

Tallah reached for the straps of her pack with her left hand, lifted it clear of the ground, and carrying it that way at ankle-height, headed back down the column toward Falt.

Rukh's eyes went to meet Hal. They stood, made private for a moment by the distance between them and the next-closest members of the Command.

"We had a break only thirty-five minutes ago," said Hal.

"Yes," she said, more quietly, "but in any case we had to stop now, and I didn't want to upset the Command any more than they are already. Come along."

She led him off into the woods. As soon as the vegetation screened them from sight, she turned left to parallel the column and led the way down alongside it for half a dozen meters. Following her, in spite of the preparation for this moment he had had in events of the past few weeks, it struck Hal like a physical blow to see James Child-of-God, seated on the ground on a rain jacket, with his back propped against the trunk of a large variform maple tree.

Child's face against the rutted bark of the tree, stained dark by the rain, was itself sun-darkened and carved, like old wood left too long in the rain and weather. His clothes, even the bulky, outer rain gear, lay limply upon him; so that it was unmistakable how thin he had become in these last few weeks. His forearms rested on his upper thighs, wrists and hands half-turned up, as if they had simply fallen strengthless there under the weight of Harmony's gravity. Legs, arms and body lay utterly still. Only his washed-out blue eyes, sunk deep in their bony hollows beneath the gray brows and above the still-impeccably shaven lower face, showed signs of life and were unchanged. They regarded Rukh and Hal calmly.

"I will stay here," he said, huskily.

"We can't afford to lose you," Rukh's voice was cold and bitter.

"Thou canst not wait for me to rest at the cost of letting the Militia catch thee—as they will within the hour if thou dost not move on," Child said. His words came in little runs and gasps, but steadily. "And it would be a sin to burden Warriors further with someone useless. It is not as if this is a sickness from which I may recover, if the Command supports me for a while. My sickness is age—that only grows more so as we wait. I could go a little farther—but to what purpose? It will be honey to my heart rather to die here, with the enemies of God before me, knowing I still have strength to take more than one of them with me."

"We can't spare you." Rukh's voice was even colder and harder than before. "What if something happens to me? There's no one to take over."

"How am I to take over now, when I can neither march nor fight? Shame on thee to think so poorly, who art Captain of a Command," said Child-of-God. "We are all of us no more than spring flowers, who bloom for a day only in His sight. If a flower dies, any other may take its place. Thou hast known this all thy life, Rukh; and it is the way matters have always stood in the Commands, or with those who testify for the faith. No one is indispensable. So why shouldst thou miss or mourn me who cannot make a better end than this? It is unseemly in thee, as one of the Elect, to do either."

Rukh stood, staring at him and saying nothing.

"Think," said Child. "The day is advanced. If I can delay those who follow us by only one hour, night will be so close that they will have no choice but to stop where they are until morning. While you, knowing they will not follow, can change your route, now; and, by morning they will have gone at least half a day in the wrong direction before they wake to their mistake. So you can gain a full day on them; and with a day's lead, perhaps, the Command can escape. It is your duty not to let pass that God-given chance."

Still Rukh stood, unmoving and unspeaking; and the silence following Child's long speech went on and on; until Hal suddenly realized that of the three people there he was the only one who could break it.

"He's right," Hal said, and heard the words sound tightly in his own throat. "The Command's waiting, Rukh. I'll give him a hand to make him comfortable here, then catch up."

Rukh turned her head slowly, as if against the stiff pressure of unwilling neck muscles, and stared at him for a long moment. Then she looked back at Child.

"James . . . ," she said, and stopped. She took one step toward him and fell suddenly on both knees beside him. Stiffly, he put his arms around her and held her to him.

"We are of God, thou and I," he said, looking down at her, "and to such as us the things of this universe can be but shadows in smoke that vanish even as the eye sees them. I will be parted from thee only a little while— thou knowest this. My work here is done, whilst thine continues. What should it be to thee, then, if for a short time thou lookest about and seest me not? There is a Command that thou must guard, a Core Tap that thou must destroy, and enemies of God that must be confounded by thy name. Think of this."

She shuddered in his arms, then lifted her head, kissed him once and got slowly to her feet. She looked down at him and her face smoothed out.

"Not by my name," she said, softly. "Thine."

She gazed down at him and her back straightened. Her voice broke out again, suddenly, whiplashing through the sodden woods under the low-bellied sky with low-pitched intensity.

"*Thou*, James. When the Core Tap is closed and I am free at last, I will raise a storm against those we fight, a whirlwind of judgment in which none of them will be able to stand. And that storm will carry *thy* name, James."

She wrenched herself around and strode off swiftly, almost running. The two men watched her until low-hanging branches of the trees hid her from sight. Then their gazes came back together again.

"Yes . . . ," said Hal, without really knowing why he said the word. He looked about, at the hilly, cut-up, overgrown land surrounding them. A little distance away, a small rise that was almost a miniature bluff showed between the wet-bright, downturned leaves.

"Up there?" he asked, pointing.

"Yes." It was more pant than spoken word, and Hal, looking back at the older man, saw how prodigally he had plundered his remaining strength to send Rukh from him.

"I'll carry you up there."

"Weapons . . . ," said Child, with effort. "My power pistol with the short barrel, to put inside my shirt. My cone rifle . . . rods of cones. Power packs. . . ."

Hal nodded. The older man was now wearing only his customary holstered power pistol with full barrel and a belt knife.

"I'll get them," said Hal.

He went off through the trees. The Command had just gotten underway once more as he rejoined it; and none of its exhaustion-numbed members bothered to ask why he untied the donkey carrying Child's tent and personal equipment, and led it toward the rear of the moving column.

Reaching the end of the line of people and beasts, he kept going. When vegetation hid him at last from sight of the rearguard, he cut off into the brush and trees once more. A short way back, he found Child sitting where he had been left, and boosted him on top of the load the animal carried.

The donkey dug its hooves in under the double burden, and refused to be led. Hal let the older man off again, and led the animal alone to the little bluff. On top, it was ideal for a single marksman, its surface sloping backward from the edge of the almost-vertical, vegetationless face that looked back in the direction the Militia would come. Hal unloaded Child's gear, set up the tent, and laid out food, water and the rest of the equipment within its dry interior. Then, with the donkey's load lightened considerably, he led it back down to where Child still waited.

This time, when the older man was lifted onto its back, the donkey made no objection; and Hal led it back up to the top of the bluff. He spread a tarp before the tent, just back from the lip of rock and earth overhanging the vertical slope, then helped Child down onto it.

"This, if necessary, I could still do myself," he said, as Hal put him on the tarp, "but what strength I have, I need."

Hal only nodded. He brought logs, rocks and tree branches to make a barricade just behind the lip, through which Child could shoot with some sort of protection against return fire.

"They'll try to circle you as soon as they realize you're alone," said Hal.

"True," Child smiled a little, "but first they will stop; and then talk it over before they come again; and when they do come, finally, still they will be cautious. By that time, I need only hold them a little while for the day to end."

Hal finished laying out the final things, the weapons, a water jug, and some dried food, beside the man who lay on the tarp, his eyes already focused upon the distance beyond the firing gap Hal had left in the barricade. Done, Hal lingered.

"Go," said Child, without looking up at him. "There's nothing more for thee to do here. Thy duty is at the Command."

Hal looked at him for a second more, then turned to go.

"Stop," Child said.

Hal turned back. The older man was looking away from the firing aperture and up at him.

"What is thy true name, Howard?" Child asked.

Hal stared at him.

"Hal Mayne."

"Look at me, Hal Mayne," Child said. "What dost thou see?"

"I see . . ." Hal ran strangely out of words.

"Thou seest," said Child, in a stronger voice, "one who has served the Lord God all his life in great joy and triumph and now goeth to that final duty which by divine favor is his alone. Thou wilt tell the Command and Rukh Tamani this, in just those words, when thou returnest to them. Thou wilt testify exactly as I say?"

"Yes," said Hal. He repeated the message Child had given him.

"Good," said Child. He lay gazing at Hal for a second longer. "Bless thee in God's name, Hal Mayne. Convey to the others that in God's name, also, I bless the Command and Rukh Tamani and all who fight or shall fight under the banner of the Lord. Now go. Care for those whose care hath been set in thy hands."

He turned to fix his eyes once more on the forest as seen through the firing slot in his barricade. Hal turned away also, but in a different direction, leaving James Child-of-God upon a small rise in a rain-saddened wood, awaiting his enemies—solitary, as he had always been; but also, as he had always been, not alone.

Chapter

> > **29** < <

It took Hal the better part of an hour to catch up with the Command. Rukh had changed the direction of its march, as Child had suggested; everyone there going off in different directions to regather later at an appointed destination. It required almost twenty minutes for Hal, circling, to pick up their new trail. After that he went swiftly; but still nearly sixty minutes had gone by when at last he caught up with them. In that last half hour, for the first time since he had left Earth, his mind dropped into certain orderly channels; standing back from the present situation as a detached and independent observer, to coldly chart and weigh its elements. James Child-of-God's last words had had the effect of making the path of Hal's own duty very clear before him; and with that his mind was set free to a hard, practical exercise of the intellect, to which all three of his tutors had trained him, but which until now he had ignored under his involvement in the life of the people around him. Now, however, under the slow abrasion of exhaustion and fever, followed by the final assault of Child's self-sacrifice, his personal emotions vanished from the equation like mist from a mirror, leaving what they all faced, clear and hard in its true dimensions.

As a result, when he at last rejoined the column of the Command, he looked at the men and women trudging along with different eyes. These people were not merely worn out—they were at the farthest stretch of all the extra strength which will and dedication could give them. It might well be that Rukh herself could never be defeated and would never surrender; but these more ordinary mortals who marched and fought under her orders had been used to the near-limits of what was physically and mentally possible to them.

He reached the head of the column and saw at a glance that Rukh had not yet faced this—and would not, could not face it. Like Child, she had an extra dimension of self-use possible to her that ordinary mortals did not have; and she had no real way to appreciate their limits or the fact that these about her now were now very close to them.

Walking at the head of the column, she turned her head to look at him as he came up.

"You did what you could for him?" she asked in a neutral voice. Her face was without expression.

"He sent a message," said Hal. "He asked me what I saw; and when I couldn't answer, he told me that what I saw was one who had served the Lord God all his life in great joy and triumph and went now to that final duty which by divine favor was his alone. He asked me to tell you all this."

Rukh nodded as she marched, still without expression.

"He also asked my true name," Hal went on, "and when I told him it was Hal Mayne, he blessed me by it in God's name. He told me as well to convey to the rest of you that in God's name also he blessed the Command and Rukh Tamani and all who fight or shall fight under the banner of the Lord."

She looked away from him at that and walked in silence for a long minute. When she spoke again, it was still with head averted, but in the same perfectly-level voice.

"The Command now lacks a Lieutenant," she said. "Temporarily, I'm going to assign that officer's duties jointly to you and Falt."

He watched her for a second as they walked together.

"You remember," he said, "that Barbage's real interest is in me. It's possible that if I were seen to be going away from the rest of you—"

"We talked about that. The Commands don't work that way."

"I hadn't finished," he said. "By tomorrow noon you'll have enough of a lead on the Militia to make some things possible. What I was going to suggest was to let Falt take over the duties of First Officer; and while you're moving forward tomorrow, and even yet today, let me start to slip the loaded donkeys, one by one, off from the line of march. The trail left by the Command will still pull the troops after it; and eventually I'll have all the donkeys away from the rest of you."

"Leaving them to be found one by one by the Militia, once they pick up our trail again?"

"No," he said patiently, "because when I take the last one off I'll head back and pick up the others, and take them off to some rendezvous point. Meanwhile the rest of you keep laying a trail forward for another day or so—then split up. Disappear into the woods individually, so that the trail vanishes into thin air. Later you can all rendezvous with the donkeys."

She pondered the idea for a moment as they moved forward side by side.

"No," she said, finally, "after all this, Barbage won't give up so easily. He'll continue to comb the area generally; and even if he doesn't find us eventually, he'll find the donkeys. No."

"He won't comb the area unless he thinks when he finds the rest of you he'll find me," Hal said. "As soon as I've got the donkeys gathered at the rendezvous, I'll let myself be seen at one of their road supply points—I'll knock out and tie up a sentry and steal a weapon or some food—and once he hears I'm alone and headed away from the area, Barbage'll follow. As I say, it's me he's really after."

She returned to her thoughts, walking with her head tilted a little down, her eyes fixed on the forest floor a half-dozen steps ahead. The silence stretched out. Finally, she sighed and looked back at him.

"What are your chances of being seen and still getting away safely?" she asked.

"Fine," he said bluntly, "if I'm on my own and don't have anyone else from the Command to worry about."

She looked forward again. There was another little silence. He watched her, knowing he had set her fear of losing the explosive materials against her duty to preserve the lives of those in the Command.

"All right," she said, finally. She looked squarely at him. "But you'd better begin right now, as you say. It's going to take time for you to get twenty-one beasts staked out away from the line of march, one by one, going off and then catching up again each time. Go get Falt and the maps from my gear, and we'll pick out a rendezvous point."

That night and into the dawn hours of the next day, Hal led laden donkeys away from the Command, taking them down the back trail to separate points before entering the woods on one side and then leading each of them far enough off so that it might bray without being overheard by Militia following the trail. By the time the Command was ready to move, he had all the donkeys staked out individually and was ready to part from the rest of its members.

"In five days," Rukh said. "Keep a watch out during the day. In five days we'll all meet you at the rendezvous."

"It'll take you at least that long to get there once you've started to move all the beasts together," Jason put in. "It's more than a one-man job. I should really come with you."

"No," said Hal. "Except when I've got the donkeys in tow, I can move fastest alone—and if something comes up, I'd rather have only myself to worry about."

"I think you're right," said Falt. "Luck—"

He offered his hand. Hal shook it; and shook hands with Jason also. They were all, including Rukh, wearing trail packs with their essential gear, now that the donkeys were gone.

"You will indeed be careful, won't you, Howard?" Jason said.

Hal smiled.

"I was brought up to be careful," he said.

"All right," said Rukh. "That should take care of the good-byes. I'll walk off a little ways with you, Howard. I've got a few more things to say to you."

They went off together, Hal balancing the full pack, heavy on his shoulders, as the power pistol Rukh had now issued him balanced heavy on his right leg and the cone rifle poised in his left hand; so that all those weights could be as easily ignored as the weight of the clothes he wore. The rain had ceased; but the skies were still like grey puddled metal and a stiff wind was blowing from the direction in which the Command was still moving, a wind that picked up the dampness from the leaves and ground, and chilled exposed faces and hands. Once out of earshot of the Command, Rukh stopped; and Hal also stopped, turning to face her.

He waited for her to speak; but, erect and stiff, she merely stared at him, with the look of a person isolated on a promontory, gazing out at someone on a ship that was drawing away from the shore on which she stood. On a sudden impulse, he put his arms around her. The stiffness suddenly went out of her. She leaned heavily against him; and he felt her trembling as her arms went fiercely around him.

"He brought me up," she said, the words half-buried in his chest. "He brought me up; and now, you . . ."

"I'll be all right," he said to the top of the dark forage cape on her head. But she did not seem to hear him; only continued to hold powerfully to him for a long moment more, before she breathed deeply, stirred and pulled back slightly, lifting her head.

He kissed her; and for another long moment again she held herself against him. Then she broke loose and stepped away.

"You have to go," she said.

Her voice was almost normal once more. He stood, watching her; knowing instinctively not to reach for her again, but feeling in him, like a sharp ache, her private pain.

"Be careful," she said.

Without warning, Epsilon Eridani broke through the heavy weight of the clouds over them; and in its sudden rich-yellow warmth, her face was clear and young and tight.

"It'll be all right," he told her automatically.

She reached out her hand. Their fingertips barely touched; and then she had turned and was going away, back through the woods to the Command. He watched her out of sight, then turned away himself, remembering as he did how he had turned from Child, only the afternoon before.

He went swiftly, thinking of the next twenty-four hours, within which so much would need to be done. At the moment he had both eaten and slept recently, enough of both so that he now went easily into the familiar adrenalin overdrive he could always draw upon; and the fatigue, the rawness of his throat and chest, and the headache that had sat like an angry dog in the back of his head on and off since the fever had begun to work on him, effectively were forgotten.

He had not staked out the donkeys individually as he had indicated to Rukh he would; though it had been necessary to lead each of them off the main trail at a different spot, so that the Militia would not realize that there had been a general exodus of the Command's animals. Trail sign of an occasional beast being led away from the line of march was not unusual. Lame or sick beasts would be taken aside before being turned loose, so that they would not be tempted to try and rejoin their fellows in the column. Once Hal had conducted an individual donkey a safe distance from the trail this time, however, he had turned and taken it to a temporary gathering spot, to be staked out there with the others he had already led away from the Command.

It was to this place he headed now. When he got there, the donkeys were patiently grazing at the ends of their long tethers, scattered about a hollow of land screened with trees on the heights surrounding it; and Epsilon Eridani was halfway up toward the noon position overhead, in a sky furnished with only scattered clouds.

He set to work making up his pack train. It was an advantage that the process of filling the trail packs of the Command members had reduced the total amount his animals were carrying, to the point where he now had five of the twenty-five beasts travelling completely without load and available for use as relief pack animals in case any of his loaded beasts could not go on.

Even with that, however, and the advantage of good weather, the handling of a twenty-five animal pack train single-handed through country like this was a monumental task. He got to work reloading his beasts with the packs he had taken off them on getting them here, and connecting them in a line with lead ropes. It took over three hours before the pack train was ready to go.

When he did at last get under way there were some six hours left in which there would be light enough to travel. He headed almost due east, down-slope toward the nearest road shown on his map, which was the closest supply artery Barbage could be using to keep his troops and equipment supplied for the pursuit. In the six hours that remained, he was able to move within half a kilometer of the road. There, he picked a resting spot very like the one in which he had left the donkeys earlier, unloaded, staked them out, and ate. He lay down in his bedsack to sleep, setting his mind to wake him in four hours.

When he opened his eyes, Harmony's moon—as he had expected—was high in the almost cloudless night sky. The moon—called Eye of the Lord—was half-full now, and the light it gave was more than adequate for the kind of travelling he had in mind.

He made up a light pack with some dried food, first-aid kit, ammunition and rain gear, and left his donkeys to the moonlight. Working his way the rest of the distance down to the road, he began a search back along it for one of the Militia's supply points.

He found one within twenty minutes. At night, its two Militiamen on guard were asleep and all ordinary lights were out; but he smelled it before he saw it. Tucked into the side of the road, in an open spot, were a tent, the still-red coals of a fire, and some piles of unopened cases and general debris. The odors of wood smoke, garbage, human waste, and a medley of the smaller, technological smells of such as weapon lubricant and unwashed tarps led him directly to it.

He took off his pack and laid his rifle aside, a few meters back in the trees, and drifted into the sleeping camp on noiseless feet. The night was so still and insect-free here in the high foothills that he could hear the heavy sleep-breathing of at least one of the men. He could possibly have lifted the tent flap in perfect safety to confirm that there were only two of them on duty there; but it was not necessary. The camp shouted forth the fact that no more than a pair of men were occupying it.

He checked the stack of boxes, but short of opening one, there was no way to tell what was in them. The weight of the one he lifted indicated it held either weapons, weapon parts, or some other metallic equipment. The unseal-and-eat meal units on which the Militia were fed in this kind of pursuit would have been packaged up into boxes that were much lighter for their size than these, as would have medical supplies, clothing and most other deliverable items. From the look of the camp and the number of emptied meal-unit cartons, it was a good estimate that these two had been holding this supply point for two days already and would be here at least another day yet. They would not be here now—they would have gone back with the last supply truck to reach them—if at least one more delivery to this supply point were not expected. Also, from the marks where the earlier deliveries had been made, at least one full day of sunshine and moisture had been at work on the indented earth where the last truck to visit had shut off its blowers and let itself settle to the ground.

Therefore, there should be at least one truck due tomorrow.

He looked once more about the camp, memorizing the distances between its various parts, and its general layout. It was not hard to imagine how it would look and where the men involved would be when a delivery came tomorrow. Having done this, he turned and left as silently as he had come. Only a little more than an hour later, moving on a slant now that he knew the relative positions of the two points between which he travelled, he was once more with his donkeys and in his bedsack, ready for sleep.

He woke before dawn and an hour later was squatting on the hillside a dozen meters above the supply point. He had thought it unlikely that the nearby Militia post, wherever that was, would exert itself to get a supply truck loaded and out before dawn. In any case, he found when he arrived that the two soldiers on duty there were still asleep in their tent; and he was able to listen and watch through the full ritual of their waking and breakfasting.

That day's delivery, he gathered from their breakfast talk, was due an hour before noon and would involve three trucks. His jaw tightened. Three trucks, each with a driver and loader, plus the two Militiamen already here, would be almost too many for him to handle. Ten minutes after hearing this, however, he was on his feet and running back toward his donkeys, having just been gifted with further information. Late in the day there would be another, single truck arriving; but not to make a delivery; and for this reason the two were looking forward to it enthusiastically. It was the truck that would pick them up and return them to barracks life in Ahruma.

The late arrival of this solitary truck offered an opportunity that had been unlikely to hope for—one that could take off some of the hardship his private plans had looked to inflict on the Command. He got back to his donkeys and went swiftly to work loading only the personal gear on as many beasts as were needed to carry it.

Loaded and with the donkeys roped together, he started out for the rendezvous point he had settled on with Rukh.

Left alone as he now was with the problem he faced, caught up in the machinery of the physical job involved in moving nine loaded donkeys in limited time twenty-odd kilometers to the rendezvous point he had originally set up with Rukh, and burning with the fever that had now taken firm hold of him, Hal went almost joyously into a state of self-intoxication in which all things were unreal except the relentless drive of his will.

He had, he estimated, at best seven hours to make the round trip—to get the donkeys there, to get them staked out and unloaded, and to return before the single truck arrived to collect the two Militiamen. It was possible only if everything went without a hitch—which was more than could be expected in the real universe—or if he could manage to move the relatively lightly loaded, if worn-out, donkeys at better than their normal pace.

Somehow he managed to so move them; and the astonished donkeys found themselves at intervals, on downslopes and in open stretches, actually breaking into a trot. For a time that lasted into midday, it seemed that fortune would smile on him and not only would he make his schedule, but beat it by an hour or so.

Then without warning, the country turned bad for pack trains. The ground became cut and seamed with gullies, heavily brushed and wooded, so that the last donkeys might be headed down a precipitous—if short—slope, with their hooves digging in to keep them from nosediving forward, while the animals in the lead would be struggling up an opposite slope that was equally steep and tangled with bushes.

In the case of a string of beasts of necessity roped together in one long line, this kind of situation produced falls on the part of some of the loaded beasts, and unbelievable tangles. By an hour past midday it became clear that, barring a sudden change for the better in the terrain, he had no hope of getting his beasts to their destination and returning in time to the supply point.

He did the next best thing. Consulting the map he had copied from Rukh's supply, he located the nearest stream, tied up his donkeys temporarily and prospected for a substitute rendezvous point along it. Having found this, he went back and brought the animals to this point, unloaded and cached the equipment they carried, then staked them out individually on "clotheslines" fastened at each end, each donkey being tethered to a slip ring that ran up and down the line, so that he could move to reach the stream and available forage.

This done, he cut a generous handful of hair from the tail of one of the donkeys and headed for the original rendezvous. There, he tacked up bunches of the donkey hair on the trunks of several trees, with an arrow carved in the tree just below each bunch, pointing a compass direction to the substitute point where donkeys and equipment were now to be found.

It was all he could do. Rukh and the others were not unaware that under campaign conditions few things went exactly as planned. Not finding the donkeys where they should be, they would instinctively look for them, and for clues left as to where they might be. Unless they had the Militia right on their heels and no time to stop and hunt, a reasonable investigation on their part would find the animals and equipment where he had left them; and this before the donkeys ran out of forage, or fell prey to the kind of accident that could occur to such creatures left tethered alone in the woods for several days. Hal shut his mind to the thought of how Rukh would feel on discovering no explosive among the loads he had cached with the animals.

In any case, he had no time to do more. Leaving the established rendezvous now, he literally ran the more than twenty kilometers back to the supply point.

He arrived no more than three-quarters of an hour later than he had originally planned. The two Militiamen were still there, although their personal gear was packed and ready for their leaving. Puzzlingly, the pile of unopened supplies was also still there; and Hal, sweating and exhausted from the past eight and a half hours of extreme exertion, was left to worry over the possibility that some of Barbage's Militiamen from the pursuit team might appear at any minute to pick them up. If half a dozen more armed men should arrive just when the truck was here to pick up the two on sentry duty, he would be facing an impossible situation.

But there was nothing for him to do but wait; and one of the advantages of waiting was that it gave him a chance to rest before the next demand upon him. He lay on the slope, accordingly, not even bothering to keep an eye on the camp below him, since his ears gave him a clear image of what was going on down there. His only concern now was stifling the urge to cough that, now the excitement and adrenalin of his earlier exertions was over, was threatening to betray his presence to the men below.

In the end it was necessary to use one of the techniques Walter the In-Teacher had taught him for emergency control of the body's automatic processes, knowing as he did that he was further draining his strength to do so and putting himself at least partially back into the berserkedness of overdrive. But the exercise effectively silenced the cough for the present; and, after a while, his ear picked up the distant sound of blowers that signalled a truck making its way up the slope of the highway to the supply point.

It was roughly an hour and a half late. He could, if he had known it would be this dilatory, have returned from where he had left the donkeys at no more than a good walking pace. So much for lost opportunities. An hour and a half overdue was almost to be expected in military schedule-keeping; but, he told himself, if he had counted on the truck being late, as surely as this day would end, it would have appeared on time.

The truck came on. The two Militiamen were standing, waiting, out by the side of the road, with their packs and other gear piled behind them. The vehicle was a heavy-framed, military version of the farm trucks the Command had made use of in the Masenvale raids on the fertilizer plant and the metals-storage point. It came on, stopped, turned about and backed up to the pile of boxes.

Clearly, it was intended to take back whatever was in the boxes to the supply center. The two Militiamen who had been waiting went back to the boxes themselves, to load. Hal, holding his cone rifle in his right hand and with the flap up on the power pistol holstered on his leg, slipped down until only a small screen of bushes and some four meters of roadside dirt separated him from them. With the back of the truck open now, he could see into the cab. The driver alone was still in the truck, behind its wheel. One other Militiaman had come out of it and was helping the two who had been on duty here to load the boxes.

Hal stepped quietly from the bushes with the cone rifle in his arms.

"Driver, get out here!" he said. "The rest of you—stand still!"

They had not seen him until the sharp snap of his voice brought their heads around. Inside the truck, the driver's head jerked back to look over the top of his seat. His face stared.

"Back through the truck and stand here with the rest of them!" Hal said to him. "Be careful—don't make it look as if you're trying anything."

"I'm not . . . ," the driver almost stammered.

He lifted his arms into view beside his head and worked his way clumsily between the two seats of the cab, then came back through the empty body of the truck to jump down and stand beside the other three. Hal turned his attention to the others. One was an older man. The two who had been on sentry duty were plainly only in their teens. Two pale young faces stared blankly at him with the expressionless terror of children.

"Are you—are you going to shoot us?" one of them asked in a high voice.

"Not yet, anyway," said Hal. "I've got some heavy work for you to do, first."

Chapter

> > **30** < <

"Take it between those two large trees there. Slowly," said Hal.

The driver was seated at the vehicle's controls beside him, with the barrel-end of Hal's power pistol touching his ribs. Behind them in the body of the truck, the three other Militiamen sat against one side of it, with their hands in their laps, looking into the small dark circle that was the muzzle of Hal's cone rifle, aimed at them over the back of the seat. Except for the fact that Hal had to keep his attention at once on the route on which he was directing the driver, the driver himself, and the three in the back, the situation was almost comfortable.

"A little farther . . . ," said Hal. "There!"

They emerged into the area holding the donkeys he had not taken to the rendezvous point.

"Over there," he told the driver, and coughed harshly. "That stack covered with tarps. Bring the truck up to it, turn around and open your back doors. We'll be loading."

The driver swung his steering knob and punched keys on his console. The truck's blowers shut off and the vehicle sat down on the ground. Hal herded the driver and others before him out the open rear doors onto the ground beside the pile of explosive materials.

"All right," he said. "All of you—yes, you too, driver—start putting everything from that stack into the truck."

It took the four of them, at gunpoint, only some twenty minutes to load what had taken Hal several hours to unload, pile, and protect from the weather. When it was all in the truck, he set his prisoners to work turning the remaining donkeys loose and shooing them out of the clearing. When the last beast had been chased off, Hal brought the men back to the truck. Leaving them standing on the ground before the open back doors, he climbed back inside alone and went forward to the driver's seat.

Taking the driver's seat, he rested the cone rifle on the back of it, covering them.

"Now," he said, "driver, I want your uniform, including your hat and boots. Take it off."

The driver looked at him grayly. Slowly he began to undress.

"Good," said Hal, when he was done. "Throw them here—all the way to me. That's right. Now, the rest of you, take off your boots and toss them in the back of the truck."

They stared at him.

"Boots," he repeated, moving the rifle sights from left to right across their line. "Off!"

Slowly, they began to remove their boots. When the last piece of footwear had fallen with a thump onto the metal bed of the truck, Hal gestured once more with the cone rifle.

"Back off across the clearing until I tell you to stop," he said.

They backed, lifting unshod feet tenderly high above rocks, sharp twigs and spiny-leaved vegetation.

"That'll do!" Hal called, when they were a good twenty meters from him. "Now, stay there until I leave. After that, you can make your own way back to the road and either wait for help, or go find it."

He keyed the truck to life and lifted it on its blowers.

"You can't just leave us out here, without boots!" the driver called. "You can't—"

The rest of his words were covered by the sound of the blowers as Hal drove off. He watched the four of them in the truck's viewscreen until trees and bushes blocked them from sight; after which he closed the rear doors of the truck and drove with all safe speed to the road.

Bootless and carefully choosing where to set their feet, and with the driver as the only one who had seen the route they had followed from the supply point, the best speed the four could make through the woods on foot would take them at least a couple of hours to find their way back to the highway. After that, they would still have to choose between trying to walk in what was left of their socks, thirty or forty kilometers of this highway down to where it intersected with a more trafficked road; or finding their way back to the supply point and waiting there to be rescued.

In two hours it would be dark and their feet would be very sore. They would almost certainly choose to wait at the supply point, where Hal had already destroyed their communications equipment. In any case, it would be several hours after dark before their return would be overdue enough to be noticed at the motor pool to which the truck belonged; and the first assumption there would be that, through accident or design, they were simply delayed and would be in by morning. It would probably not be until full morning of the next day that attempts would be made to check on them. Meanwhile, since Barbage would have assumed that by now this point had been abandoned, no one from his pursuit team would be likely to check on it.

So, it should be tomorrow before anyone learned that this truck was gone astray. He had at least the next ten hours in which to drive, with only the problem of avoiding a routine check on his credentials or his purpose for being on the road with a Militia vehicle.

Just before he turned onto the highway, Hal stopped to replace his own clothes with the driver's uniform. The driver had been both tall and heavy, so that the jacket was only a little tight in the shoulders, though the pants were enormous around Hal's waist; but even the other man's height had not been enough to provide sleeves and pant legs that were other than obviously, almost ridiculously, short on Hal. Still, wearing the uniform and the cap— which fortunately was only a little loose on his head—and sitting mostly hidden in the cab of the truck, Hal could pass a casual inspection as a Militiaman.

Dressed, he keyed-on the truck's reference screen for a small-scale map of the general area between his present location and Ahruma. The map showed the city at a distance of something over two hundred and ten kilometers, with a spiderweb of roadways multiplying and thickening toward its center.

Somewhere on the city's south outskirts was one of the local people whom Rukh's Command had been scheduled to contact, when at last it reached the city; a woman named Athalia McNaughton, who had a small business selling used farm equipment. She might be able to help him—if he could reach her. There would be the truck to dispose of and its contents to hide; and, while he had with him the identification and credit papers he had carried ever since leaving Earth, he would need information on how to use them safely. The only hope of escaping Bleys now lay in getting off Harmony.

Ahruma, he knew, because of its Core Tap and spaceship refitting yards, had a commercial spaceport even larger than that of Citadel, the city at which he had first set foot on Harmony; but any spaceport could be a dangerous place for him to try arranging passage unless he knew where to go and whom to see when he got to the terminal.

If she could help, the odds were with him. She could have no idea that he was approaching her without Rukh's approval and orders. It might be a week or more before word of the splitting up of the Command could reach Ahruma partisans. On the other hand, his name and description would be known to her, as one of the Warriors under Rukh's leadership.

He clicked off the reference screen, punched on the trip clock, and having picked his route to the city, drove out onto the highway and turned right.

He drove for half an hour before he ran into any sign of other traffic. By that time he had covered over forty kilometers and was on a double-lane Way headed generally in the direction of Ahruma. The load which had been a full one for a dozen donkeys was a light one for the truck; and the vehicle hummed along at the legal military speed limit of eighty kilometers an hour. Without problems, he could probably expect to reach the city in about three hours.

Darkness closed in about him as he drove; but as the countryside surrounding the Ways he travelled on became more inhabited, artificial lighting blossomed to challenge it on either side of his route. Seated alone in the cab above the blowers, their breathy roar tuned down by the truck's soundproofing to a steady, soft humming, and with the illumination of the instrument panel softly glowing at him below the dimness of the windshield, his alertness began to yield to the lack of that emotional pressure which had kept him keyed up earlier. His body and mind relaxed; and, as it did so, his awareness of the fever, the headache, the cough and the fatigue that rode him like vampires became more and more acute.

For the first time he was able to measure the depths of his own exhaustion and illness; and what he found alarmed him. He would need to be at full alertness, and at something like full strength, from the time he parted company with Athalia McNaughton until he was safely aboard the ship taking him to some other world. The partisans in Ahruma might not know that he had left the Command; but it could not be more than twelve hours before the local Militia would, since he had dealt with the men he had captured so as to make it clear that his hijacking of their truck had been a solitary action.

It might be the better part of wisdom to see if Athalia could provide him with a few hours' safe sleep at her place, before he tried the spaceport. He should be relatively safe until dawn. On the other hand, if he could use these same late-night hours to get to the spaceport and buy his passage unsuspected, they were probably better utilized that way. Once aboard an interstellar ship, he could sleep as much as he wished.

Mind and body were becoming very heavy. He had to force his gaze to focus on the polished ribbon of the Way, that seemed to roll endlessly out of darkness before his forelights as he went. He debated tapping his overdrive reflex, once more—and once more put it from him. It would be easy and tempting to do, but wasteful of energy in the long run; and his energy was draining fast. He clicked on the reference screen again, and studied the maze of roads before him on the edge of the city. He had been eating up the distance on the open Way; but that sort of travel was reaching its end. Now came the time in which he would have to feel his way through fringe areas of the city by road sign and map alone, to Athalia's front door. This close to his goal he could not risk stopping to ask for directions from someone who might later identify him.

The night became one continuing blur of dimly-lit intersection and street signs. He took refuge in focusing down as he had days earlier when he had needed to think effectively toward a decision through the fog of sickness and fatigue; and his vision cleared somewhat. His reflexes were slower, and he slowed the truck accordingly, driving as circumspectly as he dared without drawing attention to a military driver who seemed to be exercising unnatural caution. Time, which had been in generous supply, began to run short. He checked the trip clock and saw that he had been driving now for nearly six hours. The glowing figures of the clock at which he stared made only academic sense to him. Subjectively, the time in the cab seemed to have been, at once, endless and no more than a handful of minutes.

He found himself at last guiding the vehicle down a narrow, fused earth road into the wilderness of a dark suburb, half small farms, half ramshackle cottages or small businesses. There was no light in the buildings he passed until he came to what looked like an abandoned warehouse, with a remarkably-tall and new-looking highwire fence about it, and an invisibly-large stretch of ground behind it. At one corner of the front of the building, a window was illuminated.

Hal stopped the truck and got creakily out of it. He walked to the closed and locked pipe-metal gate of the fence and stared through it. The lighted window was uncurtained; but the distance was too great to see if anyone was visible behind it. He looked about the gate for some kind of communicator or bell to announce his presence and found none.

As he stood there, there was the sound of a snarling bark and two dark canine forms rushed the other side of the gate, setting up a savage noise at him. He stared. Like horses, dogs were not usually able to reproduce on Harmony, particularly dogs as large as these. A pair like this would be more likely to have been raised from test-tube embryos of Earth stock, imported by spaceship—and their purchase would have represented a very large expense for a business as small and poor as this one looked. He waited. Perhaps the barking would raise the attention of someone inside.

But no one came, and time—his time, limited as his strength was now limited—was going. He considered getting back into the truck and simply driving it through the locked gates. But that would hardly be the way to begin an appeal to the sympathy and help of Athalia McNaughton, if this was indeed her address. Instead, he sat down cross-legged on his side of the gate and began to croon to the two dogs in a soft, quavering falsetto.

The dogs continued to bark savagely—for a while. Then, gradually, intervals came in their clamor; gradually the volume of their barks lessened and became interspersed with whines. Finally, they fell entirely silent.

Hal continued to croon, as if they were not there.

The dogs whimpered more often, moving about uneasily. First one, then the other, sat down on its haunches. After several minutes, one of them raised its muzzle to the still-dark sky and moaned lightly. The moan continued and increased, developing into a full howl. After a second, the other dog also lifted its muzzle and howled softly.

Hal crooned.

The howling of the dogs rose in volume. Shortly, they were matching voices with him, almost harmonizing, seated on their haunches on the other side of the gates. Time went by; and, suddenly, a crack opened in the dark front wall of the building, next to the window, spilling white, actinic light in a fan of illumination out toward the fence. The dogs fell silent.

A dark, trousered figure occulted the brilliant, newly-appeared opening and advanced across the yard toward the gate, carrying a light in one hand and something short and thick in the other. As it got close, the light being carried centered on Hal's face and blinded him. His available vision became one blare of light. It approached and stopped, close enough that he could have grabbed it, if the bars of the gate had not been between him and the approaching individual.

"Who're you?" The voice was a woman's, but deep-toned.

Hal pulled himself slowly and heavily to his feet. On the other side of the fence, the dogs also rose from their sitting positions, approached the gate and stuck black noses between its pipes, licking their jaws self-consciously with occasional whines.

"Howard Immanuelson," he said, hearing his own voice echo, hoarse and heavy in the darkness, "from the Command of Rukh Tamani."

The light stayed steady on him.

"Name me five people who're with that Command," said the voice. "Five besides Rukh Tamani."

"Jason Rowe, Heidrik Falt, Tallah, Joralmon Troy . . . Amos Paja."

The light did not move away from his eyes.

"None of these are the Lieutenant of that Command," said the voice. "Name him."

"I'm co-Lieutenant, with Heidrik Falt," said Hal. "Both of us, acting only. James Child-of-God is dead."

For a moment the light held steady. Then it moved away from him to the truck behind him, leaving him lost with contracted pupils in the darkness.

"And this?" The voice came after a moment, unchanged.

"Something I need your help with," Hal said. "The truck has to be gotten rid of. Its load is something else. You see—"

"Never mind." There was a sound of the gate being unlocked. "Bring it in."

He turned around, eyes gradually adjusting to the night, fumbled his way to the cab of the vehicle and into it, up behind its controls. Without turning on its forelights again, he drove through the now-open gates to halt just outside the building. When he got down from the cab again, the two dogs pressed shyly forward against him, their noses sniffing at his pants legs and crotch.

"*Back,*" said the voice; and the two animals retreated slightly. "Come on inside where I can get a better look at you."

Within, his vision gradually adjusted to the brightly-lit room behind the window that seemed to be half office, half living room—impeccably neat, but somehow without the forbidding, don't-touch quality that often accompanied such neatness. They stood and examined each other. She was mid-thirties, or possibly a good deal older, straight-backed, wide-shouldered, handsomely strong-boned of face, with heavy, wavy hair, cut short and so rich a brown as to be almost black. Under that darkness of hair, her skin was cream-colored, reminding Hal of a face on a cameo ring he had fallen in love with, once, when he had been very young. Her eyes were also brown and wide-set, her mouth wide and thin-lipped. To only a slightly lesser extent—although they were in no way similar otherwise—she had the devastatingly-direct gaze Hal had seen in Rukh; but, unlike Rukh, the challenge of her presence was almost entirely physical.

"You're sick," she said, looking at him now. "Sit down."

He looked about, found an overstuffed chair behind him and dropped heavily into it.

"You say James is dead?" She was still standing over him.

He nodded.

"We've had Militia right behind us for nearly a week and a half now," he said, "and there's been some kind of pulmonary disease we've all caught. James got to the point where he couldn't keep up. He insisted on making a rearguard action by himself to give the Command time to change its route. I helped him set up in a position. . . ."

The words Child-of-God had given him to pass on to Rukh and the Command came back to him; and he repeated them now for this woman.

She stood for a moment after he had finished, not saying anything. Her eyes had darkened, although there was no other change in her expression.

"I loved him," she said at last.

"So did Rukh," Hal said.

"Rukh was like his grandchild," she said. "I loved him."

The darkness went from her eyes.

"You're Athalia McNaughton?" he asked.

"Yes." She glanced out the window. "What's in the truck?"

"Bags of fertilizer—to be combined with those makings we brought in before the raid, for the explosive Rukh planned to use to sabotage the Core Tap. Can you hide it?"

"Not here," she said, "but I can find a place."

"The truck needs to disappear," he said. "Can you—"

She laughed, dryly. Her laugh, like her voice, was deep-toned.

"That's easier. Its metal can be cut up and sold in pieces. The rest of it can be burned." Her gaze came back to him. "What about you?"

"I've got to get off-planet," he said. "I've got credit vouchers and personal papers—everything that's necessary. I just need someone to tell me how to go about buying passage at the spaceport here."

"Real vouchers? Real papers?"

"Real vouchers. The papers are real, too—they just belonged to someone else, once."

"Let me see them."

He reached into the inside pocket of his jacket and pulled out the long, lengthwise-folded travel wallet with its contents. She took them from his hand almost brusquely and began to go through them.

"Good," she said. "Nothing here to connect you with anyone in Ahruma. No one official's seen these since you left Citadel?"

"No," he said.

"Even better." She passed the papers back. "I can't do anything for you directly; but I can send you to someone who's probably—probably, note—safe to buy from. He's not so safe you can trust him with what you've been doing since you joined Rukh."

"I understand." He stowed the envelope with its papers once again in the inside pocket. "Can I get to him at this time of night?"

She stared at him so directly her gaze was almost brutal.

"You could," she said. "But you're ten paces from collapsing. Wait until morning. Meanwhile, I can give you some things to knock down that infection and make sure you sleep."

"Nothing to make me sleep—" The words were an instinctive reflex out of the years of Walter the InTeacher's guidance. "What sort of medication were you thinking of for the infection?"

"Just immuno-stimulants," she said. "Don't worry. Nothing that does any more than promote your production of antibodies."

She half-turned to leave, then turned back.

"What did you do to my dogs?" she asked.

He frowned at her, almost too exhausted to think.

"Nothing . . . I mean, I don't know," he said. "I just talked to them. You can do it with any animal if you really mean it. Just keep making sounds with your mouth like the sounds they make and concentrate on meaning what you want to tell them. I just tried to say I was no enemy."

"Can you do it with people?"

"No, it doesn't work with people." He smiled a little out of his exhaustion. After a second, he added—"It's a pity."

"Yes, it's a pity," she said. She turned away fully. "Stay where you are. I'll get things for you, including some different clothes."

Chapter

> > **31** < <

He woke suddenly, conscience gripping him sharply for some reason he could not at the moment recall. Then it exploded in him that he had let himself be talked into sleeping rather than continuing on his feet to whomever it was could sell him passage off Harmony.

For a moment, half-awake, he lay on whatever bed he had been given, feeling stripped and naked, as lonely and lost as he had felt in that moment four and a half years before, when he had turned away from the shadows on his terrace and the physical remains of Walter, of Malachi and Obadiah. In this moment between unconsciousness and full awareness, he was once again a child and as alone as he had ever been; and under the massive pressure of the weariness and feverishness that held him, the overwhelming urge in him was to curl up, to bury his head under the covers once more and retreat from the universe into the warm and eternal moment he had just left.

But, far off, like a strident voice barely heard, a sense of urgency spoke against further sleep. Late . . . already late . . . said his mind; and the urgency pulled him like a heavy fish out of deep water back to full awareness. He sat up staring into darkness, finally made out a faint line of something like illumination below eye-level and two or three meters from him, and identified it as light coming faintly beneath a closed door.

He got to his feet, groped to the door, found its latch and opened it. He stepped into a dim corridor with light bouncing from around a corner at its far end, to faintly illuminate the walls and floor where he stood. He went toward the light, turned the corner, and stepped into the room where he had first confronted Athalia McNaughton, a room now lit from its unshaded windows with the antiseptic light of pre-dawn.

"Athalia McNaughton?" His voice went out and died, unanswered.

He went to the only door other than the entrance in the room, and pulled it open. Beyond was a small office stacked with papers, and a tiny desk, at which Athalia was now sitting, talking into a phone screen. She switched off and looked over at him.

"So you woke up on your own," she said. "All right, let me brief you, feed you, and put you on your way."

When he rode out through the pipe-iron gates forty-five minutes later, beside her in a light-load truck, the Militia vehicle had vanished from the yard. He did not ask about it and Athalia offered no information. She drove without speaking.

He had no great desire for conversation at the moment, himself. His few hours of rest had only worked to make him aware of how feverish and tired he was. With one voice, all the cells of his body cried for a chance to rest and heal themselves. The immuno-stimulants were hard at work in him, and the fever was down slightly—but only slightly. His throat and chest burned, although the overwhelming urge to cough was now controllable by methods Walter had taught him; and that was something for which he was grateful. He had no desire to draw attention to himself with the sounds of sickness that might cause anyone who came close to him to pay particular attention to him.

Athalia had also made an offer of painkillers and ordinary stimulants. But both would interfere with his own mental control, the effects of which on his weakened body he could judge more accurately than its response to drugs; and on being refused she had turned immediately to the problems of getting him to the person who could sell him the interworld passage he needed. The man's name was Adion Corfua. He was not a native Harmonyite but a Freilander; a small shipping agent who did not sell interworld passages himself, but knew brokers from whom cancelled tickets, or those not picked up within the legal time limit, could be bought—at either a premium or a discount, depending upon the world of destination and the buyer demand.

"I'll drive you to a point close to the Terminal," Athalia told Hal. "From there you can catch a bus."

After that, it would be a matter of his following directions to the general shipping office out of which Corfua worked.

The morning had dawned dry and cool, with a stiff breeze, a solid cloud cover, but no prospect of rain. A gray, hard day. Just before Athalia dropped him off at the sub-terminal where he would catch the bus, she drew his attention to a compact piece of tan luggage behind his seat, the sort of case in which interworld employment contracts were carried by those who had business with them.

"The contracts in it are all legitimate," Athalia said, "but they're from workers who've made their round trips. They won't stand up to being checked with employers; but for spot inspection, they're unquestionable. Your story should be that you're making a sudden, unexpected courier run. It'll be up to you to come up with a destination, an employer there and a situation in which contract copies are needed in a hurry."

"Industrial sabotage," Hal said, "destroyed some files in an interworld personnel clearing house on the world I'm going to."

"Very good," said Athalia, nodding and glancing at him for a moment, then back to the Way down which they were travelling. "How do you feel?"

"I'll make it," he said.

They had reached the sub-terminal of the bus line. She handed the case to him as he got out. Standing on the pavement of the sub-terminal with the case in one hand, he turned and looked back at her.

"Thank you," he said. "Remember me to Rukh and the rest of the Command when you see them."

"Yes," she said. Her eyes had darkened again. "Good luck."

"And to all those James sent his message to, at the end there," Hal said, "good luck."

The words, once they were spoken, sounded out of place in the hard, prosaic daylight. She did not answer, but sat back in her seat and pressed the stud that closed the door between them. He turned away as she drove off in the truck; and walked over to stand at the point where he would be boarding the bus.

Twenty minutes later he stood instead at the general desk of the shipping office with which Adion Corfua was connected.

"Corfua?" said the man on the general desk. He punched studs, looked into the hidden screen before him, and then glanced off to one side of the room behind him in which a number of desks were spread around. "He's here today; but he's not in yet. Why don't you take a seat at his desk? It's the third from the wall, second row."

Hal went over, and settled into the piece of furniture facing the indicated desk. It was not a float seat, but a straight-backed uncushioned chair of native wood, plainly designed to encourage visitors not to linger. But in Hal's present physical state, to sit at all rather than stand was a welcome thing. He sat, therefore, on the edge of dozing; and after some minutes the sound of feet beside him brought him fully awake again. He sat up to see a large, slightly-overweight man in his forties with a thick black mustache and a balding head, taking the padded float behind the desk.

"What can I do for you?" asked the man who must be Adion Corfua. His smile was a minimum effort. His small blue eyes were large-pupiled and unnaturally steady as they met Hal's.

"I need a passage to the Exotics," Hal said, "preferably to Mara. Right away."

He lifted the contract case from the floor beside him to show briefly above desk-level, and dropped it to the floor again.

"I've got some papers to deliver."

"What's your credit?" asked Corfua.

Hal produced his travel envelope and extracted from it a general voucher of interstellar credit showing more than enough funds to take him to the destination named. He handed these to Corfua.

"It'll be expensive," said Corfua, slowly, studying the voucher.

"I know what it'll cost," said Hal; and made the effort necessary to smile at the other man, as Corfua looked over the top of the voucher at him. Athalia had told him approximately what the other should charge for a passage to Mara. In his present feverish and exhausted state he had no interest in bargaining; but to be too unconcerned about the cost of the trip would make people suspicious.

"What's the problem?" Corfua laid the papers on his desk.

"Some papers destroyed by industrial sabotage, there," he said. "I'm carrying replacements."

"Oh? What papers?"

"All I'm interested in with you," said Hal, "is finding a passage."

Corfua shrugged.

"Let me talk to some people," he said. He got up from behind the desk, picking up Hal's identity and voucher. "I'll be right back."

Hal stood up also and took the papers neatly back out of the other man's hand.

"You won't need these," he said, "and I've got a few things to do. I'll meet you at the central newsstand kiosk in the Terminal, in twenty minutes."

"It'll take longer than that—" Corfua was beginning.

"It shouldn't," Hal said. Now that he had actually locked horns with the other man, his head was clearing and his early training was upholding and guiding him. "If it does, maybe I should find someone else. See you at the kiosk in twenty minutes."

He turned and walked away without waiting for agreement, out of the shipping office. Once beyond its entrance and beyond the sight of anyone there, he stopped and leaned for a second with one shoulder against a wall. The spurt of adrenalin that had activated him for a moment had died as quickly. He was weak and shaky. Under the jacket of the brown business suit with which Athalia had outfitted him, his shirt was soaked with sweat. After a second he straightened up, put his papers back in their envelope and walked on.

His greatest safety in the Terminal, Athalia had not needed to tell him—although she had, anyway—lay in keeping moving. Standing or sitting still, he could be studied. Moving, he was only one more in a continually-swarming crowd of faces and bodies that, even to trained observers, could at last all come to look very much alike.

He moved, therefore, about the maze of internal streets, shops and buildings almost at random. Half the Spaceport Terminal was taken up by this Commercial Center, which was like a small city under one roof. The other half was an industrial complex that dealt with the maintenance, repair and housing of both visiting ships and those being worked over in the Core Tap–powered Outfitting Center, only a few kilometers away. Even after three hundred years of interstellar spaceflight, the phase-shift ships, even the smallest courier vessels, were massive, uneasy visitors to a planetary surface. Those landed here were of course completely out of sight of any of the people thronging the Commercial Center. But the awareness of their nearness, and the reminder in that of the great interstellar distances beyond Harmony's atmosphere, shrank the human self-concept and made for a Lilliputian feeling, not only with regard to the crowds filling the Commercial Center, but about the architecture and furnishings surrounding them.

It was with this feeling, superimposed upon the protests of his ill and overextended body and joined to the nervous awareness of a hunted animal, that Hal moved about the Center. He was stripped down to a sensation of being beaten and naked in the midst of enemies, a traitor to all who had trusted him. To save the lives of those in the Command, he had taken it on himself to remove from it not only himself, but the materials for the explosive. In effect, he had betrayed the others, knowing both actions were ones Rukh would never have agreed to, if asked. Only luck could reunite the Command now with what he had carried off in the truck, and lead it to the completion of its planned mission.

But the alternative had been death for all the rest of them; and after the self-sacrifice of James Child-of-God, Hal had found himself unable to face the prospect of more death among these people to whom he had become close.

Perhaps he had been wrong to take matters into his own hands; but there had seemed no other choice. Only, he had never felt so alone in his life— so alone, in fact, that part of him was a little astonished that he still possessed the will to resist capture, control, and possibly death. But yet he was continuing to resist, instinctively and innately. Under his mind-numbing exhaustion, his illness and the sorrow of parting with the first humans he had come to feel deeply at home with since his tutors' deaths—under the desperation of his present situation—an instinct of resistance entirely independent of his will burned steadily with the fierceness of ignited phosphorus.

He pulled himself from the whirlpool of his thoughts and emotions that was sucking him down into himself. It was almost time to meet Adion Corfua at the central newsstand kiosk.

He walked to the end of the interior street he was on and checked the map of the Center. He was only the equivalent of a couple of city blocks from the large central square, edged with sidewalk cafés and filled with plantings and fountains, that held the kiosk. He turned toward the square.

A block from it, he stepped into a clothing shop to buy a blue jacket and gray beret, of the cut he had remembered seeing on New Earth, when he had transferred spaceships there on his way to Coby. Outside the shop, he discarded in a sidewalk trash incinerator the bundle containing the brown jacket he had been wearing when he had met Corfua. Slumping to reduce his height, he went on to the square and began to wander casually around it, observing the kiosk and the people clustered about it out of the corner of his eye.

Corfua was there, standing by a wall of the kiosk and apparently absorbed in reading a news printoff he had just bought. Around the agent there was a little space with no people, the closest one being a man in a green leisure jumper who was scanning a screen with listings of book publications. Hal, who had planned to continue around the square if he had not found Corfua, turned off again up the street at the next corner. He went around that block entirely, coming back into the square at its next corner, turning back and moving in the opposite direction down the side of it he would have gone along next if he had not turned off.

Adion was still there, still seeming to read. The man in the green jumper still scanned the screen. Around them, there was still a small area without any other person.

Hal continued moving. Now that his suspicions had been confirmed, his eyes picked out five other individuals, four men and one woman, standing about the kiosk who did not fit the normal patterns and movements of the crowd in the square.

The movements of all crowds, Malachi had told him, fell into patterns which were continually changing, but only to related patterns. The old Dorsai had trained young Hal first with a kaleidoscope—a tube with a rotatable end which, when turned, rearranged triangles of color as seen through a prism—then by standing him on a balcony overlooking a shopping center square in Denver, much like this one. The day had finally come when Hal, looking down, could immediately identify all the individuals Malachi had hired to play watchers in the square. It was not by specific actions or the lack of them that Hal had come to recognize those who were anomalies within the patterns. Rather, they had come eventually to jump to his eye, subjectively; as, at first glance, in gestalt fashion, the spuriousness of a fake painting jumps to the eye of an art expert who knows intimately the work of the painter being imitated.

Just so, now, the five standing about the square jumped to Hal's eye from among the individuals surrounding them. There might well have been others seated at café tables, whom with closer study he might have picked out; but what he had now discovered was all he needed to know. He continued casually, but turned off immediately at the same corner he had turned off before. He began to walk as swiftly as he could without attracting attention.

Once again, the shirt under his jacket was damp with sweat—the sweat of tension and exhaustion. Clearly, the Ahruma area generally had now been warned and his picture made available to anyone selling interstellar passages—and particularly to such as Corfua, who probably worked close enough to the line of legality to be known to the local police. On recognizing him, Corfua, to save himself, would have had no choice but to alert the Militia.

By this time the whole Commercial Center, and possibly the whole Terminal, would be under observation and search for him. The only question remaining was whether he could get to the Terminal entrance and escape from it before he was noticed, even in his new jacket and beret, and the searching forces closed in on him.

He continued to walk, fast but not so fast as to attract undue attention. He passed nearly a dozen men and women whom he identified as anomalies in the patterns around him; although whether all of them were watching for him or for someone else, was anyone's guess. In a few minutes he had turned a final corner, and one of the entrances to the Terminal was before him, with the front end of a line of buses to inner-city Ahruma just visible outside it.

Four black-uniformed Militiamen were checking the papers of everyone entering and leaving through the entrance.

He had altered course automatically, even as he saw them, so that now instead of heading directly toward the entrance, he was headed off to one side of it. He continued, increasing the angle of his change in direction as he went until his route became a curve leading him down a corridor parallelling the front face of the Terminal.

It was a temptation to tap his adrenalin reserves once more, if only for a minute or two, simply to forget briefly the physical discomforts that were clamoring for his attention. But he was aware how little his remaining strength was. Effortfully, he put aside the alluring notion of the anesthesia of self-intoxication, and set himself grimly, as he walked, to thinking the situation through in his present fogged and fever-lit mind.

The enemy he faced, he reminded himself, was not the Militia but Bleys Ahrens. The Militia was only a tool. Bleys must fear him for greater than usual reasons, or the Other Man would not have put into motion so large an effort to capture him. The goal must be his capture, not his death; Bleys could have made sure of his destruction back on Coby by simply arranging the deaths of all those at the mines where Hal was suspected of being. From what Hal had always been given to understand, the use of such bloody means to achieve a relatively-small result would not be at all out of character for one of the Others.

Bleys, then, wanted him alive for some specific reason; therefore Hal's goal must be to either keep himself from being captured or make his capture as worthless as possible. It seemed clear that friendless, alone and ill as he was, he stood almost no chance of being able to get away from this Terminal without being taken by the Militia. There were things he could and would try, but the fact of his capture had to be faced; and the question therefore was to make that capture as unrewarding as possible.

One way he could do that was to make sure that the credit vouchers and identity papers that made it possible for him to move between the worlds were not taken if he was captured; so that if he had the luck to get free of Bleys and his people, he could regain them and with them the means to escape to another planet.

Still struggling to think of ways to do this, he had paid little attention to where he was going, turning down streets at random. He was only half a block from the square where he had been to meet Corfua, when he suddenly caught sight of a line of black uniforms, a little less than a block distant, across the street and moving toward him.

They were beginning to sweep the interior of the Terminal—or the interior of the Commercial Center, at least—for him. The thought of the mobilization of troops required for such an effort brought home to him with a chill, more clearly than anything else had done, the kind of power that the Others must wield here on Harmony. Idly, he stopped to look into a shop he was passing, gazed for a second, then as idly turned and began to move back the way he had come.

As he did, his steps quickened. He reached the end of the street and turned left, looking for a postal kiosk. A couple of blocks farther down this new street, he found one. A small amount charged against one of the Harmony-local vouchers he had been supplied with as a member of the Command caused a slot in the kiosk to disgorge a large envelope, already stamped with local postage. Hastily, he took his identity envelope from his inside jacket pocket, stuffed it into the envelope, and sealed it. He addressed the envelope to *Amid, OutBond to the Department of History, University of Ceta.* On the bottom in capital letters he printed HOLD FOR ARRIVAL. A screen on the kiosk, questioned, gave him the address of the local Maran Consulate in Ahruma. He memorized it even as he had the kiosk print it on his package. Then he slipped the sealed and addressed package into the mailing tray of the kiosk, which inhaled it with a soft, breathy sound. Empty-handed and momentarily light-headed with triumph, he turned away from the kiosk.

Now it was only a matter of taking the best of what chances were left to get free of the Terminal. There was one means that might allow him to bluff or bully his way past the Militiamen guarding the entrances to the Commercial Center. He might be able to do it if he were dressed as a Militiaman himself—preferably in the uniform of a superior officer. The problem would be to find an officer among those hunting him here whose clothes he could wear with any conviction that they belonged to him. An alternative—the thought struck him suddenly—would be to get the papers of one of the men in civilian clothes who had been stationed around the square and try to make his way out on the strength of those, in his present garb.

He was still only a block from the square. Something like enthusiasm beginning to rise in him for the first time that day, he turned away from the kiosk.

"There he is—that's him!"

It was the voice of Adion Corfua. Looking, he saw the pale, large figure, with two men in civilian clothes and five Militiamen, coming toward him from the direction in which he had just been about to go. He wheeled to escape, and saw another line of Militia just entering the intersection at the end of the block behind him.

"Get him!" Corfua was shouting.

There was the pounding of feet on the pavement behind him, and the Militiamen ahead also broke into a run toward him. He looked right and left, but there was nothing on either side of him but the unbreakable glass of shop windows. Choosing, he charged the line of uniforms he was facing.

Almost, he broke through them and got away. They were not expecting attack, and they faltered slightly at the sight of him coming down on them. Nor were they trained as he had been trained. They converged on him and he spun into them as they came close, leaving four of them on the ground and a fifth, still on his feet but staggering. But they had delayed him just long enough for the Militiamen behind him to catch up; and these swarmed over him, helped by those who could recover from the first group he had hit.

Without warning, his momentary burst of strength exhausted itself. There were simply too many of them. He went down, conscious of blows raining on him—blows hardly, it seemed after a bit, more than light taps; until, after a little while, he did not feel them at all.

Chapter

> > **32** < <

He came to consciousness to find himself lying on his back on some flat, hard, cold surface that rumbled slightly; and a second later he recognized the low, steady sound of truck blowers heard from inside a vehicle. His legs and arms ached, and he tried to move them, but they were held—ankles, knees and wrists pressed tightly together. For a moment he threw all his strength against whatever pinioned them, but they remained immovable. He slid back into unconsciousness.

When he woke a second time, he was still lying on his back; but the surface under him was softer and motionless, and there was no sound of blowers. A bright light glaring down into his eyes was in the process of being turned down slightly.

"That's better," said a memorable, resonant voice he recognized. "Now take those stays off him and help him sit up."

With unbelievable gentleness, fingers removed whatever had been holding his wrists, knees and ankles. Hands assisted him to a seated position and put something behind his back to prop him upright. There was a pricking sensation in his left arm that startled him, but not to the extent of betraying him into any sign that he was once more aware. Less than a minute later, however, warmth, energy, and a blissful freedom from pain and discomfort began to flood all through him.

With that, he recognized the ridiculousness of continuing to pretend unconsciousness. He opened his eyes on a small, bare-walled room, furnished like a prison cell, with two Militiamen on their feet and the width of the room away from the narrow bed-surface on which he lay. And Bleys Ahrens, standing tall, loomed close beside and over him.

"Well, Hal," said Bleys softly, "now we finally get a chance to talk. If you'd only identified yourself back in Citadel, we could have gotten together then."

Hal did not answer. He was face-to-face with the Other, now. The feeling of cold determination that had come on him when he had faced the fact that he was not staying at the Final Encyclopedia, nearly four years before, rose in him again. He lay still, studying Bleys as Malachi had taught him to do with an opponent, waiting for information on which to act.

Bleys sat down on a float beside the bed, which Hal felt to be some cot-like surface, covered with a single mattress of no great thickness. There had been no float beside it when Bleys had started to sit, nor had the Other Man given an order or made any signal Hal had seen. But by the time Bleys had needed it there, the padded float had been in position for him.

"I should tell you how I feel about the deaths of your tutors," the tall man said. "I know—at the moment you don't trust me enough to believe me. But you should hear, anyway, that there was never, at any time, any intention to harm anyone at your home. If there'd been any way I could have stopped what happened there, I would have."

He paused, but Hal said nothing. Bleys smiled slightly, sadly.

"I'm part-Exotic, you know," he said. "I not only don't hold with killing, I don't like any violence; and I don't believe ordinarily there's any excuse for it. Would you believe me if I told you that what happened there on the terrace that day surprised me enough to make me lose command of the situation?"

Again he paused, and again Hal stayed silent.

"Because of my surprise, I couldn't stop my bodyguards in time."

"Bodyguards?" said Hal. His voice was so weak and husky he hardly recognized it as his own.

"I'm sorry," said Bleys. "I can believe you think of them in different terms. But no matter what you think, their primary duty there, that day, was only to protect me."

"From three old men," said Hal.

"Even from three old men," replied Bleys. "And they weren't so negligible, those old men. They took out four of five of my bodyguards before they were stopped."

"Killed," Hal said.

Bleys inclined his head a little.

"Killed," he said. "*Murdered*, if you want me to use that word. All I'm asking you to accept is that I'd have prevented what happened if I could have."

Hal looked away from him, at the ceiling. There was a moment of silence.

"From the time you set foot on our property," said Hal, wearily, "the responsibility was yours."

The drug they had given him was holding pain and discomfort at bay, but still he was conscious of an incredible exhaustion; and even turned down, the lights overhead were hurting his eyes. He closed them again; and heard the voice of Bleys above him projected in a different direction.

"Lower that illumination some more. That's right. Now, leave it there. As long as Hal Mayne is in this room, those lights aren't to be turned up or down, unless he asks they be."

Hal opened his eyes again. The cell was now pleasantly dim; but in the dimness, Bleys seemed—even seated—to loom even taller. By a trick of his fever and the drug in Hal, the Other Man appeared to tower upward above him toward infinity.

"You're right, of course," Bleys said, now. "But still, I'd like you to try and understand my point of view."

"Is that all you want?" Hal asked.

The face of Bleys looked down at him from its unimaginable height.

"Of course not," said Bleys, gently. "I want to save you—not only for your own sake but as something to put against the unnecessary deaths of your tutors, for which I still feel responsible."

"And what does saving me mean?" Hal lay watching him.

"It means," said Bleys, "giving you a chance to live the life you've been designed by birth—and from birth—to live."

"As an Other?"

"As Hal Mayne, free to use his full capabilities."

"As an Other," Hal said.

"You're a snob, my young friend," replied Bleys. "A snob, and misinformed. The misinformation may not be your fault; but the snobbery is. You're too bright to pretend to a belief in double-dyed villains. If that was all we were—myself and those like me—would most of the inhabited worlds let us take control of things the way they have?"

"If you were capable enough to do it," Hal said.

"No." Bleys shook his head. "Even if we were supermen and superwomen—even if we were the mutants some people like to think we are—so few of us could never control so many unless the many wanted us to control them. And you must have been better educated than to think of us as either superbeings or mutants. We're only what we are—what you yourself are—genetically-fortunate combinations of human abilities who have had the advantages of some special training."

"I'm not like you—" For a moment, lulled by Bleys' warm, deep tones, Hal had forgotten the hatred in him. It came back redoubled, and a sort of nausea moved in him at the idea of any likeness between Bleys and himself.

"Of course you are," said Bleys.

Hal looked past him to the two Militiamen standing behind him. With eyes now adjusted to the light, at last, one of them was now recognizable as a commissioned officer. Focusing more closely on the face above the collar tabs, he recognized Barbage.

"That's right, Hal," said Bleys, having glanced over his shoulder. "You know the Captain, don't you? This is Amyth Barbage, who'll be responsible for you as long as you're in this place. Amyth—remember, I've a particular interest in Hal. You and your men are going to have to forget he was ever connected with one of the Commands. You're to do nothing to him—for any reason, or under any circumstance. Do you understand me, Amyth?"

"I understand, Great Teacher," said Barbage. His eyes went past Bleys and he looked unblinkingly at Hal as he spoke.

"Good," said Bleys. "Now, all surveillance of this cell is to be discontinued until I call you to come let me out of here. Leave us, both of you, and wait down the corridor so Hal and I can talk privately—if you please."

Beside Barbage, the enlisted Militiaman started, taking half a step forward and opening his mouth. But without turning his gaze from Hal, Barbage closed a hand on the other black-sleeved arm. Hal saw his thin fingers sink deeply into the cloth. The man checked and stood still, saying nothing.

"Don't worry," said Bleys. "I'll be perfectly safe. Now, go."

The two of them went. The door of the cell, closing behind them, relocked itself with a soft click.

"You see," said Bleys, turning back to Hal, "they don't really understand this; and it isn't fair to expect them to. From their standpoint, if another human gets in your way, the sensible thing is to remove him—or her. The concept of you and I as relatively unimportant in ourselves, but as gathering points for great forces, and in a situation where it's those forces that matter . . . that's a thing essentially beyond their comprehension. But certainly you and I ought to understand such things; not only such things but each other."

"No," said Hal. There were a great many more things he wanted to say; but suddenly the effort was too great and he ended by simply repeating himself. "No."

"Yes," said Bleys, looking down. "Yes, I'm afraid I have to insist, on that point. Sooner or later, you're going to have to face the real shape of things in any case and, for your own sake, it'd better be now, rather than later."

Hal lay still, looking once more only at the ceiling over his head, rather than into the face of Bleys. The tall man's voice sounded like some gently-sonorous bassoon in his ears.

"All practical actions are matters of necessity in the light of hard reality," said Bleys. "What we—those who're called the Other People—do, is dictated by what we are and the situation in which we find ourselves; and that situation is to be one among literally millions of ordinary humans, with the power to make our lives in that position ones in either a heaven or a hell. Either—but nothing else. Because the choice isn't one any of us can avoid. If we fail to choose heaven, we inevitably find ourselves in hell."

"I don't believe you," said Hal. "There's no reason it has to be that way."

"Oh yes, my child," said Bleys softly. "There is a reason. Apart from our individual talents, our training, and our mutual support, we're still only as human as the millions around us. Friendless and without funds, we can starve, just like anyone else. Our bones can be broken and we can fall sick as easily as ordinary mortals. Killed, we die as obligingly. If taken care of, we may live a few years longer than the average, but not much. We have the same normal, human emotional hungers—for love, for the companionship of someone who can think and talk our own language. But, if we should choose to ignore our differentness and mold ourselves to fit the little patterns of those around us, we can spend our whole lives miserably; and probably—almost certainly—we may never even be lucky enough to meet one Other being like ourselves. None of us chose this, to be what each of us is— but what we are, we are; and like everyone else we have an innate human right to make the best of our situation."

"At the expense of those millions of people you talk about," said Hal.

"And what sort of expense is that?" Bleys' voice grew even deeper. "The expense of one Other borne by a million ordinary humans is a light load on each ordinary human. But turn that about. What of the cost to the Other;

who, trying only to fit in with the human mass around him, accepts a life of isolation, loneliness, and the endurance daily of prejudice and misunderstanding? While, at the same time, his unique strengths and talents allow those same individuals who draw away from him to reap the benefits of his labors. Is there justice in that? Look down the long pages of past history at the intellectual giants, men and women alike, who've moved civilization forward while struggling to survive in the midst of lesser people who innately feared and distrusted them. Giants, crouching daily to keep their differences from showing and arousing the irrational fears of the small ones around them. From the beginning of time to be human, but different, has been dangerous; and it's been a choice between the many who could carry one lightly on their combined shoulders and the one who must carry the many all alone, with his or her much greater strength, but staggering under the proportionately-greater effort; and which of those two choices is fairer?"

Hal's head, under the effects of the fever and the drug together, spun strangely. The mental image of a giant crouching made a grotesque image in his mind.

"Why crouch?" he said.

"Why crouch?" The face of Bleys smiled, far above him. "Ask yourself that. How old are you now?"

"Twenty," said Hal.

"Twenty—and you still ask that question? As you've gotten older, haven't you begun to feel an isolation, a separation from all those around you? Haven't you found yourself forced, more and more often lately, to take charge of matters—to make decisions not merely for yourself, but for those with you who aren't capable of making them for themselves? Quietly, but inevitably, taking charge, doing what only you realize has to be done, for the good of all?"

He paused.

"I think you know what I'm talking about," he said after that moment of silence. "At first, you only try to tell them what should be done; because you can't believe—you don't want to believe—that they can be so helpless. But, little by little, you come to face the fact that while they may do things right under your continual coaching, they'll never understand enough to do what's necessary on their own, each time the need arises; and so, finally, worn out, you simply take over. Without their even realizing it, you set things in the path they should go; and all these little people follow it, thinking it's the natural course of events."

He stopped again. Lying still, watching him, a portion of his own mind remote, Hal did not reply.

"Yes," said Bleys, "you know what I'm talking about. You've already known it, and started to feel the width and depth of this gulf that separates you from the rest of the race. Believe me when I tell you that what you now feel will steadily grow deeper and stronger as time goes on. The experience your more capable mind acquires, at a rate much faster than they can imagine, will continue to widen and widen the gap that separates you from them. In the end, there'll be little more kinship between you and them, than between you and any lesser creature—a dog or a cat—of which you've become fond. And you'll regret that lack of real kinship bitterly but there'll be nothing you can do about it, no way to give them what they'll never be able to hold—any more than you could give an appreciation of great art to monkeys. So, finally, to save yourself the pain that they don't even know you feel, you cut the last emotional tie you have with them, and choose instead the silence, the emptiness and the peace of being what you are—unique and alone, forever."

He stopped speaking.

"No," said Hal, after a moment. He felt detached, like someone under heavy sedation. "That's not a way I can go."

"Then you'll die," said Bleys, dispassionately. "In the end, like those who were like us in past centuries, you'll let them kill you, merely by ceasing to make the continual effort necessary to protect yourself among them. And it'll be wasted, all wasted—what you were and what you could've been."

"Then it'll have to be wasted," said Hal. "I can't be what you say."

"Perhaps," said Bleys. He rose to his feet, the float drifting back in midair and aside from his legs. "But wait a bit yet and see. The urge to live is stronger than you think."

He stood looking down at Hal.

"I told you," he said. "I'm part-Exotic. Do you think I didn't fight against the knowledge of what I was, when I first began to be aware of it? Do you think I didn't reject what I saw myself committed to being, only because of what I am? Do you suppose I didn't at first tell myself that I'd choose a hermit's existence, an anchorite's life, rather than make what then I thought of as an immoral use of my abilities? Like you, I was ready to pay any price to save myself from the contamination of playing God to those around me. The idea was as repellent to me then as it is to you now. But what I came to learn was that it wasn't harm, it was good that I could do the race as one of its leaders and masters; and so will you learn—in the end."

He turned and stepped to the door of the cell.

"Open up here!" he called into the corridor.

"It makes no difference," he said, turning back once more as footsteps sounded, approaching them from beyond sight of the barred door, "what you think you choose now. Inevitably, a day'll come when you'll see the foolishness of what you did now by insisting on staying here, in a cell like this, under the guard of those who, compared to you, are little more than civilized animals. None of what you're inflicting on yourself at this moment is really necessary."

He paused.

"But it's your choice," he went on. "Do what you feel like doing until you can see more clearly. But when that time comes, all you'll have to do is say one word. Tell your guards that you'll consider what I've said; and they'll bring you to me, out of here to a place of comfort and freedom and daylight, where you can have time to set your mind straight in decency. Your need to undergo this private self-torture is all in your own mind. Still, as I say, I'll leave you with it until you see more clearly."

Barbage and the enlisted Militiaman were already at the door of the cell. They unlocked and swung it open. Bleys stepped through and the door closed behind him. Without looking back he walked off, out of sight up the corridor, and the other two followed, leaving Hal to utter silence when the sound of footfalls had at last died away.

Chapter

> > **33** < <

Exhausted, Hal dropped into sodden, dreamless slumber; and the length of his sleep was something he had no way of measuring. But he came struggling back into consciousness to find himself spasming with convulsive shivers that shook him with the power of an autumn gale upon a last dead leaf clinging to a tree.

The cell about him was unchanged. The light still burned with the same muted intensity in the ceiling. Complete silence continued beyond the barred door of his cell. Pushing himself upright again into a semi-sitting position, he saw the thin blanket folded at the foot of his bed, and, reaching out an unsteady hand, caught and pulled it up to his neck.

For a moment the relief of having something covering him almost let him escape again into oblivion. But the blanket was hardly thicker than his shirt; and the chill still savaged him like a dog shaking a rat. Holding the blanket tightly to his chin with both hands, he made an effort to exert some control over his shuddering body, fastening his attention on a point immeasurably remote within his own mind and striving to transfer all his attention to that remote, austere and incorporeal location.

For some minutes it seemed that he would not be able to do it. The effort at mental control was too great in his worn-out condition, and the wild plungings of his body's reflexes were too strong. Then, gradually, he began to succeed. The shuddering ceased, the tensions leaked slowly from his muscles and his whole body quietened.

He could still feel the urge of his flesh to respond to the frightening chill that had seized him. But now that urge was held at arm's length, and he could think, he opened his mouth to speak but only croaked. Then he managed to clear his throat, take a deep breath and call out.

"It's freezing, here! Turn the heat up!"

There was no answer.

He shouted again. But still there was no response; and the temperature of the cell stayed as it was.

He stayed listening to the silence, and his memory gave him back Bleys' earlier order that all surveillance of the cell be discontinued until the Other should call to be let out. Surveillance must have been resumed when Bleys left and that would mean that there was no need to shout now. Someone must be listening and possibly observing him as well, at this moment.

He lay back under the blanket, still holding down hard on the urge of his body to shiver, and looked up at the ceiling.

"I know you hear me." With an effort he held his voice level. "I think Bleys

Ahrens told you not to do anything to me—that includes letting me chill to death. Turn the heat up. Otherwise I'll tell him about this, the next time I see him."

He waited.

Still, no one answered or came. He was about to speak again when it occurred to him that if those watching him had been unmoved by his words, repeating them would do no good; while if he had worried them at all, repetition would only weaken his threat.

After perhaps ten minutes, he heard steps in the corridor. A thin, upright, black-uniformed figure appeared beyond the bars of his cell door, unlocked it and came in. He looked up into the flint-blade features of Amyth Barbage.

"It is well that thou be told," said Barbage. His voice was oddly remote, almost as if he talked aloud while dreaming.

Hal stared up at him.

"Yes," said Barbage, "I will tell thee."

His eyes glittered like polished chips of hard coal in the dimness of the cell.

"I know thee," he said slowly, looking down at Hal; and each word was like a drop of icy water chilling the feverish surface of Hal's mind. "Thou art of that demon blood that cometh before Armageddon—which now is close upon us. Yes, I see thee, if some else do not, in thy true shape with thy jaws of steel and thy head like to the head of a great and loathsome hound. *Wily art thou, a serpent.* Thou didst pretend to save my life, long since, from that apostate of the Lord, the Child of Wrath who would have slain me in the pass—so that I might feel a debt to thee; and so be seduced by thee when thou wert at last, as thou now art, in the power of God's Chosen."

His voice became slightly harsher, but still it remained distant, detached.

"But I am of the Elect, and beyond thy cunning. It hath been ordered by the Great Teacher that I let no thing be done to thee—nor will I. But there is no need that anything be done *for* thee. Immortal in wickedness and blasphemy as thou art, there is no need to cosset such as thee. Therefore call out as thou wilt—none shall come or answer. This cell is of the temperature it had when thou wert brought in. No one hath altered it, nor will. The lights thou mayest have up or down; but no other thing will be changed or brought about at thy word. Rest thee as thou art, foul dog of Satan."

He turned away. The cell door clicked closed its lock behind him; and Hal was left alone.

He lay still, trying to control his shivering and little by little the effort of doing so became less; not so much because his control was strengthening, as because his fever was once more starting to assert itself and his body temperature beginning again to rise. As he warmed, the need to control his reflexes relaxed; and he drifted once more into sleep.

But it was a light, uneasy sleep, from which he roused suddenly to find his throat so dry and sore it felt as if it would crack open with the simple effort of swallowing. The demand of the thirst upon him was so great that he managed to summon the strength to pull himself up off the bed and onto his feet. He staggered across the room to the washstand anchored to the wall next to the stool. Turning on the single tap there he lowered his head and gulped at the stream of icy water that poured down.

But after only a few swallows he found he could drink no more. The water he had already taken in seemed to fill his gullet full and threaten to nauseate him. He stumbled back to the cot, fell on it and was asleep again instantly—only to wake, it seemed, in minutes; and with the raging thirst that had roused him before once more driving him back to the water tap.

Once more, he made his unsteady pilgrimage to it; and once more he was able to drink only a few swallows before it seemed he could swallow no more. Warned now by his fading strength, he went back to the cot he had been lying on and struggled to pull it across the room until it stood next to the washstand.

The effort of moving the light cot was inconceivable. His head rang and his muscles had the strength of half-melted wax. Jerking the cot first this way, and then that, like an ant trying to move a dead beetle many times its weight, he managed at last to get it next to the washstand and fell back on it exhausted, to sleep immediately.

In some indeterminable time—it seemed only a matter of seconds, though it could have been much longer—he woke again, drank, and fell back to uneasy sleep.

So began a feverish, dream-ridden period which, on the one hand, seemed to encompass no time at all but which, looked at only a little differently, stretched out through an eternity. He woke and drank, drank and slept, woke again to drink and sleep . . . over and over again. While about him there was only stillness; the eternally-lighted cell and the silent corridor beyond produced neither the appearance of any watcher nor any change.

He was aware now that the sickness in him was raging with a violence greater than any such he had felt in his life before, and an uneasiness unknown until now stirred deep in him. Periods of fever were alternating with periods of deep chill, with the fever gradually predominating. Little by little, the unnatural states of his body took him over, first the great shuddering chills, then the wild demand of the thirst in him that choked on only a few mouthfuls of water at a time, the ringing headaches and the wakeful periods alternating with snatches of uneasy and nightmare-torn sleep.

He could feel the infection in him gaining on his life-force. The chills gave way at last completely to a light-headed unnaturalness that would have been almost pleasant by comparison if it had not also been ominous. He took it to be one of high fever—but of how high a fever, he had no way of telling. The headaches lessened, temporarily, but his breathing was becoming more and more difficult, as if his lower chest was being slowly stuffed full with some heavy material, forcing him to breathe with only a small space that remained open at the top of his lungs. Gradually, he pulled himself into a sitting position in which breathing was easier, upright at one end of the cot with his back against the rough wall to which the washstand was attached, the washstand on one side of him, the stool on the other.

Somewhere about this time, also, the ability to sleep was lost to him. His head rang and pounded, he breathed painfully in tiny gasps, and a fiery awakeness shut out any possibility of further slumber. The minutes passed as slowly as caterpillars humping their way along a tree limb, but they came endlessly, measuring out hours followed by hours that went on forever. Time itself stretched out endlessly, and still no one appeared at the barred door of his cell.

For the first time he remembered the Coby-built miner's chronometer he normally wore on his wrist, that had been given back to him, among his other belongings, when he and Jason Rowe had been turned loose from the Militia Headquarters in Citadel after Bleys had spoken to them. He had worn it all through the time he had been with the Command. He looked automatically for it at his left wrist now; and, with some surprise, saw the instrument had not been taken from him this time. The current reading of its outer ring of numerals glowed against its metal face like ghost figures of flame to tell him that, somewhere outside this cell, it was eleven twenty-three of the Harmony evening, local time.

There was no telling how long it had been since he had been brought here. But perhaps he could make an estimate. Struggling with his fevered mind to think back, he remembered that it had not yet been noon when he had been captured in the Spaceport Terminal. He could hardly have been here less than one full day of the twenty-three point sixteen Interstellar Standard Hours that made up the calendar day on Harmony. From that noon, then, to noon of the day following, plus the hours necessary to bring him now almost to midnight of a second day, would make a total of a day and a half since he had been carried in here. Fumbling in his pockets, he came up with everything that had been in his possession when he had been captured, but nothing that could mark on the smooth-painted wall behind him. With the metal case of the watch, finally, he managed to scratch a single vertical line, low down under the washstand, where the shadow of the basin would hide the mark.

They had not brought him food at any time since he had gotten here; but he did not miss it. In the heat of the fever his stomach seemed to have shrunken and contorted upon itself like a clenched fist. The only appetite he had was for water; and, after a swallow or two, that continued to choke him. His single greatest desire now was merely to breathe easily and normally, with the full capacity of his lungs. But his body was denying him that.

The struggle to breathe began to wake all his instincts for survival. On the wings of the fever in him, his total being cranked itself up; his heart hammered in his chest, faster and faster, his mind leaped and dodged and sought for a way out—a way to open his lungs to great gulps of air, to set himself loose from this place. But the lack of oxygen made any additional effort beyond mere existence too great to attempt. Seated bolt upright, with his back against the cell wall, struggling for air, he was at once physically immobilized and mentally on emergency alert; as his body tuned itself ever higher in an attempt to fight the slow suffocation that was threatening him.

He knew too little of medicine to build a full picture of what was happening inside him. But clearly his struggle to breathe against the congestion of his lungs was triggering off all the instincts and reflexes of his body that could be marshalled against it. He was barely able now to spare breath for the extra physical effort of leaning over to drink from the water tap, but his mind raced at its greatest capacity like a creature afire. Immobilized, but thinking now at life-and-death speed, he sat facing the slow, continuous movement of the hours.

There was no one to help him. Barbage had promised that none would come; and, slowly, he was beginning to understand that, barring another visit from Bleys himself, that promise would be kept. For the first time it came to him that Barbage, in his fanaticism, must actually be hoping for his death and doing everything possible within the limits of Bleys' commands to bring it about. If things as they now were with him continued to worsen, then, uncared-for—eventually—he must die.

He found himself facing that prospect at last as an actuality. He could no longer deny that it could happen. All his life until this moment, it had been easier to imagine the death of the universe than his own. But now, at last, his personal mortality had become as real to him as the walls enclosing him. His end could be only a handful of hours away, unless something—some miracle—could prevent it.

His racing mind revolted against that realization, like an animal galloping wildly around and around the circular wall of an abattoir in search of some opening to freedom and life. Deep and far off in him, like the barely-heard trumpet call of an approaching enemy, he felt for the first time in his life the pale, cold touch of pure panic. He made an effort to reach out with the semi-autohypnotic technique he had used when he had passed through the Final Encyclopedia and evoked the images of his three former tutors to help him; but his mind could not be freed sufficiently from the adrenalin released by the instinctive struggles of his body, so that he might be able to find the mental control that would make the evocative technique work.

For a second, realizing this, his panic doubled. Then, coldly, strengtheningly into him came the realization that there was no one to help him now in any case but himself. The years that had passed since the deaths of the three who had raised him had given him experience and information beyond what Malachi, Obadiah and Walter had known in him, while they were alive, and these things he must find now to use for himself.

But the brief moment of logical understanding had steadied him. He had slumped down during the past hours. Now he pushed himself farther upright with the wall at his back and set himself to consciously deal with the situation. But the fever still held him like an intoxication and with his best efforts his mind wandered and drifted off from its purpose, in a state of blurred discomfort that left him floating halfway between consciousness and un-consciousness.

Without warning he found himself dreaming with a knife-edged clarity to all his senses, discovering himself on the same mountainside to which his mind had retreated back when he had been newly landed on Harmony and in the Militia's hands before; and Bleys, not recognizing him among prisoners in the room before him, had tried to make them all captive to the Others' charisma.

But this time he dreamed that he was spread-eagled on his back, wrists and ankles manacled tightly to the rough granite upon which he lay and the icy rain, falling steadily upon him, chilled him to his bones. . . .

He forced himself awake to find himself shuddering once again with the great chills that shook his whole body. The thin blanket had fallen from him. He pulled it hastily up around him and huddled down on the mattress, to lie panting with the effort of movement. For what seemed to be a long time he fought for breath and against the shivering fit that shook him, until his fever started to swing upward once more; and—once more without warn-ing—dreams returned him to the moment earlier, in which Bleys had stood towering over him, here in the cell.

". . . You're right, of course," he heard the Other saying again. "But still I'd like you to try and understand my point of view. . . ."

As before, Bleys loomed enormous over Hal. But from somewhere else, out of the far past, the soft voice of Walter the InTeacher rose, reading, as he had once read aloud to Hal, the lines spoken by the fallen Satan in Mil-ton's *Paradise Lost*:

> ". . . *The mind is its own place, and in itself*
> *Can make a heav'n of Hell, a hell of heav'n.*
> *What matter where, if I be still the same,*
> *And what I should be, all but less than he*
> *Whom thunder hath made greater? . . .*"

But Walter's voice dwindled again and was lost while Bleys was still speak-ing. The Other's deep tones echoed in the fevered vastness of Hal's dream.

". . . None of us chose this, to be what each of us is," Bleys was saying once more to him, "—but what we are, we are; and like everyone else we have an innate human right to make the best of our situation."

"At the expense of those millions of people you talk about." Hal heard his own answer as if from someone else, speaking far off, at a distance.

"And what sort of expense is that?" Bleys' voice deepened until the whole universe seemed to resonate with it. "The expense of one Other borne by a million ordinary humans is a light load on each ordinary human. But turn that about. What of the cost to the Other; who, trying only to fit in with the human mass around him, accepts a life of isolation, loneliness, and the endurance daily of prejudice and misunderstanding? While, at the same time, his unique strengths and talents allow those same individuals who draw away from him to reap the benefits of his labors. Is there justice in that? . . ."

The deeply-musical voice rolled on, echoing and reechoing until it muttered like distant thunder in the mountains, until in its multi-layered echoes all sense of the individual words was lost. Suddenly, the mountains of his younger years were once more around Hal and he found himself standing again in the water at the edge of the artificial lake on the estate, looking up through the limbs of the bush that hid him at the terrace of the house, seeing the three figures there that he knew so well move suddenly, together . . . and fall.

It seemed he fled from that scene, fled as he had actually fled—to Coby. Once more he lay in his small room in the miner's barracks, that first night at the Yow Dee Mine, feeling that same feeling Bleys had spoken of only hours since, that difference and isolation from everyone else sleeping and awake around him within the plain walls of the building. That isolation, that he seemed to remember knowing also at some earlier time, long, long before Bleys or any Other. . . .

Suddenly, he was back on Harmony, in his dream of rubbled plain; and the tower, far off, toward which he made his slow way on foot. He had known that plain, too, from before, somewhere. He forged on now toward the tower, but his efforts seemed to bring him no nearer to it. Only the conviction held him, like the conviction of life, itself, that it was what he must reach eventually, no matter how far it might be, or how difficult the way to it.

He woke from that dream to another—of Harmony and the weeping woods, to the stumbling figures of an exhausted Command fleeing from the relentless Militia pursuit of Barbage. He left the others and by himself carried James Child-of-God up to a little rise, settling him there with his weapons and his slight barricade, leaving him there to die in delaying their pursuers.

"What is thy true name. . . ?" James asked again, looking up at him.

Hal stared at him.

"Hal Mayne."

". . . Bless thee in God's name, Hal Mayne," said James. "Convey to the others that in God's name, also, I bless the Command and Rukh Tamani and all who fight or shall fight under the banner of the Lord. Now go. Care for those whose care hath been set in thy hands."

James turned from Hal to fix his eyes once more on the forest as seen through the firing slot in his barricade. Hal turned away also, but in a different direction, leaving James Child-of-God upon the small rise. . . .

. . . And woke at last to his silent cell, which took shape around him once more.

Chapter

> > **34** < <

Here, there was no change. But something in him was aware of having just achieved movement toward some as-yet-undefined goal. From the dreams just past he had progressed, had gained something that had not been available to him before. Once more aware of the cell about him, he felt for the first time an almost perfect separation of himself into two parts. One part, from which he was withdrawing, was the suffering body, which he now understood clearly but calmly to be losing its battle for life as its temperature mounted and its lungs gradually filled, bringing it closer and closer to the moment when it would cease to function. The other, to which he had drawn nearer, was the mind, now that the tether that normally held it to the demanding feelings and instincts of the body was becoming attenuated under the fierce fire of his struggle to survive. The mind itself burned now, with a brilliance that fed on the heat of that fire.

It was a new sort of brilliance that illuminated things formerly hidden from him. He was acutely aware of the two parts of the structure with which he thought. The but and the ben of it—the front chamber and the rear one. In the front, brightly illuminated, was the long and narrow room of his conscious thoughts, where logic kept order and worked in visible steps from question to answer. But at the back of that room was the doorless wall that separated it from the rear chamber—the vast unordered attic of his unconscious, piled and stored with all the rich lumber of his experience. In just the past few hours of talk and dreams that wall had been burned thin, as the connecting link between mind and body had been thinned by his struggle to survive, so that now it was less a wall than a semi-transparent membrane. Also, the normally-blinding lamp of his instinct to survive had been turned down, until with vision adjusted to dimness he could see through that membrane into formerly-obscure corners and dark places from which his conscious vision had been blocked before.

Now he saw by the light of that gentler lamp of understanding, which illuminated both chambers alike and shone through the thinned membrane that separated them, until from the dimmed front chamber he could now begin to make out new shapes of patterns and identities amongst all the clutter that the back chamber held.

In that seeking light he could no longer deny what he knew to be true. He had indeed, as Bleys had claimed he must sooner or later, taken matters finally into his own hands. He had lied to Rukh by omission because he knew she would not agree with what he wanted to suggest, the removal of the donkeys and the explosive so that the Command might disperse and survive, the explosives taken by one person to a safe hiding place. He had chosen to do this without consultation with anyone, making the decisions for all of the rest and taking charge by main force. But he had done it with a purpose. A purpose outside himself.

And in that fact lay all the difference in the universe from what Bleys had tried to imply to such an action. For Bleys had spoken of matters taken over by the more powerful individual, alone, for his own survival and comfort. Behind the tall man's words had been the implication that there was no other worthwhile goal but this. But he had been wrong. For there was in fact a massively-greater goal—the eternal survival of the race so that it could continue to learn and grow. That purpose was toward life while Bleys' was only toward a brief moment of personal satisfaction, followed by an inevitable death that would leave behind no mark upon the fabric of the universe. The truer instinct to sacrifice a personal life that the race might survive was imaged in the brown man he had created as part of the poem he had made in the mountains, reaching out to give form to the understanding already growing within him.

It had been a form constructed by way of the pattern of words, as he had been making such constructs unconsciously with his poetry since he had been very young. Bleys' way had no form, no purpose, no value, only the building of a little comfort for a short while—before the coming of the endless dark.

The way of all those Hal had ever been close to had always been aware of the greater purpose. Malachi, Walter and Obadiah had died to ensure that Hal himself would live, and so perhaps come to this present moment of understanding. Those in Rukh's Command had fought and died for an end they felt too strongly to question, even if the exact shape of it was not visible to them. Tam Olyn had given the long years of his life to guardianship of that great lever for humanity that the Encyclopedia would one day be. And he, himself, had been driven from his earliest beginnings by a similar purpose; even if, as with those in the Command, its exact shape had continued to be hidden from him.

A powerful feeling of being close now to what he had always sought took hold of Hal. In the face of that feeling, the agonies and the approaching death of his body dwindled to unimportance. The fact of the cell about him dwindled. Pushing all things into the background now was the fact that through the near-transparent membrane, between the two compartments of his mind, comprehension was at last beginning to flow back and forth, revealing a possible solution to all problems, a victory the possibility of which had been wholly hidden from him, before.

Even now, he still could not see it clearly. But he felt its presence, unmistakably; and, knowing at last that it was there, he mined his way toward it with the twin tools of dreams and poetry, linking the two for the first time to explore, with the illumination of his reasoning front mind, the great store of human experience and unconscious understandings in the mind's darker, older twin beyond the membrane.

A sense of transport uplifted him. He foresaw these tools finally taking him to the distant tower of which he had dreamed, that was his goal and that of humanity since the beginning. The tools only waited for him to fashion them into conscious reality, out of the memories and vision that had been used unconsciously to that purpose since the race first lifted its eyes to dream beyond the prison of its present moment toward a greater and better future.

All that he needed was there in the cluttered attic of his experience. To isolate each necessary element of it he was only required to follow the two lamps that had lighted the way of every human from his beginning . . . the need, and the dream.

He let his mind take leave, therefore, of his body that was fighting and struggling for the scant breath available to it; and set his perceptions free to go on their search.

Again, he dreamed. But this time on the wings of purpose.

. . . A young man's face looked down at him, with Old Earth's summer sky blue and high behind it. It was an Exotic face, much more youthful than Walter's, the visage of a visitor to the estate. Its owner was a former pupil of Walter's, who had studied under the older man at a time when Walter had still been a teacher on his home of Mara. The pupil was grown, now, and himself a teacher of other Exotics. He wore a dark brown robe on his slim, erect body, and stood with Hal in the woods just beyond the artificial lake. Together, they were watching a sandy patch of ground at their feet and the busy scurrying there of tiny black bodies to and from the opening of an anthill.

". . . One way of thinking of them," the young Exotic was saying to Hal, "is to think of the whole community as a single creature, so that an anthill or a swarm of bees becomes the equivalent of a single animal. The individual ant or bee, then, is just one part of the whole creature. The way a fingernail might be to you, useful, but something that you can do without if necessary, or something for which you can grow a replacement."

"Ants and bees?" echoed Hal, fascinated. The single-creature image woke something in him that was almost like a memory. "What about people?"

The Exotic teacher smiled down at him.

"People are individuals. You're an individual," he answered. "You don't have to do what the hive as a whole, or the swarm as a whole wants to do. These have no choice, as you do. You can make individual decisions and be free to act on them."

"Yes, but . . ." Hal's mind had been captured. The powerful idea that had risen in him was something he could not quite visualize and which his eight-year-old powers of expression were inadequate to describe. "A person doesn't have to do what other persons want unless he wants to—I know that. But there could be something like everyone knowing the same thing, then each person could make up his own mind about it. Wouldn't that be practically the same thing?"

The Exotic smiled at him.

"I think what you're suggesting is a sort of conversation of minds," he said. "It's been speculated about for hundreds of years and called a lot of different names—telepathy is one of them. But every test we've ever been able to make shows that at best telepathy's an occasional phenomenon of the unconscious mind, and there's no way to be sure you can use it when you want it. Most people never experience it at all."

"But it could be," said Hal. "Couldn't it?"

"If it could be, then perhaps you'd be right." A single, thoughtful crease formed for a second between the eyebrows of the young Exotic. Then it went away and he smiled again at Hal. ". . . Perhaps."

They turned from the anthill and went on together to look at other things about the estate. Later, Hal overheard the younger Exotic speaking privately to Walter.

"He's very bright, isn't he?" the visitor was saying.

Walter's reply had been too low for Hal to catch. But he had been fascinated by the compliment implied in the young Exotic's final words—a compliment none of his three tutors had ever chosen to give him. But thinking about it, afterward, the feeling came even more strongly to him than it had at the time, that he had not so much suddenly stumbled then upon the question that had impressed the young Exotic, as found it already there in some part of him with which he was unfamiliar. Now, fascinated by it anew, after all these years, he let go of his dream about the visitor and came back to awareness of the cell.

That one idea was a piece of the whole that had brought him to this moment. It was also—he thought now, with his racing brain—a part of one of the tools of understanding he had just earlier imagined could be forged by a linking of the forward and back parts of his mind. He reached out to develop that idea, trying to touch with his consciousness other knowledges and awarenesses beyond the membrane, things that he could sense were there, but could still not see clearly. However, these still hid from him. It occurred to him once again that these hidden elements might be from a time farther back than his aware memory knew, that perhaps they lay shrouded partly by the darkness of that mystery about himself to which he had always hunted unsuccessfully for an answer, the mystery of who he was and where he had come from.

With that thought, it came to him that the unconscious might know what the conscious did not. Buried within it must be specific memories from before the time when he had been old enough to make conscious observations of what was around him. Memories, perhaps, of what it had been like aboard the old-fashioned courier spaceship on which he had been found as a child. He closed his eyes and leaned back against the cold wall of the cell, willing awareness of his body to depart from him again, reaching out for a vision of the past before the remembered times. . . .

But the picture that he finally summoned up, half dream, half autohypnotic hallucination was limited in ways that disappointed him. He was able to see something that was clearly like a room, but most of it was shadowy or out of focus. Parts of it—a pilot's chair, some steadily-glowing lights on a panel just above his reach—stood out in sharp focus seen with the un-marred, fresh-born attention of the very young. But the rest was remote or blurred to the point of being unrecognizable. Clearly, he thought, he was looking at the space that had combined the functions of main cabin and con-trol room of the craft in which he had been found. However, he could de-duce nothing beyond that fact to help him with the questions in his mind. There was no indication of a particular moment in which he might have been seeing this and no sign of other humans within the remembered range of his vision.

A sharp disappointment woke in him, kindling into near anger. All through the life he could remember, he had dreamed and longed to find out about his origins, imagining a thousand fanciful tales of who he might be and where he might have come from. Now it was almost as if he was delib-erately being prevented from that discovery, when it lay at his fingertips. In frustration he turned his mind upon the inmost recesses of his unconscious with all the fury of someone running down empty corridors, pounding on door after unresponsive door. Until, at last, he burst his way through one such door to a point where he found himself brought up short, face-to-face against a barrier the existence of which he had not expected.

His imagination pictured it for him as a massive, round, metal door, like that on a vault. It was an unnatural barrier, that made no secret of the fact it had been put there by someone so much more capable than his present self, that there was no hope of his forcing it open. It stood, speaking a silent, unyielding message to him from the fact of its very existence.

I will stand open when you no longer need what I hide.

In itself, it represented a defeat. But at the same time it gave a confirma-tion of what he had often suspected; and that confirmation made it not a defeat but a victory. The barrier's very existence was proof at last that he was, and always had been, something more than his conscious self had realized. Also it meant that the way blocked off was no more than one tried by an earlier self and found to be a dead end. He was being directed by this to find some other path to the goal they had both tried to reach; and a newly pos-sible means for that journey to that goal lay now in the understanding that had just come to him in this cell.

He let himself go back, therefore, to full consciousness of the cell, back to his laboring, suffering body. But with a new freedom now of will and thought, he began consciously to commence the forging of those special mental tools he had imagined earlier when it had come to him how the con-scious mind might reach back and tap not only the knowledge but the abil-ities of the unconscious. He set himself, even as he struggled to breathe, to the building of a poem, sending his desire for that which he needed through the membrane to search among the relationships between the as-yet-unclear shapes and meanings stored back there.

And the search brought those relationships to him finally, in the sharply focused, creative images of the poem itself.

ARMAGEDDON
Yes, they are only deer.
Nervous instincts, fitted with hooves and horns,
That foolishly stamp among these Christian pines
Affixed like seals to the legal foolscap of winter;
And, illiterately facing the line of the snowplowed asphalt
Scrawled by a book-learned hand among these hills,
Cross to the red-capped men.

Armageddon.

Of course. The title and the words of the poem burned in his mind's eye as the Final Encyclopedia had made his poem about the knight burn amongst the stars that appeared to surround his carrel there. Then, what he had found himself discovering in poetic form had been the irresistible inner force that was to drive him forth from the Encyclopedia, toward his years on Coby and this present moment of realization. Now, with this latter verse he had rendered a picture of the self-created cataclysm toward which the human race was now hurling itself, like a drunken man too intoxicated to realize the consequences of what he did.

Of course. Armageddon—Ragnarok—whatever you wanted to call it, was finally upon all of them. It had caught up all people like an avalanche, gaining speed as it plunged down a mountainside; and there was no one now who could fail to be aware of it on some level or another of his or her senses.

Tam Olyn had told him of it, bluntly and plainly. But he also remembered Sost, in the tunnelled corridors of Coby, referring to it. Hilary had talked about it to Jason as he had driven Jason and Hal to their meeting with Rukh's Command. . . . and, just a few hours since, Barbage had once more used the term "Armageddon," here in this very cell.

Armageddon—the final battle. Its shadow lay with a weight that could be felt on all living humans, even those who had never heard of the word or the concept. Now it was obvious to Hal that each of them, alone, could feel its approach, just as birds and animals under a blue and cloudless sky could yet feel the coming of a thunderstorm. Not only with the thinking top of their minds, but all through their beings, they could sense the buildup of vast forces about to break into conflict above their heads.

And it was a conflict the roots of which stretched back into prehistoric times. Now that Hal had opened his own eyes to its existence, it became obvious how in the last few hundred years the developing historical situation had merely briefly held back the inevitable, coming hour of conflict, while at the same time setting the stage for its final fury.

All of this was there in the poem he had just made, in allegorical form. Now that he looked for it there, he saw each large division of the race represented. The hunters could only be the Others, involved solely with their personal concerns for the brief, secular moments of their individual lives. The deer were the great mass of people like Sost and Hilary, being driven now by pressures they did not understand at last across a dividing line from safety into the hands of the hunters. Finally, there were those who stood back and saw this situation for what it was, with a vantage point like that of a reader of the poem or a viewer of the picture described. Those who could see what was about to happen and who had already dedicated themselves to prevent its happening. People like Walter, Malachi and Obadiah, like Tam, Rukh and Child-of-God. Like—

Without warning, the lighting of the cell and the small section of corridor he could see dimmed almost to total darkness. A shiver ran for some seconds through all around him. At the same time, from nowhere in particular came a deep, rumbling sound that mounted in volume briefly, then died away—as if just beyond the walls enclosing him there had been the passage of that massive, swift-moving avalanche he had imagined as an image for Armageddon.

It was an inexplicable sound to reach his ears, here in the bowels of a Militia Headquarters as this must be, in the center of a city such as Ahruma. Then the lights came back on full, again.

He waited for an explanation to offer itself—for the sound of running feet approaching or the corridor-blurred echoes of raised voices. But nothing sounded. No one came.

Chapter

> > **35** < <

Gradually, he ceased to wait. The hope that someone might come or some sort of explanation appear left him; and his mind, like a compass needle, swung back to the magnetic element of his earlier thoughts. He had been listing in his mind those he had known who were committed to fight the bringers of Armageddon and he had been about to add one more name— his own.

Because he now realized that he also was committed. But there was a difference between him and the others he had thought of. Unlike them, he had been enlisted at some point farther back than his conscious memory could reach. Even before he had been found in the spacecraft, plans must have been laid to make him part of a war that he did not then even know existed.

Once more, he came back to the fact that there were things beyond the membrane, in the shadowy warehouse of his unconscious, that belonged to a past beyond the life his present consciousness knew. He could feel back there answers that had been blocked from him, as the image of the vault door had blocked his earlier searching. But it was no dead end he followed now. A certainty lived in him that the reason he had been committed to this struggle had been with him all this time in his unconscious.

The same tools that had brought him answers so far should continue to work for him now. He closed his eyes and his mind once more to the cell about him and reached out for the materials of another poem that would give him further answers.

But no poem came. Instead, came something so powerful that he lived it beyond the definition of the words *dream* or *vision*. It was a memory of a sound once heard. It spoke in his mind with such keen clarity that there was no difference between that and his hearing it with his physical ears, here in the cell, all over again. It was the sound of bagpipe music. And he found himself weeping.

It was not for the music alone he wept, but for what it had meant, for the pain and the grief of that meaning. He followed sound and pain together as if they were a braided thread of gold and scarlet leading him first into darkness and then out once more into a cloud-thick, chilly autumn day, with tall people standing around a newly-dug grave, below willows already stripped of their leaves, and the high, cold peaks of mountains.

The people about seemed so tall, he realized, because he, who was there with them, was still only a child. They were his people and the grave had been filled in though the coffin it held was empty—but the music was now filling it, for the body that should have been there. The man playing the pipes and standing across from him, up near the head of the grave, was his uncle. His father and mother stood behind the gravestone, and his great-uncle stood opposite his uncle. His only other uncle, the twin of the one playing the pipes, was not there. He had been unable to return, even for this. Of the rest of the family present, there was only his one brother, who was six years older than himself, sixteen now and due to leave home himself in two years.

At the foot of the grave were a handful of neighbors and friends. Like the family, they wore black, except for five of them with oriental faces, whose white mourning robes stood out starkly amongst the dark clothing around them.

Then the music ended and his father took a limping half step forward, so that he could close one big hand over the curved top of the gravestone, and speak the words that were always spoken by the head of the family at the burial of one of its members.

"He is home." His father's voice was hoarse. "Sleep with those who loved you—James, my brother."

His father turned away. The burial was over. Family, neighbors and friends went back to the big house. But he, himself, lagged behind and drifted aside, unnoticed, to slip away into the stable.

There, in the familiar dimness warmed by the heavy bodies of the horses, he went slowly down the center aisle between the stalls. The horses put their soft noses over the doors that locked them in and blew at him as he passed, but he ignored them. At the barn's far end he sank down into a sitting position on a bale of new hay from the summer just past, feeling the round logs of the wall hard against his back. He sat, looking at nothing, thinking of James whom he would never see again.

After a while a coldness began to grow in him; but it came, not from the chill of the day outside but from inside him. It spread from a point deep within, outward through his body and limbs. He sat, remembering what he had listened to the day before, with all of the family gathered in the living room to hear from the man who had been his dead uncle's commanding officer, to tell them how James had died.

There had come a point in the talking when the officer, a tall, lean man of his father's age, named Brodsky, had paused in what he was saying and glanced over at him.

"Maybe the boy . . . ?" Brodsky said. Small among all the rest, he had tensed.

"No," answered his father harshly, "he'll need to know how such things happen soon enough. Let him stay."

He had relaxed. He would have fought, even in the face of his father's command, being sent away from what the officer had to tell.

Brodsky nodded, and went on with what he had been telling them.

"There were two things that caused it," he said slowly, "neither of which should have happened. One of them was that the Director of the Board at

Donneswort had been secretly planning to pay us with the help of some pretty heavy funding promised from William of Ceta."

Donneswort was one of the principalities on the planet called Freiland; and the small war there in which James had died had been one of the disputes between communities on that populous world which had escalated into military conflict.

"He'd kept that from us, of course," the officer went on, "or we'd have required a covering deposit in advance. Apparently no one at Donneswort, even the other members of his Board, knew. William, of course, had interests in controlling either Donneswort or its opponent, or both. At any rate, the contract was signed, our troops made good progress from the first into opposition territory and it looked like we were ready to sweep up, when—again, without our knowing it—William reneged on his promise to the Board Director, as he'd probably planned to do from the beginning."

Brodsky stopped and looked steadily at his father.

"And that left Donneswort without funds to pay you off, of course," his father said. His father's dark gaze glanced at his uncle and brother. "That's happened before, too, to our people."

"Yes," said Brodsky, emotionlessly. "At any rate, the Board Director decided to try and hide the news of this from us until we'd got a surrender from our opposition—it looked as if we were only a few days from it, at that time. He did keep it from us, but he didn't manage to keep it from spies belonging to the opposition. As soon as the other side heard, they stuck their necks out, borrowed Militia from adjoining states they wouldn't be able to pay for unless they won, and we suddenly found a force three times the size we'd contracted to deal with thrown at us."

Brodsky paused and he saw the officer's dark eyes glance briefly, once more, over at his own small self.

"Go on," said his father, harshly. "You're going to tell us how all this affected my brother."

"Yes," said the officer. "We'd had James on duty as a Force-Leader, with a unit of local Donneswort Militia. But of course, since he was one of ours, his orders came only down our own chain of command. Because he was new in command and because his Militia weren't worth much, we'd held his Force in reserve. But when the Board Director heard of the increase in opposition forces, he panicked and tried to throw all of us, all available troops, into an all-out attack—which would have been suicidal, the way we were positioned at the time."

"So you refused," said his uncle, speaking for the first time.

"We did, of course," said Brodsky, looking over at the uncle. "Our Battle Op rejected the Director's order, for cause, which he was free to do under the contract, and as he would've in any case. But those companies of Militia not under our own officers received the order and followed it. They moved up."

"But the boy got no order," said his mother.

"Unfortunately," Brodsky sighed softly, "he did. That was the second thing that shouldn't have happened. James' Force was part of a unit positioned off on the left flank of our general position, in touch with the overall Command HQ through a central communications net that was staffed almost totally by local Militia. One of these was the man who received the message for the troops in James' area. There, all the units except James' were commanded by Militia officers. The Militiaman on net communications to their sector made up move orders for all units before someone pointed out to him that the one to your brother could only be sent if it was authorized by one of our own Commanders. Because the Militiaman was ignorant of the overall situation, and apparently also because it was simply easier for him than checking with our Command, he put the name of James' Commander on the order to James without authority, and sent it out over the net to your brother."

Brodsky sighed softly again.

"James moved his Force up with the rest of the Militia around him," he went on. "There was a road they'd been ordered to hold; and they made contact with opposition forces almost immediately. James must have seen from the beginning that he and his men were caught up in a fight with numbers and equipment too great for his men to hold. The Militia under their own officers on either side of him pulled out—ran, I should say. He checked back with the communications net, but the same Militiaman who'd issued the order panicked, just as the Board Director had, and simply told James no orders had come in from the Dorsai Command for him to pull back."

The officer stopped speaking. The silence in the living room was uninterrupted.

"So," said the officer, "that's the last contact that was had with his Force. We believe he must have assumed our own people had some reason for wanting him to hold. He could still have pulled back on his own initiative under the Mercenaries' Code, of course, but he didn't. He did his best to hold until his position was overrun and he and his men were killed."

The eyes of all the rest of them in the room were dry and steady upon Brodsky.

"That particular Militiaman was killed an hour or so later when the net position was overrun," the officer said softly. "We would have dealt with him otherwise, naturally, and also there would at least have been reparations for you as a family. But Donneswort was bankrupt, so not even that much was possible. The rest of us who were there got the funds to return home from the opposition. We threatened to hold the Donneswort capital city on our own, against them, if they didn't pay us what we needed to evacuate. It was a lot cheaper for them to bear the expense of sending us home than to pay the cost of taking the city from us. And if they hadn't taken the city within a week, they'd have been bankrupt themselves, unable to keep the borrowed Militia they needed to control Donneswort."

He stopped speaking. There was a long silence.

"Nothing more than that's required, then," said his father, harshly. "We all thank you for bringing us word."

"So." It was his uncle speaking, and for once his open, friendly face was no longer so. In this dark moment he was the mirror image of that grim man, his twin brother. "William of Ceta, the Board Director, and the dead net communicator. We've all three to hold to account for this."

"The Director was tried and executed by Donneswort, itself," said Brodsky. "He got a lot of his own people killed, too."

"That still leaves—" his uncle was beginning, when his father interrupted.

"It does no good to fix blame now," his father said. "It's our life, and this sort of thing happens."

A deep shock went through him at the words; but he said nothing then, watching as his uncle fell silent and the rest of the family got to their feet. His father offered a hand to the officer, who took it. They stood, hands clasped together for a moment.

"Thank you," said his father, again. "Will you be able to stay for the funeral?"

"I wish I could," Brodsky answered. "I'm sorry. We've still got wounded coming back."

"We understand—" his father had said. . . .

—The stable door creaked open now and the scene from the previous day evaporated, leaving him only with the perfect coldness that held him as if he had been frozen into a block of ice. Remotely, he was aware of his uncle coming toward him with long strides down the aisles between the horse stalls.

"Lad, what are you doing here?" his uncle asked, in a concerned voice. "Your mother's worried about you. Come back into the house."

Hal did not answer. His uncle reached him, abruptly frowned and knelt so that their faces were on a level. His uncle's eyes peered into his own, and his uncle's face suddenly altered into a look of pain and deep shock.

"Oh, boy, boy," his uncle whispered. He felt the big arms gently enclosing his own stiff body, holding him. "You're too young for this, yet. It's too soon for you to go this way. Don't, lad, don't! Come back!"

But the words came remotely to his ears, as if they had been addressed to someone other than himself. Out of the coldness in him, he looked steadily into his uncle's eyes.

"No more," he heard his own voice saying. "Never any more. I'll stop it. I'll find them and stop them. All of them."

"Boy . . ." His uncle held him close as if he would warm the smaller body with the living heat of his own. "Come back. Come back. . . ."

For a long moment it was as still as if his uncle were speaking to someone else. But then, in a moment no longer than that of a sigh, the iciness drained out of him. Half-unconscious in the reaction from what he had just been feeling, he fell forward against his uncle's shoulder, and as if in a dream he felt himself lifted up like a tired child in the powerful arms and carried out of the stable. . . .

He woke once more to the cell. For a brief moment, still anesthetized by unconsciousness, he had thought that he was well again; and then an uncontrollable coughing seized him and for a moment he found his breathing completely stopped. Panic, like the shadow of some descending vulture, closed its wings about him and for a long minute he struggled vainly for breath. Then he managed to rid himself of the phlegm he had coughed loose, and momentarily the illusion of being able to breathe more deeply came to him, then was lost in a new awareness of his fever, his violently-aching head and his choked lungs.

His sickness had not lessened. But for all that, he felt a difference. A small increase of strength seemed to have been restored to him by the sleep; and he felt a clearheadedness in the midst of the pain and the struggle to breathe that he had not known before. Where he had thought of himself until now as thinking with a fever-fueled overpressure of brilliance and insight such as he had never touched before, he now, like someone recovering from a massive dose of some stimulant drug, discovered a different and stronger order of perception, an awareness of subtle elements in all of what he had so far perceived and remembered—and the connections between them, that he had been blocked off from previously.

Moreover, with this awareness he found himself caught up for the first time in a tremendous sense of excitement—the excitement of a searcher who has at last stepped over the crest that has been blocking his view and for the first time sees his goal undeniably and clearly. He felt himself on the edge of something enormous, that thing he had been in pursuit of all his life—in fact, for longer than his life, an incalculable amount of time.

Sitting upright once more with his back against the cell wall, he probed the difference this new feeling implied. It was as if all the universe beyond his limited view of the cell and the corridor had suddenly taken a gigantic step toward him. He no longer guessed at the vague shapes of possible understandings just beyond his reach; he knew they were there and that his road to them could not be barred.

So thinking, he let himself go, following the inner compass needle of his will; and passed almost without effort into a condition he had never experienced before. Awake—he dreamed, and was conscious that he dreamed. He could see the cell around him; but at the same time, with as much or more clarity, he could see the landscape of his dream.

He was back in his vision of the rubbled plain and the tower toward which he had been journeying so long and so painfully on foot; while the tower itself had seemed to move back from him as each footstep brought him closer to it.

For the first time now, all this was changed. He had taken one great step that brought him close in to the tower. Now he looked at it from relatively close at hand. Only a short distance separated them. But at the same time he saw that he had covered only the easy half of his journey to it. What remained ahead was less in distance, but so much greater in difficulty that he realized only his training and toughening by the long, arduous travel to this point made it possible for him to hope he could cross the final stretch of forbidding ground that lay between them.

Looking back over his shoulder, he discovered now that his journey to this moment had been subtly upslope, so that only now did he stand on a high point from which he could see what lay before him. Slowly the massive rubble before him began to reveal a form. He stood on the broken and crumbled stones of what had once been the outer ramparts of some great defensive structure, so enormous in extent that the historic Krak des Chevaliers of Old Earth could have been dropped into it and lost, among the very shadows of the massive building stones that had formed its inner structures. It was a castle old beyond memory, and time had all but destroyed it. Only the tower, which had been its keep, its innermost defense, still stood and waited for him.

It would be among that maze of ruined inner walls and outer walls, of fallen baileys and rubble-choked courtyards, chambers and passageways that he must climb and crawl, to make his way at last to the entrance of the tower. And it was a journey that would have been inconceivable to him, even now, if it had not been for the changes in mind and body that had come upon him over the years, the counterpart of the hardening absorbed in his dream of the long, solitary trek across the rubbled plain. Now older, more skilled and firm of mind, there had grown in him a relentlessness that he had not recognized until now and that not even what lay before him could halt. As someone might enter hell for some strong purpose, he stepped forward and down off the broken ramparts into the rocky and treacherous wilderness before him; and with that step forward his mind was at last committed and at peace.

Going, he left behind that part of him that had carried him through the long earlier parts of his journey and which he no longer needed. Grown and different, he returned to his self that was still in the cell, where he could now begin to see the work that lay before him and the path he must take to its doing.

Chapter

> > **36** < <

. . . He woke.

It was not a sudden wakening. He came gradually out of deep slumber to the knowledge that he had been sleeping heavily for some little time. With consciousness, the awareness of his fever, his weakness and his struggle to breathe came back to him. . . . but now there was a difference.

He broke into another heavy fit of coughing, almost strangling, as he had strangled before when the matter in his lungs choked and closed completely the airway that brought him the oxygen of life. But this time the panic that had hovered on dark wings above him as he fought to clear his airways did not materialize. Some new fierceness within him, burning more hotly than the fever itself, more inextinguishably than the attack of whatever microscopic entity was working to destroy him, fought back and routed it.

Gasping, he leaned back limply against the wall. It was strange. Nothing was changed, nothing about his physical condition had improved, but internally he felt as if the universe had swung half a cosmic turn about him and settled in some new order that gave strength and the certainty of hope. Triumph lifted its head in him. Death had been pushed back now, and for some reason, he no longer gave it credit for the power to overcome him.

Why? Or rather, if this was so, why had he ever had a fear of it in the first place? He sat, propped up against the wall of the cell in a sitting position, with the thin blanket pulled up over him; and the realization came slowly to him that the difference he now recognized was one of mind and will, rather than of body.

When Barbage had named him a hound of Armageddon, and left him to die, a small part of him had acknowledged a rightness in the Militiaman's attitude. Barbage was what he was. His faith, though twisted, was real. He listened to and was used by Bleys, but only because he believed Bleys spoke with the words of Barbage's own personal God; not, like Bleys' other followers, because he either feared or worshipped the man himself.

Unnaturally turned as it was, still the quality of that faith had had the power to touch and weaken Hal. Because of the strength of it, for the first time in his life he had acknowledged the possibility of his own personal death; and in doing that he had, in effect, accepted the possibility of dying. But now, that acceptance was gone from him. In these last hours of fever-vision and dream-memories he had found and confirmed instead a reason why he could not afford death. There were things to be done first, the most urgent of these being the necessity to translate into clear, conscious terms the unconscious reasonings that had given him the necessity to survive. He cast his mind back.

At first, after Barbage, his journey into understanding had not been toward survival, but away from it. His first dream had been of himself, manacled on the mountainside, slowly being destroyed by the pitiless and invincible rain of Bleys' logic. The words Bleys had spoken had carried the argument Milton had put into the mouth of his Satan in *Paradise Lost*—"I am greater than either the concept of Heaven or that of Hell."

And it was true. Only, it was true in that sense not just of Bleys or the Others, but of any human being who was not afraid to face that greaterness. It was in his avoidance of that universality of possibility that all of Bleys' arguments had betrayed their weakness. The isolation Bleys had spoken of and Hal had remembered feeling on Coby was also true enough, but it was a self-made thing. Nor was it necessary to understand this fact logically in order to put that feeling aside. Anyone with sufficient faith could put it aside without understanding, as James Child-of-God had put aside any consideration of personal cost in the matter of his death on Harmony.

Bleys' arguments, like Bleys' chosen way, were personal and selfish—they closed their eyes to the proven rewards, equally personal but greater, of working not for the self but for humanity as it was personified in one's fellow humans. And it was humanity, the race itself, that was the key to all puzzles. No, not just the race, but the understanding of it as a single creature, concerned with its own survival and apportioning its parts among partisan groups that struggled with each other, so that strengths might be revealed which would point the best direction for future actions and growths by the race as a whole. A race-creature regarded its parts as expendable and unimportant, setting up a web of historic forces that built always forward, containing and controlling the great mass of humanity—that great mass that since time began had been driven like the deer by forces they did not understand, to the waiting, red-capped hunters. Sost and John Heikkila, Hilary and Godlun Amjak, the farmer who had sought reassurance for the future from Child, and had not gotten it—all driven and trapped by the warring factions that had now dwindled to two, the Others and those who opposed them.

And he was one of the opposed. Hal realized suddenly that it was from his understanding of that, that his new strength had just come. He knew himself now. Once, at some graveside, he had made a commitment; and this present moment in which he found himself was simply an extension of that commitment. He had been barred, until now, from knowing his own past, for a reason he could not see. But now he saw.

Until now, this present moment, he, who had made the commitment, had not known how to get to where he wanted to go. It had taken this present life he could remember, up until this moment in the cell, to uncover that way and make it plain. He had seen it now, in allegory in his dream of his path to the tower—which, that still lost and hidden past of his now whispered, might yet be not dream, but reality. Reality of a different order only, than the here and now.

But it was in the here and now that he presently existed; and so what he must do immediately, was translate that unconscious and allegorical understanding of a path, into hard and logical understandings of the real forces that must be worked upon to produce the end toward which he had worked all this time. He let the effort of that translation take him; and the overriding excitement in his new capacity for understanding flowed purposefully over all that he had mined from his unconscious. The image of the human race as a group entity, an amoeba-like race-animal with an identity and a purpose apart from the individual identities of its component human parts, now stood as a valid model of what he must deal with. The race, pictured as a single creature, a sort of primitive individual with its own instincts and desires—chief among these the instinct to survive as an entity, and a willingness to sacrifice its parts in continuous experimentation to satisfy that instinct—explained all that followed.

Such experimentation would have been a steady process from the time the race-animal became conscious of itself. The drives to develop, through its human components, first intelligence, and later, technology, would have been expressions of that instinct at work. So, too, would have been the twentieth century's probing off the planet of its birth into space, in unconscious search for more living room, the rise of the Splinter Cultures—each an experiment in the viability of human varieties in off-Earth environments—and now, finally, the emergence of the Others.

What made the Others a racial experiment, he understood now, was their need to take over and control all the rest of the race. In that need lay the way to an answer to why the racial-animal should have birthed them in the first place. Bleys had answered it himself, in this cell. Whatever else was true about the Others, two things were undeniable. They were human, with all ordinary hungers and wants, including that of always wanting more than they had; and they were very much aware that they were too few to risk the rest of humanity realizing how their sheer lack of numbers made them vulnerable. It was a vulnerability that nothing less than total control of the rest of the race could ever remove; and such control could only be achieved by the establishment of a single unvarying uniform Culture. Only a Culture in which all things were permanently fixed and unchanging could release them from the need to stand on guard against those they dominated; and turn them loose at last to enjoy their advantage of a natural superiority over the majority of humanity.

And the only way for them to obtain both ends was to first achieve a situation of complete stasis, an end to the long, instinctive upward development of civilization. History must be brought to a halt. To do that, they must remove or render harmless to them those other humans who could never accept an end to that development, those who would have no choice but to oppose the Others' building of that stasis.

The strengths of the Others would lie, first, in their charismatic skills; and, secondly, in the fact that individually they were the equals, in minds and bodies, of the best that could be brought against them. And those strengths would be magnified because they would be able to marshal most of the populations of ten worlds to act on their orders.

On the other side of their ledger lay their lack of ability to value the future. Other weaknesses . . .

. . . But so far they seemed to have no other weaknesses. In a strict sense, one thing that could be labelled a weakness was the smallness of their actual numbers. Their opponents included, for all practical purposes, the total populations of the Dorsai and the two Exotic Worlds—plus, on Harmony and Association, the minority of true Faith-holders such as Child-of-God and Rukh. To these would be added, in the long run, a large share of the population of Earth—although any hope of getting all the diverse inhabitants of the Home World to voluntarily join together in any kind of effective response to the danger the Others posed, would be wishful thinking.

The possible numbers of those opposed—putting Old Earth aside—would equal only a fraction of the fighting strength and resources the Others could raise from the ten planets they effectively controlled even now, if it came down to worlds fighting worlds as in the old days of Donal Graeme. Therefore, from the start, the Others' best tactic had been to work for an Armageddon, a final battle under the cover of which all those they could neither dominate nor persuade could be destroyed or neutralized.

It was easy now for his mind to see how they might aim at this; but hard to see any way by which they could be stopped or turned back. In any case, the war that was beginning even now would not be one fought so much with material weapons for physical territories, but one waged by opposing minds for the support of the driven deer, the mass of uncommitted individuals making up the human race; and, in such a war, the charismatic abilities of the Others ought to make their victory a foregone conclusion.

Hal sat, struggling for breath in the silent cell, his body burning like a live coal, his mind thrusting and dissecting like a surgeon's tool of ice.

What those who opposed the crossbreeds must have, as soon as possible, was, first, a long-range plan that promised at least the hope of victory; and, second, a weapon to match the charismatic abilities of the Others. It would have to be a weapon that the Others either did not have, or could not use— any more than those opposing them could probably expect to use charismatic skills successfully against them.

That there must be at least the potential of a counter-weapon was sure, since the Others themselves were an experiment in survival by the racial-animal. It was necessary to look at the racial-animal itself for an understanding of the real forces at work, those historic forces of which the

Others—like the Dorsai, the Exotics and the true Faith-holders, and like himself—were merely manifestations.

It had been as if the racial-animal—thought Hal—on becoming aware in the twentieth century that space was physically reachable, had been both attracted and frightened by what lay outside the warm, reliable place that was the planet of its birth. History showed at that time two attitudes among people: one that shrank from space, speaking of "things Men were not meant to know"; and another that was fascinated by it, dreaming of exploration and discoveries, just as dreams of the Indies had moved minds four hundred years earlier when some foresaw only ships sailing off the ocean-edge of the world. When at last it became possible to go into space, and particularly to go beyond the home solar system, both the fears and the dreams had spawned thousands of smaller groups, looking for a place to build a society in the pattern of their own desires.

What the racial-animal had wanted, Hal thought now, was proven survivor types, both in the way of individuals and societies; and so it had given free rein to the experimentation of its parts. Out of the diversity of that diaspora had emerged the most successful survivors of the so-called Splinter Cultures, the three greatest of which had been the Dorsai, the Friendlies and the Exotics. These three had flowered for two hundred years during which they performed functions that made the off-Earth, interplanetary society of their time stable, by making war, trade and conflicts safely controllable within the fabric of that society.

Then, with the necessary development of the pattern of that society as its diverse elements were brought under one system of control by Donal Graeme, the need for the Splinter Cultures' special elements dwindled and the Cultures themselves had begun to die. Meanwhile, the racial-animal, thriftily crossbreeding the new human strains that these Splinter Cultures had developed, so that what had been gained should not be lost, had begun at last to produce the unopposable dominants for which part of its nature had always yearned. So had been rounded out the growth that had gone from development of intelligence—to technology—to the overpopulation of Earth—to space—to the Splinter Cultures who were experiments with survival types of humans off-Earth—to the recombination of these Splinter types, into the new dominants who called themselves the Others.

Only, these dominants now looked to be unremovable as the new leaders of the race; and the millennia-proven growth of historical progress that had always come from the new human talent of each generation deposing the old from authority was in danger of being ended for all time—unless the Others could be shown, after all, to have a weakness.

So much, then, thought Hal, for the position of the Others. Their opponents' position was simply that, since the coming of the Others to power meant an end to all human change and growth, it was a situation not to be endured. To that part of the racial-animal the Others' opponents represented, to cease growing meant a death to all hopes for the future; and to avert that universal death, personal death was a small price to pay.

Something clicked in Hal's mind.

Of course. The reason Earth alone had shown such a resistance to the influence of the Others would be that Earth was still the original gene pool of the race. Its people were full-spectrum human—unspecialized in any of the myriad ways that had resulted from the racial-animal's experimentation with the breeding and adaptation of its individual parts for their life on other worlds. Within all of those who were native Earth-born—as opposed to just some of those on the Younger Worlds—lived not merely a portion, but all of the possibilities of the human spirit, good and bad; and one of those possibilities was a portion with the faith of the Friendlies, the independence of the Dorsai, and the vision of the Exotics, that could not endure an end to change and growth.

Sudden hope kindled in Hal. Earth, then, was at least part of a weapon the Others could not use.

At least part . . . Hal's leaping mind fastened on a new point. What the Earth's population of native-born, full-spectrum individuals represented to the Others, as to the race as a whole, was genetic insurance, in case their dominance should result in patterns of human specialization that would lack the ability to survive. Some of the variforms of plants and animals had already shown themselves unable to flourish on certain of the Younger Worlds. No one could be sure what several hundred generations from now would produce in human adaptations to the newer planets. Earth was the one world the Others dared not decimate; and also the one they absolutely must control, in order to ensure the survival of their interstellar kingdom once they had established it.

Others, then, equalled stasis. Others-opponents should therefore equal . . . evolution?

Evolution . . . the word rang, like a massive gong hammered once, in Hal's mind. Evolution had been the great dream of the Exotics—their great, unfulfilled dream, that mankind was indeed in the process of evolving; and that the Exotic students of mankind would eventually identify the direction of the evolution, foster it, and eventually produce an improved form of human.

But the Exotics were dying now, their dream unfulfilled, if their purpose was still in existence, as was that of the Dorsai and the Friendlies. But meanwhile their place was being usurped, along with that of everyone else, by the Others. The Exotics, like the rest of the Others' opponents, had no solution of their own to the situation. If there had been a way within the reach of the Exotics that would stop the Others, they would have found and used it by now.

But, even though the Exotic Culture—if not yet the people themselves—was dying off, evolution as a concept still existed—for the moment at least. It was not just the private property of the Exotics and never had been, but a property of mankind in general. In short, all these years that the Exotics had sought it, perhaps evolution and the means for it had been in operation under their noses, unrecognized. Perhaps mankind could have been building toward the future of the race without knowing it, just as for centuries humanity had built toward a home on other worlds without knowing it—

Hal chilled. So profound was the shock of discovery, that even with the candle of his life guttering within him, for a moment he forgot the cell around him, his fever, even his struggle to breathe.

The Final Encyclopedia.

The Encyclopedia was the one weapon the Others did not have, and could not use, even if they had it.

Because it had been designed as a tool for learning that which was not known; and, by definition of the stasis toward which the Others worked, there would be a positive danger for them in a tool that promised the addition of new knowledge, in a Culture where they wanted no increase and neither growth nor change.

And that, of course, explained the division and the upcoming conflict.

Because the racial-animal was purely concerned with survival, at root it would have no partiality for either side. It was allowing its parts to fight each other only to find out which would win. Therefore, both sides must have been allowed by it to unconsciously develop means and weapons toward the inevitable moment of conflict—not just the side that had spawned the Others. The Final Encyclopedia could be the weapon that balanced the scale for the adherents of evolution against the Others' weapon of charisma.

Hal wiped his forehead with the back of an unsteady hand and it came away damp. With a shock he realized that, in this last burst of mental struggle with the problem obsessing him, something had changed in his physical condition. Strangely, now, the chill he had felt at the first shock of discovery was still with him. His fever no longer seemed to burn so fiercely inside him; and even his breathing appeared easier. He coughed; and it was not the dry, struggling cough that it had been before. This cough brought up phlegm more easily and seemed to clear a little extra breathing space in his over-stuffed lungs. His head had almost stopped aching. He put a hand to his forehead, again, wonderingly, and again brought away a palm wet with sweat.

His fever had broken. But so great was the turmoil of discovery in him that he could not yet rejoice.

Within his mind, now, he could feel massive shapes and patterns of understanding beginning to take form, like the underwater ghosts of great icebergs in a murky, polar sea, as known facts fell together with conclusions that suddenly were obvious—all shaping so rapidly that consciously he was not able to read the full meaning of what he was just now beginning to understand. It was as if one block, pulled from a towering and meaningless jumble of other such blocks, had caused an earthquake-like tumbling and rearrangement through the entire pile; so that when the motion at last ceased, as in his last dream of the tower, the jumble stood as a recognizable structure—complete to the smallest detail; while he stood, with the one removed block still in his hand, and marvelled. Even the charisma had come from some element buried in the full spectrum of human capabilities. Somehow, they who would fight the Others would find it and use it equally.

Now that he had found this knowledge—now that he held, safe within him, the understanding that the Final Encyclopedia was indeed the tool he had blindly reached for, the weapon unconsciously prepared over time to be used against the Others—he could hardly believe it. He sat with it in mind, dazed by the fact of his understanding, as Arthur Pendragon who was to be king might have felt dazed at finding the great sword come smoothly from the stone into his hand, deaf to the cheers of the watching multitude in his realization of what he had done.

Now that Hal understood, he realized that this understanding was more precious than anything in the hands of the race. Now that he had it, he must live to escape from here and get himself and his knowledge to safety.

As this other had been solvable, so that, too, must be.

Chapter

> >**37**< <

Sitting exactly as he was, a great sense of accomplishment and relief came over him, like a runner who has raced some incredible distance and won. Still thinking of what he must do, not only to escape with his present understanding but afterward, he fell into a doze, as his worn-out body took advantage of the fact that the fever had now broken and his breathing was slightly easier; and the doze, still without a change of position, became deep and exhausted sleep.

He woke from an apparently-dreamless sleep to find that, without waking, he had slid down into a position flat on his back on the bed and pulled the thin blanket up over him. He struggled up again into a sitting position. The effort brought on a coughing spasm which produced more yellow-green phlegm, but the coughing did not hurt so much; and he found, after the first breathlessness from the effort was over, that he seemed to be more successful at getting air into his lungs now than he had been for some hours, although he was still a long way from normal. About him, the silent cell still showed no change.

His first and most desperate need was to empty his bladder. He threw back the blanket and discovered he had barely strength to get to his feet facing the stool. Finished, he fell back onto the bed and lay for a moment, while he collected enough energy to turn, crawl across and raise himself on his knees beside the washstand on the bed's other side. He drank, this time, at last, deeply from its tap, stopping to catch his breath and then drinking again, revelling in again being able to swallow more than a few mouthfuls. Finally, with moisture at least partially restored in him, he sat back against the wall at the head of the bed and put himself to the labor and pain of coming fully awake.

Asleep, he had for a short while forgotten the struggle to breathe; and now for a little while he had attention only for that, and his general weakness and discomfort. But gradually, as he woke more fully, his mind began to gain something of its normal ascendancy over his body; and all that he had thought his way through to, in the long hours just past, came back. The urgency in him reawoke. Even before he remembered fully why it was so, he remembered that he must get out of here.

Under the stimulant of that necessity, he began to come back to a normal state of alertness; and his struggle to breathe eased even further, until it was almost possible to ignore it. He coughed and raised a certain amount of phlegm, but the effort ate brutally into his slim supply of strength. He gave up trying to clear his lungs and sat back once more against the wall of his cell. Remembering his chronometer, he looked at it. It showed 10:32 A.M.

His first concern now that he was fully awake was to check the structure of understanding he had built before sleep kidnapped him. But it was still all there, only waiting for deeper examination to give up its details. He was free to devote his attention to getting out of the hands of those who held him.

It was obvious that the situation was one in which it was not practical for him to escape in any physical, literal sense. His only real chance was to persuade his jailers to take him out of the cell. As a last resort, if they would not, he could ask to speak to Bleys; and tell the tall man that he had agreed to think over the possibility that he might be one of the Others.

But it was absolutely a last resort, not because it might not get him out of the cell, or because of any physical danger inherent in it, but because face-to-face contact with Bleys at any time was perilous. Bleys was not only an Other, but—unless matters had changed among his kind—second-in-command of their organization. He was not the kind of individual whom someone possibly as much as ten years younger could confidently expect to delude.

Leaning back against the wall, Hal shut his eyes and let his mind focus down on the question of escape, until everything else was shut out but the edge of his physical misery, niggling on the horizon of his consciousness, and the massive shape of the structure he had conceived, standing mountainous in the background of his thoughts and throwing its shadow over everything.

All together, the physical discomfort, the situation and his new understanding, gave birth to a plan. He opened his eyes after a time, got up from the bed and took two unsteady steps into the center of the room. For a long moment he merely stood there, feeling upon him in his imagination the attentive eyes of the invisible watcher keeping his cell under surveillance.

Then he opened his mouth and screamed—screamed as impressively as he could with the hoarse throat and miserly breath that were all he had to scream with—and collapsed on the floor of his cell.

He had let himself fall as gravity took him; but he had also relaxed in falling, so that the impact upon the bare concrete floor was not as painful as it might have been. Once down, he lay absolutely motionless, and set about doing a number of things to himself internally that either Walter or Malachi had at different times taught him to do.

As individual exercises, most of these were not difficult; and they tended to reinforce each other in the effect he needed. Slowing his respiration was in any case part of the techniques for slowing his heart rate and lowering his blood pressure. These latter two, in turn, helped him achieve the more difficult task of decreasing his body temperature. Taken all together, they decreased his oxygen need, thereby easing the task of breathing with his secretion-choked lungs; and gave him the plausible appearance of having passed into a deep unconsciousness. At the same time the state they helped him achieve made it possible for him to endure without moving the long wait that he expected—and was not disappointed in having—before those watching him finally became convinced enough to send a guard to his cell to see if something had indeed happened to him.

In the end, he lay where he had fallen for over three hours. A small part of his mind kept automatic track of the passage of that time, but the greater part had withdrawn into a state of near-trance; so that he was very close to being honestly in the condition in which he was pretending to be. When his guards finally did reach the point of checking on him, he was only peripherally aware of what was happening. He lay, hearing as if from another room, as the first guard to come into the cell and examine him relayed his conclusions over the surveillance microphones; and after some consultation at the other end, a decision was made to get him to a hospital.

There had been a certain delay, the small, barely-interested, watchdog part of his mind noted, resulting from the fact that Barbage was not on duty and his inferiors fretted, caught between their fear of the lean Captain's displeasure if they did anything unjustified for the prisoner and their awe and fear of Bleys' reaction if anything happened to Hal. In the end, as Hal had gambled it would—even if Barbage himself had been present—their respect for Bleys' orders left them no choice but to get Hal to someone medically knowledgeable as soon as possible.

It seemed that there had also been another reason for their hesitation, having to do with conditions outside the building; but what this was, Hal could not quite make out. In any case, he eventually found himself being lifted onto a stretcher and carried out of the cell and along corridors to a motorized cart. This took him—now buried under a pile of blankets—for some distance until they passed finally through a tall pair of doors into cold, damp air. He was lifted off the motorized cart onto another stretcher, which was then carried into some sort of vehicle and suspended there, in a rack against one of the vehicle's sides.

A door slammed, metallically. There was a momentary pause, then blowers came to life and the vehicle took off.

Heavily depressed as his body now was, it resisted his efforts to wake it. The resistance was not active but inert, of the same sort that makes an unconscious man harder to lift than a conscious one. The near-trance in which he had put himself had shut out all the pains and struggles of the last few days; and his present comfort drew him the way a drug draws its addict.

It was only by remembering the structure of understanding that he had finally put together in his mind, and its importance, that he was able to rouse himself to push back the torpor he had created. But once he managed to lift the effect slightly, his work became easier. He felt a touch of relief, momentarily. He did not want to bring his body all the way back to normality too soon, in case he should find himself in competent medical hands before he had a chance to take advantage of being out of his prison. There was too much danger of being turned around and sent directly back to his cell.

On the other hand, he needed to be alert enough to take advantage of an opportunity to escape if one should come up. He went back to rousing himself with his original urgency, therefore, toward the point where he believed he would be able to get to his feet and move if he had to; but he could feel that his pulse remained in the forties and his systolic blood pressure was probably still only in the nineties, and his original concern returned. His body was lagging in its response to his efforts to wake it.

With all this, however, he was still becoming once more able to pay attention to what was going on around him, although his emotional reactions to what he saw and heard remained sluggish. He saw that he was alone in the back of what was obviously a military ambulance capable of transporting at least a dozen stretchers hung three-deep along its two sidewalls. A couple of enlisted Militiamen were occupying the bucket seats before the controls up front in the open cab area.

A band of windows ran along each side of the vehicle in the stretcher area; and beside him as he lay on a top-level stretcher the upper edge of the window glass was just below the point of his shoulder. He lay on his back. By turning his head only a little, he could get a good view of the streets along which they were passing. Although it would be early afternoon by this time, no one was to be seen in the streets; and the small shop fronts he passed were closed tight, their display windows opaqued.

It was a dull, wet afternoon. It was not raining now; but the street surface, walkways and building fronts glistened with moisture. He caught only an occasional glimpse of a corner of the sky between far-off building tops when the ambulance passed through the intersection of a cross-street; but it seemed uniformly heavy and gray with a thick cloud cover. After a little while, he did indeed see one pedestrian who turned his head sharply at the approach of the ambulance and ducked up an alley between two shops.

There was tension in the cab of the vehicle. Now that his senses, at least, were working normally, his woods-wise nose could catch in the still, enclosed air of the ambulance, the faint harsh stink of men perspiring under emotional stress. They were also directing the vehicle oddly, travelling only a few blocks in a straight line, pausing at occasional intersections for no visible reason, then turning abruptly to go over several blocks to the right or left before returning to their original direction of travel, as furtive in their movements as the first foot traveller he had seen.

As they went on, their progress slowed, almost as if the man controlling the vehicle had lost his way. Now, they began to see more pedestrians, all in a hurry, nearly all going in the same general direction the ambulance was following. At last, Hal's dead-seeming body was beginning to respond, although it still felt as though it weighed several times its normal amount. He faced the fact that, far from being in danger of recovering too soon, he had underestimated his exhaustion and the effort it would need to lift himself from the attractive state of near-unconsciousness. Elementally, his body was desperate for the rest it felt it needed to survive; and it was resisting being forced back to a higher level of energy expenditure.

In his concern to get himself back to a state in which, if necessary, he could stand and walk, Hal all but forgot the vehicle around him and the streets through which it was passing. He was barely aware that they were proceeding more and more cautiously; and that more and more often the ambulance halted briefly. Slowly, his stubborn body was returning to life; and at last he was beginning to have confidence that he could raise and move it for a short distance, at least. He lay under the blankets, clenching and unclenching his hands, flexing his arms and legs, shrugging his shoulders and making every movement that was possible without unduly risking the danger of attracting the attention of the two men up front.

He was all but completely occupied with these exercises when the ambulance slowed suddenly enough to slide him forward on his stretcher, then abruptly revved up its blowers for a second before throttling all the way back to idle. The vehicle halted.

Hal stopped exercising and looked out through the window glass beside him.

The ambulance was surrounded by people, a still-gathering crowd not yet so tightly packed that those in it could not move without other bodies moving out of their way. Clearly, it had just become impossible for the vehicle to continue forward; and glancing back the way they had come, Hal saw more people filling in behind them. It was already impossible to turn around and go back.

They were in a large square that was rapidly becoming jammed with people, having apparently just emerged from one of the streets feeding the square. The faces of those around the truck, glancing in at the pair of Militiamen, were not friendly. Hal could now smell more strongly the stink of emotion from the two. He pulled his head back to look forward as far as was possible. Less than thirty meters in front of them, with a solid stand of human bodies in the way, was the entrance to another street that would have led them beyond the square. Clearly, the driver had gambled that he could get across to it before the crowd barred his path completely—and the driver had lost.

The ambulance was trapped like a mastodon in a tar pit. It would remain that way, unless the driver chose to simply bulldoze a way through the people in their path; and that sort of action would clearly be a suicidal thing to try, judging from the scowling faces glancing at the Militia uniforms. With an explosive inhalation somewhere between a sigh and a grunt, the driver cut the blowers entirely and let the vehicle settle to the pavement. The Militiaman beside him was muttering into the vehicle's phone unit.

"Stay put!" crackled an answering voice from the interior speaker unit of the vehicle. "Don't do anything. Don't attract any attention. Just sit it out and act like you're enjoying it."

Silence fell inside the cab. The two Militiamen sat, pretending to be engaged in conversation and refusing to meet the dark stares of those who glanced in at them. Looking again out the window glass beside him, Hal saw that their attempted route had been across one corner of the square. They were grounded broadside onto the open space of its middle; and, without having to move, he had an excellent view of the central area where the crowd was thickest.

It had pressed in tightly there about a pedestal supporting a stark brownish cross of granite, that towered at least three stories into the air. From where Hal lay on the stretcher, looking out through the moisture-streaked side window of the ambulance, the upper part of the cross seemed to loom impossibly high over them all, giving the illusion of floating against the dark, swag-bellied rain clouds overhead. The figure of a man in a business suit was beginning to climb down from the pedestal, having just finished a speech that Hal had been minimally conscious of hearing from repeaters worn or carried by those in the crowd close around the ambulance.

Applause began, and sounded for a few moments as the business-suited man climbed off the pedestal. After a second another man, this one wearing the familiar bush clothes Hal had seen around him through the past weeks, began to climb up. The ascending man reached the top of the pedestal, took a grip on the upright shaft of the cross to steady himself on the narrow footing, and began to speak. His voice came clearly to Hal's ears; plainly he was wearing a broadcaster which the repeaters were picking up, but from this distance Hal could not see it anywhere visible on his clothing or body. All around the ambulance, the tiny, black repeaters pinned openly to lapels or defiantly held up overhead threw his words out over the listening crowd. They penetrated the walls of the trapped vehicle.

"Brothers and sisters in God—"

Hal's attention woke to a new alertness. The voice he was hearing was the voice of Jason Rowe; and now that he had identified Jason, he recognized the square-shouldered, spare figure standing as he had been used to see it stand.

"—In a moment the one who will speak to you will be Captain Rukh Tamani, who planned the complete blockage of the Core Tap shaft accomplished by her Command, yesterday—who not only planned it; but gathered, with her Command, the materials out of which the necessary explosive was assembled; and trekked those materials halfway across the continent under threat of attack by Militia at all times, and under actual pursuit and attack much of the time. Brothers and sisters in the Lord, we have as of yesterday testified to the fact that our faith in God remains whole and able to strike at those very points where the Belial-spawn consider themselves strongest. As it was yesterday, so shall it continue to be until the Others and their dogs no longer harry our worlds and our people. Brothers and sisters, here is Rukh Tamani now, Captain of the Command that sabotaged the Core Tap and shut down the spaceship-outfitting station—and *my* Captain, as well!"

A roar built up from the crowd and continued as Jason descended from the pedestal. Then there was a moment in which the cross stood still and alone in the midst of them and the roar slowly died away. Then it began again as a slim figure in dark bush clothes began to climb into view.

It was Rukh—it could be no one else. She climbed up on the pedestal and paused, holding one arm around the vertical shaft of the towering granite cross. It lifted high above her, its polished surface gleaming dully with moisture.

For a moment she stood there, looking like a black wand in the grey light. Gradually, the sounds from the square died away like the sound of surf when a heavy curtain is drawn across an open window. The crowd was silent.

She spoke, and the repeaters carried by people in the square picked up her words and threw them audibly over the heads of everyone there.

"Awake, drunkards, and weep!"

It was, Hal recognized, a quotation from the Old Testament of the Bible, from the first chapter of Joel. Her clear voice reached even through the walls of the ambulance to Hal's ears, like a sharp needle prodding him in his efforts to regain full conscious control of his body.

"All you who drink wine, lament," she went on:

"—For that new wine has been dashed from your lips.

"For a nation has invaded my country,
mighty and innumerable;
its teeth are the teeth of lions,
it has the fangs of a lioness.
It has laid waste my vines
and torn my fig trees to pieces;
it has stripped them clean and cut them down,
their branches have turned white.

"Mourn like a virgin wearing sackcloth
for her young man betrothed to her.
Oblation and libation have vanished
from the house of Yahweh,
the priests, the ministers of Yahweh,
are in mourning.
Wasted lie the fields,
the fallow is in mourning.
For the corn has been laid waste,
the wine fails,
the fresh oil dries up."

She stopped; and after the clear cadence of her voice, the silence seemed to ring in their ears. She spoke again, slowly.

"When did we come to fear death?" She turned her head, looking at all those about her. "For you, I see, fear death."

The silence of the crowd continued. It was as if they had no power to make a sound, almost no power to breathe, until she should finish with them. Hal struggled against the reluctance of his body to return to life.

"Today"— her voice reached him again through the glass window in the ambulance—"you crowd the streets. Today the Militia does not come out to disperse you. Right now you are willing, in your hundreds, to take up weapons and march against the Belial-spawn and Antichrist."

She paused, watching them all.

"But tomorrow"— her voice continued—"you will think better of it. You will not say you will not march; but you will find a thousand reasons to question the time and manner of marching, and so never leave Ahruma at all.

"When did you come to fear death? There is no death to fear. Our forefathers knew this, when they came from Earth. Why do you fail to know it now?"

The crowd neither moved nor made a sound.

"They knew, as we should know," her voice went on, "that it does not matter if our bodies die, as long as the People of God continue. For then all are saved, and will live forever."

Hal got his legs moving, and stirred them quietly on his stretcher, to get the blood moving in them. They made a small rustling sound between the stretcher surface and the covering blankets. But the two Militiamen in the bucket seats up front in the ambulance paid no attention. They were as caught up in Rukh's speaking as the crowd outside.

"There is a man," went on Rukh; and the repeaters in the crowd flung her words against the concrete fronts of the buildings facing the square on all four sides, "who has been in this city before today and will be here again, who is called by some the Great Teacher."

She paused.

"He is a teacher of lies—Antichrist incarnate. But he envies us our immortality—yours and mine, sisters and brothers—for he is only mortal and knows he will die. He can be killed.

"For God alone is independently immortal. He would exist, even if Mankind did not; and because we are part of God, you and I, we are immortal also. But Antichrist, who comes among us now for our last great testing, has no hope of long life except in Mankind. Only if we accept him, and his like, can they hope to live.

"But because Mankind is of God, though the Enemy may slay our bodies he cannot touch our souls unless we give them freely to him. If we do, we are lost, indeed.

"But if we do not; then, though we may seem to suffer death, we will live eternally—not only in the Lord but in those who come after us, who will because of us continue to know our God.

"For only if we betray him by giving up the power to choose Him for ourselves, can we lose immortality. If we will not be dogs of Antichrist, we shall be part of our children's children's children—who, because of our faith and our labors, will still belong to our God, our faith and, therefore, to us, forever. If the race continues free, none of us shall ever die."

She paused; and for the first time, there was a sighing, no more noticeable than a vagrant wisp of breeze, that travelled across the surface of the crowd and died against the buildings surrounding.

"There are those"— when she went on, her voice had changed slightly— "who say, 'But what if we should all be killed by those who follow Antichrist?' And the answer to that is, 'they cannot.' For there would then be not enough to serve the Belial-spawn as they wish to be served. But even if it was possible for our enemies to kill all who are steadfast in the faith, that killing would be useless to them. For even in their slaves the seeds of faith would still lie dormant, awaiting only the proper hour and the voice of God, to flower once more."

She paused and once more took a slow survey of the square.

"So, pick up your courage," she said. "These who oppose us can only destroy bodies, not souls. Come, join me in putting off our fear of death; which is, after all, only like a child's fear of the dark, and testify for the Lord, praising Him and thanking Him that it is to us, to our generation, that this great and glorious moment has been given. For there is no reward like the reward of those who fight for Him; knowing that they cannot lose because He cannot be defeated."

She stopped.

"Now," she said. "Testify with me, my sisters and brothers in the Lord. Let us sing together that God may hear us."

She let go of the upright of the cross and stood there balanced upon the narrow upper edge of the pedestal top. Standing so, she began, herself, to sing. Her voice came clearly and joyfully from the repeaters, making the dark hymn Hal had heard led by Child in the house of Amjak into a paean of triumph.

> *"Soldier, ask not—now or ever,*
> *Where to war your banners go.*
> *Anarch's legions all surround us.*
> *Strike—and do not count the blow. . . ."*

The crowd was singing with one voice. Up in the front of the vehicle, the two Militiamen were silent, but they sat crouched in their seats as if they, too, had been captured by the music. Hal, who had also been caught up in the power and sweep of Rukh's speech, woke suddenly to the fact that he was letting his chance to escape slip through his fingers.

As quietly as he could, he pushed the blankets off him to the window side of the stretcher, swung his legs out over empty air and let himself slip quietly off the stretcher surface until he was standing on his feet.

Up front, the two Militiamen stared out through the side window next to the driver's left elbow, blind and deaf to anything taking place behind them.

Hal swayed a little on his feet. His balance was unsure, and the effort of keeping himself erect was a large one; but he felt a tremendous surge of happiness at being able to stand by himself. He moved as softly as he could to the door in the back end of the ambulance, through which he had been carried in. One step. Two. Three . . . he reached the door.

He put his hand on the rounded, cold, metal bar of its latch lever, ready to push it down; and glanced back over his shoulder at the front of the vehicle. The two Militiamen still sat in profile to him, unnoticing.

He turned to the door again, and pushed down on the lever. It resisted him as if it had been set in concrete. For a moment he thought his weakness was to blame, and he threw all his weight upon it to force it down. But it held.

Then his mind cleared. He looked more closely at the latch and saw that it was locked by a horizontal sliding bar that needed to be drawn before the lever could swing down. He took the knob of the bar gingerly in his fingers and pulled. It held as if stuck. He pulled harder. It held for a second more; and then, with a rasp and a clang that seemed to echo like a beaten alarm through the ambulance, it sprang back. He seized the lever.

"Stop!" said a tight-throated voice from the front of the ambulance. "You push that handle down and I'll shoot!"

Still holding the lever, he looked again over his shoulder. The faces of both Militiamen were watching him above the upper edges of their bucket-seat backs; and, down between the seats, its slim, wire-coiled barrel projecting through, was one of the stubby hideout-models of a void pistol. It was aimed squarely at him, held low by the driver so that his body and that of the man beside him would shield it from the eyes of any of the crowd who might happen to look in.

"This doesn't make any noise," said the driver. "Go back to your stretcher and get back up on it."

Hal stared at them and the shadow of the structure in his mind seemed to fall between him and the two of them.

"No," he said. "If I fall out of here dead, you two won't live five minutes."

He pushed the lever down, leaning against the door. The latch released. The door swung half-open under his weight before it was stopped by the body of someone standing in the way; and Hal fell into the opening, which was too narrow for his body to pass but let him get his head outside.

"Help, brothers!" he croaked. "Help! The Militia've got me."

He had been braced instinctively for the silent blow of the charge from the void pistol against his back. But nothing happened. He was aware of startled faces turning toward him; then suddenly the door gave fully and he fell through the opening.

He would have tumbled to the pavement, if hands had not caught him and held him upright.

"Help . . . ," he said again, weakly, feeling the last of the small spurt of strength he had been able to summon up draining from him in the sudden relief of still being alive. "They've had me in their cells. . . ."

A fainting spell misted his vision for a few seconds. When it cleared, he became distantly aware of being half-pulled, half-lifted forward for a little space; then lifted again by many hands to the head-height of the crowd. Dimly, he realized he was being passed along by an unending succession of hands above the heads of the multitude—and, at the same moment, became crazily aware that here and there about the square there were the figures of other casualties of the tight-packed gathering—men, women, and even some children, being passed toward the outskirts of the crowd by the same means.

In his present exhausted, slightly confused state, it was a curious sensation, rather like floating across strangely-uneven ground, while receiving innumerable pats on the back; and, strangely, it brought back the dream he had had of starting out on foot, alone, across a plain to a tower seen far off in its distance. He was conscious mainly of a naked feeling from the cold, wet air cooling him through the thin shirt and trousers that were all his captors had left him to wear in his cell. After a while the number of hands beneath him became less; and, a few moments later, he was let down into an upright position with his feet on the pavement of one of the streets leading into the square.

"Hang on," said a man's voice in his ear.

There were two of them, one on either side of him. He had an arm over the shoulders of each, and they each had an arm about his waist. They half-carried, half-walked him forward through a lesser thickness of people for a little distance, and then abruptly brought him back into warmth, for which he was grateful.

They had helped him up a ramp into the body of a large truck that seemed to have been fitted up as a first-aid station.

"Put him there," said a woman with a stethoscope hanging from her neck, who was working over someone on a cot. Her elbow indicated an empty cot behind her.

Gently, the two men carrying Hal put him down on the cot.

"See if anyone outside knows him," said the woman briefly. "And shut the door as you go out."

The two went. Hal lay basking in the warmth and the growing joy of being free. After a while, the medician with the stethoscope came over to him.

"How do you feel?" she asked, putting her fingers on his wrist at the pulse-point.

"Just weak," said Hal. "I wasn't in the crowd. I just got away from a Militia ambulance. They were taking me to the hospital."

"Why?" asked the woman, reaching for a thermometer.

"I had a bad cold. A chest cold, that went into bronchitis, or something like that."

"Are you asthmatic?"

"No." Hal coughed thickly, looked around for something to spit into, and found a white tray held under his nose. He spat; and the sensor-end of the thermometer was tucked beneath his tongue for a moment, then was withdrawn.

"No fever now," said the woman. "But you're still wheezing. You're not moving air well."

"Yes," said Hal. "The last few days I had a pretty high fever, I think, but it broke early this morning."

"Roll up your sleeve," she said, producing a pressure gun and thumbing an ampoule into it. His fingers fumbled clumsily with the fastening of his sleeve cuff, and she laid the gun aside to pull loose the cuff closure and push the sleeve up. He watched the nose of the pressure gun pressed against his upper arm, felt the coolness of a drug being discharged into the muscle, and himself rolled his sleeve down and fastened it once more.

"Drink this," said the woman, now holding a disposable cup to his lips. "Drink it all."

He swallowed something that tasted like weak lemonade. Less than a minute later, a blissful miracle took place, as his lungs opened up, and shortly thereafter he became busy coughing up large amounts of the secretions that had clogged his constricted air passages.

The door to the truck by which he had been brought in opened and closed again.

"—Of course I know him," a voice was saying as it approached him. "He's Howard Immanuelson, one of the Warriors in Rukh's Command."

Hal looked and saw the round, determined face of one of Gustav Mohler's grandsons from the Mohler-Beni farm, coming toward him with a man behind him who might have been one of those who had carried Hal in earlier.

"Are you all right, sir?" the grandson asked. Hal had never known his name. "Is there someplace I can take you to? I drove in earlier this week in one of our trucks, and I can bring it around in a moment. You needn't worry, sir. We're all faithful people of God, here!"

A blush stained his skin on the last words. Hal appreciated for the first time that the urging of the truck driver with the accordion that Hal be put off from the Command, that evening at the Mohler-Beni farm, might have been a source of embarrassment to their host and his family.

"I don't doubt it," he said.

"He can't go like that," said the medician sharply, from another stretcher at which she was working, "unless you want him back down with pneumonia, again. He needs some outdoor clothing. Somebody out there ought to be able to spare a jacket or a coat for a Warrior of God."

The man who had come in with the grandson ducked back out of the truck.

"Don't worry, sir," said Mohler's grandson. "There's lots of people who'll be glad to give you a coat. Maybe I'd better go get the truck and bring it here so you don't have so far to walk to it."

He went out, leaving Hal to wonder if someone out there would actually be willing to give away an outer garment and expose himself or herself to the temperature Hal had just felt, at the request of someone else who was probably a stranger.

However, the man came back before Mohler's grandson had a chance to return; and his arms were filled with half a dozen coats and jackets. Left to himself, Hal would have taken any one and been grateful for it; but the medician took charge and picked out a jacket with a fleece lining that wrapped him with almost living warmth.

"Thank whoever gave it, for me," said Hal, to the man who had brought it.

"Sir, he's already thanked," said the man, "and proud that a member of Rukh's Command would wear a garment of his."

He left with the rejected coats. A moment later, Mohler's grandson came in and helped Hal out to a light truck that was now standing in the street beside the first-aid truck, surrounded by a considerable crowd that broke into applause as Hal came out, his elbow steadied by the young man.

Hal waved and smiled at the crowd, let himself be helped into the other truck, and sat back exhaustedly in his seat as the grandson lifted the vehicle on its blowers and the crowd made a lane before it to let it move off.

"Where to, sir?" asked the grandson.

"To—I'm sorry, I don't know your name," said Hal.

"Mercy Mohler," said the other, solemnly.

"Well, thank you, Mercy," said Hal. "I appreciate your identifying me; and believe me when I say I appreciate this ride."

"It's nothing," said Mercy, and blushed again. "Where to?"

Hal had put his memory to work to turn up the address he had written on the mailing envelope containing his papers. Nothing that he wanted to remember was ever forgotten; but sometimes it required a certain amount of mental searching to turn it up. At the last minute, he changed slightly what his memory had given him. There was no need to advertise the fact he was going to the Exotic Consulate.

"Forty-three French Galley Place," he said. "Do you know where that is? Because all I have is the address."

"I'll ask," said Mercy.

He stopped the truck, lowered the window at his shoulder and put his head out to speak to those in the crowd immediately outside. After a second, he brought his head back in, put up the window and restarted the truck.

"French Galley's right off John Knox Avenue, below the First Church," he said. "I know where that is. We'll be there in ten minutes."

But it took closer to twenty minutes than ten, before French Galley Place was found. It turned out to be a circle of very large, comfortable three-story houses; and, seeing the flags displayed on various of the doorsteps, Hal realized that the Place itself was evidently a favorite location in Ahruma for off-world Consulates. So much for hiding the fact that he had been heading for a diplomatic destination. A somewhat puzzled Mercy dropped him off before a relatively-smaller, brown establishment between what were obviously the Venus and New Earth Consulates.

"Thanks," said Hal, climbing out. "I can't thank you enough. No thanks, I can manage fine by myself. Let me see you safely on your way now—and say hello for me to your grandfather and the rest of your family when you get home."

"It's been my pleasure—and an honor, sir," said Mercy; and put the window up between them, before waving and driving off.

Hal waved back and watched the truck continue around the traffic circle on which the houses of the Place were built, and disappear between the trees on either side of the entrance into Knox Avenue. He breathed out, heavily. Merely being polite had drained his small supply of strength.

He turned, and walked slowly and unsteadily around the circle to Sixty-seven French Galley Place, four doors away. The walk in from the gate was a short one, but the six steps leading up to the front door were like a small mountain to climb. He reached the top at last, however, and pressed the annunciator button. There was a wait that stretched out to several minutes. He was about to signal the annunciator again when its grille spoke to him.

"Yes?" said a voice from within.

"My name is Howard Immanuelson," he said, wearily leaning against the doorframe. "A few days ago I sent some papers—"

The door before him opened. A figure hardly shorter than his own, in a saffron-colored robe but with a full-fleshed, round and ageless face stood framed in the relative darkness of the interior.

"Of course, Hal Mayne," said a soft baritone voice. "Amid asked us to do whatever we could for you; and said that you'd be along shortly. Come in, come in."